THE VISIONARY

KAMRYN BLACK
KRISTIN HARRIS

KRISKAM
PUBLISHING

The Visionary

by Kamryn Black and Kristin Harris

This book is a work of fiction. Characters, incidents, names, and places are the product of the author's imagination or are used fictitiously. Any resemblance to actual events, or persons, living or dead, is purely coincidental.

Cover art by Aprampar

Edited by Maryssa Gordon

Formatted by Kristin Harris

Kris Kam Publishing

P.O. Box 24

Owingsville, KY 40360

kriskampublishing.com

Originally published in hardcover and ebook by Ingram Spark 2025

Library of Congress Control Number: 2025906598

ISBN 979-8-9927383-0-8 (hardback)

ISBN 979-8-9927383-1-5 (ebook)

Printed in the United States of America

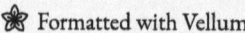 Formatted with Vellum

To Becky, who has always encouraged us to tell our stories.

CHAPTER
ONE

I know that before the timer on the oven goes off, the vase of flowers on the kitchen island will shatter. Water will spill everywhere, ceramic shards will litter the floor, and my adoptive mother, Mrs. B, will cut her hand trying to clean it up.

I see things. Flashes of things that I can't explain. Sometimes, it's things that haven't happened yet. Sometimes, it's years ago.

"Jade, honey, the new school can't be *that* bad," she said, completely oblivious to both my feelings and the fact that her elbow was too close to the vase as she tried to toss the salad without spilling lettuce everywhere. It was a losing battle. "What about the kids? You've been at Pinewood for a month, haven't you made any friends? Benji and I had a great time back when we went to school here."

"You guys went to college here, not high school. It's different," I said, leaning out of the way as she moved to add the cherry tomatoes.

Mrs. B raised an eyebrow. "So I take it that's a no on friends then?"

"Some guy said hi to me the other day, but I'm pretty sure he was forced to. Mr. Goodman is pretty cool, but I don't think teachers count, and he was gone all last week," I rolled my eyes. "Oh! I stopped a ball from hitting someone in the face. They called me a freak, but somehow, *I* am the one who got in trouble for it. Does that count?"

1

Mrs. B frowned. "Do I need to talk to your teacher?"

"Because that worked out so well the last time," I muttered.

"Jade, the attitude isn't necessary."

She turned to pull out the plates for dinner, and I quickly moved the vase out of the danger zone. "You just need to be a bit more... approachable. This isn't going to be like your last school. Not every kid is going to be another Ashley."

I tried not to wince at the name. Yeah, we were in a new school in a new town, and as much as I wanted to believe I'd get a fresh start here, I'd learned my lesson about making friends at my last school. Couldn't Mrs. B see that it was just better to fly under the radar?

"I liked Ashley. She was cool...unlike you," my little brother, Tommy, said as he walked in the back door. His sandy hair was sweaty, and his new blue soccer uniform was covered in mud. Of course, the little twerp wouldn't miss an opportunity to butt into our private conversation. Our parents knew not to broach the Ashley topic too much, but Tommy seemed to think testing my patience was his purpose in life.

"You stay out of this," I warned as he snatched a gluten-free breadstick from the tray when his mother wasn't looking. "We don't talk about her anymore."

"Whatever," he said, crunching loudly.

"Judging by your clothes, I'd say the first practice went well," Mrs. B said cheerfully. "You're not eating with dirty hands, are you?"

"No!" Tommy said through a mouthful of bread, distorting his voice to sound like the little goblin he was. Mrs. B waved him toward the sink as the kitchen timer sounded. I let out a sigh of relief, scribbling *broken vase* into my weathered journal.

The Bensons didn't know about my visions. I'd kept them hidden and written them down for as long as I could remember. An old leather journal, with its pages practically about to fall out of its spine, was my only connection to my real family. Wherever I actually came from. It came with me the night I was dropped off at a hospital where my adoptive dad used to work. The inside had a curling signature, faded from all the times I'd traced my finger over it: *Vivian Kastel*. The woman who left me behind. My mother.

That was it. The hospital and social services had found my mother extremely hard to track, minus a few basic records from when I was born. A faded journal, a mysterious name, no message in invisible ink. I'd like to think maybe she gave me the journal to help me sort out my visions as if every word I wrote in it was silently asking for her help. I knew that was wishful thinking.

"Anyway, Jade, the point is still the same," Mrs. B said, smacking Tommy's hand away before he could grab another breadstick. "Once more people get to know you, you'll have friends in no time. *Real* ones. They'll be lining up for miles!"

Tommy started chuckling. I shot him a glare.

"What's so funny, twerp?"

"Stop with the name-calling, Jade," the larger version of Tommy said automatically as he came in, hanging up his car keys.

Mrs. B smiled at him. "How was work today, sweetie?"

My adoptive dad, or Benson as I'd taken to calling him over the last few months, shrugged. "Busy as usual. You know."

Meaning the exact same answer he'd given ever since we'd moved to Pinewood for his job a few months ago. In truth, I wasn't even sure he'd wanted the new position at first, but after what happened at my old school...no, I wasn't going to think about that again. Not right now, anyway. Mrs. B swatted her husband away as he reached for the breadsticks, too. How a father and son could be so similar and so annoying was baffling.

Looking at the three of them, it was hard not to feel like I didn't belong. It was clear as day that I was adopted. They were almost the definition of the perfect, white, cookie-cutter family. And then there's me. The girl with light brown skin, dark eyes, and long chestnut curls. As dumb as it was, Ashley had been right- I'd always be an outsider to my own family.

"Who would want to be friends with *Jade*? Ew!"

"Tommy!" Mrs. B scolded. She didn't raise her voice very often, especially not to her precious baby, but she hated when we fought. Benson's blue eyes watched me carefully to see how I would react. He looked like he wanted to say something, but seemed to decide against it.

"Well, it's true! She never talks to anyone. She's always zoned out or

3

in her stupid journal," he said, swiping the leather-bound book from the counter beside me.

"Give that back!" I yelled at him.

"Why?" Tommy mocked, thrilled to get under my skin. "It's only a book."

He flipped slowly through the pages, taunting me, holding it just out of my reach. His greedy blue eyes drank in the drawings and words I had forbidden anyone to see. My secrets.

"Tommy, you know not to touch your sister's things," Benson scolded while I bit my tongue to retort the sister comment. "Give it back."

Tommy, being the obedient son he was, immediately started to shove the journal in my direction. The only problem: it was a very old journal, already about to fall apart. The force of Tommy incorrectly holding the journal and swinging it toward me caused pages from the spine to scatter on the floor in a confetti of papers.

For a moment, time seemed to stop. Tommy looked as stunned as I felt, and somewhere deep inside my mind, I knew he hadn't meant to. But the second I saw my mother's handwriting on the ground—the only thing I had left of her, my *real* family—I saw red.

"WHAT DID YOU DO?" I screamed at him. We yelled at each other all the time, but not like this. I'd never actually gone off on Tommy before. I tore the remaining pages out of his hands and shoved them back into the journal, tears prickling at the ends of my eyes.

"Jade, please calm down. We can put the book back together," Mrs. B intervened, trying to diffuse the situation. She knew how important that journal was to me, but she didn't even try to stop Tommy. She always took *her* kid's side.

"What was the *one* thing I told you!" I whirled on Tommy. "You do not touch this! *Ever*!"

I shoved him out of my way and made a break for the back door. I needed to escape. To be alone for a while so I could calm my racing heart.

The issue was that I shoved him a little harder than I meant to, and Tommy tumbled to the floor. Hard. His hand caught one of the plates on the island, and it shattered against the floor. The timer on the oven sounded again—I'd missed Mrs. B resetting the time.

It was the exact scene from my vision. Only the vase had been replaced by the plate.

"Jade!" Mrs. B said sharply, crouching to pick up some of the larger shards. She winced, and a bead of blood quickly began to form on her hand.

"Let me help," Benson said, rushing over to his wife. "I'm a doctor."

Mrs. B waved him off as she went to rinse off her wound. "That's still not funny, and you're a geneticist, dear."

Tommy sat on the floor, completely stunned. I had never *ever* done anything like that to him before. As nasty as the kid could be, sometimes it was easy to forget he was only nine and, at least for the moment, smaller than me.

I caused this. I had to leave. *Now.*

"I'm sorry!" I said in a panic. My breaths were erratic as I snatched my bag from the hook. I looked behind me—I couldn't have them chasing after me, thinking I was running away again. "I'll be back in a little bit."

"Jade Benson! Come back here!" my adoptive father ordered.

I stared at him. Cold. "I'm not a Benson."

I slammed the door behind me.

The eerie chill dried my watery eyes and calmed my nerves faster than anticipated. It was Friday night, yet the streets were deserted. Storm clouds, creepy ones, loomed overhead. I loved weather like this: the ominous sky painted with swirls of dark gray and purple, threatening to unleash its wrath at any moment. An oddity. Just like me.

I thought back to the Bensons, how I freaked out on Tommy. We fought like cats and dogs, but I had never laid a hand on him before. He might call me a monster, but that didn't mean I wanted to actually *be* one.

It's going to be bad when I get back. I sighed.

A red sign caught my attention as a gust of wind caught the chimes around the door, sending them swaying frantically. *Yan Mei's Cafe,* it declared. I allowed myself a smile. My favorite place in town, with a view of the storm. Perfect.

I walked into the small building and was immediately filled with the smell of savory meats and spices. Oh, sweet, comforting Chinese food.

The Bensons and I had gotten takeout from here when we first moved in, a tradition when we settled into a new place. We gorged ourselves with bourbon chicken and chow mein on the living room floor surrounded by unpacked boxes. It was so delicious that I found myself becoming a regular here.

The shop was a little hole-in-the-wall cafe with spread-out square tables and a tall counter where one of those lucky cats waved endlessly at customers. The walls were decorated with silk tapestries of deep reds, greens, and golds. A beautiful watercolor painting hung at the back.

"I'm rather fond of that." A woman with a heavily accented voice jolted me out of my skin.

"Oh, sorry! You scared me," I yelped, catching my breath and willing my heartbeat to return to a normal cadence. A petite Asian woman was suddenly beside me, an elegant bun framing her fair skin. The first traces of silver were just starting to show in her ebony hair.

"You didn't see me coming?" she asked with an innocent smile, brown eyes warm. *If only she knew.* I smiled politely and shook my head.

"You come here often enough to seat yourself, you know. I'll put in an order for your usual," the woman said. I looked down at her to see a "World's Best Grandma" T-shirt. Someone was lucky to have her as a grandmother. She was the owner of the place, Mrs. Yan Mei. I'd talked to her a few times since we'd moved to Pinewood and she'd always been really nice. She'd sometimes tell funny stories about her grandson or how she loved cooking and always dreamed of owning a restaurant after she immigrated from China.

I thanked her before moving to an abandoned table near the window. Only a few booths were taken. It was the perfect place for my escape into solitude.

I wondered how long I would last here. The last school year flashed through my mind, and I cringed. I wasn't sure if I could handle another incident like that or another fake friend like Ashley. It was hard to be optimistic, but maybe Pinewood *would* be different. So far, it was the most pleasant location we'd moved to. Not too hot or cold, and the food was top-notch.

But I had to face my inevitable reality: I space out, see things, and then act. I couldn't explain *why*. My last school had questions that I couldn't answer. I would just ignore the visions, but then what kind of person would *I* be? I'm no superhero, but I would like to believe I'm a good person. Not including today's events.

I sighed. Pinewood's a joke. We had five months here, six tops.

"Excuse me?"

For the second time today, I jumped.

"Oh, sorry. I didn't mean to scare you," a male voice said softly. He looked to be my age, several inches taller, with light brown hair and blue eyes that somehow felt familiar. Someone I passed in the hallway? A classmate? He was slightly attractive, I guess. A sheepish smile crossed his face, and his shoulders raised. A plate of hot, steaming food was in his hands.

"You didn't," I said, holding back a glare. I usually tried not to be hostile, but it had been a *really* bad day, and I wasn't in the mood for pleasantries. My plans included running away from my problems and stress eating.

The boy cleared his throat. "You're in some of my classes. At Pinewood High. I go there too, obviously, since I'm in your class. My name's Dylan," he said so quickly that it was almost unintelligible.

"Nice to meet you, Dylan...I guess. Can I have my food now?"

His eyes went wide. "Right, sorry. I babble when I'm nervous—I mean, here's your food! Please enjoy!" he said with an overly cheery voice as he set my food down. The smell of sweet bourbon chicken invaded my senses and made my mouth water. I started to reach for the plate. "Be careful, it's hot!"

For a moment, I felt our fingertips graze each other. My vision hazed, and my ears rang. I didn't feel my body hit the floor.

CHAPTER
TWO

My body ached. Smoke burned my lungs. I opened my eyes, and the desolate twilight sky was above me. Not a cloud in sight. I slowly picked myself up from the rubble and tried to regain my bearings.

Panic filled my body. I was near the cafe, but in what must've been a terrible nightmare.

Buildings were either demolished or ablaze, the fire's rustling loud and consuming. Glass shards and rubbish littered the streets. The smell of gasoline and smoke was nauseating. It was an utter wasteland. What *was* this?

Snow fell like a blizzard, but I didn't feel cold. Instead, I felt the residual heat from the flames. Ash. I walked on what once was a street, hearing it crunch under my shoes with every step.

As I walked, I became aware of a tiny sound. I followed the noise, desperate to find *something*. My shoes stomped the ground faster and faster as I clung to the only sign of life. Anything would surely be better than the deadly quiet and desolate wasteland. The noise got louder and more distinguishable. *Crying*.

I sprinted until my legs ached and my heart throbbed in my chest. Someone needed help. As I got closer to the sobbing, a stench got stronger: blood. I braced myself. Whatever the reason might be, I was going to help.

Then I saw him.

Dylan. The boy who was just serving my Chinese food was now hunched over on his knees, sobbing in front of a body. He looked worse for wear, with bruises and cuts scattered across his skin, his left arm limp at his side. My hand shook as I covered my mouth.

A wave of grief rammed into my body, nearly knocking me onto my knees. The closer I got to Dylan, the more potent the grief felt, and—something else that I couldn't put my finger on. Something that burned and caused my chest to ache and stomach to sink.

"This wasn't supposed to happen," Dylan sobbed, lowering his head to the body before leaning to stroke their face. "This wasn't supposed to happen."

He chanted it over and over as if saying it enough would make it true. Even though I had only ever said a few words to him, I wanted to run up to him and offer some form of comfort. But my feet froze when I saw the Bensons.

Mrs. B was sobbing into her husband's shoulder, her clothes tattered and brunette hair frayed messily from her usual tidy ringlets. It was off-putting seeing her so disheveled. Benson had messy stubble and dark purple under his eyes. Tommy was on his knees, but he looked a few inches taller. His blond hair was nearly black from the ash, and there was a nasty-looking cut on his lip.

Mrs. Benson slowly pulled Tommy off his knees and clutched him tightly while Benson walked over to Dylan. He put his arm around him, and Dylan's piercing cry was deafening.

"You did everything you could, son," Benson said, tears rolling down his cheeks. He gasped as he looked down at the body and squeezed Dylan's shoulder. The air was filled with quiet sobs before Dylan spoke again.

"I loved her. I loved her *so much,*" he cried.

"She knew. She knew how much we all loved her," Benson said.

My feet shot forward automatically. I was drawn—forced closer to the pair with a pull like a magnet. The stomp of my shoes was thunderous to the mournful scene, but the others paid it no mind. Nobody looked in my direction or startled at the sound of my approach. I found myself directly beside Dylan and Benson.

Right in front of the body.

A girl with brown skin who looked sickly pale, dirt-filled curls framing her sleeping face. Her arms were out to her sides. The young woman could only be slightly older than me. Her skin was covered in little scratches, patches of dirt, and bruises. But no blood. The smell had to come from somewhere else. Her lifeless body sat unmoving, and I found myself unable to look away. *Who is she?*

"Jade," Dylan cried out.

My heart stopped as my head turned to the broken young man clutching my adoptive father, but his eyes weren't on me. They were on *her*. I let out a bloodcurdling scream as I realized I was looking at myself.

The dead girl was *me*.

A blinding light stung my eyes, making me blink hard. The ringing in my ears faded to a gentle voice. Someone was calling my name. My eyes snapped open, and I tried to make sense of my surroundings. I was lying on the ground, back in the restaurant. My stomach rose into my chest as I saw Dylan hovering over me.

"Jade, are you okay?" he asked softly.

My heart pounded. I couldn't think, couldn't breathe. My nose still stung from the smell of gasoline and fire. My dead body, with Dylan and Benson sobbing over me, flashed through my mind. I scrambled up as quickly as I could. I had to get out of here.

"Jade," Dylan tried again, his gentle touch burning my arm. I shoved him away like a hot coal.

"Don't touch me!" I snapped.

Dylan's terrified eyes broke me out of my frenzy. His face was no longer cut or bruised, and his arm seemed fine. No terrible sorrow in his eyes. He wasn't grieving. He was frightened...because of me. *Get a grip, Jade.*

I took a breath and looked around. A gentle rain tapped against the windows. *Was that really a vision?* My heart ached from what I'd seen, but embarrassment coursed through my body as my mind finally caught up to the present situation. I had passed out in the middle of a restaurant. Dylan must have caught me before I fell completely out of the booth. A boy who would one day be crying over my dead body.

"Sorry," I muttered. "That's never happened before."

Dylan let out a relieved breath, relaxing a bit. "We were worried about you."

I looked up, realizing Yan Mei was behind me. Thankfully, there weren't many people in the restaurant, but I'd managed to get everyone's undivided attention. Could this day get any worse?

Yan Mei seemed to notice the unwanted attention and motioned for everyone to go back to their food. "She's alright, everyone. As you were." She turned to me. "You sure you're alright, dear? Your father is Mr. Benson, isn't he? I can call him if you—"

"No! No, I'll be okay," I said, getting to my feet, which was harder than it looked because I was shaking all over. "Sorry for scaring your customers."

Yan Mei shrugged. "It'll take more than that to scare them away. Everyone always stays for my food—it's my own special recipe, you know. Speaking of which, I bagged your food for you. We thought we might have to call an ambulance."

"Oh...thanks. I should really get going. Sorry—again." I reached into my bag and shoved a twenty into the older woman's hands, snatching up the plastic bag. "Keep the change!"

I made a break for the door, but Dylan followed me. I turned, seeing him reach out his arm before thinking better of touching me again.

"Are you sure you're okay?" he asked. "I can give you a ride home if you need it."

"Thanks, but I-I'm good," I said, still not sounding very good at all.

Dylan nodded, confused and unsure what to make of my odd behavior, before settling on giving me an awkward wave. "I guess I'll see you at school, Jade?"

I raised an eyebrow at him, suddenly realizing something. "I never told you my name."

Dylan cringed. Clearly, something he didn't want me to pick up on.

"Like I said, we have a few classes together," he mumbled, though he still looked uneasy.

"Right," I said. My mind flashed to his grieving confession. It was all too weird, too fast. I needed to get out of here. *Away from him.*

For the second time today, I stormed out. Past the beaded door, I trudged through the rain. Droplets fell in a cold drizzle, prickling my skin as I thought back to whatever *that* was.

I had *never* passed out from a vision before. A few headaches or zone-outs, but never anything that couldn't have been passed off for more than a daydream. Certainly not a fainting spell of an apocalyptic town foreshadowing my demise.

None of it made sense. Why would Pinewood—some little town in the middle of nowhere—look like Armageddon had just gone down? Earthquake? Volcanic eruption? Nuclear fallout?

Most importantly, why would Dylan—the server from a Chinese food place who could barely talk to me—somehow be close enough to me to be crying over my dead body? I had *felt* his emotions: sorrow, desolation, anger, and—maybe the scariest—love. He had been wholeheartedly in love with me—to the point where he openly shared the sentiment with the *Bensons*. My death would destroy him, *all* of them. But *how*? I didn't exactly make a habit of getting close to people.

It's my future, I thought, shivering from the cold of the September rain. I shook my head—none of that was happening now. All the streets were still here in one piece—the school, the restaurants, all the houses I'd passed on the way to Yan Mei's Cafe.

Still, I couldn't shake the vision out of my mind. If what I'd seen was really going to happen—the downtown warzone, the Bensons, the boy I didn't know loving me, and me...dead—then it seemed alarmingly close. Maybe only two or three years in the future, judging by how Tommy, Dylan, and I had looked. If that was true, then—*WHAM!*

I was on the ground. My bag went flying, littering the wet sidewalk with pens and money and receipts that had gone there to die. All the papers Tommy had just torn scattered as my journal hit the pavement, but I kept the take-out bag securely in my hands. You can't say I didn't save what was important.

"Sorry, sorry—I wasn't looking," I said, face burning as I scrambled to pick up the discarded contents of my bag.

"It's alright," the guy on the ground in front of me said. I'd been so shaken up by the vision that I hadn't even seen him coming out of a doorway. I had plowed right into him. "You're Jade, right?"

I hung my head. "Why does everyone in this town know who I am?"

"What?" he asked, eyes panicked.

"Nothing," I said, quickly trying to untangle myself from him.

A memory appeared in my head. I knew this boy—he sat a few rows behind me in English with Mr. Goodman. I had an odd feeling we had worked together on something this week for class, but I couldn't remember what the project was. I shook the thought out of my mind.

"I think this is yours," I said, handing him a box of Earl Grey tea that had definitely not come from my bag. I looked up at the shop he'd just come out of: The London Fog. Were there enough people in Pinewood to have a whole shop devoted to tea?

"Thanks," the guy said, stuffing it back into a bag packed with about six other mega-sized boxes of various kinds of tea.

"Looks like you're planning to go wild this weekend," I said, dusting my jeans off as I stood up.

He smiled sheepishly. "I'm a bit of an enthusiast."

He looked like it. His brunette curls were cropped short, and his skin was brown. He was dressed nicer than most high school guys would be: dark gray cable-knit sweater, nice jeans, expensive-looking shoes. Definitely from a family with money. My heart pounded when I saw what was in his hands: my journal. For the second time today, it was in the hands of someone else, but for some reason, I got the strange feeling this guy wouldn't hurt it. He cradled it almost reverently.

"Kastel, huh?" he said, eyes glancing over my mother's signature. "That's a beautiful name."

"Um, thanks," I said awkwardly. "Can I have that back now...?"

"Julian. Julian Graves," he said, smiling politely as he stood up and handed me the journal.

I tucked it quickly into my bag. "Well, nice talking to you, Julian, but I'd better get home—"

"I can walk you home if you want—"

"Jade! Jade!" Benson's frantic voice yelled as he came running toward us. He was drenched from the rain as if he'd run all the way from the house. "There you are! Are you alright?"

"What?" I said, crossing my arms over my chest. "Benson, what are you—"

"The lady from the Chinese food place called," he said, hunching over breathlessly. "Something about you passing out? Has that happened before? Do you need to go to the hospital?"

"I'm fine," I said, waving him off. Had Mrs. Yan Mei called Benson behind my back? My face was burning. I couldn't tell if Julian was worried or trying to keep from laughing.

Benson seemed to notice Julian for the first time. "Who are you?"

"Benson!"

Oh my gosh, could this day get any more embarrassing?

Julian chuckled and stuck out his hand. "Julian Graves. I was just asking if Jade needed help home."

"Graves? Like Dominic Graves?" Benson asked.

Julian winced at the name. "He's my father, sir."

Benson nodded with distracted approval, though he was still staring at me as if he thought I might keel over any second. "Well, I appreciate you helping out my daughter. We'd better get you home before the rain picks up again, Jade."

I started to turn back down the street toward home before my adoptive dad decided to cart me off to the hospital. "Really, I'm fine—"

A loud horn cut me off as a sleek black car pulled even with us. One of the blacked-out windows rolled down, revealing a man in an expensive suit. He had sunglasses on even though it was nearly dark out.

"Julian," he said curtly, "we need to go."

Julian's friendly expression clouded over into an irritated frown. "In a minute, Bartley."

"No can do, kid," the man insisted, softening his tone. "Your dad's already worried enough that you took off like that."

Julian looked down, fidgeting with his sleeves, but he nodded. Apparently, I wasn't the only one who'd had a rough day. Julian gave Benson and me an apologetic smile.

"I'd better go," he said, reluctantly stepping toward the car. "See you later, Jade."

"Sure," I said.

As soon as he was inside, the black car peeled up the street.

"Huh," Benson said, pushing his damp hair out of his face. "Is today Moody Teenagers Run Off Day?"

"Not your best joke," I said, rolling my eyes as we started back toward the house.

I expected him to give me a hard time about shoving Tommy and running off like I did, but he didn't seem to have the heart to. He was so soaked that he might have been out looking for me long before Yan Mei called him. I caught his gaze. Benson still looked really worried.

"I'm okay, Benson. Really."

"You're sure?" he said, seeming to choose his words. "I mean, you'd tell me if something was wrong?"

Like dying in the middle of a destroyed street sometime in the near future?

I handed him the bag from Yan Mei's. Having premature visions of your death will do wonders for getting rid of your appetite. "Make sure Tommy gets that, huh? It's his favorite."

I thought Benson might have smiled, but it was hard to tell since it was getting darker. "You understand we'll have to talk about what happened earlier, right?"

I nodded. "I know."

Benson slung his arm over my shoulder. "Come on, let's get you home."

CHAPTER
THREE

Since my freaky death vision—the mega-vision, as I'd started calling it—you could say I'd been...a little on edge. I brewed over it all weekend. How long did I have? Why was the town the way it was? And, most importantly, how exactly did I die? This was what happened when you were a sixteen-year-old psychic. Hormones and magic abilities were probably not a good combination.

Then, there was Dylan. The shy and kind of babbly white guy who worked at the Chinese food place, somehow already knew my name, and who would one day fall in love with me. I still didn't know how to process that. Should I avoid him? Would that keep me alive longer? Did being close to him keep me from dying sooner? If I was being honest, I kind of liked the thought of having someone who cared about me. Self-imposed isolation so no one discovers your freaky powers did kind of get old. It would be nice to have someone who *wanted* to be around me. If only that wasn't also related to me dying. Sounded like my life.

So, I wasn't 'stalking' per se, merely *observing*. Really, you could say it was for the good of the future. I was trying to save my life here and, you know, potentially trying to stop a town from being destroyed. It was for a good purpose. What if he's evil? Maybe he got close to me just so he could off me and pretend to be the sad little boyfriend to my clueless adoptive family? That was a bit of a stretch from what I knew about him already. But hey, a girl can't be too careful.

Even then, it still felt incredibly weird peeking up from the book that I was pretending to read, waiting for Dylan to come in. English was the first class we had together, and I was determined to keep an eye on him. People were filing through the door left and right in their little cliques, smiling with each other like their own imminent demise wasn't lingering in the back of their minds...which, in retrospect, was probably a good thing.

Finally, Dylan walked in with an Asian guy I'd noticed he seemed to always be around, although I didn't know his name. His brown eyes were excited and he flailed his arms about, dark hair flying messily as he retold something very dramatic. Still pretending to read whatever book I'd picked up from the library, I watched them take their seats beside one another.

A few more students straggled in. One I recognized as the boy I ran into Friday, Julian. His brown eyes looked straight into mine. I panicked, feeling caught, and awkwardly smiled, starting to raise my hand up halfway before his gaze suddenly dropped to the floor, and he made his way to his desk. He never looked in my direction again. *Weird.* Certainly a different reaction than when we last spoke, but perhaps he was just being polite then?

"All right, class. Settle down," Mr. Goodman said. The chatter of the classroom slowly diminished, though Dylan's friend seemed to have a hard time stopping his laughter. "I know you all thought you'd gotten rid of me, so I'm sorry to disappoint, but I am back and feeling much better after my week of treatments."

A couple of students whispered. I was glad to see Mr. Goodman back since he was one of the few teachers that I actually liked at Pinewood. He looked much better than he had at the beginning of the school year—his skin was less pale and sickly looking, dark hair no longer brittle and lifeless, and he appeared to be a more healthy weight. He must have had *very* good doctors.

Mr. Goodman then continued with the morning announcements,

and I started to tune out. Something about a new unit. Normally, I was very attentive in class, but I couldn't focus. My eyes kept glancing over to Dylan, who was absentmindedly flicking his pencil up and down his desk. Over and over.

"This will be a semester-long project that you *will* have to work with a partner on—" Mr. Goodman said as the class groaned.

Wait, what?

I'd always had a problem with the whole "partner" thing every time we moved. Nobody ever wanted to be partnered up with the new kid. *Mr. Goodman, why did you have to betray me like this?*

Mr. Goodman called the class back in order before telling us to split off to join partners. People started shuffling around, switching seats and snatching their friends. I looked over at Julian again, not very hopeful but wondering if maybe I caught him at a weird time? On Friday, he did seem like a very nice person and someone I *could* be friends with. Plus, I'd never really seen him with anyone else in our classes. We seemed like we were the same.

I started toward him, but he caught my eye and quickly plopped down in the seat beside Miss Princess. Victoria Harper: head cheerleader, class president, frequent wearer of the color pink. The borderline perfect type—blonde, pretty, and popular. She greeted Julian with a soft smile.

I probably stared at them longer than necessary as I tried to wrap my head around what had just happened. The tea enthusiast, who seemed like he didn't hang around anyone, was potentially friends with Victoria Harper. I guess I could see it. I could totally understand why he would want to work with her. A pretty, smart, and outgoing leader seemed like an optimal partner. Still, it kind of stung he'd clearly not wanted to work with me.

This place was shaping up to be just like all the others.

Someone snickered, bringing me back to reality. I was standing in the middle of a silent room. Everyone was seated with a partner, leaving me, once again, all alone. Piercing eyes stared at me from every desk. Even Mr. Goodman looked uncomfortable, counting quietly to himself to confirm that I was, indeed, the only person without a partner.

"Over here!" Dylan's friend exclaimed. My eyes shot wide with horror as he waved both arms in the air like someone trying to flag down a helicopter.

As if I wouldn't notice?

Dylan stared at his friend wide-eyed before giving me a shy look. "You can work with us...if you want."

I glanced around. Clearly, no one else was going to volunteer to let me join their group. I gave Mr. Goodman a pleading look.

"Can I just do the project by myself?" I asked, already knowing the answer.

He frowned. "Sorry, Jade. But no-can-do. You should join Dylan and Henry. They're nice..." he said. I glanced at the pair to see Henry with a larger-than-life grin. It was unnerving.

I sighed and collected my things. I dragged a chair to their desk while Mr. Goodman went over the project details, saying he would allow class time for groups to discuss and plan. A paper and visual representation of our key interpretations of *Macbeth*. It sounded long and like a lot of talking. Given my history of group projects, I would inevitably be stuck with the brunt of the work while the duo signed their name on it. English was slowly losing its title as my favorite subject.

Someone poked me in the back. I turned to see Julian, eyes turned downward, offering a paper with the unit instructions to me. I took it from his hands, maybe with a bit more force than necessary, and he drifted silently to the next table.

"Ugh," I muttered.

"I know, right?" Dylan's friend sighed. He was leaning with his head in his hands, gazing toward the table with Victoria Harper. I didn't need psychic powers to know who he had a crush on.

Dylan cleared his throat. "So...Jade, Henry, how do you guys want to split up the project?"

"Wait! We haven't even introduced ourselves yet!" the boy—Henry —said. *Do high schoolers still do introductions?*

"You know who she is!" Dylan said with a flush, fidgeting with his pencil once again.

"Rude," Henry said with a sarcastic glare. He turned toward me with his hand out. "Hi, I'm Henry. I heard you passed out at Grandma's restaurant Friday! That's so cool!"

"W-What?" I asked, looking at him with wide eyes before checking to make sure nobody else heard his strange but true accusation. Everyone was absorbed in their own projects or playing on their phones discreetly under their desks.

Did he say *Grandma*?

"What he meant was that we are very happy you are alright," Dylan interjected, sending Henry a glare. Henry rolled his eyes, and I noticed he was wearing a "World's Best Grandson" T-shirt.

Ah, I can see the resemblance. Henry had a darker skin tone than Yan Mei, but their features were very similar. Plus, I had never seen matching grandmother-grandson outfits. They were definitely one of a kind. And she was the owner of the restaurant where Dylan worked. It all clicked together. Which meant they *all* knew about my fainting. Thankfully, the intercom saved me from having to continue our conversation.

"Mary Milford, please come to the office," Principal Porter's voice crackled over the speakers. "Mary Milford to the office."

"Isn't she in our class?" the boy behind me asked.

Everyone looked around. Mr. Goodman did another headcount. I realized there was someone missing—that quiet redhead that sat a few rows behind me. That must've been what threw off the group numbers. A small seed of hope settled into my chest that I might get out of the Dylan/Henry group after all.

"Work amongst yourselves for a few minutes," Mr. Goodman said, propping the door open and heading off down the hall toward the main office. Weird. Mary should have been in AP history with me this morning, too. She'd never shown up. But why would they be calling for her at school when she hadn't come today?

"Okay, game plan," Henry said, interrupting my train of thought. "Why don't we meet up at the cafe after school and try to get a head start on this? I've got a shift until five, and Dylan's got swim practice today, but could we meet later? Five-thirty? Six?"

"Works for me," Dylan said blankly, starting to flick his pencil again. He seemed determined not to look in my direction. Did every boy I meet want to avoid me after talking to me?

"Six is fine," I said. "I just need to clear it with the Bensons first."

"The Bensons?" Henry asked.

I cringed. I'd forgotten how much I dreaded going through the whole explanation of me and the Bensons each time we moved.

"My...family," I said, pretending to scribble something in my notebook so I wouldn't have to say anything else.

"You call your family the Bensons? But I thought your last name was—"

"Henry," Dylan said, looking directly at me for the first time since I'd first spoken to him, "maybe she doesn't want to talk about it."

Henry winced. "Oh, sorry. I didn't mean—sometimes I just start talking and don't really know how to stop."

Eccentric and impulsive were definitely things I'd observed in the short time I had actually paid attention to him. It wasn't necessarily a bad thing, but I could see where that might rub someone the wrong way. "It's alright," I said, giving Dylan a thankful glance. Shy or not, Dylan seemed to be very mindful of their words and how I would interpret them. It was kind of sweet, actually. He turned his attention back to his pencil flicking.

Henry decided to fill the silence. He promised to bring a batch of Chinese donuts to our impromptu group meeting to "start things off on the right foot," which to me translated as *please accept this food. I'm sorry I pried into your business.* Which was unnecessary, but I was always up for food. The eccentric boy wasn't so bad after all.

The other groups started moving around and talking freely. Mr. Goodman had been gone for at least fifteen minutes now with no sign of returning. Henry launched into some story about how one of the basketball guys had hurled a frantic cross-court shot at the end of the last game and nailed him in the gut. Henry was apparently the secret identity of Pinewood High's mascot: Prickly the purple porcupine. *Far too much alliteration.*

"And then she slapped me!" Henry said, beaming.

"Wait, what?" I asked. How much of that story had I zoned out on?

Dylan flicked his eyes toward the back of the room where Julian and Victoria were sitting. Victoria seemed to be chatting politely, but neither she nor Julian seemed too interested in the conversation. Julian had turned most of his attention to a stray thread on his jacket sleeve. It didn't matter. It would be a lot easier to keep an eye on Dylan now that I was stuck in a semester-long group project with him.

I quickly looked back at Henry's dreamy expression. "Miss...I mean Victoria? She slapped you?"

Henry wasn't fazed. "Yes! To get me to *regain consciousness*. She was concerned about my well-being!"

Dylan snorted slightly, going back to flicking his pencil. Henry rolled his eyes, immediately starting in on some other story I didn't pay much attention to. I found myself watching Dylan's pencil roll up and down the table. It was strange. There were a few times it went right up to the edge and seemed like it was going to fall. But it always came back down. The bell rang, snapping me out of my thoughts. Henry was *still* talking, possibly another Victoria story.

"Dang it," Henry said sadly. "I'll finish that story later. Don't forget: Grandma's at six." He turned to me. "Oh, and Jade, please don't faint this time."

I winced. I'm sure he meant it as a joke, more of that *speaking before thinking* that I was learning was very difficult for Henry. Dylan was still zoned out and rolling his pencil, causing Henry to elbow him.

"What? Sorry, I was totally zoned out," he said. He rushed to get his stuff. The pencil lost its momentum and rolled back down the tabletop. I thought it was going to hit the floor, but it rolled back up again before going over the edge. The only strange thing being that Dylan's hands were still digging around in his backpack. Weird.

I looked at Henry in case he'd noticed, too, but he'd already drifted across the room toward Victoria while she gathered her things. Julian caught my eye again, and then suddenly became very interested in his shoes.

"Hey, Dylan?" I asked. He stared back at me with his eyes slightly widened. "Did you see that pencil? It looked like it was moving on its own for a second."

Dylan coughed before snatching said pencil and tossing it into his backpack. "Oh, that's weird. I guess the wind caught it."

I looked over to the windows to see that they were all firmly shut, and I was positive there wasn't a draft in the room. Dylan quickly excused himself and bolted out of the room.

Was he nervous because he's shy? Or for another reason? There's no way he could...No. I was crazy. I was sleep-deprived from my weird death vision and not thinking clearly. I was the only weirdo around here. But, even so, all the more reason to not let Dylan Mason out of my sight.

CHAPTER
FOUR

The more I followed Dylan Mason, the stranger he seemed to get. First, for one of the top jocks on the swim team—literally the only sport Pinewood was good at—he seemed remarkably isolated.

He kept to himself, didn't talk much beyond being polite. Instead of grouping up with all the other kids who wore Pinewood's atrocious purple and green letterman jackets, Dylan sat with Henry and a bunch of other nerdy-looking kids at lunch, swapping lunchbox snacks and theories about some TV show I'd never heard of.

I only had one other class with Dylan after English—calculus—so it was hard to see much of him beyond a few passing glances in the hall, but even those had been weird. He seemed to always be helping people: moving heavy stuff for teachers or popping open jammed locker doors. One time, I'd even seen him break down the hall at a full run, carrying a giant heat lamp. Maybe a favor for science class?

"You're going to do fine, Jade," Mrs. B said, craning her neck as she backed out of the driveway. "Tommy's game should end at eight, so I'll be back to pick you up around then."

I nodded, stomach already twisting in knots at the thought of a whole evening trying to sort out a project with Dylan and Henry.

Mrs. B raised an eyebrow. "You must have made a pretty good

impression if these boys asked you to join their group. I told you it would just take a little time."

"I was standing awkwardly in the middle of the room," I said, crossing my arms over my chest. I made a point not to meet her eyes. "They probably felt embarrassed because no other group wanted me."

"Still, they sounded nice. That boy—what'd you say his name was?"

"Henry."

"Henry," Mrs. B repeated, clearly already running away with the idea that he and I were going to be great friends. "He went out on a limb for you, Jade. Maybe you should do the same for him."

"Come on," I protested as we turned out of the subdivision. "These guys think I'm a freak—they both know I passed out at Yan Mei's the other day. It was horrifying."

"Speaking of that," Mrs. B said, giving me a concerned glance, "you've not had any more episodes, have you? No headaches? Lost time?"

I fixed my eyes on the trees passing outside the window, the first traces of yellow and orange already starting to creep into their leaves. "You sound as bad as Benson. Wasn't he supposed to be dropping me off tonight anyway?"

"That wasn't an answer, Jade," she said, still sounding worried. "Your da—Benji got held up at work. Something about his boss fast-tracking some kind of new project."

"He's a geneticist?" I asked, pretending not to notice that she'd nearly said *your dad*. I hadn't addressed Benson as that in months. "What on earth could be so important in somebody's DNA that he needs to work overtime?"

Mrs. B shrugged. "Something big, apparently. Graves Research is one of the biggest medical firms in the world. Maybe they've found something that could help cure cancer or diabetes or something."

I sat up straighter. "Did you say *Graves* Research?"

"I thought you knew what Benji's new company was called?" she asked, raising an eyebrow. "Graves. As in, the founder, Dominic Graves."

As in Julian Graves, I thought, though I kept my mouth shut. Hadn't he said his dad's name was Dominic? So, Julian was the heir to a genetic research empire. No wonder his dad had been able to send that fancy car after him. Why hadn't I realized the connection sooner?

"What? Is something wrong?"

"Nothing," I said, turning back to the window as storefronts started to pass by. "His son's in my class. Kind of a jerk."

"He hasn't said anything mean to you, has he?" Mrs. B asked warily, clearly ready to break out her Protective Mom powers if I gave the word.

He just acted nice to me then ignored my existence.

"No."

Mrs. B nodded as she pulled up to the curb in front of Yan Mei's Cafe, clearly relieved that she didn't need to bust heads at the next PTO meeting. The cafe didn't look too crowded since it was still a little early for dinner. I could see Dylan and Henry at one of the tables inside, waiting for me. Henry was talking a mile a minute as usual. Dylan raised a hand in a shy wave as he noticed me in the car.

"Those your study buddies?" Mrs. B asked, waving back at him cheerfully.

I cringed. "Please don't call them that. Dylan. Henry."

"Oh, they are just adorable!" Mrs. B said excitedly. "Maybe I should come in and introduce myse—"

I was already out of the car. "I'll see you at eight, Mrs. B."

The familiar beaded door jingled as I walked inside the restaurant, breathing in the competing smells of rice and fried beef. It was strange... I had expected to feel weird coming back to Yan Mei's after the mega-vision, but the place only felt familiar. Comfortable. Like some place you were always meant to be.

"Jade! Over here!" Henry shouted, giving me another exaggerated wave. Several of the customers looked up at him, but none seemed surprised, as if they were used to Henry randomly yelling across the restaurant at people. He and Dylan had taken up positions at a table near the kitchen. Dylan gave me a small smile when I caught his eye. I gripped my bag tighter and made my way over to their table.

"Sorry to keep you waiting, guys," I said.

Dylan fumbled to pull out the chair beside him, nearly knocking it over in the process. "Oh, no worries. We're still waiting on our food."

"I thought we were going to work on the project?"

The boys shrugged. "Sure, but that doesn't mean we have to be hungry! It's kind of an obligation to get food when you go to a restaurant. Especially your grandma's," Henry said, motioning for me to sit down.

"That...actually makes sense," I agreed.

A sweet confectionary aroma filled the air, and I turned my head to see Yan Mei walking toward our table with a plate piled high with Chinese donuts. She was wearing a Pinewood High T-shirt and a matching purple and green hairpiece. Obviously, Henry's grandma had more school spirit than anyone who actually went to Pinewood.

"Nice to see you again, Jade," Yan Mei said, placing the plate down on our table. "My grandson said he owed you an apology that could only be repaid in donuts."

"It's no big deal...But I will always take some donuts," I said, reaching toward the plate. Wow, that really was nice of Henry to do that for me. "Thanks, Mrs. Yan Mei."

"Yeah, I hope we're all good now, Kastel," Henry said, smirking at me.

A gasp brought every eye to Yan Mei. She was staring directly at me, eyes wide. I paused mid-donut, not sure what to do. Why was she staring at me? Had I done something wrong? The boys looked just as confused as I felt. Her dark brown eyes stayed locked on mine, frozen like a deer in the headlights. She looked like she wanted to say something but couldn't quite seem to manage it.

"Grandma?" Henry asked, suddenly sounding more serious than I'd ever thought he could be. His grandma was still staring at me with that same weird expression. Shock? Horror? Disbelief? I couldn't place it before she seemed to snap herself out of the daze.

"Ex-Excuse me," she said before rushing back into the kitchen.

"Grandma?" Henry called worriedly, standing up to rush after her.

Dylan and I just sat, staring at each other for a moment—both weirded out and not sure what to say without Henry to buffer the conversation. Finally, Dylan cleared his throat.

"I don't think she was feeling well today," he said before pointing at the donuts on the plate. I hadn't even realized I was still clutching the one from earlier. "Are you going to eat those?"

"Absolutely. And if you don't take some now, I *will* eat them all," I said, taking a bite from my donut. Still warm. The sweet, sugary pastry melted in my mouth. I must have made a silly face as I ate it because Dylan chuckled before grabbing one himself.

"These are *so* good!" I said. I could practically hear Mrs. B chiding me for not being very ladylike, but I didn't care. The donuts were too good. Plus, Dylan was smiling at me.

"Yeah, Yan Mei is the best," he said, taking a bite. "Really, she's good at everything. And she *knows* everything. It's literally impossible to keep anything from her."

"Sounds like you guys are close."

He nodded. "Yan Mei and my mom go way back. Henry and I have been best friends since, like, birth. We've sort of always had each other. I know he may seem like he's a lot, but he really is great. Never a dull moment with him."

I smiled. "It certainly seems that way. It must be nice to have a friend like that."

I hadn't meant for it to sound sad, but I'm sure that's how it came out. Dylan looked at me like he was concerned but didn't say anything. I could almost see the question in his mind that he didn't want to ask.

"Hey! Save some donuts for me, guys!" Henry shouted as he ran back over to the table.

"How's your grandma?" I asked as he snatched a donut from the plate. I cringed as the entire pastry disappeared into his mouth, and he started to blubber out incoherent words.

"Chew, Henry," Dylan chided. Henry gulped down his food and took a large swig of his drink. He sighed contentedly.

"Man, those are good," he said, reaching for another. "She's fine. Just said she'd remembered something sad and wanted some tea."

Tea reminded me of Julian...how he'd dropped half a dozen different brands of the stuff when I'd run into him. He seemed so friendly then. But I suppose his true colors came out when we were at school, in front of everyone. He was just another person who wanted nothing to do with me.

Watching Henry stuff donuts into his mouth and Dylan silently doodle on one of the napkins, I could tell they were different. They knew who I was, that I zoned out. They had been nice to me and shared good food, even if it was under the guise of a school project that clearly was not a priority right now. It was almost like we were three friends just having a good time.

"So, Dylan, why were you carrying a lamp down the hallway earlier?" I asked awkwardly, not sure what else to say.

Both boys went pale. Suddenly, I was worried that the three donuts Henry had just inhaled were going to make a reappearance.

"It's a gift—" Henry started.

"Carrying it to the teacher's lounge—" Dylan interrupted.

"What?" they said in unison, looking at each other blankly.

"It's a gift for the teacher's lounge," Henry said, refusing to look at me.

I raised an eyebrow. It was clear that both of them were lying, but it didn't make a lot of sense to me why they'd be so flustered over a lamp. Maybe I didn't want to know the real reason. Also, why did Henry chime in? It wasn't like he had been there too. "O-kay..."

"So, how do you know Julian?" Dylan asked, shaky voice indicating his desperation for a subject change.

Now, it was my turn to be flustered. "What?"

"I saw you start toward him when we were picking groups," he said, sounding embarrassed. "You looked...sad."

"Ooh, stalker much?" Henry chided.

"No!" Dylan and I shouted. We looked at each other with wide eyes. Silence fell throughout the entire restaurant. Everyone had gone quiet, looking at us with a mix of confusion and annoyance. Dylan flushed cherry red. I sunk down in my chair.

"I just meant..." Dylan fumbled for the right words.

"It's okay," I said, making sure to keep my voice low. Most of the people in the restaurant had gone back to their conversations and food, but the people at the next table over were still glaring at us. "I met him a few days ago...buying an obscene amount of tea. He seemed nice enough, so I thought maybe he'd want to work with me. Obviously, I was wrong."

"Well, clearly, you ended up in the better group. We're way better than that dude," Henry said. "I don't know why she would want to work with him anyway. He's obviously brainwashed her."

Dylan laughed. "There's no way we'd get anything done if Victoria was in our group."

"It's not like we've gotten a lot done anyway," I said, interrupting Henry before he could argue. I pulled out my notebook and script for *Macbeth*.

"I guess we can be good students now and *actually* work on the project," Henry said, rolling his eyes. Dylan and I raised our eyebrows at him. "What? I can be good sometimes."

As expected, we didn't get much done. But we did eventually get a better understanding of what we needed to do for our project and how we were going to split the tasks. Surprisingly, when focused, the pair could actually be pretty productive, though it took a few redirects on Dylan's part since Henry got distracted *very* easily. Usually, with group projects, I ended up doing all the work, and the other members would only speak to me when necessary. But I could tell Dylan and Henry were actually trying to contribute.

We bantered back and forth between whether or not we were going to do a reenactment of the three witches for the visual portion—something I was *heavily* against.

"But it's *perfect*!" Henry said, slurping the last drops of his third Dr. Pepper. "We are the *only* group of three. It would be a crime to *not* do it! Tell her, Dylan."

"Well, it seems easier than creating something from scratch," Dylan said.

"But that means getting up in front of *people*," I said, cringing.

"You know, Jade has a point," Dylan agreed. I was sure he wanted to get up in front of everyone about as much as I did.

Henry threw his arms up in the air. "Whose side are you on?"

"Jade's," he said quickly.

Henry sighed. "But I don't want to make something...*creative*. That just sounds like a lot of work," he whined.

"You do have a point there," I said.

Henry's face lit up in a smile. "See, I knew you were cool, Jade."

30

"But we're still not doing a reenactment," I said. His face dropped, and Dylan and I laughed at him.

My phone buzzed loudly from my bag, making me jump. It was an *I'm here* text from Mrs. B. Was it eight o'clock already? It had to be—Mrs. B was nothing if not punctual.

"Well, that's my ride," I said, standing up to gather my things. Funny enough, I was actually reluctant to leave. For the first time in my life, I felt *normal*.

"Aw, it's already eight?" Henry gasped.

"Guess I should start heading back home, too," Dylan said.

I started toward the door. To my surprise, the two boys were right behind me. There was a shuffle of quiet steps, and I realized Yan Mei had reemerged as well. I hadn't seen her at all since she'd taken off into the kitchen. Her eyes watched me for a long moment before her face eased into a gentle smile.

"It was good to see you, Jade. You should come by again soon," the older woman said. Her voice was rough, almost like she'd been crying.

"Yeah, we would love to see you again," Dylan chimed in.

"You're basically stuck with us now," Henry said, grinning from ear to ear. Sugar from the donuts glinted all over his chin.

"Still not doing the play," I said cheerfully, heading toward the car. Tommy grinned at me triumphantly from the front seat, meaning I would have to squish in behind him in the back. Yan Mei and Henry vanished back into the restaurant after a small wave, and Dylan started up the street. I'd barely had time to close the car door before Mrs. B lurched it forward...pulling even with Dylan's fast pace. The sound of a window lowering made my eyes go wide with panic. *No way. No, no, no...*

"Excuse me! Young man, excuse me!" Mrs. B yelled, halfway leaning over Tommy.

"No! Mrs. B, don't—" I started but groaned. Dylan looked terrified that someone was screaming at him out a car window, but he had stopped. This could *not* be good.

"Uh...yes, ma'am?" Dylan said, still confused and slightly terrified.

"Oh, you are such a doll!" Mrs. B gushed, breaking into a wide

31

smile. "Why don't we give you a ride home? We have plenty of room here in the back—with Jade."

"Mrs. B!" I hissed. Tommy looked ready to die of laughter.

"I wouldn't want to intrude. I don't live that far from here, Mrs...?"

"Benson. Charlotte Benson, Jade's mom."

"*Adoptive* mom," I said. "You don't have to go with us—"

"Yes, you do!" Tommy interrupted excitedly, popping the locks on the doors. Mrs. B grinned.

Dylan clearly saw it was a losing battle and quickly made his way around the car to take the seat behind Mrs. B.

I'm sorry, I mouthed. Dylan shrugged like it was no big deal. Maybe suburban moms tried to kidnap him all the time. He did seem like the typical charming teen who got in every mom's good graces.

"So, Dylan," Mrs. B said, trying hard to hide the excitement in her voice, "Jade has told me so much about you."

"I have not!" I protested. "I told you his name two hours ago."

"And you told me about the project," she insisted. "How'd that go? You three get a lot of work done?"

"Some," Dylan said. "We basically just split the project up. Our other partner, Henry, wants us to act out a scene for the visual part of the project."

Mrs. B smiled at him in the rearview mirror. "Ooh, that would be fun! I don't think Jade's been in a play since she was in third grade...She ended up knocking half the set over, but it still made a cute video to send to Nana Benson."

"Yeah, what'd you play again, Jade? A princess?" Tommy asked, grinning innocently.

"No, no, it was a fairy princess," Mrs. B corrected happily. "What was that cute little song you had to sing, Jade? Something about 'Rain-bowland'?"

Dylan politely stayed silent, but he looked like he was trying hard not to laugh. I put my head in my hands. This. This was what hell looked like.

"If it makes you feel any better, Henry once had to dress up as a lamp in elementary school to explain household objects, and he's never really forgotten about it," Dylan said, careful to keep his voice low from Tommy and Mrs. B.

I laughed. "I'll be sure to remember that for later."

"So, I suppose this means you two will be spending quite a bit of time together for this project, huh?" Mrs. B said, trying to sound nonchalant. She failed miserably.

"It's a semester-long project. We'll probably need to meet at least once a week," I said. Her smile was practically blinding in the rearview mirror. Wuh-oh.

"Are you sure you just don't want to spend more time with *Dylan*?" Tommy teased.

"Tommy. Stop," I hissed. He turned smugly in his seat with a triumphant grin on his face. I was grateful for how dark the sky was tonight. Hopefully, Dylan couldn't see my deadly expression.

"Um, my house is just up here, Mrs. Benson." Dylan pointed out sheepishly. "On the left."

Mrs. B stopped in front of the house he'd indicated: a big white building with a long front porch and a two-car garage. Little electric candles burned in all the windows, and an expansive flower garden had been carefully planted along the front of the house. It was a nice place—the kind that was probably always unnaturally clean and got decorated outside for every holiday.

"Thanks again for the ride, Mrs. Benson," Dylan said. When he opened the door, a symphony of different-pitched wind chimes clinked in the cool night breeze.

"Oh, anytime, honey! Anytime!"

Dylan reached in to get his backpack, though I'd already grabbed it to hand to him. For the briefest second, our hands bumped on the top strap, and I felt my gut wrench with the unmistakable feeling of a vision.

The world was loud and echo-y and bright. A strong chemical smell invaded my nostrils, making me feel lightheaded with the drafty breeze. People were talking, but everything seemed...garbled, like a crowd speaking all at once. A shrill noise tore through my mind like a whistle blast, making me double over in pain.

Breathe, I thought. *You have to breathe, Jade.*

I clapped my hands over my ears and tried to concentrate. The overwhelming brightness slowly started to recede to a tolerable level. I could see the floor under my feet now—dark gray concrete that was wet underneath my boots. The mess of voices seemed to untangle themselves: a little girl laughing, a man talking, then one that sounded amplified somehow—like an announcer.

Suddenly, I heard a loud splashing noise. I forced myself to stand up. I recognized this place. It was the back building where the pool was at Pinewood High—I'd seen it during orientation, then again today when I was trying to keep an eye on Dylan. A wide open room with big windows on either side to let in the sun, though it seemed duller now, like it was closer to dusk. The pool in the center had been divided into rows with long lap lanes. The stands were packed with people—parents, students, teachers. A swim meet.

Usually, when I had a vision, it wasn't hard to tell if something was wrong, but the scene in front of me looked completely normal. The crowd cheered as a big group of kids headed for the diving boards—half decked out in purple and green, the rest in black and yellow. The Birchwood Beavers, Pinewood's top rival (hey, I know *some* stuff about my school). Nothing seemed out of place, though. Why was I seeing this?

I looked closer, familiar faces emerging out of the crowd. Victoria was in the front row, chatting away with one of the girls from the school newspaper as she fiddled with her camera. Someone was obviously making their rounds as class president. Henry wasn't far behind her, but he didn't seem to be able to get a word in edgewise between the two. I spotted Julian at the end of the stands, sticking out like a sore thumb in his dark clothes. He was deep in conversation with Mr. Goodman.

A laugh caught my attention, drawing my eyes back to the side of the pool. Dylan was a few feet away with the next round of Pinewood kids waiting to swim. He was talking to a boy a little younger than him.

A whistle sounded. Sixteen kids hit the water at lightning speed. Suddenly, an eerie feeling washed over me, like I was being watched. I felt myself lurch forward, just like in the mega-vision, as if it was physically moving me toward something I needed to see. My boots slipped across the floor, unable to find traction. It was all I could do to keep my balance.

I shuddered. An angry, predatory feeling, like I was being hunted, spread through my chest like ice. No one around me let on like anything was wrong. The swimmers were halfway across the pool. Henry was still on the stands, though Victoria seemed to have vanished from sight. I didn't see Julian or Mr. Goodman now either.

The vision yanked me forward until I was standing right in front of the Pinewood team. Someone—*something*—was heading straight for Dylan. I don't know how I knew, but suddenly, I was sure that's who the predator was after. I tried to call out for him to move, but he couldn't hear me, still laughing obliviously with the other boy.

The force was getting closer now—practically right on top of him. I couldn't see or hear it, but somehow I knew it was there. He had to move.

He had to move.

~

"Jade? Jade!" Mrs. B's voice brought me back to reality.

"What?" I asked, heart still pounding against my chest. Both Tommy and Mrs. B had turned around to look at me in concern.

"Honey, I asked you if you wanted anything for dinner like three times," Mrs. B said worriedly.

Out the windshield, I could see Dylan was already on his front porch, safe and sound. A small blonde girl had opened the door for him.

"Aw, she zoned out again, Mom," Tommy sneered. "Probably daydreaming about her next study date with *Dyl-an*."

I kicked the back of his seat.

"Jade!" Mrs. B chided, but her eyes were watching me knowingly. There wasn't any anger in her tone.

"I-I think I just want to go home," I said, yanking out my journal to log the vision. It was too dark to sketch it out right now. *Dylan, swim meet, evil force.*

Two visions about Dylan in under a week. He had to be going for a record. One thing was for sure: Dylan Mason was starting to take up a lot of my time.

CHAPTER
FIVE

I didn't normally do this. I normally *avoided* the popular people at all costs. Even Henry was surprised when I asked for his help, though he'd happily obliged. I wove my way up through the crowded hallway, searching for the one and only Victoria Harper.

It wasn't like I *wanted* to talk to her, but this wasn't about me. This was about Dylan and saving him from whatever invisible *thing* was hunting him in my vision. I needed information. The vision clearly hadn't happened yet, as the swim season had just started, and Dylan was alive and well. I had tried to figure out when the swim meets were, but the schedule wasn't posted yet. Even Dylan wasn't sure. I tried a few more people who were very clearly confused as to why I was talking to them and why I was so interested in the swim meets, but they all gave me one answer: "Ask Victoria."

Apparently, no one cared enough about the swim team except our class president. Something I completely understood but, in this circumstance, was extremely unhelpful.

Finally, I caught sight of a tall blonde at the end of the hall by the chemistry lab. Right where Henry said. I chose not to think about how well he knew her schedule as I started toward her. But she wasn't alone.

Beside her, dressed in his usual button-up and khakis, was Mr. Goodman. I debated on what to do. Should I approach them and ask to speak with her? Should I wait until he went away? I'd rather walk away and not talk to *either* of them, but that was out of the question. Something bad was going to happen to Dylan if I didn't stop it. My mind flashed to Mary Milford, the girl who disappeared—was that what happened to her? All the more reason I *had* to save Dylan. I took a deep breath and marched up to the pair.

"I just have a bad feeling about it," Victoria said. The pair hadn't yet noticed my presence, and I was awfully curious as to what our class president would have a bad feeling about. Mr. Goodman reached out his hand but hesitated over her shoulder before giving her a quick pat.

"Everything is going to be fine," Mr. Goodman promised. "Just look at me. I was basically on death's door until everything turned around for me."

He winced slightly, but Victoria didn't seem to notice. It was weird like he was in pain and trying to hide it. She looked calmed by his pep talk. The tension in the air released, and a smile appeared on her face.

"Yeah, you're right. Sorry. I've been a little stressed lately," she told him.

"I completely understand," Mr. Goodman replied before turning to face me with a pleasant smile. "Can we help you with something?"

Victoria's piercing eyes turned toward me as well, and I suddenly felt very out of place. Even though I had been standing there with the intention of getting noticed, I still felt like I had intruded on a private conversation.

"Can I talk to you for a moment, Victoria?" I asked, cringing at how embarrassing this whole situation was. *If only I could disappear through the wall and pretend this never happened.* Her eyebrows shot up before quickly composing herself. Mr. Goodman smiled.

"I have to run back to class, but I will see you both later."

Victoria raised an eyebrow. "Sure, what do you need, Jade?"

Yet again, another person I hadn't spoken to before knew my name. At least it made more sense with her because she was the class president, and we shared a few classes together.

I noticed she was bouncing restlessly on the balls of her feet. *Was I scaring her or something?*

"I need to know when the swim meet is."

She raised her eyebrows. "Which one, exactly?"

I blanked. How was I supposed to know which one I had seen in my vision? I could've seen any upcoming meet. *Think, Jade. Which team were they up against?*

"Um...Birchwood. I need the swim meet date for the Birchwood Beavers."

"Oh, that's actually this Friday. It starts at five at the Rec Center across the street," Victoria said.

Friday? That means I had three days to figure out a way to save Dylan. It wasn't a lot of time, but I supposed I would have to figure something out. I *had* to.

"Thanks, Victoria," I said, trying not to sound awkward but failing miserably. She gave me a polite smile, twisting a knot deep in the pit of my stomach. I knew the resemblance was only passingly similar, but there was a part of me that couldn't help picturing my supposed former friend, at a different school, a different hallway. *Not every kid is going to be another Ashley,* Mrs. B's voice echoed in my mind. I shook away the thought. Victoria was not Ashley- she was too tall, too preppy, hair a more honeyed blonde, eyes blue instead of brown. Still, I was very cautious. Just because she hadn't yet didn't mean she wasn't about to start.

"No problem, Jade," Victoria said. "Though I am kind of surprised why you would be interested in that sort of thing."

I stammered for a moment, trying to come up with a reasonable excuse to show up. I tried to think of something in my vision that might explain my sudden interest in aquatic sports, but I came up blank. So, I just started saying words, and I hoped it would work.

"Oh, well—Dylan is on the swim team," I stammered. Victoria's face lit up in a grin, and I suddenly realized I had made a huge mistake.

"I see," she said, smirking. I waved my arms in panic. *No, not her, too!*

"No, no, I mean—we're friends, I guess. And I want to...support my friend!"

Her smirk didn't waver for a second. *This was a bad idea.*

"Yes, I am sure you do. Well, I have to get to history, but it was nice talking to you. Oh, and good luck *supporting* Dylan at the swim meet!" she said with a wink, patting my shoulder before starting toward the stairs.

I didn't even have time to cringe at my embarrassing exchange as a wave of nausea hit and my vision distorted. I braced myself on a locker.

~

I was standing in the same hallway, though everything seemed...duller, faded. Like an old movie playing before my eyes.

Victoria was in front of me again, leaning against the junior lockers, even though I had just seen her walk toward the stairs a few moments prior. But this wasn't the Victoria I was just talking to. Her hair was pulled up into a ponytail instead of down, and she was wearing jeans and a pep-squad T-shirt instead of a dress.

I'd only ever had a few visions of the past, but I was confident that I was seeing an event that had already happened. Only Fridays were pep squad days, and the clock on the wall had moved from a little after 12:30 to well after four. Victoria didn't look much different, so it had to have been recent. Last Friday, maybe? But why was she here so late, hanging out near someone's locker?

Footsteps drew my attention down the hall. A group of teens streamed out of one of the empty classrooms, and Victoria turned toward the group. The chess club? What would Victoria want with—

I froze.

It was *her*.

A short girl was fighting her backpack zipper as she headed straight toward Victoria and me, not paying any attention. Her curly red hair flew everywhere, and the lenses on her bright purple glasses were so thick that her eyes had a constant frazzled sort of look to them. Mary Milford, the girl who went missing.

From what little they told us at Pinewood High, no one had seen Mary for several days. Supposedly, she'd spent the weekend at a friend's house (though no one seemed to know *which* friend), and her parents had come to school on Monday looking for her, causing those weird announcements from Principal Porter. Mary hadn't shown up today either. Every class she'd been in had been interrogated to see if anyone knew where she might have gone. No one did. I'd heard a couple of kids say she might have run away.

This *had* to be last Friday—right when I'd had my freaky death vision and ran into Julian. Before Mary Milford had gone missing. But why was Victoria here? They never appeared to be friends, and I had heard Victoria say to Principal Porter that she hadn't seen her since English on Friday. Why had she lied?

Victoria cleared her throat, making Mary jump before glaring at the class president.

"I told you, I'm not interested," Mary said, keeping her eyes low and opening one of the lockers.

Victoria sighed. "Come on, Mary. Please? You're the best at guessing, and we *need* you!"

Mary kept her eyes firmly on the inside of her now-open locker. "I don't *guess*."

"Even more reason to help us! My boss would love to meet you. Just this once? Then you'd never have to help again, I *promise!*" Victoria pleaded.

"I said no, Victoria," Mary said, slamming her locker door shut. Her voice was forceful and commanding. She looked around to make sure no one else had heard them, but the hallway was empty except for the two of them. "I'm sorry, but my answer is no. Please stop asking."

Victoria sighed. "Okay, if that's what you want." She pushed herself off of the locker she was leaning against and started walking away. Mary bolted toward the stairs in the opposite direction of Victoria.

Suddenly, the same terrible feeling I got from my prior vision washed over me. The same gripping force shot me forward. Straight toward Mary. I looked around, but Victoria was nowhere to be found, having likely already left.

A scream shattered my ears as the force slammed into Mary Milford. A chill ran down my spine. My fears were correct. She hadn't run away.

She had been taken.

~

Someone's hand was on my back, holding me upright. My head was spinning. I felt like I could throw up. Three visions in a week? I had never had that many visions before in such a close time frame.

"Are you alright, Jade? You had me worried for a second."

Before my eyes was none other than Julian Graves. Irritation surged through me, but I was far too tired to act on it. I nodded and pushed out of his reach.

"Just got a little dizzy," I lied, rubbing my temples.

Julian looked concerned. "Does that happen a lot?"

I glared at him. The lights hurt my eyes. "Why do you care? Also, no. It doesn't."

Julian shrugged off my comment. "Maybe your blood sugar dropped." He fished out a couple of crumpled dollars from his pocket. "Why don't you get a candy bar or something sugary to drink? I can tell Mr. Nicholson that you aren't feeling well since we have the same class."

I pressed my forehead against the cool of the lockers. I didn't even care that they weren't mine. Even my brain hurt. "That might actually help a lot. Thanks, Julian. I owe you."

He gave me a kind smile, similar to when we first met, before heading off. "It's no problem, Jade. I hope you feel better soon."

I don't know how long I stood there trying to make sense of what I'd just seen, probably long enough to get behind in psychology class. So, Victoria wanted Mary to do something, and she'd refused. Victoria also mentioned her boss wanting to meet Mary? Was this a job interview about guessing? None of it made any sense.

But then Mary was taken by some *invisible force*? No one would believe that. Not that anyone would believe I could see the future and past either, but still. This was extremely confusing. To make matters worse, Victoria had *lied* about seeing Mary. She may not have taken her, but she was the last person who saw her before she vanished. Maybe she was scared of getting in trouble? That would be problematic for her. Could that have been why she was talking to Mr. Goodman? Class presidents have a reputation to keep. But something about that seemed off to me. What was Victoria talking about, and what was she hiding?

One thing was for sure, though. Mary Milford did not run away, and whatever took her was going after Dylan next. I had three days to think of a plan to save him.

CHAPTER
SIX

"I need your help," I said to Mrs. B reluctantly as she pulled away from the curb of Pinewood Elementary. We had just dropped off Tommy, and the next five minutes in the car would be the only time I'd be able to say something to her without one of the Benson guys around. I was pretty sure I would regret talking to her about this, but I was out of options and running out of time.

I needed to stop that vision from happening. I would have to get Dylan far away from that swim meet—the trouble was that it was kind of difficult since he was *on* the swim team. I was starting to get the feeling the visions were sending me on a wild goose chase to make sure Dylan Mason stayed alive.

She perked up as we started down the road toward Pinewood High —it was a rare occasion I ever asked her about anything. "Yes, dear? What is it?"

I took a deep breath and tried to choose my words carefully. "Well, let's just say that you want someone to...hang out with you. How would you go about that without seeming like you're demanding?"

Mrs. B paused, eyes widening before her mouth spread into a wide smile. She squealed so shrilly that I covered my ears. "Could this be a certain *boy*, perhaps?"

"Yes, actually. How did you—" I stopped when I realized *why* she was so happy. "It's not a date! I am trying to make friends like you told me to!"

Her smile didn't falter. In fact, I was certain you could have told her the world was ending, and her grin wouldn't have gone down in the slightest. Who knew this was the key all along to making her happy?

"Of course it's not a date, honey," she said, winking at me. "But if you wanted to ask this *boy* on a not-date, perhaps you could try something simple. Why don't you invite him over after school?"

"What? No, I couldn't—" I sighed. "Okay...hypothetically, how would I even ask? Wouldn't I need a reason? And we aren't exactly alone very often—"

"Honey, if you don't have a reason, make one up." Mrs. B laughed. "That's how your da...Benji and I got together. Back in college, I let the air out of my own tires just so he'd offer to drive me home."

I raised an eyebrow. "And he didn't notice they weren't actually slashed?"

Mrs. B shrugged. "Benji isn't always the most observant man. I'm just saying, maybe you need a more creative solution."

"Meaning, lie?"

"I didn't say that exactly. But inviting someone over might be a good start."

"I could," I pondered, weighing the pros and cons. "But that isn't very private."

Mrs. B grinned widely, determination spreading across her face. She was one step away from laughing maniacally.

"You just leave that to me, dear," she said. "I'll take care of Benji and Tommy. I will make sure you get some time with Dylan."

I sighed in relief. "Thanks, Mrs. B—wait, how did you know I was talking about Dylan?"

"A mother just knows these sorts of things, Jade. Even adoptive ones." Mrs. B smirked as she pulled into the drop-off line for Pinewood High. "You'd better hurry if you want to ask him now. You're about to lose your chance."

Mrs. B nodded out at the sea of kids streaming in from the parking lot. Sure enough, there was Dylan, walking with his quick, quiet pace toward the front doors. She motioned me out of the car, still grinning enthusiastically. It didn't really seem like I had a choice in the matter anymore. She probably would have sat there all day, waiting to see if I talked to Dylan, but a honk from the car behind us saved me from total humiliation.

Regardless of her misunderstanding my intentions, I was grateful for the help.

"Thanks, Mrs. B," I said. "But it's still not a date."

"You leave *Operation Not-a-Date* to me!" she said with way too much enthusiasm. She was giving off Henry-vibes, and I was not at all prepared for it. "Now, let me plan. Go—do whatever it is you do most of the time."

Ponder my short mortal existence?

I shook my head and darted for the school.

"Jade! Don't chicken out!" Mrs. B called, halfway leaning out the window.

"Please go away!" I yelled back at her. I could see her laughing as she pulled out of the drop-off zone. I might have created a monster.

I looked around. Dylan was already at the doors—so much for asking him now when no one else was around.

You have to keep him from going to that swim meet, my brain said.

Yes, I know that, Brain, I thought miserably.

I took a deep breath. I had two classes with Dylan: English and calculus. That was two more chances to try to talk him out of swimming Friday. With any luck, I'd never even have to invite him over at all.

The only problem was that I apparently didn't have any luck.

English was a bust because we were discussing our group projects, and Henry was around the whole time. He was still dead set on doing a "dramatic interpretation" of the three witches scene at the beginning of the play, and Dylan and I spent the entire forty-five minutes arguing against it.

Mary Milford's seat was empty again—apparently, she still hadn't turned up. That was five days she'd been gone. I tried to watch Victoria for any sign that there might be something to that weird vision I'd seen of her and Mary, but she and Julian seemed consumed with their scene of Macbeth and his wife.

It wasn't until calculus that I finally caught a break.

Mrs. Watson was handing back our tests. I had switched seats with some kid a few days ago, so I'd have the one across from Dylan since I'd been trying to keep an eye on him after my mega-vision. The second Dylan looked at his test, he flipped it over and hung his head, though I'd seen the giant *D* at the top written in red ink.

As discreetly as I could, I leaned over and poked him with my pencil. Dylan jumped so high his knees banged into the table.

Mrs. Watson turned around in concern. "Are you alright, Mr. Mason?"

"All good," he said, clearly not all-good, but she turned back to the board anyway. He raised an eyebrow at me.

"What's wrong?" I whispered. "Was it that bad?"

Dylan nodded. "If I fail again, I'm never going to make swim captain."

I gave him a sympathetic frown. From what I was learning about him, his two main priorities were Henry and the swim team. He probably dreamed about being team captain.

"That's rough, Dylan," I said. I wanted to offer more comfort, but a sympathetic shoulder pat would only make things awkward—plus, if I touched him, I could get *another* vision, and I already had enough I needed to keep from happening. *Figure out what Victoria has to do with Mary disappearing, stop Dylan from getting attacked, and not die in two to three years.*

Wait. Dylan needed help with his calculus. Mrs. B's advice popped into my head. *I think I just found my reason.*

Mrs. Watson launched into a lesson on derivatives, something I was already familiar with. I still took notes absentmindedly, but my mind wandered to the gloomy-looking boy flicking his pencil up and down again, something he always seemed to be doing. I tried to watch to see if he really was touching the pencil each time he flicked it up the desk, but it was too close to call. There was the tiny hope again, fluttering up from the pit of my stomach—no. There was no way it was possible that Dylan could have powers, too.

What if that's why there's been so many visions about him? A rebellious part of my brain whispered. *You've never had so many of the same person so consistently before.*

Before I knew it, the bell had rung, and everyone around me was packing up their stuff. Dylan mournfully shoved his test into his backpack. Now or never. I couldn't believe I was taking advice from Mrs. B on, God forbid, *boys*.

"I can help you with that," I said, not sure if I'd regret this.

Dylan looked up in surprise. "What?"

"Your test...Mrs. Watson will let you do a retake," I said, keeping my voice low as the other kids headed past us. "We already covered this stuff at my last school. I can help you with it if you want."

"Seriously?" he asked, some of the tension easing out of his shoulders.

"Seriously."

Dylan beamed at me. "Really? That would be great!"

I shrugged as if it was no big deal. He didn't have to know I'd been planning this all day. "Sure. My house around five-thirty?"

"Awesome! You're the best, Jade!"

A nervous feeling fluttered through my stomach, but if my expression gave it away, Dylan seemed too happy to notice. "I'll see you then."

Dylan gave me one last smile before heading out of the room. Okay, so I had my chance—all I had to do tonight was convince Dylan not to go to the swim meet and try not to completely embarrass myself. I could do that, right?

Panicking. I was panicking. Dylan would be at my house any moment now. A whole evening with him stuck in the same house as me and the Bensons.

"Jade, quit pacing. You're going to wear a hole in the floor," Mrs. B chided, passing by with a basket of clean laundry. She looked remarkably excited, which made me even more scared about whatever this "plan" was she had to help me out with Dylan. Why? Why had I ever thought this was a good idea? It'd been a long time since I'd had a friend over and I'd never seen Mrs. B this excited about anyone.

I heard a car door slam shut outside. I peeked out the window—sure enough, there was Dylan getting out of his car. He was heading toward the house now. Thirty feet. Twenty.

"Remember, you all promised not to be weird," I hissed, eying Tommy and Benson in the living room.

Tommy rolled his eyes. "You're the only one being weird, Jade."

I jumped out of my skin as the doorbell rang. This was it. All the Bensons stared at me expectantly. Mrs. B gestured for me to open the door.

"*Hihowareyoudoing?*" I said, probably unintelligibly, as I yanked open the door. *Smooth, Jade.*

"Um, hi...everyone?" Dylan said, eyes widening as he took in our whole family staring at him. Or were they staring at me? Dylan raised an eyebrow in my direction. "Are you okay? How much coffee have you had today?"

"Unfortunately, none," I muttered, running a hand over my face. "My room's upstairs, on the left."

"You're taking him to the Room of Doom?" Tommy asked in mock horror. Benson nudged him to leave me alone.

"Ignore him," I said, pointing up the stairs. Dylan led the way, though he looked slightly more nervous than before. Mrs. B tried to wink reassuringly at me before I could follow. It didn't have the desired effect.

We'd barely made it halfway up the stairs before Benson called, "Remember, doors need to stay open at all times, Jade Margaret!"

"Benson!" I yelled back down at him.

Dylan looked horrified. Great. Now we'd scared him to death, and he knew my middle name. No one knew my middle name.

"I thought we could start by walking through what you didn't understand on the test," I said quickly as we stepped into my room. I plopped down on the rug where I'd spread out my calculus notes. "What?"

Dylan had froze, trying to take in my bedroom. I had done a quick shove-everything-in-the-closet cleaning, but suddenly, I felt self-conscious. He picked up a candle, looking at it like it was radio-active.

49

"Violet walls, scented candles, stuffed animals..." he said in confusion. "Who *are* you?"

"What stuffed animals?" I asked, looking around worriedly. I thought I'd hidden all of them.

Dylan picked up the little stuffed owl on top of my bookcase, holding it up for me to see.

"Oh, that's Mr. Hootsworth," I said, cringing at the name. "He freaks Tommy out, so it keeps him from stealing my books...Geez, I sound like a five-year-old."

Dylan chuckled, his eyes scanning the books piled sloppily on the shelves. "No, it doesn't. My six-year-old sister named her owl Mr. Hooty-Toot, so I think you're safe. *Connecting with Your Inner Psychic Abilities*?"

I winced. How had I missed hiding that book? I'd gotten it a few years ago when my powers had first started getting stronger. The inside was completely covered in notes and scribbles I'd made over the years. *Please don't open it, please don't open it...*

"Tommy gave that to me as a joke."

Dylan raised an eyebrow. He didn't really look like he believed me, but he didn't argue. He sat down beside me and pulled his test out of his backpack. "I think had the most trouble on—"

"Knock, knock!" Mrs. B called, announcing her presence unnecessarily loud. She had the biggest tray of snacks I'd ever seen in her hands. Apparently, she'd gone all out: a pepperoni rose in the center surrounded by rows of cucumbers, crackers, cheeses, grapes, and hummus with a side of freshly baked chocolate chip cookies. "Hope I'm not interrupting anything."

I looked up at her in shock. "Did you buy the entire grocery store?"

"This is a special occasion, Jade," Mrs. B said cheerfully.

"You didn't even know he was coming over until...recently," I said, barely catching myself before revealing this had been a more in-depth plan.

"Thank you, Mrs. Benson," Dylan interrupted, smiling politely and saving me from an argument. "It looks wonderful."

Mrs. B practically squealed. "Oh, you are such a doll! Let me know if you need anything else!"

"Goodbye, Mrs. B," I said flatly, motioning for her to go.

"Oh, right. Got it," she nodded, winking at me as she backed up toward the hall. A master of subtlety, ladies and gentlemen.

I blew a curl out of my face. "What were you saying before...all that?"

"Well, I think I started having the most trouble on section two," Dylan said, handing me his test. "I think I've figured out what I did on these first two. But I have no idea what went wrong after that...Sorry."

"Don't apologize. You were actually pretty close on this one. See? You just copied a number down wrong on the last step."

Dylan hung his head. "That's the problem, though. I get all mixed up and make stupid, little mistakes that mess up the whole test."

I gave him a sympathetic look. "It's okay, Dylan. We can work on it together until you're confident with it, and then you won't have those same little mistakes."

He seemed to cheer up slightly. "Thanks, Jade." He smiled. "I really do appreciate you helping me."

His smile sent a weird feeling in the pit of my stomach. Every coherent sentence had suddenly turned into gibberish. Since my words were failing me, I decided to just smile in return. It was nice to have someone appreciate my help, even if it was just math.

We spent the next half hour walking through the rest of Dylan's test. The floor was covered in scrap paper and notes, but he seemed to be getting the hang of the problems he'd missed. Anytime I'd met with Dylan before, Henry had always naturally dominated the conversation. Without him here, though, I felt like I was actually getting to hear Dylan talk for the first time.

It turned out he could be just as funny, though it wasn't as over-the-top as Henry usually was. He listened intently as I explained, asking questions if he needed to. I noticed he'd sometimes get this cute look on his face when he was really concentrating. He even pretended not to be weirded out by the Bensons' antics, like Mrs. B running in, yelling about how she forgot the lemonade or the fact that Benson had made fifteen suspicious-looking passes in front of my door.

Finally, our brains were fried, and we gave up on math for a while, digging into the snacks piled high on Mrs. B's tray.

"Do you always get a full charcuterie board for an after-school snack?" Dylan asked.

"Are you sure you want to ask that?" I said. "Because you only get five questions."

Dylan grabbed a petal from the pepperoni rose and chewed thoughtfully. "Well, if I get five, you get five. And no, that wasn't my first—"

"Too late, you already asked one." I grinned, dusting cookie crumbs off my hands. "No, the fancy tray and fresh-squeezed lemonade isn't normal. Mrs. B was just feeling really extra today. My question: how do you know what a shark-cutie board is?"

"Shar-coo-ter-ee," Dylan enunciated, trying hard not to laugh. "My mom's a caterer—she knows all about that fancy-schmancy food stuff. Second question: Margaret? Really?"

I groaned. "Don't say it out loud. What about you?"

"James. What's your favorite color?" Dylan asked, looking around the room. "My money was on black, but the violet throws everything into question."

I pursed my lips. *Hmm...how would a normal person respond to a question like that?* "Well, the default answer is black, but maybe on a good day violet. Maybe a dark blue or red."

"Not sunshine-y yellow?"

"Do you really want to waste a question on that?"

Dylan shook his head and motioned for me to continue.

"Okay, so has Henry always been so...Henry?" I asked, not sure how else to phrase it.

He gave a slight smile. "He's not so bad when you get to know him. Sure, he's always kind of hyper and in-your-face, but there's a lot more to him than that. Nobody cares as much as Henry," Dylan said, going for another piece of pepperoni. "If you had one superpower, what would it be?"

Definitely not seeing the future, that's for sure.

"I don't know. Powers are stupid," I said quickly. "What's—"

"No! Wait a second!" Dylan interrupted. "You have to answer the question—it's in the rules."

"What rules?"

"The ones I just made up," he said matter-of-factly. "You have to answer any question that's asked. That's the only rule."

I rolled my eyes. "Fine—um, teleportation, so I can just pop away when I don't want to talk to anyone? What would you pick? Telekinesis?"

Dylan choked on the cracker he'd just eaten. "That's...oddly specific."

I shrugged. "Is that what you would pick?"

He considered the question. "If I had powers—which I don't—I think I'd want something useful. Maybe telekinesis, empathy...if I could read minds, I might finally be able to figure out what you're thinking."

My face was burning. I kept my eyes low, devoting my full attention to spreading an unnatural amount of dip onto a cracker. Dylan stayed silent, but I could feel his eyes on me. There was that stupid fluttery feeling again in the pit of my stomach. No, don't look up. Put the cheese on the cracker. There wasn't anyone staring at me. Were Dylan's eyes always that blue? No, bad Jade. Look at the cracker. Only the cracker.

Five minutes or five hours could have passed before he finally spoke again.

"We're both at four questions," Dylan said softly. "Can I ask something serious? You don't have to answer if you don't want to."

"Go for it," I said, surprised at how level my voice sounded.

"What's the deal with you and the Bensons? Why do you keep yourself separate from them—you know, like the different last name, not ever talking about them?"

I sighed and got up to check the hallway. Benson hadn't been past in a while, and nobody seemed to be upstairs. I could hear the TV in the living room, so hopefully, everyone was still there. As silently as I could, I shut the door.

"The truth?" I hesitated, the words I'd never had the courage to say heavy on my tongue. "I've never really felt like part of the Bensons. I mean, I used to, sort of...but it's kind of obvious I don't fit in," I said, gesturing at myself as I sat back down beside him.

"And Kastel?" Dylan asked cautiously.

I pulled my bag over and showed him my journal, careful to open it only to the front cover where my mother's signature was. "Benson said the night he, well, *got* me, that a woman ran up to him while he was on break at work. It was the middle of the night...he said she looked scared, maybe even hurt.

"Apparently, the lady just shoved me into his arms, told him my name and to keep me safe, then ran off again. Nothing else, no explanation...She'd left a bag with him, too—I guess that's where Benson found the journal when he took me back inside the hospital. I guess he sort of felt responsible for me after that, and he and Mrs. B didn't have any kids at the time, so he volunteered to take me home."

"You're saying Mr. Benson just called from work one day like, 'Hey, honey, do you randomly want a kid?'" Dylan asked in surprise. "How did Mrs. B take that?"

I shrugged. "Like I said, they didn't have any kids at the time. Until Tommy came along, I don't know if I even realized how different I was from the rest of them. I mean, I *knew*, but—" My voice failed.

"Tommy made it feel even more obvious," Dylan finished for me, voice quiet. "You think Vivian Kastel is your real mom?"

"She has to be," I said, terribly aware of how desperate the hope in my voice sounded. "Same last name the lady told Benson. I've tried to search a couple of times, but it's like there's no Vivian Kastel on the face of the earth. I'd have no idea where to even start on my dad."

I took a deep breath and put the journal back in my bag. Dylan looked sad but didn't try to say anything comforting, which I was grateful for. "Okay, my last question: why are you taking calculus when you clearly hate it? It's an optional class—you didn't have to do it."

Dylan sighed. "My dad's a science professor at Pinewood University. Being bad at math isn't an option in my family."

"And is there a reason he's not helping you right now instead of me?" I asked, raising an eyebrow.

"All of this stuff just comes really easy to him, you know? Anytime he tries to help me, he just can't understand why I don't get it. It's like he thinks I'm stupid if I don't get it on the first try."

"I'm sure he doesn't think that, Dylan," I said, awkwardly putting a hand on his arm. "You really do know a lot of this, and it's a hard subject. No one's going to get it on the first try."

"Yeah, well, he never walked through it with me like you did," Dylan said, eyes flicking down to my hand. "Hey, Jade? Can I ask you another question?"

His eyes were back on me, and I felt like my brain went completely blank. "You already used your five."

"Just a general one," he said, lowering his voice. "Did you actually ask me over here just to help me with my test, or was there another reason?"

This was it! I could finally warn him not to go to the swim meet and save him from getting snatched by that...whatever it was. I opened my mouth, but nothing would come out when suddenly—

KNOCK! KNOCK! KNOCK!

"Why is this door shut?" Benson's voice came from behind the door. *I am so dead.*

I ran over to my door and opened it. Benson was angry, face clenched as he scanned the room, then Dylan, then me, looking for any sign we were up to something. Dylan looked mortified.

"Sorry, Benson," I started nervously. "I just wanted to talk about something private."

He raised an eyebrow. "Why would you need to shut the door for that?" Benson took an audible breath. "I trust you, Jade. But you need to respect our rules."

Oh great, it's not like I needed even more *attention from Benson after the journal incident.*

"That's fair. I'm sorry," I said, trying to smooth things over before they could get any more out of hand. Dylan sat rigidly, not daring to move in case it would make the situation worse. To my surprise, Benson actually seemed to find it funny.

"You literally haven't moved an inch since I last checked on you guys, Dylan. You can relax." He chuckled.

Dylan exhaled loudly. "Actually, I need to get home. Mom wanted me back before dinner."

Mrs. B seemed to appear out of thin air with a plastic container.

"Oh, dear. You'll have to stay for dinner next time you're over," Mrs. B said before heading over to our barely dented platter of food. "But let me get something for you to take home. You never know when you might need a snack."

Dylan started to wave her off. "Oh, I couldn't—"

"I insist," Mrs. B said with a smile that made it clear he had no choice in the matter. He relented and accepted the food after she filled the container.

"Thank you, Mrs. Benson," Dylan said.

She grinned like she had just won the lottery. "Oh, you are such a doll!"

We all chuckled, even Benson, who seemed to have lightened up after the whole door incident. Still, I had a feeling it would be a long time before I could invite anybody else over if I wanted to stay low on the Benson's radar.

"I'll walk you out," I said. Dylan and I made our way down the stairs and through the front door, stopping in front of his old car. We paused awkwardly, neither of us really sure what to say.

"If you want, I can help you with your math some more," I said, trying to hide the nervousness in my voice. "In the library. Not here."

Dylan chuckled. "But the library doesn't have charcuterie boards, though."

"Don't encourage her," I said, rolling my eyes. "We could meet up again Friday. If you want."

Dylan frowned. "Can't. Swim meet."

"Oh, right. I mean, I don't suppose you could skip that, could you?"

"Tempting, but I can't. Maybe Saturday?"

Assuming you live that long, I thought, watching him climb into his car. Well, warning Dylan hadn't worked.

Two days and counting.

CHAPTER
SEVEN

I had twenty minutes to save Dylan. If I didn't stop him before the swim meet started, I had no guarantee of stopping whatever that *thing* was from grabbing him. He was probably already there. The swim team was released prior to dismissal, making things all the more complicated for me.

This past week, I'd tried everything to keep Dylan from going or even stopping the swim meet from happening. I even tried to convince the coach that the pool's water seemed too acidic to allow the swimmers in. Of course, they laughed in my face.

Since nothing was working, I was out of options. I was going rogue. There was no plan other than grabbing Dylan and forcibly keeping him safe until after the swim meet was over. Easy.

Now, I just had to find him before the *thing* did. There was a good-sized crowd forming. Teens and family members were starting to fill the stands while swimmers stood around the pool end, talking and adjusting their swim caps. Dylan wasn't out on the pool deck, which meant he was likely near the locker rooms. I walked on the already wet concrete floors to what I assumed to be the door to the locker rooms.

"What are you doing over here, Jade?" a teasing voice said, stepping out in front of me. I winced, finding myself face-to-face with Victoria. Where had she come from? The hall was deserted a second ago.

A flash of our prior conversation ran through my mind. *She thinks I'm here to see Dylan and 'confess my feelings' or something stupid like that. Great.* I tried to think of something to save myself from any more embarrassment.

"Actually, I was just...looking for Henry?" I said as I caught sight of him at the end of the hall. He wore a red and white T-shirt for Yan Mei's Cafe like he'd just come from work. There was a big purple and green sports bag swung over his shoulder. "Hey, Henry! I've been looking everywhere for you!"

"Jade?" Henry said in confusion. *Well, it wasn't like she was going to buy my lie anyway.* He quickly turned his eyes to Victoria standing next to me and rushed over toward us. "Hello, ladies. Nice to see you in this lovely...chlorine-scented hallway."

"Henry," Victoria said, rolling her eyes. "What are you doing down here?"

He straightened up like he was trying to make himself look taller. Which didn't help. He was still nearly a whole head shorter than Victoria. "Dylan left his swim bag in his car. He asked me to bring it down."

Who forgets their bag at a swim meet?

"Right!" I said, snatching the bag from him. "Yeah, Dylan asked us to run this down to him. Henry, you walk Victoria back up, and I'll take this to Dylan."

Victoria's eyes widened. "You can't go into the boy's locker—"

"Sounds good!" Henry interjected and shot me a wink. "You're a real pal, Jade."

He tried to link his arm through Victoria's, which she promptly slapped away.

Henry waved his hands apologetically. "Right, sorry. I respect your boundaries."

She sighed. "Let's go."

I didn't stick around to see Henry's reaction, but I imagined he was grinning from ear to ear as I went further down the hallway and busted into the boy's locker room. I quickly locked the door behind me. It looked empty at first glance. I walked around the corner.

"Jade?" Dylan called, making me turn. He was standing in the doorway of the room I'd just passed, clad in just his swim trunks. I quickly averted my eyes. *Bad Jade.*

My brain had slowly started to catch up with my rashness. I had stormed into the boy's locker room without a second thought. Someone could have been naked. *He* could have been naked. I flushed. I *really* needed to think before I acted.

"What happened to Henry?"

"Victoria," I said breathlessly, awkwardly thrusting the bag into his hands. He accepted the bag and started digging through it for something. I kept my eyes firmly on the ceiling.

"My eyes are down here." He chuckled, a pair of goggles in his hands. I laughed, trying to sound normal, but I was so nervous it almost sounded like I was choking. "Are you alright, Jade?"

I shook my head, laughing nervously again. "Yeah, yeah, I'm fine."

He smiled, starting to step toward the door. "Well, thanks for bringing my bag. We'd better go."

I quickly stepped in front of him, blocking his path. "No! You can't!" I said a little louder than necessary. I glanced around. We seemed to be the only people in the locker room.

Dylan started to look worried. "What? Why not?"

I swallowed hard. There were footsteps coming down the hall. Maybe Victoria had ditched Henry and come back to bust me for going into the boy's locker room. *Think, Jade. It's now or never.*

"It's just—you—over here!" I said, shoving him backward toward the more hidden lockers. I kept my voice down. "Look, I didn't *want* to do this, but—"

"Jade," he cut me off in a more serious tone than I'd ever heard from him before. "What is going on? Why did you lock the door, and why are we hiding?"

I ran a hand over my face. I *really* wasn't good at stuff like this. "I'm sorry. I can't explain, but I need you to trust me. I can't let you go to the swim meet today."

He stared at me like I was crazy. I didn't blame him. I *knew* I sounded like a lunatic. "Why can't I go to the swim meet?"

A perfectly logical question that had a completely *illogical* explanation. "You just can't."

"That doesn't make any sense!" he said, widening his eyes and definitely not lowering his voice. He tried to make another move for the door, forcing me to pull him back again.

"I know it doesn't, but I need you to stay calm!" I whisper-shouted. "Your life could be in danger, and I'm trying to—"

Dylan threw his hands out in a *time-out* gesture. "My *life*?"

Ooh, that definitely wasn't the right thing to say. Maybe I should have spent a little less time on planning how to save Dylan, and more on what I was actually going to say to him to convince him I wasn't insane. *This is why I'm not good at people-ing.*

"Who are you?" he asked frantically. "Witness protection? The mafia? Are you kidnapping me right now? I thought you were flirting with me. I didn't think I was going to *die*!"

I slapped my hand to my face. This was probably the worst way this conversation could have gone.

"You're not going to die, Dylan! It's a precaution, and I'm here to save you and—"

"Help!" Dylan yelled, trying to get away from me again. My eyes went wide as I grabbed his arm. "Henry! Anybody!"

"Shut up!" I hissed.

"Or *what*? HEN—" I grabbed both sides of his face and looked into his wide eyes before smashing my lips to his. I could never have seen this coming, not even in a vision. My first kiss to calm down a frantic boy who thought I was going to kidnap and murder him. *And he's half naked.* My grip was firm, but I couldn't feel any resistance. Actually, it seemed like—

A jolt of the door opening, followed by Henry's concerned voice, bolted us apart. We were both out of breath and flustered. It didn't take a psychic to know what we were doing. *This was actually the most embarrassing day of my life.*

"Dylan? Oh...*oh*. Sorry, I thought I heard you call for me, but you're *clearly* okay. More than okay, it seems. I'll just," he said, gesturing to the door, which I clearly remembered *locking* so something like this wouldn't happen. "...see myself out."

"No, wait!" Dylan snapped, coming out of his stupor and stepping closer to Henry to get a safe distance between us. "She is holding me hostage!"

Henry raised an eyebrow. I tried to speak, but Henry beat me to it. "Yeah, it didn't really seem like you minded."

Dylan's face flushed bright red. I pushed past him. "No, that is definitely not what was happening."

"It wasn't?" Henry asked, confused.

"No! I keep telling him he can't go to the swim meet today!" I said, throwing out my arms in exasperation.

"But *why*? I know how to swim!"

"I told you you can't go. And I can't tell you why!"

"Then *why* did you kiss me?"

"BECAUSE!" I shouted. "You wouldn't shut up!"

"Simmer down, confused lovebirds," Henry interjected, silencing both of us. "There's no need to fight about...wait, is this your first fight? And your first K-I-S-S? That *was* your first, right? Are you guys together now? Am I the third wheel? Why don't you tell me these things, Dylan? I thought I was your best friend! I thought—"

"You are. We aren't together. Yes to the other two questions," Dylan groaned, frowning and putting his forehead against one of the lockers in defeat. "Apparently, my life is in *danger*," he mocked.

"Look," I snapped. "You want to get snatched up like Mary Milford by some freakish invisible thing? Be my guest because I am out of here!"

I shoved past Henry, who looked *very* confused. The second I touched the door, I froze. Ice spread through my chest as I felt a vision. The invisible *thing* was coming right toward us. Different paths flashed through my mind: the front hall, the trophy cases by the pool entrance —another turn would take it straight down the hall to the locker rooms. I hadn't saved Dylan. I'd isolated him. If he were actually *swimming* like he was supposed to be, he wouldn't have been able to be taken. Stupid, I was so stupid.

"It's coming," I said, turning to face the boys. "We have to go. *Now!*"

Dylan started to say something, but Henry cut him off.

"You saw something, didn't you? You saw something that hasn't happened yet," Henry said with a more serious tone than I had thought possible for him. His face had gone ashen as he stepped up to me.

I froze. "What?"

"Is it true?" Dylan asked softly.

"How...could you know that?" I whispered. This was bad. This was very, very bad. I didn't think just moving away would fix things this time. How did they figure it out? What were they going to do now that they knew?

"I'll tell you later. Right now, we need to get you to my grandma," Henry said. His grandma? This was certainly the start of an interesting ransom. The old lady from the Chinese restaurant?

"The thing you saw...how close was it?"

I didn't get a chance to answer. The locker room door slammed open, knocking Henry forward.

"Down!" Dylan yelled, throwing out his hands. I took the hint and dropped, barely missing getting plowed over as one of the benches flew across the room. No one was in the doorway, at least no one we could *see*. But we heard a grunt of pain, indicating that Dylan had hit his target.

I stared at Dylan with my mouth agape. "You *do* have powers! The pencil, the *lock*—I was right!"

Dylan opened his mouth to say something but ended up shaking his head. "Yes, but now is really not the time for explanations," he said finally, pointing to the opposite end of the room. "Grab Henry and run!"

He was right. I couldn't see the thing that was after us, but that bench wouldn't hold it back for long. I yanked Henry to his feet and charged out after Dylan. An emergency exit led us to the back of the parking lot, where an old white van sat mostly to itself. On the side was a cartoon painting of Yan Mei herself holding a big bowl of noodles.

"Our getaway car is a *noodle van*?" I groaned.

Henry smiled and patted the side of the van. "She's an oldie but a goodie!" he said as he swung himself into the driver's seat.

"Come on!" Dylan said, throwing open the back doors and jumping in. I followed in after him. Henry peeled out of the parking lot, throwing me backward into Dylan. I think he intended to catch me, but we both lost our footing and ended up sprawled on the van's floor. Something crunched underneath me.

"Is this a delivery order?" I asked, pulling a smashed container out from under Dylan's shoulder.

"Yeah, we're going to have to deliver that on the way back. Fifteen minutes or it's free!" Henry said cheerfully before glancing at the smashed container in the rearview mirror. "Well, it is a little rough, and I am *very* late, so I will give them a gift card."

"Remind me to never order takeout from you again," I muttered. To my surprise, Dylan chuckled. Even though we'd just run for our lives, he seemed to have collected himself some. Suddenly, his eyes narrowed before giving me a worried look.

"Are you bleeding?"

I looked down, confused. I didn't think I was hurt, but my shirt was soaked in something red and sticky. I wasn't in any pain, and it was too light to be blood, and it smelled...sweet? I glanced at Dylan. The stuff was all over him, too—on his shoulders and back. I hadn't even realized it, but he hadn't grabbed anything when we ran. He was still just in his Pinewood swim trunks...he didn't even have shoes on.

Dylan followed my gaze and quickly wiped some of the stuff off of his shoulder. He smelled it, then touched some to his tongue. "Henry, we're going to need more sweet and sour sauce."

Henry laughed. "That's what we should call your relationship!"

I glared at him in the rearview mirror. "And what exactly is *that* supposed to mean?"

Henry, wisely, did not answer. Dylan handed me a box of tissues nearby to try and wipe away the worst of the sauce.

"Sorry I freaked out on you back there," he said, careful to keep his voice low, though I doubted Henry would be able to hear him over his obnoxious radio blaring. "I should have believed you—it's just...you kind of took me by surprise, you know, with the holding me hostage and...kissing and all."

Ooh, I'd almost forgotten about that. I winced. "Sorry about that. I kind of panicked."

"It's okay. It could have been much worse." Dylan froze. "Wait, no, that's not what I meant. I just mean...I don't exactly do well under pressure."

"At least you didn't turn into a lamp," Henry muttered, punching the van's radio preset button in irritation as the song ended. I raised an eyebrow at Dylan.

"You'll see," he said.

It took over twenty minutes to get to Yan Mei's, though the majority of that time was Henry apologizing to angry customers. Luckily, there weren't many people in the restaurant, though we had to make a sauce-covered walk of shame past the few people eating an early dinner.

Yan Mei herself was at the cash register, her warm eyes sizing us up intently.

"No shoes, no shirt, no service, young man," she said, clearly trying hard not to smirk at Dylan.

He rolled his eyes. "I work here, Yan Mei."

"Well, at least put on an apron," she responded matter-of-factly, holding up one that said *Kiss the Cook*. I wondered how many suggestive aprons she kept on hand in case her employees showed up half-naked.

Henry wiggled his eyebrows at me. I smacked him away. "Mrs. Yan Mei, Henry said I needed to talk to you."

She raised an eyebrow, though I could tell she wasn't surprised. "Let's go to the back."

Together, the four of us made our way behind the counter and through the doors into the back of the restaurant. The two chefs managing orders ignored us as we passed, focusing intently on boxing up a couple of large take-out orders. The room smelled so good it made my mouth water. Sizzling meat and steamy rice. I would have stayed there forever if Yan Mei hadn't led us through another door at the back of the kitchen.

The next room was smaller, with a desk toward the back. There were a few chairs set in front and a small couch up against a wall. Similar to the dining area, a few long silk tapestries hung along the walls in gorgeous colors, each meticulously embroidered with elegant Chinese script.

Other than that, the room had little more memorabilia than a few pictures on the shelves behind the desk. The first was a photo of Henry and Yan Mei wearing matching T-shirts with large, ear-to-ear smiles. Beside it was a photo of Yan Mei standing beside a man around her age with dark skin and large brown eyes. He had his arm around her, and she leaned into him; both had a soft smile. Clearly, someone she was close with.

But it was a picture to the right that caught my eye: a man who looked to be an older version of Henry with a large, over-the-top grin stood next to a woman with dark, curly hair and skin just a few shades darker than my own. If I had to guess, the male was likely Henry's father? He'd never mentioned him before. But it was the woman in the picture that I felt drawn to. Like I *knew* her, even though I was very certain I had not seen this woman before. *Who was she?*

"Jade?" Yan Mei asked, breaking me of my thoughts. Henry had already propped his feet up on the couch, and Dylan and Yan Mei were seated by the desk, all staring at me.

I shook my head, taking a seat across from Henry's grandmother. "Sorry, I was distracted."

Yan Mei glanced at the photo, and I saw Henry give her a somber look. "I'll get straight to the point," Yan Mei said, lacing her fingers together on the desk like she'd routinely had this conversation. "We've had a feeling since you first came to the cafe that you may have *special* abilities. After you passed out, I was almost sure, but I asked the boys to keep an eye on you before I risked confronting you about it. As you know, we can't exactly reveal to the public *what* we are."

"There's *more*?" I asked, dumbfounded. I really wasn't the only one. I know, I'd just found out about Dylan, but I hadn't really had time to process. All my life, I thought there was no one else like me. Like I was abandoned because I wasn't *normal*. Did my parents have powers, too? There were so many questions buzzing in my head. I needed to write them all down in my journal.

I could feel Yan Mei's dark eyes watching me. She always seemed to get this strange expression when she looked at me—a somewhat hopeful, caring look like the way she looked at Henry, but at the same time, there was a heaviness to her eyes as if I reminded her of something sad.

"It's not often those with abilities do not know about the greater community at large, but I have seen it happen occasionally," Yan Mei said as if reading my mind.

For a horrible second, it occurred to me that maybe she *could*. I tried to think of something funny, like a bear on a unicycle slipping on a banana, but Yan Mei's face remained unchanged. Well, that certainly was a good thing. I'd admittedly stared just a little *too* long at the *Kiss the Cook* server. Only because it was weird and hard *not* to stare at the practically half-naked boy.

"Usually, if someone does not know about others with powers," Yan Mei said, breaking my thoughts, "it is because their connection to the community has been severed. The proficiency for powers is handed down genetically, though sometimes it does not occur for many generations, and families forget. Other times, the answer is simpler. Dylan told me you were adopted?"

I nodded, feeling a little awkward explaining it with so many eyes on me. This was much harder than talking to Dylan in my room. He gave me a reassuring smile. "Clearly, I'm adopted," I started. "But I never knew much about where I came from or who my parents were. From what Benson told me, my mother found him outside a hospital and asked him to take care of me. She handed me off with nothing more than a bag, and he never saw her again."

Yan Mei nodded slowly, a grimace on her face, but she remained silent for a moment before asking, "You chose to keep your original last name, not Benson?"

"I used to go by Benson," I said, mouth dry. "But we had a fight, and Benson let me change my name back to Kastel. It was the name on this."

I fished my journal out of my bag and handed it to Yan Mei. She held it sadly. It almost reminded me of when Julian picked it up outside of the tea shop. She eyed my mother's name on the inside cover and then glanced up, silently asking for permission to continue.

I nodded. It was weird. I had never let *anyone* know about my journal, let alone *showed* it to them. But something told me I could trust her. Silently, she flipped through the pages, eyes scanning drawings and passages about different visions I'd had throughout my life. There were some pretty intense visions in there, but Yan Mei remained expressionless. Her face faltered slightly when she got to the last few pages: the vision of my death, the invisible force taking Mary Milford and also attempting to take Dylan.

"Dylan, Henry, please leave us for a moment," she said, voice eerily blank.

Henry leaned forward, clearly excited. "Come on, Grandma, we haven't had someone new in—" he froze with one sharp look.

"Let's go, Dylan," Henry said as he jumped off the couch and was out of the door at record speed. Dylan took his time, giving me a hesitant look. I had a feeling he was curious about what could be in my journal that would provoke a reaction like that from Yan Mei, but I was grateful that the older woman had given us some privacy. It was hard enough to talk about it with one person.

"I'll talk to you later, Jade," Dylan said as he walked out.

"Sorry I tried to kidnap you," I called out to him. I heard him chuckle as the door shut, leaving us alone. The silence was eerily loud; the room felt even smaller without the boys. Well, better get this over with.

I turned to Yan Mei. "So, what do you want to know?"

CHAPTER
EIGHT

"He cares for you," Yan Mei said carefully, "though I suspect you already know that."

She set my journal on the desk between us, open to the page where I'd sketched out everything I could remember about the mega-vision: the Bensons, the destroyed street, Dylan kneeling over my dead body. Just seeing it scrawled out on the page was enough to bring an ashy taste to my mouth. I didn't know what I was going to say, but Yan Mei held up a hand to stop me the second I tried.

"You have been given a rare gift, my dear," she said, taking a deep breath as if to steel herself. "There are not many people powerful enough to see the future...Many stories do not end well. There is a very high price to knowledge."

"What do you mean?" I asked, not sure I wanted to know the answer.

"Knowing the future is a double-edged sword, unlike any other ability. It provides you insider information on how to live your life—how others behave, how they feel, how events will play out. Perhaps worst of all, it provides you the temptation to attempt to change it, as I see you've already tried."

"Yeah, but it doesn't work!" I said, flopping back against the chair.

"Look at the notes yourself! Every vision I've tried to change has come true in some way or another: you stop a vase from breaking, you get a busted plate instead. Tommy's supposed to break his ankle. He messes up his arm. I've never been able to stop a vision from coming true."

"That must be very distressing for you with a future like this," Yan Mei said as casually as if she were discussing the weather. "To know one's own fate must be a terrible burden. To see your death, know the hurt it will cause those you love."

I felt myself squirming under her gaze. "You're not talking about the Bensons, are you?"

"By knowing the future, you have automatically put yourself on a path toward it. Dylan is like a grandson to me. He has always been so caring, so doubtful of himself—something I suspect you can relate to. I just don't want to see him hurt. Or you."

I pursed my lips. "Look, Mrs. Yan Mei, I'm not trying to hurt Dylan or anybody else. Nobody wants this vision not to happen more than me—"

"Yet you play to feelings you know he'll have one day when you're not even sure you'll care for him yourself," Yan Mei said, eyeing me warily.

She was right. The mega-vision had shown me everything about Dylan's feelings toward me in the future, but I had no idea how Future Me might feel about him. Would I love him too, or did I see a one-sided obsession like Henry had with Victoria? I wasn't trying to lead Dylan on, but Yan Mei did have a point. Maybe I was only drawn to him because I had seen the future. I didn't like that idea.

I swallowed hard. "Is that why you wanted to talk to me without Dylan or Henry around?"

Yan Mei sighed. "Unfortunately not. You said you had never been able to change a vision? Not even in the slightest?"

"Never. Like I said, if I try to change something, sometimes the same thing happens, but differently, or sometimes it switches."

"So, if you saw Dylan getting snatched by someone invisible in a vision but prevented it, then is it possible that someone else took his place?" Yan Mei asked ominously.

My stomach dropped. By stalling Dylan from the swim meet, had I just caused someone else to get taken instead? I had never even considered that saving one person might sacrifice someone else.

"You know something about this invisible person, don't you?" I asked, lowering my voice as the talking got closer in the kitchen. "Are they taking people? There was a girl that went missing a few days ago—"

"Mary Milford," Yan Mei confirmed, tugging aside the closest tapestry to reveal a map pinned up to the wall. There were scribbled notes and pictures taped up around it—one of them was definitely Mary. "The fifth in the last few months, to be exact. All those who have been taken were people I suspect or know to have powers. All were gone at least a week, and none remembered being taken or missing."

"You mean four other people went missing and had no idea they'd been gone?" I asked, moving to get a better look at the map. Yan Mei had a full-blown conspiracy board going: names, dates, times, places disappeared and reappeared. Some of the photos had powers like *Emotion Manipulation* or *Mind-shield* scrawled across the bottom. Mary's picture had *Suspected* written on it, though no one had written down any ideas for what powers she might have had.

"They all seemed to have perfectly valid excuses—vacations, hospital stays, business trips," Yan Mei said, looking the board over worriedly. "Even stranger is that within a few days, most of the people closest to them seemed to believe the same things."

I thought back through all the rumors I'd heard about my missing classmate over the last few days. "Like running away? Mary had only been gone a day or two before everyone started saying she'd mentioned taking off before."

"Implanted memories," Yan Mei agreed. "Most likely an accomplice covering the tracks of their invisible friend. If they can implant memories, maybe someone is doing all this without even knowing."

"You don't know of anyone who has invisibility?"

Yan Mei shook her head. "Someone is going after people with powers. We don't know why. You can see how being able to see through time could be very helpful in figuring out who that is. I have my suspicions, but I pray they're wrong."

I raised an eyebrow at her. "Didn't you just chew me out for using my powers?"

"Not your powers, just your reaction to what you were shown, dear," Yan Mei said with a knowing smile. "The reaction makes all the difference in someone with abilities as powerful as yours. We could use your help, Jade."

"My help? How could I help? I don't have any control over my powers—sometimes I just touch somebody, and boom! Vision."

"You can't control your powers because you haven't been shown *how* to control them," Yan Mei said gently. "You think Dylan just woke up one day and was able to throw a table across a room? It took years and many, many bruises before he was able to manage something like that."

I glanced down at the sketch of the mega-vision. The little version of me lying there on the page surrounded by people I didn't understand. The destroyed street. The fire. Maybe I was imagining it, but I could have sworn a smoky smell started burning inside my nose. My lungs ached. It was getting harder to breathe.

"I may not have years to learn how to use my powers, Mrs. Yan Mei," I said, quickly shutting the journal to get that awful nightmare out of my sight.

"Then we'd better start now," she agreed, standing up. "How far into the future have you been able to see before? A few days? A month? Years?"

"The mega-vision's about the farthest out I've seen, maybe two or three years in the future," I said. "Sometimes it's easier to see further if I'm looking at the past. It's more fixed in place."

Yan Mei froze like I'd slapped her across the face. "You can see into the future *and* the past?"

"Is that weird?"

"No, not necessarily...Just surprising," she said quickly, not reassuring me at all. "Show me what you can do."

I stared at her. "Um...I can't just do it. I don't know what causes it really, but—"

"You can't do it because you're not trying hard enough," Yan Mei said matter-of-factly. "Your visions seem to come about when your emotions are in flux—embarrassed, scared, flustered. You're not in control of yourself, so you're not in control of your powers."

71

Yan Mei went to the shelf of pictures behind the desk and pulled down the frame I'd been staring at, the one with Henry's father and the curly-haired woman who seemed so familiar.

"This one caught your attention, didn't it?" she said, extending a hand out to me. "What can you see about this woman?"

I wanted to argue that it was pointless—I'd tried to force myself to have a vision eight million times and never had any luck, but I could tell I wasn't getting out of this. Reluctantly, I took the old woman's hand and waited. As expected, nothing happened.

"Calm your mind," she said softly.

I tried to focus on the room around me: the face of the woman in the picture, the rhythm of my breathing, the ticking of the clock on the wall. Suddenly, the clatter from the kitchen dulled to a murmur. My sight narrowed, but slower than it normally did with a vision. I could feel myself swaying on my feet, but Yan Mei's hands held me steady.

Slowly, a different room began to take shape around me: a living room a little larger than the office I'd just been standing in. The room had the same faded look that visions of the past always seemed to have, but I would've been able to tell even without that. The TV in the corner was big and clunky, with a stack of black rectangles scattered around it. Tapes? Beyond that, the room was covered with an explosion of blankets —on couches, chairs, the floor—you couldn't go a foot without finding one. A bassinet to the side of the couch. A stack of clean laundry no one had gotten around to folding piled high in a chair. Pictures filled the walls, and the room had a messy, lived-in sort of feel. Like a real home.

"Can I hold her now?" Yan Mei's voice asked excitedly, though the old woman I'd been standing with a moment before looked nothing like this one. This Yan Mei was clearly much younger—smoother skin, traces of gray only beginning to show in her hair—though her expression looked worn and weary. Instead of the silly T-shirts I'd gotten used to seeing her in, younger Yan Mei wore a simple white cardigan and jeans.

"Be my guest. But if she throws up on you, don't say I didn't warn you," a woman said from a chair, gingerly passing a swaddled newborn into the younger Yan Mei's arms. It was the same woman from the photo, though she looked considerably rougher. Her curly hair was tied back into a tight ponytail, and she looked like she'd been living in the same pair of stained pajamas for a week. "I can barely move. I haven't slept in three days—nobody told me that newborns never sleep."

Yan Mei smiled gently at the baby. "It will get better, Vivian. It always does."

A chill went through my whole body.

Vivian.

As in, Vivian Kastel, the name inside my journal?

I stared at the young woman with newfound awe. Was it possible that this exhausted woman was really *my* mother? I suppose I did sort of look like Vivian—dark hair, similar sort of build, but there was also plenty about us that didn't match up. Her skin was a little darker than mine. Her features were sharper. Mine were softer.

Wait, did Yan Mei try to make me have this vision on purpose? Had she *known* my birth mother? Was that baby squirming in her younger self's arms actually *me*? How did the lady from the Chinese food place know absolutely everything?

"I'll believe it when it happens," Vivian sighed. "I'm convinced I'll never be normal again."

Yan Mei chuckled and started rocking the baby gently. "You were never normal to begin with."

Vivian smiled knowingly. "You got that right. How is Henry?"

Yan Mei grinned, though there seemed to be a tinge of sadness to it. "He is good. Healthy and growing...I think he's resilient like his father."

A heavy silence seemed to fill the room.

"I can't believe Trisha didn't make it," Vivian said, picking distractedly at a stray thread on her chair's blanket. "She was doing so well. I can't imagine what Michael is going through raising Henry all on his own. We were supposed to all be doing this together—me and Lance, Michael and Trisha, and now Jessica and Chris. It seems like yesterday we were going out for lunch. It all seemed so normal then."

A gentle rain started drizzling down the windows. Odd. It wasn't even cloudy five minutes ago, but now the sky was dark and dreary. Almost like it was sad.

"It's very hard on Michael right now. Jessica and I are doing the best

73

we can to help with Henry, but I'm afraid only time will help him. I'm sorry, Viv, I've been meaning to check on you more, too."

Vivian shook her head, and the rain dissipated, revealing the previous sunrays through the window. "Michael needs you right now. We'll be okay...I'd help out myself if I didn't have my hands full right now."

That *definitely* wasn't normal. Yan Mei had said that my powers were tied to my emotions. Was it the same for my mother? Did her powers control the weather? I imagined erupting volcanoes and tsunami-like storms every time she got into an argument. She was probably terrifying when she was angry.

"How is Lance handling fatherhood?" Yan Mei asked.

"*Somehow,* he is getting enough sleep to work on a formula dispensing device so that we can measure bottles correctly at three AM."

"Sounds just like something he would do." Yan Mei chuckled.

A strange sound that was a mix between a snort and yawn came from the baby, drawing the attention of Yan Mei and Vivian.

"Why, hello, sweet girl," Yan Mei cooed. "I am so happy to see you! Let's get lots of sleep and drink all your bottles so you can grow big and strong. Please tell me you and Lance are closer to settling on a name? I feel ridiculous not knowing what to call her."

Vivian rolled her eyes. "We're working on it. Lance says it's hard to name humans—you can't pick wrong because they'll be stuck with it forever. Joke's on him. I filed the papers this morning. You know he was never going to actually settle on anything."

"And you're not going to tell me, are you?"

"Nope." Vivian smirked, popping the *p* in the word.

Yan Mei laughed. An odd feeling washed over me. I hadn't seen much, but anyone could tell my mother and her were close. If I hadn't ever been separated from my parents, would Yan Mei have also been more in my life? Would I have grown up with Henry?

A phone started ringing loudly, causing the bundled baby in Yan Mei's arms to start squirming again. She gently shushed the baby while she pulled out her phone.

"It's Lance," she said with a worried tone, setting the baby gently into the bassinet. "I'll be right back."

Yan Mei left the room as a small cry erupted from the bassinet. Obviously, the baby wasn't happy about not being rocked anymore. Vivian rushed over and gently offered a pacifier, instantly calming the baby.

"Don't cry, baby girl. You'll wake your brother."

Brother?

My sight tilted. The world seemed to flicker between the living room and the office at the back of the restaurant. I could feel Yan Mei's hands gripping my arms again, holding me upright. I was losing my control over the vision.

No! Not yet! Not yet!

I lunged forward, trying desperately to get a look inside the bassinet. Sure enough, there was *another* tiny form tucked inside, though this one had on a blue hat.

"Michael's in trouble," the younger Yan Mei said worriedly, flickering in and out like a bad TV signal. "I have to hurry!"

The living room spiraled out of sight. My hands hit the floor as Yan Mei lost her grip on me. I was back in the present—the din of the restaurant kitchen, the smell of steak frying, the older Yan Mei leaning over me in concern. My head was pounding. Everything seemed too bright, too loud. Still, I managed to raise my head and look into the older woman's eyes.

"Tell me everything," I said hoarsely.

CHAPTER
NINE

"Here, tea will help you feel better," Yan Mei said, passing the steaming cup to me. My hands were still shaking so much from the vision that I could barely hold it.

"Is it magic?" I asked hopefully.

"No, it's oolong." She smiled, retaking her seat across the desk from me.

"Oh, right. Well, that's embarrassing," I said, accepting the tea. "And this is why I'm more of a coffee person."

Yan Mei smiled. "Same as your mother."

Interesting. She clearly knew my mother pretty well. The picture, visiting her after I—we—were born, knowing her interests. They seemed to be far more than old acquaintances. I took a sip of my tea before Yan Mei cleared her throat.

"Alright, you said you wanted to know everything," she said. "But I think that it would be rather difficult to explain *everything* right now. Let's start with your vision. What did you see?"

I quickly recounted the vision in my head, the vivid dream I never wanted to forget. "You came to visit her, *us*. She wouldn't tell you our names, but I had a twin. A brother."

Yan Mei's face lightened. "That was the first and only time I got to meet you before you showed up in my restaurant a month or two ago. Your family disappeared before they got a chance to tell me. There was supposed to be a 'name reveal' party."

"A name reveal? Did it really take that long to name two people?" I asked.

"Your parents said it was hard to name two humans, insisting they had to get to know you a little bit first," she said. My mind flashed back to my mother's words in my vision. I would hold onto that memory of her for as long as I could, which made me think of a question.

"Would you be able to show me more memories of my mother?" I asked.

Yan Mei smiled. "As much as you'd like, but not today. You're still coming into your powers, and you don't want to exhaust your strength so quickly."

I figured I wouldn't get any more today, and I *was* very tired. But the thought of being able to see my mother some more through the visions and being able to hold onto more pieces of her made me excited.

"How did you know her so well?" I asked. "Were you close friends?"

She shook her head. "I suppose your vision didn't show you everything. Jade..." Yan Mei trailed off, almost with a nervous look. "Vivian is my daughter."

Wait, what? Her daughter? *That would make her...*

"You're my grandmother?!"

She chuckled before grabbing the photo I'd noticed earlier of her and the man. "Vivian and yourself look a bit more like my husband, William. He was your grandfather."

I could see where we got our darker skin tone. Recalling my mother's face, I could see a faint resemblance in their facial structure with their prominent cheeks and smaller foreheads...Wait, *was* my grandfather?

She continued, and I was grateful I didn't have to ask. "William passed away shortly after you and your brother were born. That is something I wouldn't like to share right now. I want to make my first *real* talk with my granddaughter a happy one."

Clearly something unexpected, but I definitely wasn't going to ask at the moment. I was insanely curious about every detail, but I also wanted this to be a happy moment of being with my family...my grand-mother. Man, she was nothing like Nana Benson.

"I would like that too," I said in a shy voice. "I can't believe I ran into your restaurant by accident!"

She frowned. That was weird. "Fate has an interesting way of being kind or cruel. I hope that it was simply time for us to reunite," Yan Mei said. I looked at her, confused, but she shrugged me off. "Don't worry about it, dear. Is there anything else you would like to know?"

Was there anything I *didn't* want to know? I had *so* many questions, but it seemed like some of my answers would have to wait. I wanted to know everything about my mother and my family as much as I could. Speaking of which...

"I know when my mother gave me to Benson, she was alone...did you ever hear about my brother? My father?" I asked softly, almost afraid to ask for what I might hear.

Yan Mei frowned. "I'm sorry, Jade, but I haven't heard or seen anything of the Kastels in nearly seventeen years. Until I realized who you were, I had lost hope of ever seeing any of my daughter's family again. I don't know what happened to them," she said.

I had a feeling that was what I would hear, but it still stung. I wanted to know what had happened—where my mother and father and brother had vanished to, if they were *alright*. Plus, why had my mother decided to leave me at a hospital? Why had she been alone? I could tell from Yan Mei's face that she'd asked herself the same questions a million times. It must have been difficult for her too, not knowing what happened to her family...

"Could you tell me what you knew about my parents?" I asked, trying to lighten the conversation.

"Well—" she started but stopped short when the door flew open. An overly excited Henry busted inside the office and nearly tackled me in a bear hug.

"Cuz!" Henry exclaimed.

My eyes widened in alarm, processing a thought I hadn't before. Henry was Yan Mei's grandson. If I was Yan Mei's granddaughter...

"I'm related to *you*?!"

"Yeah! Isn't it great?" he said before letting me go. "My long-lost cousin! We meet at last. Well, we've already met, but now we know, and you know—" he said before Yan Mei cut him off.

"Let's give Jade some time to process everything. It has been quite the day for her," she said, for which I was grateful. It was all too much, too fast. Much like everything that had happened since we moved to Pinewood. I had a family. I'd *met* my family. I had a grandmother and cousin who I could talk to anytime now. In a way, if we never moved again, I could be with a piece of my family forever. I liked the sound of that.

"Oh, right. Sorry," Henry said, rubbing his arm.

"It's fine! Anyway, I'd better go home. I'm sure the Bensons are waiting on me now," I said. Yan Mei nodded, and Henry smiled but still had a sad look in his eyes. Clearly, he was very excited about having a long-lost cousin. I sighed. "Henry, do you want to walk me home?"

He perked up immediately and was nearly out the door the moment I finished asking the question. I turned to Yan Mei.

"I guess I'll see you later...uh, is it okay if I still call you Yan Mei?" I asked awkwardly.

Yan Mei gave me a small smile. "Of course. I am just happy to see you. I'll let you see more as soon as you're ready," she said.

I smiled before walking out the door and made my way to the overly excited Henry, who was tapping his foot like Victoria sometimes did.

"Where's Dylan?" I asked as we walked.

Henry gave a nervous laugh. "Oh, his mom called and told him to go home."

I nodded, a little confused, but I figured Henry was probably still just acting weird from finding out we were family.

"I wonder if we'll ever find my brother," I said quietly.

Henry looked at the sky with a smile. "If he's out there, we'll find him," he said with confidence. I couldn't help but notice how he said *we* like we were a team. Like we were a family. As obnoxious as he could be at times, he really did care.

We talked for a little bit before Henry uncharacteristically grew quiet. I followed his gaze to see none other than Julian Graves. He was alone, just like when I first ran into him. This time, he was walking out of the Pinewood Library, headed in the opposite direction across the street. Instead of boxes of tea, he was holding what looked like a book, pen, and a notebook. Studying perhaps? It didn't look like a textbook, but I didn't want to stare long enough for him to catch me looking. Henry didn't bother hiding his dislike for him.

"C'mon, Henry. Put down the pitchfork," I said, tugging him along behind me.

The sun was starting to set when we said our goodbyes, and I walked through my front door. The Bensons were setting the table for dinner, and Tommy was in his seat, gulping down his drink. I hadn't thought about what it would be like seeing the Bensons after my vision with Yan Mei. I couldn't help but compare. My mother seemed pretty laid back—not worried about the chaos of clothes and blankets scattered about with two twins on hand. Even after Tommy was born, Mrs. B always seemed like she was tidying up something. She was a master at stress-cleaning.

If my biological family was still together, I wouldn't have a younger brother. I would have one my own age. Someone to grow up with. I wasn't always close to the Bensons, especially in the past few months, but I didn't know how to feel about it.

"Jade?" Mrs. B called out. "There you are, we were starting to get worried."

I walked closer to the kitchen. "Oh, I went to the swim meet and then to Yan Mei's for a little bit. Henry walked me home."

"Henry? Another boy?" Benson asked, slightly panicked. My mind flashed to the incident in my bedroom with Dylan.

"No, Benson. He's my friend. Just like Dylan."

"I love that you're making friends, but I wish they were girls," Benson sighed.

Mrs. B rolled her eyes. "He means we are very happy for you, Jade. Are you hungry?"

I shook my head. After today's events, I definitely did *not* want to sit down with the Bensons and pretend to feel normal. I needed some time to myself to reflect on all the bombshells that had been dropped today.

"No, I already ate. Thank you," I lied, ignoring their confused looks. Even Tommy, who eyed me silently as I turned away and went up the stairs to my room.

I shut the door behind me and sighed. I pulled out my journal and started to write down the details of my vision and my talk with Yan Mei afterward. Each sentence sparked more questions: What was my father like? What happened to my family? To everyone? I wasn't the only one who had lost their family...Yan Mei and Henry, my new family I hadn't known existed until today, were also wondering.

A slight knock startled me from my thoughts. I peeked out the door to find a small plate of cookies and a note that said *Sorry about your journal.* I picked up the plate and smiled. I guess I needed to talk to Tommy soon. Judging from the slightly burnt edges, he'd likely baked them himself without assistance from Mrs. B. Sometimes, he wasn't so bad. Making a mental note to thank him for the cookies later, I plopped one into my mouth and laid down on my bed.

Pulling out my phone, I saw that I had a couple messages from Dylan.

Sorry I had to leave early. I'm glad you know everything now. It's been hard keeping it a secret.

Henry is so excited.

Hey, I think I'm going to get grounded for skipping the swim meet, so I may have to postpone our next study session.

If you still wanted to do that, that is.

Skipping the swim meet...I'd made him skip the swim meet! I had potentially saved his life and prevented him from being taken by the invisible thing, but in doing so, I'd probably gotten him in trouble with both the swim team that he was already rocky with grade-wise and his family. I had to take the fall for this somehow...but *how?*

I had absolutely no way of explaining *why* I had trapped him in the boy's locker room, and...the kiss replayed in my mind. Oh, that looked bad. Very, very bad. Why did I *kiss* him? Of all the things I could've done! I could have slapped him, shoved him down, tied him to a chair, almost *anything* would have been better. What if the school found out? What if the Bensons found out? Wait. What if Dylan's *parents* found out?

As if my thoughts could be heard, I felt my phone buzz. I had a strong feeling I knew who this message was from, and it made me extremely hesitant to look. I paused for a moment as if the phone would explode if I didn't tread carefully. Finally, I got enough courage to look at my screen.

1 new message from Dylan.

I was right. It was from him. I debated not looking at it, but if I didn't, I wouldn't sleep all night worrying about what he had said. But when I looked at the message, it wasn't from Dylan.

This is Dylan's mother. We need to talk. Come to our house for dinner Monday. I will talk with your parents.

CHAPTER
TEN

This was the worst-case scenario. For someone who could literally see things coming, what I did at the swim meet was extremely stupid. I knew I threw caution to the wind, but I did *not* foresee all of this happening. It was bad enough that Dylan's mother wanted to *meet* with me, but no, it had to get worse. I swear, sometimes I think I'm cursed. Couldn't this just be a nightmare so everything would be fine again when I finally woke up?

"Hey, new girl," a tall guy with an annoying voice said, materializing beside me. I sighed, just trying to get my books from my locker in peace. "Do you meet with any guy during their games, or is the swim nerd your exclusive?"

"Be careful, or she might curse you," another boy in a Pinewood jacket warned, wiggling his fingers at me like he was casting a spell. The pair laughed.

"Yeah, just like Tyler."

I turned, slamming my locker shut, ready to make a snarky response and potentially punch at least one of them in the face when someone tugged my arm.

"Alright, Jade. Let's get to class now," Henry said, pulling me away from the pair. I resisted for a moment before letting him pull me along.

The two boys laughed and made another joke I couldn't hear, but I was sure I didn't want to know. I knew I shouldn't try to get myself into even more trouble than I was already in, especially after what happened at my last school, but for a moment, it was tempting.

"Why couldn't *they* be the ones attacked by the invisible monster?" I grumbled. "I'd gladly feed them to it myself."

Henry chuckled nervously. "Remind me never to make you angry, cuz," he said, dodging hurriedly through the cramped hall.

I could feel eyes on me from every direction, people whispering under their breath. Henry puffed out his chest and tugged me through the crowd as if he were my own personal bodyguard, which was kind of sweet, minus the fact that he was barely any bigger than I was. There was no way he would be able to stop a raging football jock or a rabid cheerleader...a sickly freshman, maybe. Still, his presence was reassuring, like his hand on my arm was somehow calming my nerves. I decided it was nice to have family looking out for you.

Not for the first time, I found myself wondering what sort of powers Henry had. Neither he nor Yan Mei had explained at the restaurant Friday night, and I hadn't heard from Dylan since the fateful Mom Text of Doom. It was hard to imagine Henry being able to hurl something across a room with his mind like Dylan or pick up a car with his bare hands. What was Henry good at? Talking? Jokes? Knowing a bunch about Victoria Harper? Could those count as superpowers?

"I'm sorry everyone's being such jerks," Henry muttered, ducking into a thankfully emptier hallway. "I don't know how everyone found out about the K-I-S-S."

I rolled my eyes. I was pretty sure spelling out words you didn't want people to know didn't work with high schoolers. Besides, I had a feeling I knew *exactly* how the entire school had found out. Only four people had been near the locker rooms when I kissed Dylan before that invisible monster came at us: me, Dylan, Henry, and Victoria. Three of those people I knew for sure hadn't said a word.

The door to Mr. Goodman's classroom loomed ominously at the end of the hall. Here it was: the moment I'd been dreading all day.

Henry led the way, glaring at anyone who dared look in my direction. Thankfully, Mr. Goodman was already at the board, scrawling out notes for today's group work, so the general reaction was relatively quiet. A few snickers and hidden smiles, but certainly not the worst thing I'd heard since I got to school that morning. Silently, I took my now usual seat beside Dylan.

Someone let out a loud cat-call whistle, making the room erupt with laughter.

I was mortified. For the first time since I'd seen him, Dylan's usually kind face looked very, *very* angry. His hands weren't anywhere near it, but I could hear the plastic water bottle in front of him starting to crunch under the force of his powers. I quickly grabbed it before he could send it flying across the room without touching it. The last thing we needed was more attention.

"Okay, okay, settle down, everyone," Mr. Goodman said, clearly confused about what was going on. At least, apparently, the teachers weren't gossiping about us, too. Yet.

I tried to send a glare back at Victoria, but she was dead to the world, hurriedly scribbling in a colorful notebook that I'd never seen before. She must have been writing something important because she never took notes like that during English. Her foot tapped incessantly against the floor like she was anxious. As if she had something to be nervous about—the whole school wasn't talking about her behind her back.

I felt another pair of eyes on mine, as, for the first time in days, Julian held my gaze. Instead of the laughing, malicious looks everyone else had been giving me all day, he seemed genuinely sad. As if he actually felt sorry for me.

I huffed and turned away from him. Like *he* would know. No one was whistling at him in the middle of class or laughing when he walked by. In fact, no one *ever* seemed to bother Julian, which was really weird since I wasn't sure I'd ever seen him talk to someone other than Victoria.

"I'm so sorry all of this is happening," Dylan whispered sadly. "I didn't...I mean, I never—"

I raised an eyebrow. "I'm the one who got you benched from the swim team, and you're apologizing? I've had worse, Dylan, really."

That wasn't exactly true. I mean, there was my last school...but I wasn't too keen on thinking about all that again. With as many schools as I'd been in, I'd definitely been up against stupid rumors and bullies before, but I was pretty sure I'd never had the entire school against me within the first month before. Go big or go home, I guess.

"These idiots aren't our only problem," Henry said, keeping his voice low. Henry had forfeited his original seat beside Dylan to me and opted to turn around a chair from the next row when we did group work for our projects. He'd claimed he was being chivalrous, but I had no doubt it was actually because it gave him a much better view of Victoria and Julian's table. Today though, Henry looked dead serious, only sending the occasional glance toward the banes of my existence, so I could tell something really, really bad was up. "Tell Jade what you told me this morning, Dylan."

It took Dylan a second to find his words. "Yan Mei told us what you said about your visions switching if you tried to change them," he said, swallowing hard. "I-I think that happened."

I suddenly felt sick. No wonder Dylan had such a guilty look on his face—it wasn't just the rumors bothering him. Yan Mei had been right... by saving Dylan, I'd only traded him out for someone else.

"Who was it?" I asked, mouth as dry as sandpaper.

"Tyler Martinez. He's a freshman. Friday was the first meet he was supposed to swim in," Dylan said, keeping his eyes low. "He was, you know...like us."

Meaning he had powers. I glanced at Henry, and he silently tugged on his ear.

"Ear powers?"

Henry face-palmed. Dylan seemed to be trying hard not to fall out of his chair laughing.

"Ear powers? What the heck are ear powers?" Henry whispered harshly. "No. As in, do you HEAR what I'm trying to tell you?"

"Super-hearing?" I asked in awe. I thought seeing the future was bad enough; I couldn't imagine having to hear everything in Pinewood happening at once. He probably knew more gossip than Victoria.

Suddenly, I remembered something. One of those idiots who'd been teasing me had made a joke about me putting a curse on a guy named Tyler.

"I think the invisible dude might have grabbed him after we got away," Dylan said, pretending to write something about *Macbeth* as Mr. Goodman did a lazy pass in front of our table. "As far as I can figure, Tyler made it out of the meet and went back to the locker room but was gone by the time everybody else got down there. I've tried to ask around on the team to see if anybody saw him after that, but nobody really wants to talk to me at the moment."

I winced. "Sorry."

"Oh, don't worry about him, Jade. It's his mom you've got to worry about," Henry warned. Dylan glared at him. "What? She needs to be prepared! Your mom's scary, man—she can read you like a book."

"Well, that's comforting," I groaned. My stomach was already tying itself into knots over having to go over to Dylan's after school.

As promised, Mrs. Mason had called Mrs. B over the weekend, and they had talked for over *two* hours. I didn't know what exactly they'd found to talk about for that long, but Mrs. B hadn't seemed mad when they'd finally hung up, so I assumed nothing had been said about me getting Dylan suspended from the swim team. Mrs. B had seemed in a remarkably good mood this morning, too—stuffing a giant box full of cookies for me to take over and reminding me to wear "Something nice." Needless to say, the yellow sweater she'd not-so-discreetly hung on my closet door did not make it outside.

"Now remember, never look directly into her eyes," Henry warned ominously. "Mrs. Mason can smell fear."

Dylan kicked him under the table. "Shut up, dude!"

Henry opened his mouth to say something else, but the bell cut him off. Had class gone by that quickly?

"Pick you up around five-thirty?" Dylan asked, looking about as thrilled as I felt about me having to go meet his parents. "Henry's just joking. Mom's really not that bad."

Henry snorted, not making me feel much better. I nodded anyway. "Sure."

Julian and Victoria made their way past our table. Victoria still looked distracted, clutching her notebook tight to her chest like she was protecting it. Julian tried to give me another sympathetic look, making my blood boil. I didn't try to hide my laughter as Henry practically lunged in between them and nearly sent him toppling into another group of kids heading for the door.

"Hey, Victoria, I was thinking—" Henry said quickly, raising his voice as she made a break for the hallway. "Victoria! If I could just have a moment of your time—"

"Jade, can I have a word with you?" Mr. Goodman asked quietly, coming up behind me.

"Um, sure," I agreed, slinging my bag over my shoulder.

"Privately," Mr. Goodman said awkwardly, shooting Dylan a silent glance.

"You got it," he said, grabbing his stuff and heading for the door. "See you later, Jade."

Mr. Goodman didn't speak until everyone else was out of the classroom. "Um, this is sort of an awkward thing to ask about, but is something going on, Jade? I've heard quite a few concerning rumors going around today—not that I believe any of them are true, of course—it's just..."

"It's alright, Mr. Goodman," I interrupted. He was clearly floundering on what to say without insulting me. "Somebody started a stupid rumor about me and Dylan. That's all. No big deal."

Mr. Goodman didn't look convinced. "Jade, if people are bullying you and Dylan, I can help."

As if any of the teachers at my last school ever helped anything. Getting a teacher involved was the last thing that would help people lay off Dylan and me.

"It's just a stupid rumor. No one will even remember it in a week or two," I said, shaking my head. "I'm sure everyone was just happy for a chance to make up stuff about the new girl. I've been there before."

"But Dylan *did* get put on probation from the swim team, didn't he?" Mr. Goodman asked quietly.

"What?" I squeaked, unable to believe that Mr. Goodman, one of the few teachers who had been really nice to me at Pinewood, would ask such a thing. For the first time, I realized his dark eyes were unnaturally sharp. Still, his face looked pained—maybe that had just come out wrong. Maybe he wasn't asking if the rumors were true but allowing me to tell my side of the story.

"He did," I said, choosing my words carefully. I couldn't very well tell my English professor that we'd been fighting off an invisible, super-powered being. "But it wasn't for the reason everyone else is saying."

Mr. Goodman nodded as if that explanation was good enough for him. "You know, if they don't stop bothering you, I would reconsider letting you switch groups..."

"No!" I said, a little louder than I aimed to. "Sorry. No, please. I really like working with Dylan and Henry. They...understand me."

"Alright, if that's what you want," he said, giving me a reassuring smile. "You'd better get going, or you'll be late to your next class."

"Right," I said, realizing we'd talked through most of the five minutes between classes. I'd have to run to get my books in time. "Thanks, Mr. Goodman. For, you know, looking out."

"No problem. I've got your back, Jade."

I nodded, hurrying out of the room to get my stuff before my next class. *Wow, that was a weird conversation.* I mean, it seemed like Mr. Goodman was trying to help, but wasn't it odd that he'd be so concerned with a stupid rumor about a teenager's love life? Plus, if he'd offered to help out me and Dylan, then why had he been so adamant that Dylan leave the room *before* we talked? Maybe he thought that the conversation might not go well with both of us? Still, with the way he'd been looking at me, I couldn't help but feel a little like I'd just been interrogated. I shook the thought out of my mind as I grabbed my biology textbook out of my locker. *He's just trying to look out for you, Jade. All this invisible force stuff is making you paranoid.*

The bell rang, signaling the start of the next period. I took off at a run. The last thing I needed right now on top of everything was being late.

CHAPTER
ELEVEN

"Okay, I'm panicking," I said, unable to stand the awkward silence that had filled Dylan's car since he'd picked me up from my house. Well, not total silence, but I was not feeling Dylan's *Car Jamz* playlist. "What exactly did Henry mean?"

"Not to be rude, but Henry says quite a lot...could you be more specific, please?" he asked, turning stiffly into the neighborhood where Mrs. B had dropped him off a few days before.

"About your mom. How does she...*smell* fear?" I asked, feeling a little silly. "I mean, can she actually do that? Like, does she have super-smell or something?"

For the first time since we'd gotten in the car, Dylan actually laughed. "No, she doesn't have super-smell...I don't know anyone with that power, actually."

"But does she have powers?" I asked, picking anxiously at a stray thread on my sweater.

"Yeah, we all do," Dyan said. He was practically radiating nervous energy, which only amplified my own. "Mom told me not to tell you what she can do. She said it's more fun when people find out on their own."

I tried to imagine what it would be like to grow up in a family full of powers—like I was supposed to. How *normal* everything would be, even though we were entirely the opposite.

"Do I get to know about anyone else?" I asked. "Their powers, I mean." I watched the beautiful homes pass us as we wound through his subdivision. Houses of brick with large windows lined the road. I didn't remember which one was his since we'd been here at night, and I'd been busy having a freakish death vision, but I could tell we were getting close.

"Well, I doubt you'd have to worry too much about Dad—his powers are...*unconventional,*" Dylan said with an odd look on his face. His features were scrunched like he was cringing. I supposed I would find out why soon enough. "Now Sophie, on the other hand...you might want to keep an eye on her."

I remembered the little girl who'd opened the door for Dylan when we'd dropped him off.

"Your little sister?" I asked.

"She pulls her weight," he said, smiling like I was oblivious to an inside joke.

Dylan pulled the car into a driveway on the left. I could hear the wind chimes clanking in the breeze on the porch. Quickly, one of the curtains snapped shut in a window like someone had been watching for us but didn't want to get caught. Dylan rolled his eyes.

"You look nervous," he said, his eyes now looking into mine. "It'll all be alright. They're going to love you."

I smiled for a moment, his words filling me with confidence. Maybe it wouldn't be so bad. After all, they had powers too. They knew what it was like to be different. But I couldn't help but shake the weirdness of it. It felt like I was meeting the in-laws for the first time instead of going to dinner at my friend's house. The problem was, I had never had dinner at a friend's house, not even Ashley...the nerves all started to rush back. I couldn't screw this up. I was vaguely aware of Dylan saying something, but I couldn't really tell what it was over my own internal panic.

A light tap on my shoulder broke me from my thoughts. He was holding a lavender bag out to me. "Sorry, it's a little smushed. It's kind of silly, but I wanted to, you know, say thank you...for helping me with my test."

"You already made the test up?"

Dylan smiled. "I got an eighty-six. Mrs. Watson told me today."

"That's great!" I said, opening up the bag. Inside was a plush, snowy owl with large, black eyes. No one had ever gotten me a gift before. Only the Bensons, who you could argue, were obligated to.

"I figured Mr. Hootsworth might enjoy a friend," Dylan said sheepishly. "Besides, that one looks pretty real—I figured you could use it to scare your brother if you wanted."

I stared down at the plush owl, gently running my fingers down the soft faux feathers. "I—I don't know what to say. Thank you so much."

Dylan looked back toward his porch. Whoever was peeking out of the curtains must have been impatient because they were clearly watching us again.

"We'd better head inside," Dylan sighed.

For a moment, a panicked look crossed his face, and he practically lunged out of the car, running to open my door for me. "Sorry, I almost forgot."

"Um, thank you?" I said, not sure whether to be flattered or concerned.

Together, we made our way to the porch, but before we could reach the steps, the front door whipped open, and a tiny girl blocked our path. She was maybe about six, dressed in a shimmery multicolored dress with a tiara placed primly on top of her blonde hair. Her eyes were a piercing blue.

"Mommy! Dylan and his girlfriend are here!" she yelled, making me cringe awkwardly.

"Is it too late to make a break back to the car?" Dylan whispered.

"Yes, it is, young man," an older woman said, materializing in the doorway. How had she heard him from that far back? Was there another person with super hearing?

I tried to put on a polite smile, but judging from the small girl's face, I was failing miserably. Dylan's mother gave a small laugh before gesturing us inside.

The interior was as beautiful as the exterior. Neutral walls with sandy furniture expertly laid out. It was an area I instantly felt calmer in. That was until I looked over to see Dylan's mother beaming at me.

What was I supposed to say? I couldn't think of a single thing. The blank was back, and the words were not happening.

"It's nice to meet you, Jade," Dylan's mother said, extending her hand to me. I debated on the proper way to shake someone's hand. Softly? Firmly? Was that only a dumb man thing?

"It's nice to meet you too, Mrs. Mason," I said, trying to shake her hand without her noticing my hand was *actually* shaking. Her hair was also blonde and fell neatly into waves. She wore a simple light blue shirt and dark-washed jeans. Her eyes were the same deep blue like Dylan and his sister.

Why did they all have to be beautiful?

I mentally smacked myself. No, bad Jade. I stopped that train of thought before it could continue on. I did *not* need to be ogling at anyone, particularly the handsome boy currently staring at me.

"Dinner's already on the table," Dylan's mom said, looking like she was trying to keep herself from laughing. That was weird. Did I say something wrong? Was it my face? "Sophie, why don't you go get your father?"

Sophie pouted, crossing her arms over her chest. "But I want to hang out with Dylan's girlfriend—"

Mrs. Mason gave her a knowing look. "I know *exactly* what you're trying to do. Wait until after dinner, at least."

"You *always* know!" Sophie pouted, running off toward the back of the house. A door slammed like she'd gone into the backyard.

"As you can see, Sophie's very excited to see you, Jade," Mrs. Mason said, leading the way through the house to a neatly set dining room.

As long as she doesn't make me wear a tiara, I thought as the three of us took our seats. There it was again: that weird little smirk like Mrs. Mason was trying to keep from laughing. I had to figure out what I was doing to my face so I could make it stop. Dylan shot her a wary glance across the table.

"So, Jade, I feel like I know all about you," Mrs. Mason said, motioning for us to start plating our food even though Sophie and Mr. Mason hadn't come in yet. I could definitely believe what Dylan had said about his mom being a caterer. Everything was out on the table with perfect precision: shepherd's pies in ramekins, broccolini, salad bowls, and a pitcher of freshly made sweet tea.

"Anything else you want to share?"

I choked on my tea. She hadn't said it in a hostile way, but something in Mrs. Mason's tone told me that there wasn't much I could say that would surprise her. Suddenly, I had an eerie feeling that she knew *everything*—that I'd asked Dylan over to my house, me kissing him in the locker room, all of us running away from school to meet with Yan Mei.

"BEHOLD, THE PAPAYANAPPLE!" a brunette-haired man announced, holding a weird, spiny-looking orange fruit. The man in the doorway was covered in dirt like he'd been out digging around in a garden all day—on his clothes, his hands, smudged across the lenses of his glasses. "I told you I could do it!"

Dylan sank low into his chair beside me. "Dad, not now..."

"There's always time for science, my boy! Now, see, I crossed several generations of pineapple with papaya—"

"Chris, honey, did you forget we have a guest tonight?" Mrs. Mason chided amusedly. "You'd better go clean up."

Dylan's dad froze, eyes focusing in on me as if he'd just noticed I was there. "Oh...Do you want to try the papayanapple? It's very...rejuvenating, makes you feel like you've drank two cups of coffee."

"I'm good," I said as politely as possible, suddenly aware of a chair scooting within an inch of mine. Instead of taking the empty seat next to me, Dylan's little sister shoved a stuffed owl with gigantic purple glitter eyes in the chair.

"This is Mr. Hooty-Toot," Sophie said matter-of-factly, taking the next seat over. "He is the Supreme Overlord of The Owl Kingdom and wishes to be very good friends with Oliver."

I raised an eyebrow at her. "Oliver?"

Sophie pointed at the stuffed owl Dylan had given me in the car. I hadn't even realized I was still holding it. Dylan's sister cast him a worried look. "You did explain everything, didn't you?"

"No, Sophie," he said, face flushed with embarrassment. "I did not explain the three-hour backstory you gave a stuffed animal that isn't yours."

Sophie's jaw dropped, scandalized. "But then how will Jade know all about Oliver's tragic backstory! He doesn't have am—am—"

"Amnesia?" I offered, a little worried she was going to hurt herself saying the word the way she was scrunching up her face.

"Yeah, that. Oliver has been through a lot in The Owl Kingdom— Dylan's just too embarrassed to tell it. Mr. Hooty-Toot and I will, though. We helped pick Oliver out. We're experts on owls, you know."

"Oh, got it," I said, awkwardly setting my owl—Oliver, I guess—in the chair beside Sophie's.

Mrs. Mason looked momentarily confused but then suddenly seemed to put the pieces together as she glanced between me, Sophie, and Dylan.

Never look directly into her eyes, Henry had said.

My fork banged into my plate so loud that everybody jumped. A terrible hunch sent a chill up my spine like I'd just been dunked in an ice bath.

Mrs. Mason smirked at me knowingly. "You've figured it out, haven't you?"

I swallowed hard. "Y-You can read minds, can't you?"

"Unfortunately," Dylan muttered, chewing a bite of broccolini mournfully.

I felt like my head was spinning. Mrs. Mason didn't just seem to know everything about me. She *did* know everything. Henry had said she could read people like a book—she had probably pulled everything about me out of my head the minute I stepped through the door. That was, assuming she hadn't read Dylan's mind before that. She really did know about *everything*.

"I appreciate what you did to try to save my son, even if it has brought you trouble," Mrs. Mason said calmly, apparently used to people being terrified of her.

She knew about the vision I'd had of Dylan getting snatched at the swim meet. Instantly, my mind started to drift toward the mega-vision where I'd seen Dylan crying over my dead body, but I quickly shut down the thought. *Don't think about it. Don't think about it.* Mrs. Mason raised an eyebrow but didn't seem to get anything before I blocked her out. I had a terrible feeling that if she really wanted to know something, she'd be able to find it in there whether I wanted her to or not. The thought made me shiver.

"You're taking it better than most," Mrs. Mason said, giving me a kind smile. "Poor Henry nearly has a panic attack every time we have him over."

"He's worried she will find out about his not-so-secret crush on Victoria." Mr. Mason chuckled, returning to the dining room some- what cleaner than before. I'd been so distracted with Sophie and Mr. Hooty-Toot that I hadn't noticed him slip away.

"He could do better," Sophie mumbled, examining a piece of broc- colini with disgust.

"Henry's, like, ten years older than you," Dylan said. "Quit claiming all my friends."

"You have one friend."

"And you're not allowed to date anyone until you're thirty, young lady," Mr. Mason interrupted. He had tried to sound firm, but his face was so kind that the threat seemed kind of ridiculous.

Sophie put her ear to the stuffed owl's beak. "Mr. Hooty-Toot says I'm old enough to date in The Owl Kingdom."

"So, Jade," Mrs. Mason said, trying to course-correct the conversa- tion before her husband and daughter could start arguing about how time flowed in The Owl Kingdom, "Yan Mei tells me you're going to be helping us with the people in our community going missing. You've had two visions concerning people with powers who've disappeared?"

I nearly asked how she knew that since I hadn't said anything about my vision of Mary and Victoria to Yan Mei before I realized she had seen it in my mind.

Mr. Mason looked up at me with renewed interest. "You mean you can see through time? What an incredible power! If only mine was that interesting."

"Trust me, I'd give it to you if I could," I said, earning a concerned look from Dylan. I ignored him. "Isn't having any power cool?"

Mr. Mason sighed. "Cool, maybe. Helpful, no. I'm good with plants—can tell when they're ripe or not doing well. Not very helpful when you're trying to save people."

"You're helping just as much as the rest of us, Chris," his wife said, squeezing his hand reassuringly. "We're just not having much luck right now."

"Wait, you're all helping Yan Mei look for the missing people, too?" I asked, sitting up a little straighter in my seat. "I thought it was just Henry and Dylan."

"Oh, Henry and Dylan aren't getting anywhere near this," Mrs. Mason said firmly. "They both barely know how to use their powers, and I'm not about to let them put themselves in harm's way. It's bad enough Dylan's already drawn enough attention for someone to go after him."

"But why does Jade get to help when I can't?" Dylan protested. He was usually so quiet and agreeable that it was weird seeing him try to argue against something.

"Having a power strong enough to see through time makes Jade much stronger than you—and more vulnerable," his mom said. "She's seen two of the people that have been targeted, so Yan Mei hopes we might be able to figure out who's in danger so we can find them before they vanish. That means trying to control her powers in a safe location. There's no way she'd risk putting her own granddaughter out in the field, not when we've just found her again."

Then, Mrs. Mason did something that surprised me. She reached across the table and took my hand. A dozen rapid-fire images tore through my mind—I wasn't sure if they were visions or if Dylan's mom was letting me see the world the way she did. There were two teenage girls—one with dark skin, one with blonde hair. I saw them laughing together, sitting on swings at a park. I saw a rainy day where the girls were drenched. One girl looked angry while the other made a face at her. I saw the girls with three guys, one of whom looked very similar to Henry.

"That was very...interesting," Mrs. Mason said, interrupting my thoughts.

I blinked a few times, snapping back to reality. My head was pounding. Geez, did my powers always have to feel like this?

"You could see my visions?" I asked. Dylan and Sophie's jaws dropped dramatically like they were in Disneyland or a pig started to fly.

"That is so *cool*!" Dylan said.

"Jade is the coolest!" Sophie shouted, moving her hands to make Mr. Hooty-Toot nod, too. I flushed before thinking back to what I saw.

Was that Dylan's mom and my mother?

"Yes, it was," Mrs. Mason confirmed softly. I had forgotten momentarily she could read my thoughts before she continued. "We were best friends...it wasn't often you would find people like us. Everyone was much more scattered back then, but Yan Mei would find us, teach us how to get control. I miss Vivian."

"Thank you for allowing me to see her, even if it was just the past," I said. She smiled and reached over to squeeze my hand again.

The rest of the dinner was primarily dominated by Sophie and Mr. Mason, though occasionally Dylan and his mom popped in to add a comment before being overpowered by the two and their enthusiastic personalities. There were several intense discussions about The Owl Kingdom.

The moment Sophie was done with her plate, she was out of her seat and running toward me. "Jade! You need to meet the other animals in Mr. Hooty-Toot's kingdom! You and Ollie have to be initchy-aited!"

"Initiated?" I asked.

"Yes! That one!" she exclaimed, grabbing my hand and the stuffed owls. I had to be at least twice Sophie's size, but she yanked my body along like it was a feather in the dainty little girl's hands. I could faintly hear Mr. and Mrs. Mason laughing. Dylan was yelling for her to come back.

"How strong are you?" I said in awe as my feet were dragged out of the kitchen and into her room.

Sophie shrugged. "Very."

I hadn't known Sophie long, but her room was exactly what I had imagined it would be. Pink paint, rainbow posters, drawings on the wall, and stuffed animals *everywhere*. On the floor, the bed, the desk— there was no place within her room that there wasn't a soft plush nearby. It was like being trapped on the inside of a claw machine.

"Okay, Jade! Let's go ask Mr. Hooty-Toot about Ollie's noble quest to join The Owl Kingdom!" Sophie said, running around with the stuffed owls before jumping on her bed.

"Wait, now it's a quest?" I asked, confused.

"I don't make the rules, Mr. Hooty-Toot does!"

"Ah, yes," I said. "Mr...Hooty-Toot."

Tommy was never interested in things like this. He always stuck to sports and pranking me. This was all new territory for me, and I, frankly, had no idea what to do. Thankfully, it seemed my rescue was coming.

"Sophie, I'm taking her back now. Jade has to go home soon," Dylan said, leaning against the doorframe.

"No, no! I just got started playing with her!" Sophie shouted, jumping off the bed. "You just want to keep her all to yourself, don't you? She's mine, and we haven't even begun the magic quest to save The Owl Kingdom!"

"Sophie, put it down," Dylan said, raising his hands slowly. I turned to see a *very* angry six-year-old with her princess bed raised above her head like it was nothing.

"How can you lift that?" I exclaimed, backing up a safe distance beside Dylan. Or maybe that wasn't a safe distance since he looked like he was about to get a big pink bed thrown at him.

Sophie continued to glare at her older brother, ignoring me.

"Sophie, don't make me tell Mom," Dylan said, giving her a knowing look. The young girl huffed before setting the bed down with a *thump*. How often did this happen?

"You better not tell!"

"Come on, Jade. I promised the Bensons I would have you back before eight," Dylan said. I nodded and followed him out of her room into the living area, still perplexed by the whole exchange. I looked back at the sad little girl.

"It was nice to meet you, Sophie," I said, bending down to look her in the eyes. "We'll have to go on that quest some other time."

Sophie beamed like she'd just won the lottery. She ran out of her room and placed Ollie in my hands before hugging me with the force of a boa constrictor.

"It's actually a secret mission, but that's okay," she said, squeezing me until I felt like my ribs were about to crack.

"Too. Much. Can't. Breathe," I choked out. Her grip loosened, allowing me to breathe.

Dylan rolled his eyes and pulled me out of Sophie's reach. "You'll see her again soon."

"I will?" she asked hopefully.

"She will?" I asked, still lost.

Dylan flushed, letting go of my arm to scratch his head. "Oh, well, I mean, if you want to, that is."

My mind blanked. In the past ten minutes, my entire brain had shut off. Thankfully, Mr. and Mrs. Mason joined us in the living room, saving me from responding.

"We certainly would love to see you again, Jade," Mrs. Mason said.

"Yes! You are much *quieter* than Henry," Mr. Mason joked. Mrs. Mason jabbed him in the arm with her elbow. We all laughed before saying our goodbyes and heading to the car.

"No sneaking off to locker rooms, you two!" Mrs. Mason shouted from the doorstep. Dylan and I paled.

"Mom!" he shouted, clearly mortified.

"Kidding! Kidding!" she said, failing miserably to hold in her laughter.

Where is a hole that I can crawl into and hide for the rest of eternity?

We made a break for the car, and Dylan peeled out a little faster than necessary, desperate to get away from his parents before they could embarrass him more. We didn't talk much on the way back to my house. The first few minutes were a little awkward, but the quiet settled into a peaceful silence. Before I knew it, Dylan had pulled the car to a careful stop in my driveway.

Once again, I was unprepared for the hustle of Dylan jumping out of the car and sprinting to my side to open the door.

"You know, you don't have to open the door for me," I said. "I am more than capable of doing that myself."

Dylan looked straight ahead as if recalling something terrifying. "If my mother found out..." He trailed off. "Which she *would*. It would be bad. Very, very bad. No disrespect to you or anything. I know you are more than capable, but please let me do this so I don't have to face the wrath of my mom."

I laughed at his terrified face. "Okay, but only because of your mother," I said. "Thanks again, for Ollie."

He smiled. "I'm glad you like it. I know it's been—kinda weird lately with everything going on. I wanted to cheer you up."

I was about to respond when I thought I heard something squeal nearby. I looked toward the house to see a *very* excited Mrs. B standing in the open doorway. Dylan seemed to notice, too, and gave her a polite wave.

"He's not coming inside! He has to go home!" I shouted. Her face fell slightly before sighing and shutting the door. I turned back to Dylan, though his attention was elsewhere. His eyes were locked curiously on my bedroom window.

"What is it?" I asked him. I followed his gaze to see the blinds were open, and there was a light on. *Weird.* I didn't remember leaving a light on.

"Nothing, nothing. I better get going," Dylan said. "I'll—see you tomorrow, Jade."

We both stared at one another for a moment, not really sure what to do. I guess we *were* friends now. Should we hug? Shake hands? I remembered my internal panic with Mrs. Mason earlier and smiled.

"I'll see you tomorrow, Dylan," I said, waving before turning to go into my house.

He waited until I was inside before he drove off. I ignored Mrs. B's shouts of him being a *doll* and how nice he was to give me a gift. I hadn't thought she'd seen the stuffed owl, but I had had to promise her a full debriefing about the dinner before she'd let me upstairs. I walked into my room and shut the door behind me.

I paused. Something felt off. I looked around and noticed a lamp I had never seen before sitting on my desk. I walked over to see a note scribbled on an index card.

To Jade. Please place in her room. Thank you! ~ Love, Dylan

From Dylan? How? *Why* did he—

My thoughts were stopped short when the lamp flickered off on its own and suddenly was replaced with an overly excited Henry, swinging his legs back and forth rapidly as he sat on top of my desk.

"Okay, spill it. Tell me *everything* that happened at dinner!"

CHAPTER
TWELVE

"What are you doing in my room!" I yelled before realizing I needed to keep my voice down. The last thing I needed was Benson breaking down the door to find a boy in my bedroom. "Henry! What the—how did you...were you just a lamp?"

Henry huffed. "Does Dylan never tell you anything about me? Get with the program, cuz. I'm a shapeshifter. Now, what happened at dinner? Was his mom mad? Did she know about the K-I-S-S? Spill the tea!"

"What? I don't have any tea," I said, mind wandering back to the tea shop I'd seen Julian coming out of.

"No, no, no!" Henry said, jumping down and pacing around my room. "The tea! The juicy stuff! The hot gossip! What went down with Mrs. Mason and her creepy mind-reading powers?"

My brain felt like it was running on fumes. Henry could shape-shift? Dylan's mom had been best friends with mine? Tea was slang for gossip? Entirely too much had happened today for me to be able to think clearly.

"Mrs. B said something about Dylan leaving me a gift...She meant you—the lamp, whatever—didn't she?" I asked, slowly putting the pieces together. "She didn't know anything about the owl."

102

"Owl? What owl?" Henry beamed. "Did Dylan get you an owl? Oh, no, did his sister make you play Owl Kingdom? Let me tell you, once you get in Owl Kingdom, you never—"

"Henry!" I said, snapping at him to focus. "What are you doing in my bedroom?"

Henry plopped down on my bed, thumbing through the book on my nightstand. "I just wanted to check on you. I mean, we are family now, and meeting the parents is a big step in any relationship."

"Dylan and I aren't in a relationship," I said, snatching the book away from him. "How long have you been up here?"

"Couple hours." Henry shrugged. "Long enough to know you need better taste in music. That's the saddest record collection I've ever seen."

I pinched the bridge of my nose. "So, let me get this straight. You turned yourself into a lamp, got Mrs. B to bring you inside, and have been snooping around my room for hours?"

Henry puffed out his chest. "It's called covert ops. I even thought of a great codename for you: Fortune Cookie! Get it? Because you can see the future? I'm still working on mine and Dylan's, though...food-related puns aren't as easy with our powers."

I sat down on the other end of the bed, realizing that Henry clearly wasn't going anywhere. I said a silent prayer that the Bensons would all stay downstairs. "So you really can shape-shift? Like, can you turn into anything?"

"Well, not exactly," Henry said, slumping back against my headboard. "My powers are sort of...temperamental. They don't work so well when I'm under pressure. I can do just about any kind of lamp as long as I've seen it, though."

I stared at him. "You mean you can *only* turn into lamps?"

For the first time since I'd met him, Henry actually looked embarrassed. "I mean, every once and a while, I've been able to turn into something else. A pen, a coat rack, a toaster...I almost managed an ant once."

"You mean, when I saw Dylan running with that heat lamp a few days ago..."

"That was me," Henry sighed, running a hand through his hair. "Victoria asked me if my grandma could make a reservation for the speech team next week. I panicked."

I rolled my eyes. "What's your whole deal with Victoria about anyway? She hardly ever talks to you—she practically ran away from you earlier today. There's probably a ton of people nicer than her at Pinewood, Henry."

"She doesn't mean to come off that way," he said, voice softening slightly. "Victoria's actually really nice if you get to know her. You just don't understand her."

I raised an eyebrow. "And you do?"

"Victoria and I used to be pretty good friends back in the day. When I was eleven, her family moved into the house beside me and Grandma. She was...nice. Like, she really understood me. She didn't think I was some weirdo like everybody else does."

I tried to ignore the pang of guilt I felt at that. Hadn't I thought Henry was loud and weird when I first met him, too? I wasn't sure I would have ever become friends with him if I hadn't gotten stuck with him and Dylan on our English project. If I hadn't, would I have ever even found out we were related? I swallowed hard, not sure I liked the thought of suddenly not having a cousin looking out for me.

"If you guys were so close, why does she give you the cold shoulder now?" I asked.

Never before had I seen Henry look so...sad. It definitely didn't suit him. The Henry I'd come to know should be obnoxious, loud, happy—not all sad and serious. I thought back to my vision with Yan Mei...how my mom had made it sound like Henry's mother was dead, then Yan Mei rushing off because his dad was in trouble. If Henry lived with Yan Mei now, had something happened to his dad, too? Had he lost his parents and a best friend? How could he always be so happy carrying all that grief around on his shoulders?

I suppose he doesn't smile all the time...

Henry was giving me a weird look.

"What?" I asked.

"Let me try something," he said excitedly. "Grab my hand."

"What? Why?" I asked, glancing nervously back at the door. Having Henry in my room was way less awkward than Dylan since we were related, but Benson wouldn't know that if he came barging in. Maybe Henry could just turn into a lamp if we needed a quick cover? If his powers were as unpredictable as he said, would they even work if we needed them to?

"Come on, Jade. I have an idea," Henry said impatiently. "I'll sort out the Bensons if we need to. It's not like I'm Dylan trying to put the moves on you."

"Yeah, but they don't know that!" I said, my cheeks heating at the comment about Dylan trying to *put the moves* on me. "They don't know anything about you or Yan Mei or my real family."

"Bringing us to why we need to talk about your sharing skills," Henry said, rolling his eyes. "Just take my hand already!"

Suddenly, I realized what Henry was trying to do. Reluctantly, I took his hand, relaxing my mind and searching for the memory of the past he was trying to show me.

I imagined I was standing in a hallway full of doors. Dozens stretched out in either direction, but the doors behind me seemed much more solid than the ones in front. Each one looked different: plain wooden doors, sliding glass ones. Some even had big locks on them, like a bank vault. All the doors in the hallway in front of me seemed eerily transparent, flickering in and out randomly.

Suddenly, the doors began to vanish. One by one, they dropped out of sight until there was only one left a few feet behind me. It was a strange flowy fabric, more of a curtain than a door, really. The stripes on it reminded me of a circus tent. Silently, I pulled it aside and stepped through.

The heat hit me first. A blazing sun shone above me, the air hot and humid like the middle of summer. Slowly, other things filled my senses: loud music like there was a band playing somewhere, children laughing and begging their parents to walk faster, the smell of funnel cakes and popcorn and lemonade. I squinted up at a tall shape towering above me. A Ferris wheel. There was a loud clicking as a small roller coaster whizzed past off to my left. There were vendors everywhere, bright lights flashing from gaming tents. A fair?

"Come on, Henry. We're holding up the line," a familiar voice said, drawing my attention to one of the booths to my right. It was one of those games where you have to throw a baseball to try to knock down a tower of bottles to win a cheesy prize. There was a massively backed up line for the game, irritated people sweating in the sun and grumbling at the kids in front to move.

"Just one more try. I'm sure I'll get it this time," a boy with dark hair insisted, swallowing hard as he handed over his final game ticket. There was already a massive pile stacked up beside him on the counter.

"Sure thing, kid," the girl behind the counter said as she handed him three baseballs, not sounding too convinced but clearly trying to boost his confidence. "Try again."

The boy was obviously Henry, though he was way younger—maybe eleven or twelve. He wore a tuxedo T-shirt and neon yellow shorts. There was a glittery green dragon painted on one of his cheeks. He looked dead serious as he wound up for his first throw. It was a wide miss. The crowd let out a collective groan.

Henry adjusted his stance, clearly trying hard to ignore them. He swallowed hard, then threw the second baseball. A little closer, but still not quite there.

"Henry, we can just go. I really don't need you to win me anything," the first voice I'd heard muttered quietly. I hadn't been able to see her very well for all the people, but there was a tall girl standing beside Henry, looking like she was trying hard to melt into the fabric of the tent.

"No, no, I've got this," Henry said confidently. "One last throw."

With a shock, I realized the girl was Victoria—but she didn't look anything like, well, Victoria. This girl was gangly and shy, bouncing nervously on the balls of her feet. Her blonde hair was pulled back into an intricate French braid, and she wore a Pinewood Middle School T-shirt and capris. A patch of freckles dusted her nose under a pair of black-framed glasses. Braces gleamed on her teeth. I felt like I had whiplash.

Henry pulled back his arm to take his final throw. The baseball flew through the air, much closer than the first two but still just a little too wide. Henry's shoulders slumped. I half expected him to start crying.

"It's okay, Henry," Victoria said, starting to pull him away, but the girl behind the booth stopped them.

"Here, kid," she said, handing Henry a cheap-looking necklace with a frog charm on it. "For trying so hard."

Henry beamed at the girl, speechless. He immediately handed it to Victoria.

"I *told* you I would win you something," he said, puffing out his chest as he and Victoria headed away from the booth.

"I don't know if that counts as a win." Victoria laughed, slinging on the necklace anyway.

Henry waved off the comment. "Boy, Dylan doesn't know what he's missing. Stupid swim camp."

"You do realize he's only gone for a few hours?" she said, raising an eyebrow at him. "We're literally supposed to see him later tonight."

"I know, I know," Henry agreed, running a hand over his face and smudging the dragon all over his cheek. "It's just...Dylan's my best friend. We've been together since birth—the peanut butter to my jelly, the mac to my cheese—what if he's busy and some crazy supervillain attacks the city? I'd be running around without a sidekick...I don't know, Victoria. I just don't think I could handle that kind of pressure."

Victoria fiddled with the frog on her new necklace. "Well...what if you had a backup sidekick? I mean, in case Dylan was busy. He's got a lot going on with swimming and his baby sister."

"But who would I get?" Henry said, considering the idea. "Grandma's always busy—"

Victoria punched him in the arm. "*Me*, doofus! I could be your sidekick."

A serious look flashed momentarily on Henry's face. He lowered his voice. "Are you sure?"

"'Course I'm sure," Victoria said, giving him a bright smile, braces and all. "I'm your best friend too."

I swallowed hard as my room reformed around me.

"Wow. That was trippy," Henry said, blinking hard like he'd just looked too long at a bright light. "What'd you see? It tickled."

"You mean you could *feel* me poking around in your memories?" I asked, running a hand through my hair as my mind tried to catch up. Henry nodded.

So, my cousin hadn't been lying after all. He and Victoria had been friends at one point—really good ones. But what had happened? Surely there had to be a reason she avoided him so much now?

Suddenly, the vision I'd seen of Victoria and Mary filled my mind. I looked over at Henry, who had braced himself on the bed as if the room was spinning.

"Yan Mei said it gets better after a minute," I assured him, trying to choose my next words carefully. "Henry, is there any reason you know of as to why Victoria might have been hanging around with Mary Milford before she vanished? Maybe something she might have wanted her to do? Someone she wanted her to meet?"

"Mary kept to herself a lot, even when we were younger," Henry said, wheels clearly turning in his head. "I mean, we were all friends in a classmate-y sort of way. Victoria slayed at board games, but she never could beat Mary. They used to compete against each other all the time. Mary's wicked smart—I think Grandma always suspected she had some sort of computing or probability power."

"Meaning something that might be really helpful in the wrong hands," I said, feeling the same cold chill I got whenever I thought about that invisible force that had come after us.

Henry nodded. "I don't think Victoria and Mary have been friends for a long time, though. Not since she got..." He gestured helplessly.

"Popular?"

"Different," he decided. "Why do you ask?"

"Just wondering," I said, a bad feeling starting to take root in my mind.

"Welp, I guess I'd better get back before Grandma gets worried," Henry said, standing up and stretching. "By the way, she wants you at the restaurant tomorrow after school. Training sesh number one, Fortune Cookie."

"Please don't call me that."

"Too late. It's already stuck." Henry grinned, opening my bedroom window.

"Wait!" I said, stopping him halfway out the window. "Training? Is that an every-night thing? What am I supposed to tell the Bensons if I'm gone all the time?"

"There's a Yan Mei's Cafe T-shirt in your closet, Fortune Cookie— just tell them you're at work. We people with powers have been doing this a long time, you know," Henry said, glancing down at my front yard two stories below in the dark. His face went pale, and he quickly ducked back into the safety of my room. "If I turn back into a lamp, can you carry me downstairs and set me outside?"

"I can throw you out the window if you're too scared," I joked, fighting off a grin.

"I don't know if I'll shatter, so let's not do that," Henry said, looking at me worriedly. "I mean, I can always stay here, but if that Benson dude came in and found me—"

"Light it up, Lamp Boy. Let's go."

CHAPTER
THIRTEEN

"Pretty good crowd tonight," Henry commented, turning the noodle mobile into the parking lot of an expansive mall.

"Are we going shopping?" I asked, craning my neck over the dashboard to get a better look at the building as we wound around it. I didn't see what Henry meant about there being a crowd—there was a max of forty cars. The lights looked like they were on in the main atrium, but other than that, there didn't seem to be many signs of life. Most of the signs for stores were out or flickering. The posters on the theater advertised movies that were several years old. Not exactly the normal teen hang-out for a Tuesday night, though that wasn't shocking. Beyond the university and a few residential areas, there wasn't much on this side of Pinewood.

"Would you quit with the questions? You're killing my vibe," Henry said, drumming his fingers on the steering wheel. "It's the Jonas Brothers Jam, Jade." He looked up at me through the mirror with wide eyes and an overly excited grin. "Tongue twister! Jonas, Jam, Jade. Jonas, jum—No!"

"Please focus on the road, Henry," Dylan said before turning to me. "Don't worry, we'll have you back before you need to go home."

"Okay, but the Bensons think I'm at the restaurant...what if they show up to embarrass me and I'm not there? They *would* do that," I said.

"It's all good, cousin-dear," Henry said, taking an epically off-beat drum solo on the steering wheel. I was suddenly regretting not forcing Dylan to drive. Henry brought the van to a stop in what seemed to be the most populated section of the parking lot. The sign for the food court glared down at us in bright red neon from a tall triangular entrance. "If the Bensons ask for you, they'll just say you're out on a delivery."

"That's even worse because I can't drive!" I panicked.

Henry shrugged. "Dylan and I can, so they'd just say you're out with us. The other staff have powers too, they know how it is. They'll look out for you."

First, did literally everyone in this town have powers? I could have saved myself a lot of emotional turmoil if I had been able to live here my whole life. Second, I was sure Benson would be *thrilled* hearing I was out with two boys.

"Ground rules for training," Henry said, looking at me with stern eyes. "Always enter through the food court—who knows what you'll walk into somewhere else. Two: stay focused inside and outside the training rooms. Three—"

"Henry, she'll be fine," Dylan said, pushing open his door and offering to help me down. "You'll see for yourself when we get in there."

Together, the three of us made our way toward the entrance to the food court. The mall was massive, to say the least. Nice, too, for someplace that seemed pretty deserted. The food court extended into a long, wide corridor leading up to the central atrium. Large, decorative pieces hung from the ceiling high above us in various shapes: the sun, clouds, and birds. The two far pillars had been hidden with platforms that looked like large trees, anchored to which was a mesh net about twenty feet below the ceiling like on a military training course.

"Are there people on that?" I asked, watching a group of dark shadows run over the top of our heads.

"That's Course One," Henry said, leading us forward. All the restaurant signs were out, and most were shuttered up, though a few still offered drinks or snacks. "It extends over the entire mall—tight spaces, ten-foot drops, obstacles in your way. It'll definitely cure any fear of heights."

"Henry and I have rigged up nearly half a dozen courses since Yan Mei bought this place to train in," Dylan said with a proud smile. "We're working on a blackout course in the old glow-in-the-dark mini golf now. You'll have to completely rely on your senses."

"Minus a few neon giraffes and alligators," Henry added.

The main corridor of the mall was where the action really was. Giant decorative sea creatures "swam" over top of a twenty-foot-wide tiered fountain, the bottom glistening with wishing pennies. An older woman stood in the water with three kids of various ages, each of them trying to maintain a single spout of water by holding out their hands.

Laughter echoed as forms ran past at exceptionally fast speeds or jumped from the turtle to the whale hanging from the ceiling.

Everywhere I looked, there were people using powers: a kid disassembling and reassembling a computer rapidly, a man healing an angry-looking bruise on a boy's head with a single touch, and a teenage couple who were clearly arguing with each other, though neither were saying anything. Every storefront was filled with different ages: young children, teens, or adults split up into different classes or skill levels. I saw Dylan's sister in a group of younger kids. Sophie waved at me through the glass.

I felt like my brain was on sensory overload. How could there be this many people with powers? In one place? Two weeks ago, I thought I was the only person in the world with powers...there had to be over a hundred here.

"Well, this is me," Dylan said, nodding toward a small group milling around an empty storefront. The store's original sign had been taken down and replaced with a graffiti-style mural marked: *Course Three*. An older man, a boy about seven, and a girl who was maybe fifteen were waiting for him. "Good luck on Day One, Jade."

He jogged off toward the others, making me wonder if they were all telekinetic. The girl high-fived Dylan as he got close, laughing about something, and I suddenly felt my face burn. Who was this girl that he was such good friends with?

"Got a problem there, Fortune Cookie?" Henry smirked.

I shoved past him, heading farther into the mall as Dylan and the others scrambled into their training course. "Where am I supposed to start? I doubt you've got a class for people who can see through time?"

"Nope," Henry agreed, jumping back as a burst of air tore right between us. "Stop running between people, Zack! It's rude!"

Laughter echoed as something raced back down the other side of the corridor impossibly fast. Henry sighed, looking a little sad. *Weird.* But he seemed to snap out of it quickly.

"Anyway, people like you and me...where we're sort of one-of-a-kind, we usually do our own thing," Henry explained. "I'll probably do Course Seven. It's an instinct course—throws obstacles at you fast, so hopefully, you'll just react naturally. I've been trying every week to see if I can manage something that doesn't require a sixty-watt bulb."

"Should I do that too?" I asked.

"No, you've been tasked with a different obstacle today," Henry said, pointing down the corridor to one of the very last storefronts. Yan Mei was waiting out front, silently watching us with that same wistful look she always seemed to get when she looked at me. "Our grandma said you go specifically to her."

Henry darted off into a training room to our left. The windows had been blacked out, and loud music blared. Someone yelled from somewhere inside, followed by a loud *THUNK!* If Henry had failed the course in under five seconds, he was probably going to have a very long night.

"What do you think of my facility?" Yan Mei asked when I reached her. She was in front of an old bookstore—drastically calmer than the rest of the building with its earthy colors, soft music, and overpowering smell of fresh coffee. I smiled. This was the kind of place I'd make the Bensons leave me when they went shopping.

"This place is...amazing," I said, not sure what else to say. "I mean, there's so many of us."

Yan Mei cracked a knowing smile and beckoned me inside the store. Instead of being empty, many of the shelves were stacked with all sorts of things: books, strange-looking artifacts, maps. A girl was up on a ladder pulling out scrolls. Literal crumble-to-dust scrolls. I was utterly bewildered.

"Your mother had the same reaction, too...back at my old facility.

113

She spent a lot of time there," Yan Mei said, leading me down the center aisle. We passed a boy in the former "Mystery" section who was reading books in seconds flat. He had three finished before we passed him. "Of course, back in the old days, we didn't have something like this. Every piece of evidence, every historical documentation I have been able to find about our people is in this room, Jade."

"You're researching powers?" I asked, staring at the stacks of books in awe. She had half the store full...if there was this much information out there about people like us, we might have been around for centuries. Maybe longer.

"Among other things, though, that's not why I've asked you here tonight," Yan Mei said, heading toward the far end of the store where the kid's section had obviously been at one point. The carpet changed into a space pattern, and the entrance was a massive pink fairy castle. "Not the most sophisticated of locations, but good for our purposes."

The shelves had been moved to make a sort of wall from the rest of the store. Several colorful chairs and bean bags had been set up in the back corner, probably a story time section. It was then that I realized that Yan Mei and I were not alone. I froze.

There, sitting half-sunk into a bright orange beanbag, was Mary Milford.

~

"What the—Mary?! Are you alright?" I asked, staring at the red-haired girl in shock.

Mary jolted like she hadn't noticed us come in, making her constantly frazzled look even worse than usual. "Jade? Y-You mean, you're one of us, too?"

I nodded slightly. "Yeah, yeah, I am, Mary."

Her eyes lit up. "I knew it! There wasn't a huge chance, but I had a feeling—"

Yan Mei cut her off with a chuckle. "Yes, dear. We know. But that is not why she is here right now. We came to talk about you, Mary." Yan Mei's eyes turned to me. "Mary has an empathic friend named Elyse, who convinced her to talk to us. Apparently, Mary reappeared at home sometime over the weekend with no memory of what happened, just like all of the others."

I remembered what Yan Mei had told me at the restaurant about how people with powers were getting taken, vanishing for about a week, then popping back up like nothing was ever wrong.

"You want me to see her past, don't you?" I asked, keeping my voice low. "Find out what happened during her lost time."

Yan Mei nodded. "I suspect you'll have some false memories to get through, but you might be the only one strong enough to find out the truth. If someone is going after people with powers, then everyone in this building needs us to figure this out."

I swallowed hard and made my way over to Mary, pulling close an absurdly small chair. I probably looked like the most ridiculous therapist ever, but I had to try. "Mary, do you remember anything about last week?"

Mary fidgeted nervously with her glasses. "Why does everyone keep asking me that? I was on a trip with my grandma. Ask my parents."

So, someone had manipulated Mr. and Mrs. Milford's memories too? Probably when whoever had taken her had returned Mary back to her house.

"What about farther back? Two Fridays ago," I said, trying to keep my voice calm. "Do you remember having a conversation with Victoria Harper? Maybe after school?"

Mary's eyes got a cloudy look. "I'm not sure. Maybe."

"She wanted you to meet with someone. You told her no and walked off...Do you remember anything after that?" I asked.

"I told you...I was with my grandma."

"You went on a vacation with your grandma a month into the school year?" I asked, choosing my words very carefully. "Mary, if you thought that was true, why did you agree to come here?"

Mary looked like she was about to cry. I felt bad for pushing her, but I wasn't going to get anywhere with her adamant denial. Looking into her eyes, I doubted she would have been able to talk if she wanted to.

I offered her my hand. "Show me."

She looked at me like I was crazy, but reluctantly reached out.

Once again, I imagined the same long hallway I had when I looked into Henry's memories. Doors of every shape, size, and form stretched out in either direction. Two weeks ago...the door had to be somewhat close by.

A loud, staticky sound filled my mind—like when one of Nana Benson's old VCR tapes cut off at the end of a movie. A door behind me caught my attention. It was wide and heavy-looking with a number over the top, like one of the classroom doors at school. Still, something about it felt wrong. That buzz was getting louder, and the door seemed to fizzle and flicker uncertainly the same way the future doors seemed to look. None of the other doors leading to Mary's past memories looked that way.

Tampered memories, I thought, pushing open the door.

I was back in front of the lockers by the chemistry lab. The exact same place I'd seen Victoria confront Mary in my previous vision.

There they were, ten feet in front of me, just as I'd seen them before. The vision had the same faded-film look it'd had when I'd pulled it from Victoria's memories, but something was wrong. Everything seemed to shudder with static like Mary's memories were getting poor reception.

"I said no, Victoria," Mary said, slamming her locker door shut. She looked around the hallway again. "I'm sorry, but my answer is no. Please stop asking."

Victoria sighed. "Okay, if that's what you want." She pushed herself off of the locker and started to head toward me.

Wait. This was wrong. That was not how it happened. Mary was hurrying toward the stairs like she was supposed to, but Victoria was only halfway down the hall. When I'd had my vision, she'd been long gone by the time Mary had started down the steps. This time, there was no invisible force coming after Mary, no scream shattering the silence of the school.

I hurried after Mary, desperately trying not to trip down the steps as I ran to catch up. She was heading for the front door toward the parking lot. It didn't make any sense. Mary hadn't made it past the steps last time.

"Have a good weekend, Mary," Mr. Goodman said cheerfully, stepping out of the teacher's lounge with his jacket and bag. "Say hello to your grandparents for me!"

"Will do, Mr. Goodman," Mary said quietly.

I watched her until she disappeared into the light of the parking lot. The vision started to fizzle and faded to blackness—the reel of memories had finished.

This wasn't real. This was not how it happened. How could the two visions be so different and still the same? Could I fix it? I had to try. I took a deep breath.

Show me the truth. Show me what really happened.

The doors reopened. Mr. Goodman reappeared beside me. Mary backed back down the hallway at lightning speed, like someone had put her on rewind. Did it work? She was scrambling back up the stairs, and I sprinted, panting with every step as I tried to keep up.

Stop, I willed my vision. This is what I needed to see. *Play.*

"Okay, if that's what you want," Victoria said again, turning to head back down the hallway.

The vision fizzled and cracked, fighting me. Almost like...the vision didn't want to be seen. It was blocked. I fought harder through the cracks. The air hissed so loud I worried my eardrums would burst. It was like time was splitting apart, revealing layers and layers of the same scene like a superimposed image. I could see Victoria heading down the hall at the same slow pace as the fake memory, but I could also see her pop in and out of sight in other layers—she was there in one moment but gone in the next. Could the fake memory be distorting the real one?

Mary headed for the stairs. That same eerie chill as before ran up my spine. The invisible force was coming for her, just like it had before. Time fizzled—Mary was screaming on the stairs in some layers, fighting against something strong and unseeable, while in others, she safely made it to the bottom and talked to Mr. Goodman. I concentrated on Mary struggling. My head ached like it was going to split in half. Focus, *focus!* What happened next?

Show me what happened to Mary after she was taken.

The scene around me faded as if I'd entered a completely new memory. I was in an expensive-looking office: glassed-in windows, steely gray walls, dark hardwood floors. Modern and cold. No personal touches. Just empty. Utilitarian. Sterile.

Mary sat in a chair in front of a big mahogany desk with a large mirror, looking worse for wear but relatively unharmed. Her red hair was matted and frizzy like she'd been lying down, and a plain white hospital gown hung loosely on her shoulders. Angry purple bruises dotted up her hands and arms like she'd been jabbed with something several times. The biggest was right in her elbow. An IV, perhaps?

"I've heard you put up quite the fight when we took our samples," a deep, mechanical voice said. It seemed to come from everywhere in the room at once like it was coming through a speaker somewhere. Mary's eyes widened, her chest rising and falling at an alarming speed. She thrashed her head around, looking for the source of the creepy voice, but it was nowhere to be found. My eyes were drawn again to the mirror behind the desk. Maybe it was two-way?

The office door opened, and a figure emerged, locking it swiftly behind them. I squinted, but I couldn't make out more than a blur. They were blocked from my vision. I could tell enough to make out that it was a woman with dark skin and long hair.

"Now, now, little one," the woman's voice said, approaching with small steps. "It's alright. We just need to ask you a few things." She reached out and took Mary's reluctant hand.

"Sleep," she commanded. Mary's eyes gently came to a close, her body relaxing in the chair. The woman positioned her head to be more comfortable.

"Much better," the deep voice said. "Now, Miss Milford, I know you have some remarkable talents. Let's start off with some basic questions. I'll have my assistant give you information, and you will tell me the probability of it happening."

Mary remained still. The woman stared down at Mary's sleeping figure and squeezed the hand she was holding a little tighter.

"It's done," the woman said.

"Good. Now, Mary, what is the probability that the Pinewood swim team will win the finals this year?" the deep voice asked.

"Seventy-two percent," Mary said automatically, though her voice sounded off...like she was talking in her sleep.

"Excellent. Just a few more questions, my dear, and you will be on your way home," the voice said. Mary once again stayed quiet.

"She will only answer in the form of probabilities," the woman said. "I'm blocking everything else out."

"That's enough," the voice snapped. "Now give her the next set of information."

The woman did the same motion as before, squeezed Mary's hand, and gazed at her before loosening her grip. "It's done, sir."

"Alright. Now, what is the probability for someone with powers to produce a child also containing the genetic marker for enhanced abilities?"

"Eighty-seven percent," Mary recited.

"How probable is it for a couple—both of whom have powers—to produce twins with powers?" the voice asked.

"0.0002 percent."

The woman chuckled. "Of course, it'd have to be Vivian and Lance who'd beat the odds."

My heart pounded. Vivian. My mother. They were asking about twins and my mother, which meant...they were asking about *me*.

"The Kastel children," the voice said. The thumping of my heart almost drowned out the voices, but I willed myself to listen. "One is most definitely alive. What is the likelihood that both twins survived?"

"One hundred percent."

The voice hesitated over the intercom. "You're absolutely sure?"

"My calculations have a .05 percent margin of error," Mary said. "I'm hardly ever wrong."

"There's an old rumor among our people," the voice said, choosing their words carefully, "about twins...why they're so rare, what they might be able to do—together. Is it possible..."

"The phenomenon of Amalgamation is a theoretical concept recorded several times in historical literature," Mary agreed without question, her eyes still blank and foggy. "Operating on the assumption that both twins had powers—complementary ones would be best—and they learned how to harness said abilities in tandem, then there would be roughly a 49.4 percent chance that Amalgamation could be achieved."

The voice laughed. "You mean it's actually possible?"

"Possible, not probable."

"One last question before I let you go, Miss Milford. My friends and I have been working on a device, a very important one, but we've had several delays. You've seen our schematics through my assistant...When do you estimate it will finally be completed? A few months? Maybe a year?"

"Judging by your current rate of work speed, technology, current funds available, plausible room for error...about sixteen years."

"W-What?"

"Sixteen years is the earliest a device like yours could be completed," Mary said, still zombie-eyed and completely unfazed by the voice's outburst. "The technology to mass distribute supernatural abilities just isn't here yet. You don't have enough data to be even remotely close to completion. Insufficient data means setbacks, not to mention potential unforeseen events."

"But—but we have the most advanced technology in the world. Surely, you've made some kind of mistake?"

Again, Mary stayed still and silent.

"That's not a probability question—"

"I know it's not!" the voice yelled, making the woman jump. She didn't look like she was having such a good time now. "Get her out of here! Call in Code 325!"

The voice crackled and then was silent.

"Wake up!" the woman commanded, hauling Mary to her feet and out the door. I caught the briefest glimpse of a sterile-looking hallway, sort of like a hospital.

The vision dissolved. I had fallen out of my tiny plastic chair and was sprawled over top of several planets on the brightly colored carpet. Mary was looking down at me in concern—or maybe that was her normal face? She always looked so worried it was hard to tell.

"Jade," Yan Mei's voice broke through my haze. She was standing over me, though I couldn't tell if I was imagining the birds spinning over her head or if they were actually rigged from the ceiling. "What did you see?"

"What do you know about something called the Amalgamation?"

CHAPTER
FOURTEEN

"The Amalgamation?" Mary asked. "That sounds familiar..." She trailed off, deep in thought, like she was fumbling for a memory that wasn't there anymore.

Yan Mei, on the other hand, looked very, *very* worried. "The A-Amalgamation? You're sure that's what you heard?"

"One hundred percent," I said, pushing myself up off the floor. "What is it?"

Yan Mei shook her head, a deep frown already stretching across her face. If I wasn't mistaken, she almost looked scared. "Nothing you need to concern yourself with. Mary, will you please wait here? Jade, go find Henry...have him show you around the rest of the mall. I-I need to talk to the Core 5."

Without waiting for an answer from either of us, Yan Mei hurried out of the kid's section and back into the rest of the Archive. I made sure to stay right on her heels.

"Wait, wait, wait—you can't just have me jump into Mary's mind and then shut me out like that! What's the Amalgamation? Who's the Core 5?"

"The Core 5 is a nickname Henry gave to the leaders of Pinewood's powered community. Unfortunately, it stuck," she said, quickening her pace even more like she was trying to lose me. I was sure now. My grandmother was definitely scared...and I didn't like the idea of anything that could scare Yan Mei.

"And the Amalgamation?" I asked, trying to get in front of her as we crossed back into one of the mall's main corridors. "What is it? And there was a voice in Mary's memories...they were asking questions about my brother and me, Yan Mei. Mary said there was a one hundred percent chance that both Kastel twins survived! My brother's still out there! Isn't that great news?"

I wasn't sure what sort of reaction I'd been expecting Yan Mei to have, finding out her *second* long-lost grandchild was alive a few days after discovering the other one was, but it wasn't what I got. Instead of looking happy or thrilled or even shocked, Yan Mei looked positively sick.

"Henry! Dylan!" she called instead, waving to flag the boys down at the far end of the hall. Both must have finished up with their training courses and were laughing about something. How long had I been in Mary's memories? Henry must have realized something was up as they got closer—he kept his grin, but his eyes darted nervously between me and Yan Mei.

"Everything alright, Grandma?" he asked as they finally reached us.

"Of course," she lied, not very convincingly. "Can you boys please take Jade to see Palo and Skylar? I think it'd be a good idea if she started training."

Dylan and Henry exchanged a look.

"You sure, Yan Mei?" Dylan asked, trying not to sound rude. "It's her first day."

"Take her to them," Yan Mei said firmly, quickly hurrying off in the other direction.

Henry looked at me in horror. "What on earth did you see? Grandma's never started anyone with Palo and Skylar so soon."

"Who are they?" I asked, keeping my eyes on Yan Mei until she vanished out of sight into the next hallway.

"They're the mall's self-defense trainers," Dylan said, motioning for me to follow him back down the hallway.

"Self-defense? Why would I need to know self-defense?"

"It's just a precaution," Henry said, shrugging. "Grandma insists on everyone being able to protect themselves. Besides, it's not all that. They help people get a better handle on their powers, too."

Dylan led the way to an escalator leading up to a higher level. From this high up, I could appreciate just how big the mall was. A thought I'd been curious about since we'd entered the mall needled at the back of my mind.

"Henry, Yan Mei owns the mall, right?" I asked.

"Correctomundo."

"Does the cafe pay the electricity bill for this place?"

Henry shrugged. "Nah, the cafe is just for fun. Something she always wanted to do."

"But then how—"

"Nobody really knows. She doesn't like when we ask questions," Dylan interjected, eyes following a pair of kids across from us as they jumped between two cloud-shaped flats suspended from the ceiling.

"I see."

Yan Mei was an ever-growing mystery I didn't think I'd be able to solve. We rose slowly up over the food court where we'd come in. When we reached the upper floor, we turned left into a brightly lit room with soft flooring and a rope fence forming a circle like a small arena. A Serta mattress guarantee poster was plastered on the walls. *Comfort to combat.*

The room was filled with people standing around the roped-off area, cheering on the two adults preparing to spar. One was Indigenous—tall, lean, and covered in angry red scars that looked like the remnants of burns. He had dark eyes and hair pulled back into a knot with the sides shaved. The most terrifying part, aside from the scars, was what he wore around his neck. Various teeth—at least a dozen—bounced grimly on a thick leather cord. The other man sparring was broad-shouldered and muscular, his fair-skin highlighted by bright red hair. Freckles dotted his cheeks, and he smirked at his opponent.

"I don't suppose I get out of self-defense if the ring's kinda occupied?" I asked hopefully.

"Unfortunately not. This match will be over quickly," Dylan said.

"I give it a minute, tops," Henry agreed.

I looked at the roped-off area where the two men were circling each other. A bell chimed, and the fight began. The red-haired man opened his arms wide, and red feathers that faded into orange emerged from his skin. His face protruded, revealing a long beak. The man leaped into the air above his opponent, hands that were now talons, ready to strike.

Okay, so the bird-man was a bit scarier than I had initially thought.

But the other man stood tall, unconcerned about the incoming attack. Just as Bird-Man's talons lashed out, his opponent howled. In an instant, the dark-haired man's eyes turned an inhuman yellow, narrowing as sharp teeth emerged and claws protruded from his hands and feet. He charged up to meet the bird-man, and the shadow of a gray wolf enveloped his body.

An animalistic *roar* silenced the crowd as the wolf-man swiped his opponent, tearing several feathers from the man before sending him painfully to the ground. The wolf-man was on top of him in seconds, claws raised in the air, ready to strike again.

"I concede!" The bird-man coughed, feathers fading away to normal skin. The crowd cheered. Henry had his hands up in the air, cheering for the wolf-man who stood unamused by the crowd's antics. A dark-skinned woman in bright athletic clothes nearby helped the red-haired man out of the ring. He didn't seem hurt badly but was complaining about how long it would take for the feathers to grow back.

"There's always next time, Peter," she said, flashing him a warm smile.

"Alright, Jade, you're up," Henry said excitedly, pushing me toward the stage. "Palo, Skylar, special training orders from Yan Mei!"

I looked at him like he'd grown three heads. "Excuse me?" I asked in a panic. "Are you *trying* to kill me?"

"They're going to be your teachers," Dylan said, giving me a reassuring smile. While it helped a little, I was still absolutely terrified of the man. He'd nearly clawed the other guy in half.

"Oh, don't worry about him, Jade, was it?" the woman asked, gently moving me toward the ring. I hadn't realized it before, but she and the man could only have been a few years older than me- maybe early to mid-twenties at most. Everything about her radiated style and confidence even in just gym clothes: the intricate way her hair was braided into thick twists, the bright glint in her brown eyes, the way she held herself despite having such an intimidating partner. "Palo's just a big teddy bear when you get to know him. I'm Skylar. Nice to meet you."

When we got to the ring, the man looked at me, all wolf features faded away, and stuck out his hand. He was tall and broad, those angry scars still evident on most of his exposed arms.

I looked back at Dylan and Henry, who cheered me on, and took the man's hand, climbing under the rope and onto the stage. By now, most of the people had started to clear out, the excitement of the short match now over. Not having an audience was a small comfort.

"Teddy bear, dear," Skylar said, poking Palo in the side as she followed us into the ring. Despite himself, he couldn't help the inadvertent smile. It was almost...shy, in a way. I looked back and forth between the two of them. Okay, so they were definitely a couple then, although I doubted they had been for long. They still seemed kind of awkward and smitten.

I held my elbows as I looked around the ring. The lights above us were bright and hot, already making me sweat. Was I even wearing proper training attire? I suppose jeans and a T-shirt would have to do for now. Maybe next time, I would pack some workout gear.

Next time? Oh, geez.

Palo stood silently in front of me like he was waiting for my internal monologue to shut up. Skylar cringed like she could tell this was already off to an awkward start.

"So, as you can see, Jade," she said, clearly deciding to take the initiative, "this is the Arena, where we do all our powered and non-powered training. Typically, I coach those with defensive powers while Palo here does offensive. Introduce yourself, Palo."

"Palo Chavez," the man greeted, more in a grunt than actual words.

"Do you have any idea which side your powers might fall more on, Jade?" Skylar asked, obviously trying not to roll her eyes at her boyfriend of few words.

"Um, not really," I said unsurely. I doubted seeing through time and nearly passing out would hardly count as *offensive*. "I'm going to guess defensive."

"Alright, my team then!" Skylar said excitedly, slinging an arm around me like she was claiming me. "Little different from the boys then. Dylan, you're with Palo. Henry, me as usual…Boys?"

We all turned to see Dylan and Henry trying to sneak out of the room. Next thing I knew, Palo had leaped into the air with a blood-curdling howl, somehow materializing in front of them.

"Ah, come on! Grandma said Jade had to train, not us!" Henry whined.

"Get in the ring," Palo commanded, pointing back toward me and Skylar.

"Yes, sir," Dylan sighed. The trio made their way into the ring, Dylan and Henry looking much more nervous than before. Well, Dylan looked nervous. Henry looked terrified.

"The boys are lazy," Palo said to me as if looking for agreement. The boys protested, but he raised a hand to cut them off. "Training to protect yourself is not just about strength. It's about using your abilities more effectively than your opponent. You must learn to enhance your strengths while protecting your weaknesses."

"Except *he* doesn't have any weaknesses," Henry muttered.

"He's actually really scared of seagulls," Skylar whispered to me conspiratorially.

"If you are so quick to speak, how about you and I give your cousin a demonstration?" Palo asked.

Henry panicked, letting out an "*EEP!*" before turning into a lamp at the side of the ring. The lamp had a brown base with a camouflage shade as if that was supposed to make him less visible. Skylar let out a long-suffering sigh.

"It seems like you could use some extra training. I will be sure to inform your grandmother," Palo said. Lamp-Henry blinked on and off rapidly, like a panicked *oh, no*. "Dylan, you were the one I wanted to use for a demonstration anyway."

Dylan made an audible gulp before stepping toward Palo. Skylar and I sat down next to Lamp-Henry, who I'm sure was purposefully choosing to remain a lamp at the moment.

"You are the attacker. I will defend," Palo instructed before turning to me and Henry. "You two, watch his technique."

I nodded, and Lamp-Henry's light flickered on, then off again.

Dylan and Palo took up wide stances, staring into each other's eyes before Dylan went for the attack.

The shelves on the walls around us started shaking. I had been so focused on the fight between Palo and the bird-man that I hadn't noticed the room was stocked to the gills with practice combat instruments: wooden staffs and swords, riot shields, nunchucks, maces...basically any weapon humanly imaginable. Dylan thrust his hand out, sending a barrage of plastic ninja stars hurtling toward Palo.

He dropped instantly, rolling and coming up as a six-foot-tall wolfish humanoid. His teeth extended into fangs. His eyes got a beady, soulless glint to them. I didn't see how Dylan could stay standing against someone so terrifying. Having successfully avoided the ninja star storm, Palo lunged at Dylan, though he didn't get far.

Dylan threw out his hands, yanking the larger man's feet out from under him. Palo toppled but was up again almost instantly. He swatted with his claws, but Dylan dodged. It was almost impossible to see, but something seemed to be forcing Palo back. His clawed feet skidded across the floor, struggling to find traction. Dylan's telekinesis! He was holding him back mentally.

How was Dylan—soft-spoken, shy *Dylan*—holding his own against this gigantic wolf dude? Every time Palo tried to move, something seemed to mess up his strike: his arm whipping in the wrong direction, his legs sliding out from under him. For a moment, I actually believed Dylan might be able to beat him.

Then, the moment was over.

Palo lunged again, though this time Dylan's powers didn't stop him until he was within arm's length. Palo was still fighting against a wall of force, but his mouth had twisted up into a wolfish grin. He *knew* he was going to break through this time.

"Go, Dylan! Keep him out!" Skylar yelled.

Dylan shook, trying to hold him back. The wall of force between them was clearly flickering. Dylan was tired, scared, losing his hold on the one thing protecting him.

Suddenly, Dylan's mental dam broke. Palo swatted him aside with the flat of his paw-ish hand. Dylan skidded halfway across the ring, groaning as he tried to push himself up. Even though it had obviously hurt, I could tell Palo was going easy on him. If Dylan had been a real adversary, Palo's claws would've torn him to shreds.

Dylan thrust out his hand again. One of the riot shields from the wall flew securely onto his arm.

Palo clicked his tongue. "I thought I was the one who was supposed to be defending?"

Palo came at Dylan with renewed force. He snarled and slashed. Each attack was fiercer than before. Dylan backed up onto the ropes. The only reason he lasted as long as he did was the shield, the heavy black surface barely able to hold Palo back. He got in one lucky shot, smacking it into Palo's snout with an exaggerated *BONK*, but Dylan's luck was quickly running out.

Why wasn't he using his powers? Dylan had nearly won within the first few minutes of the fight. Maybe he *couldn't*? He was trembling, face drenched with sweat. Had Dylan used so much energy trying to keep Palo back that he'd momentarily sapped his powers?

He swung the shield again, but the bigger man easily dodged. Palo took a lazy swipe at Dylan, his claw barely grazing his left cheek. A small line of red quickly appeared.

"Dylan Mason, always on the defensive," Palo said sadly, knocking the shield out of Dylan's hands. He pushed him down, pinning Dylan with his foot to make it clear the fight was over. "Defending is good, but you can never win a battle on that alone. You've not been preserving your powers like I told you to."

Palo offered a hand down to help Dylan up, and he took it. "I've been trying...it's just—"

"You panic. Much like your illuminated friend over there," Palo said, nodding knowingly. "Henry, Jade, you're up."

Henry reluctantly turned back into himself, moving glumly to the opposite side of the ring. Dylan took Henry's spot on the floor and gave me a reassuring smile.

Palo eyed me curiously as I took up the spot where Dylan had started. There it was again, that same fascinated look that everyone in the mall seemed to get around me.

"Am I attacking or defending?" I asked as Skylar stepped up beside him.

"Let's just see what you can do," Palo said, giving me a small wink. "I'm curious as to what kind of powers Vivian's daughter has."

Vivian. Wait, did Palo know my mom? I started to ask him what he meant, but Palo motioned for Henry and me to start sparring.

Unsurprisingly, Henry started his attack by running headfirst at me, screaming some horrifying banshee-like karate yell. I didn't even move—the screaming tackle run was one of Tommy's signature moves. I decked Henry straight into the mat. The fight was over.

"Oh, dang!" Skylar yelled in surprise. "That's going to leave a mark."

Palo held out his arms approvingly at Dylan. "And *that* is how you attack!"

"My eyes!" Henry groaned, rolling around the floor. "I'll never look upon Victoria's beautiful face again! I'll only be able to listen to *Star Wars* from now on! There will be no sunlight, only darkness!"

"I'll go get him an ice pack," Palo said, rolling his eyes as he stepped down from the ring. As he left, I noticed Yan Mei, Mary, and several other adults lurking by the entrance of the training room. They must have sneaked in sometime during Dylan and Palo's fight. The grownups were whispering to each other, and Skylar quickly made her way over to them once she noticed them too. With Skylar there, I suddenly realized there were four of them besides Yan Mei. The Core 5? One was Dylan's mom, who sent me an encouraging thumbs-up. Yan Mei nodded at me in acknowledgment but shook her head embarrassingly at Henry.

"Wow, Jade, way to go," Dylan said, suddenly at my shoulder.

"Don't congratulate her! She's blinded me!" Henry complained, squinting angrily in the wrong direction.

"I barely touched you, you big baby," I said, helping him up. "Maybe you shouldn't have yelled if you didn't want me to know you were coming."

Palo returned with the ice pack, slapping it not-so-gently against Henry's left eye. "I've got to say, that might be the shortest fight we've ever had. Neither of you even used your powers."

"I was getting there." Henry pouted.

"Palo!" Sophie's voice called excitedly. She was covered in stuffing like she'd squeezed a pillow to death. Maybe that's what the super-strong kids were doing in training tonight.

The tiny blonde girl jumped straight into Palo's arms without any fear, and the man's harsh face melted instantly. "I heard you got a bear's tooth in your collection. Which one is it?"

"This one," Palo said, softer than I would have ever imagined possible. He held up a sharp-looking incisor on his necklace of teeth. "I put it right beside the wolf's and the crocodile's."

"That's a good idea," Sophie agreed, inspecting the tooth curiously. "Do you think I could fight a bear if I wanted to, Palo?"

"Probably so, Miss Sophie." Palo chuckled, though he suddenly fixed Dylan's sister with a serious look. "Are you brushing all the way in the back like I told you to?"

Sophie grimaced. "Sometimes?"

Palo clicked his tongue like he had done to Dylan in their match. "You don't want any more cavities, now do you?"

"No, Palo," Sophie said dejectedly as he gently put her down.

I stared at the large man in surprise. "Wait a second, are you a *dentist*? Is that why you have all those teeth on your necklace?"

"Pediatric dentistry," Palo said with a shrug. "The kids think it's cool."

"It is cool!" Sophie agreed emphatically, though she suddenly froze as if just realizing the three of us were there too. She batted her eyes at Henry. "Oh, hi, *Henry*."

"Is there something you want, Sophie?" Dylan interrupted, stepping protectively in front of his friend.

"Mom said we're leaving. She wants you home by ten-thirty."

Dylan nodded, motioning for her to shoo. Sophie gave me a brisk wave, then gave Henry a hug that lasted quite a bit longer than necessary before running off.

My phone started buzzing in my pocket. There was a text from Mrs. B: *Tommy's game just ended. Heading your way now. Bust out the menus!*

"I need to get back to the restaurant. ASAP," I said, getting Dylan and Henry's attention. "Benson-related emergency."

"We'll continue this later," Palo agreed. "Next time, you fight Dylan."

Dylan chuckled nervously. "Y-You're joking, right?"

Henry huffed, still holding the ice pack to his eye but clearly able to see again. "Please, all Jade would have to do to knock you out is kiss you again."

"*What?*" Skylar asked, suddenly behind me again and trying hard to hide her amusement.

"Shut up, Henry!" I snapped, face burning.

"We'll save that for a Plan B." Palo laughed, scratching his scarred face. "Until next time, little ones."

We headed out of the training room, hurrying back through the mall to the food court entrance. It seemed most of the classes had broken up, but there were still plenty of people around—scrambling through the overhead course, eating dinner in the food court, big pods of kids laughing about something. It made me sad, having to leave this place so soon after finding it. There were dozens and dozens of people here just like me, and I'd hardly met anyone. I could barely pull my eyes away from it all until we were out the doors and in the parking lot again.

From the outside, this magnificent place didn't look like anything but a half-deserted mall. Isolated and forgotten by the normal people of Pinewood. Suddenly, I was worried that everything I'd seen tonight was just some crazy dream. Surely, it was too good to be true that there were so many people with powers all in one little town.

I felt something momentarily brush my hand. Dylan was walking much closer to me than he had been a minute before. He kept his voice low as we rounded Yan Mei's van, even though I was pretty sure Henry had already climbed in.

"It'll still be here waiting for you tomorrow," he promised, almost as if he could read my thoughts. "You're one of us now."

CHAPTER
FIFTEEN

Today was the day.

My stomach churned as I walked through the cafeteria. I was about to make the biggest proclamation of loyalty according to high school standards. Twenty feet. Fifteen. As if it even mattered, half the school was still running wild with speculation about what went down between me and Dylan at the swim meet last Friday. What did I care what all these other people thought? Ten feet. Now or never.

I slammed my tray down beside Dylan a little more forcefully than necessary at the lunch table. He jumped but smiled when he realized it was me, and I wasn't actually angry. I looked around, waiting for the inevitable reaction of the new girl finally siding with a group. Beyond a few quiet whispers, no one seemed to be paying that much attention to me. Huh. Maybe the Dylan-Jade scandal of Monday was old news by Wednesday. That would be *really* nice.

"Oh. Hey, Jade!" Henry greeted cheerfully, shooting a straw paper at me from his spot across the table. I glared at him before shrugging it off. I did deck him pretty hard...I would let it slide.

His left eye was covered with a giant purple-ish yellow bruise that clashed horribly with his Hawaiian shirt. "Decide you were finally ready to sit at the cool table?"

"Sure, let's go with that," I commented, not entirely convinced this was the "cool" table. Besides Dylan and Henry, there were only three others: a brown-skinned guy in a *Star Trek* T-shirt, a girl with straw-colored hair braided back so tight it looked painful, and a boy who seemed to be trying desperately to curl his wispy, virtually nonexistent mustache up into handlebars.

All three of them looked at me like I'd just dropped from outer space, which I suppose was ironic since it sounded like they'd been arguing about something not far off from that topic.

"Guys, this is Jade," Dylan said. "Jade, this is Kazi, Katie, and Spencer."

"Oh, we know who she is," Spencer said distractedly, though he froze when he seemed to realize how it'd probably come out. He twisted his pseudo mustache nervously. "I mean—I didn't—not to say...it's nice to meet you, Jade."

"We don't believe a word of those rumors," Katie offered kindly, looking at the boys for backup. She elbowed Kazi when he didn't say anything. "Don't we, boys? Dylan would never do anything like these bozos are saying."

Henry laughed knowingly into his Dr. Pepper. Dylan and I both kicked him under the table.

"So, Spencer, you were saying something about that new game?" Henry asked, wisely transitioning away from the topic of me and Dylan.

"That game is called *Chronos-Blue*," Spencer corrected matter-of-factly, suddenly dead serious.

"Hey, I've heard about that. My little brother plays it," I said, grateful to have something to chime in about. Suddenly, I realized that saying my nine-year-old brother played the same video game as a bunch of sixteen-year-olds was maybe not a particularly flattering comment. I swallowed hard. "It's supposed to be really good, right? Something about Arthurian legend?"

Kazi laughed at my floundering. "It's going to be the number one most downloaded game of the decade soon. It's an interactive MMO with an online or in-person feature. It's like King Arthur but in space—quests, monsters, cool artifacts. There's so much to do!"

"Fernando's Comic Shop does this massive tournament for it every month," Katie said excitedly. "See, the game is set up regionally, so like everyone in Pinewood would be one kingdom. You work your way up—page, squire, etc.—until you try to reach one of the top twelve spots. These are the best players in your region—essentially, the Round Table level knights, if you will—and they get the most dangerous players to wage war on other kingdoms."

I wasn't sure I caught all of what she was saying, but I thought I was getting the gist. "So, these gaming tournaments let people watch these quests?" I asked.

Kazi nodded. "Or if someone wants to make a play for one of the top spots, they can challenge for a duel," he said, snickering slightly. "That's exactly what happened to Spencer last night."

Henry nearly choked on his pizza. "You mean you lost your top spot?"

Spencer hung his head morosely. "I know, I know...but this guy just came out of nowhere. I mean, there were some rumors about someone working their way up through the levels really fast, but I never thought they'd show up and challenge me!"

"Someone new who's *that* good?"

"CobaltChaos," Kazi said, shivering slightly at the name. "They wanted to play for Tyler's spot but couldn't since he wasn't present. You still haven't heard anything?"

Dylan shook his head sadly. It had been six days since Tyler disappeared, and I had a bad feeling he was probably in that empty office having a chat with the deep voice and blurry woman I'd seen with Mary.

"Without Tyler, I had to take the challenge...Didn't even stand a chance," Spencer sighed. "This guy had skills—knew all my weaknesses, had the perfect strategy, and was wicked fast. It was all over in twenty minutes. Even weirder, no one has any idea who it was."

"But challenges are done in person," Dylan said, taking a bite of his PB&J sandwich. "How could nobody have seen them?"

For a moment, I had a terrible feeling that maybe the invisible force had shown up at the gaming tournament to look for more victims, but that seemed a little ridiculous.

"I mean, we saw them." Katie shrugged, putting my mind at ease that no one else had gone missing. "We just couldn't tell who it was.

They had this really intricate cosplay—all cobalt, helmet, gloves, the works. Every inch of them was completely covered."

"Ooh, someone who doesn't want anybody to know they're a gamer," Henry said, rubbing his hands together like he was enjoying the mystery. "Was it someone from here?"

"Hard to say," Spencer said, eying the other kids around us suspiciously. "Skinny, kind of tall. They kept their helmet on, so I couldn't see their hair or anything. Oh, hey! Victoria, over here!"

"What! Where?" Henry yelled, trying to hide behind his lunchbox.

Spencer kept waving, clearly determined that he not be ignored. It seemed to take forever for the blonde girl to come to a stop behind me and Dylan.

"Is there a reason you're screaming at me across the cafeteria, Spencer?" she sighed, fingers drumming quickly against a fast food bag stuffed with hamburgers. The name WUZZIES hung over a cartoon fuzzy yellow monster. How had she gotten Wuzzyburgers for lunch? The nearest one I knew about was like twenty miles away.

"Yes, there's a reason!" he huffed. "I need the names of every kid on a Pinewood gaming team. I don't care if it's chess or checkers or—"

"We don't have a checkers team," Victoria said, looking longingly at her gigantic bag of burgers. Was she feeding the whole football team? "Why? Is this because somebody beat you at the *C-B* tournament last night?"

"How do you know about that?" Kazi asked.

"I'm class president. I hear everything that goes on concerning Pinewood." She shrugged. Still, it seemed weird to me that Victoria had referred to the game by its abbreviated name rather than full, though I figured if even I vaguely knew about the game, then it was possible Victoria did too. "I'll see what I can find out."

Victoria started to walk off but stopped short when she saw Henry shrugged down behind his lunchbox. "What happened to your face?"

Henry winced. "Ha-ha! Oh, this thing?" he asked, dropping his lunchbox and trying to play it cool. "Got into a little fight last night. It's cool—stuff like this happens to me all the time! You should see the other guy."

"I'm right here," I muttered, poking at a substance on my lunch tray that I was about 80% sure was banana pudding. Henry looked like he might die of embarrassment, though he perked up some when Victoria did something that surprised me. She actually laughed.

"Wow, you got him good," she said, fingers still drumming absently on her bag. Now that I thought about it, Victoria seemed nearly as hyper as Henry, though in a much quieter way. The drumming fingers, the constant foot tapping in class, the restless shifting in the hall when I'd asked her about the swim meet. Victoria gave Henry what seemed to be a genuine smile. "Did you ask Nurse Jones for an ice pack?"

Henry shrugged shyly. "Kind of. I don't think she likes me very much after I threw up on her freshman year."

Victoria looked like she was trying hard not to laugh. Suddenly, I felt another presence behind me and realized Julian was there with his tray, too.

"Hey, Jade," Julian said, earning a very confused look from both me and Dylan. "Sorry you lost your game last night, Spencer."

In a very un-Julian-like gesture, he put his hand on Spencer's shoulder, though quickly removed it. He hurried away but cut the corner too fast and brushed into both Katie and Kazi, voicing a quick apology to the duo.

One of the football guys was yelling for Victoria back at her usual table. She gave Henry an apologetic look. "I'd better go. Meet me at the nurse's station after lunch. I'll make sure she gives you an ice pack and a sucker."

Henry was dumbfounded. "R-Really?"

Victoria smiled and headed off, a glow seeming to radiate from her. If Henry's powers had been for flight, he would've probably been in the stratosphere by now.

"Did anyone else see that? Was that real, or was I dreaming?" he asked, running a hand over his face.

"I hope it wasn't a dream," a new voice said from right beside me. "I don't want anything to do with what you probably dream about Victoria."

Dylan's fork clattered against the table. Sitting a few inches away from me—where no one had definitely been sitting a moment before—

was Tyler Martinez, the boy who'd been taken in Dylan's place at the swim meet.

Tyler raised an eyebrow. "What? Why are you all staring at me?"

"Um...Maybe because you just popped out of thin air," Henry said, eyeing him warily.

Kazi laughed. "What do you mean he just popped out of thin air? Tyler's been sitting here the whole time."

"Dude, you just asked where he was ten minutes ago," Dylan said. "Don't you remember that?"

Kazi shrugged. Katie was looking at us like we were crazy. I was 100% sure Tyler had not been sitting beside me all lunch. Dylan and Henry's gaping mouths said they obviously felt the same way.

"Jade, do the poke," Henry muttered, nodding his head indiscreetly at Tyler.

"Why do I have to poke him? I don't even know him!" I protested.

"You know!" Henry insisted. "So you can do the *thing*—that thing only you can do. Besides, I'm not about to touch him if he's been abducted by aliens or something."

"Are you all insane?" Tyler asked, staring at us worriedly. Me especially. Great, he'd never let me get near enough to have a vision now, thanks to Henry. Tyler probably thought I was the one with the alien disease.

"So, Katie, did you think up a new *D&D* strategy for next week?" Dylan interrupted, trying to diffuse the situation. I felt a small force pulling me further down the bench, though it took me a minute to realize it was Dylan's powers—quietly moving me away to give the clearly weirded-out Tyler some space. I suddenly realized that was what Dylan was best at: quiet, subtle direction. He could keep people calm and under control, even when they were freaking out.

While Katie launched into a terribly complicated spiel about raiding some kind of enchanted castle, I tried to study Tyler out of the corner of my eye. His dark hair flew in tousled curls, framing his tanned skin and brown eyes. Just like Mary, he didn't look much different than he had when I'd seen him in my vision before he'd been taken. No visible injuries that I could tell, though he had on a long-sleeved T-shirt, so I couldn't see if he had the same injection bruises Mary had had in my vision. He seemed fine. As if he'd never left—just like all the others that had been returned.

A terrible feeling crept up my spine. If Mary and Tyler, the only two people with powers Yan Mei had known to be missing, had been returned, then was the man behind that mysterious voice going to try to snatch someone else? Was he going after anyone with powers or specific people? And what was he even trying to do? All those questions about my parents and that thing...What had he called it? The Amalgamation? He'd nearly blown a gasket when Mary had said their project was going to get sidelined for years.

"Good lunch, young Shakespearians," Mr. Goodman said, startling me out of my thoughts. I hadn't even seen him stop at our table. He handed a piece of bright yellow paper to Dylan, Henry, and me. "Care for some extra credit?"

"Are we going somewhere, Mr. G-Man?" Henry asked, skimming over his paper before folding it up crookedly and stuffing it into his shirt pocket.

"The Pinewood Players are doing *Macbeth* in their fall season. I was able to get enough tickets for our class, but I had to make it an extra-credit assignment since the last performance is on Saturday. Figured it would help with your projects," Mr. Goodman said, smiling before heading off to pass out more slips to Victoria and Julian's table.

"Awesome. Extra credit and the perfect inspiration for how we should approach our reenactment," Henry said cheerfully, digging out a fortune cookie Yan Mei must have stashed in his lunch box.

"We are not doing a reenactment!" Dylan and I said at the same time.

Henry rolled his eyes and cracked open his cookie. "'An unforeseen surprise will find you soon.' Hey! This one's actually true! I get a whole two-minute walk with Victoria after lunch! Unforeseen surprises!"

"Henry, come on, you don't actually believe those things, do you?" Dylan groaned, finishing off the last of his sandwich.

"I could probably do better," I muttered jokingly, though I instantly regretted it by the crazed look that flashed in Henry's eyes.

"Oh my gosh! Of course you could!" he exclaimed, smacking

himself on the forehead and wincing as he hit his bruised eye. "Why didn't I think of that sooner? You could write all our fortunes!"

"No, wait, I didn't—" I started, but the bell signaling the end of lunch cut me off.

Tyler was up in seconds, making a hasty retreat from our table—probably mostly me. The lunch room erupted in kids trying to throw out their stuff and get to fifth period. I had psychology next with Julian. Great, a whole forty-five minutes of him watching me in that eerie way of his.

"Nope, you've got a new job," Henry insisted, zipping up his lunchbox and standing. "We'll talk about it more tonight at the mall. Now, if you'll excuse me, I have a date with Vic—"

Henry had just turned to walk off from the table when he slammed straight into Julian, who was coming to throw his tray away. Henry's lunch box went flying as both boys hit the floor, along with half the stuff in Julian's backpack. People were laughing. Henry's face, hair, and shirt were covered with banana pudding.

"Okay...so maybe *that* was the unforeseen surprise," Henry said, groaning and wiping his eyes. He licked his lips. "The pudding's pretty good today, huh?"

Julian looked shocked, his mouth wrinkled in disgust as he scrambled away from Henry and hurriedly tried to pick up his spilled stuff. The scene looked so similar to the first day I'd run into Julian outside the tea shop that I felt sorry for him even though he'd decided to ignore me for weeks on end. I bent down and started to gather up the stuff from his backpack that had rolled to my side of the table.

We were both crawling around under the table, trying to get all his notebooks and pencils and papers picked up. Neither of us was paying much attention, so we didn't notice we were going to head-butt each other until it was too late.

"Ow!" Julian winced, though the sound distorted as my mind swirled into a vision.

~

Main Street formed around me with the same cinematic crackle, a definitive sign of the past. The street was soggy. I could smell the fresh scent of the rain, but it was sour somehow. Storms and rain were things that usually brought me comfort, but in this vision, it felt...sad.

The sound of a buckle made me turn. I heard a loud *click* and saw Julian sitting beside me. We were in the back of a fancy car with dark windows. The man in the front seat wore an expensive-looking suit and sunglasses despite the weather and darkness outside.

I hadn't known Julian long, but there was a deep scowl on his usually impassive face. If only I could've had the vision start at an earlier time to see what had caused such a dramatic expression. He turned to look out the window, and his face softened.

Two figures were standing outside on the sidewalk. A blond man and a dark-haired girl with darker skin than the pale man...wait. Why was he looking at me and Benson?

Suddenly, it became clear what was going on.

The day I first met Julian. A Friday, outside the tea shop where we bumped into each other. *The day of the freaky death vision that I am actively avoiding.* A fancy car had come to collect Julian. That's right. His dad had sent this man to get him...he was upset with Julian for taking off.

"That wasn't smart," the driver said softly, gunning the car away from the curb. "You know you weren't supposed to meet her yet. It's not—"

"Not time yet, I know," Julian said, crossing his arms over his chest. "I'm starting to think it'll never be time, Bartley."

Bartley's reflective glasses stared back at us blankly in the rearview mirror. Why was he wearing them anyway? The sky was so dark outside already. "It was dangerous, running off like that...especially here. Not with them so close."

Them? Who was *them?* If it was a dangerous kind of *them,* I didn't know if I liked *them.*

Julian's eyes fixed firmly on the window. "I had to see her, Bartley. To know if there really was someone like me."

I stared at Julian in awe. Someone like him? As much as I loved other fellow introverts, I had a feeling that wasn't what he was referring to. Did he know I had powers? Did *he* have powers, too?

Well, practically everyone in this town had powers. It shouldn't have really been that surprising at this point, but...he was looking for me. Specifically.

"You know you have to stay away from her," Bartley said after a long moment. His voice was firm but sad. Like a parent denying a child a toy. "At least for now...until we're sure."

Sure? Sure of what? Of me? Of the ever mysterious *them*? At least I knew why he went all *ice queen* on me afterward.

"It's just...she's—"

But I didn't get to hear what it was.

Bright lights surrounded me as a voice called my name.

"Jade! Jade, are you alright?" Dylan asked. He was crouching beside me, shaking my shoulder. He looked at me with wide eyes, and I suddenly felt like consoling the worried boy.

Julian was shoving stuff into his backpack. He had a similar look on his face, but then he frowned...a distant look in his eyes. Had he sensed that I'd gotten a vision off him? Could people tell that? I didn't get an answer because as soon as he finished zipping up his backpack, Julian took off for the hall without a word.

Dylan put his hand on my back and leaned in close, his voice barely above a whisper. "What did you see, Jade?"

"I-I'm not sure," I said, mouth dry. I wasn't even sure what to make of what I saw. Julian may or may not have had powers, but either way, he had intentionally sought me out that day in the rain. To talk? It didn't add up, but what was I supposed to do? Confront him? With my luck, it would be something completely different, and he would get me a one-way ticket to a grippy sock vacation.

"Aw, yuck," Henry said, trying to scrape as much pudding off of himself as possible. "Now I'm going to have to walk around all day with a black eye *and* covered in pudding."

"At least you get to walk with Victoria to the nurse's office?" Dylan suggested, helping me up. He handed Henry another wad of napkins.

"Oh, radishes! I was supposed to meet Victoria!" Henry yelled, smoothing back his hair and spreading even more banana-flavored mush onto his head. "Find my lunch box! I'll talk to you guys later! Victoria, wait up!"

I looked at Dylan. "Radishes?"

"He spends too much time with my dad," he sighed.

I braced myself on the table, watching as Henry ran into the fading crowd and wishing I was the one who only had to worry about a black eye and banana pudding.

CHAPTER
SIXTEEN

"I'm sorry!" Dylan said, wincing as I hit the floor for about the hundredth time.

"Quit apologizing! You. Are. The. Attacker!" Palo groaned from his place on the side of the training ring. He was teaching our second official training session alone today- not too long after we'd started warming up, an older man and woman who looked a lot like Skylar (her parents, I assumed) had hurried in, speaking in hushed tones. Skylar had quickly excused herself and left with the others, looking worried, although if Palo knew what had made his girlfriend rush off so quick, he wasn't letting on.

"I can handle myself, Dylan," I said, pushing myself up off the floor. "Look at Henry's face!"

"Yes, my beautiful, horrendously injured face!" Henry shouted, jamming another handful of popcorn into his mouth. Only Henry would bring popcorn to watch my and Dylan's sad version of *Fight Club*. Besides, what was he even complaining about? His eye looked way better than it had this morning—you could barely even see the bruise now.

I balled up my fists like Palo had shown me. Dylan looked like he was going to be sick but raised his hand again, sending a tidal wave of pillows left over from the mattress store hurtling at me. I dodged, hurriedly diving out of the way just as they flew over my head.

"Pillows are not threatening!" Palo barked at Dylan, running his hands over his face. "Look, I know you don't want to hurt your girlfriend—"

"She's not my girlfriend!" Dylan said quickly, though he froze and looked at me in confusion. "Wait, you're not my girlfriend, are you?"

I took the opportunity to swing at him while he was distracted. Just like every other time, my fist collided with an invisible wall of pure force, stopping the strike in place. "What kind of question is that?"

"I don't know! I mean, we never really said we weren't!" Dylan said. I could feel my sneakers skidding backward against my will, his powers forcing me back.

"Ooh! Good point, Dylan!" Henry cheered, spilling half his popcorn bag on the floor by accident. "Aw, man."

"Shut up, Henry!" I said through clenched teeth. I was still losing ground. Dylan's telekinesis seemed able to hold off every shot I threw at him. Every time I got even remotely close, his powers would just shift my strikes away. I needed to distract him...he couldn't block me if he couldn't concentrate.

Maybe kissing him again isn't such a bad Plan B...

No. I was going to win this fair and square. I tried to kick his legs out from under him, but Dylan jumped back.

"Use his weaknesses, Jade," Palo coached from the sidelines as Dylan started to recover the ground I'd made him lose. "Run down his powers, force him to make bad moves."

"Hey, I thought you were supposed to be helping me!" Dylan complained.

"And I thought you were supposed to be attacking," Palo said, crossing his arms over his chest. "Without Skylar, I'm coaching offense and defense."

Dylan rolled his eyes and yanked my feet out from under me in one quick gesture. He winced again. "Sorry."

"Quit apologizing!" Palo and I said in unison.

Weakness...Weakness...What could I do to get Dylan's guard down?

Another burst of force slammed into me, and I barely managed to stay on my feet. I ran at Dylan, taking a swing I knew instantly was bad. He dodged it easily.

"Jade, you are the defender! Your job is not to attack!" Palo said, moving quickly out of the way as I went after Dylan again. I could feel his powers pushing against me, but I forced myself forward anyway. I punched and kicked and elbowed, trying desperately to hit him, but nothing ever came close. He practically had his own personal forcefield.

Dylan suddenly looked worried. "Uh, Jade, you okay?"

No, of course, I wasn't okay. I knew it was dumb to be frustrated but I'd been stuck in this stupid ring for over half an hour trying to get one measly hit in, and nothing. How was I ever going to be able to protect myself from the invisible force if I couldn't even do it in a fake match?

I wasn't looking until it was too late. Dylan raised his hand, and a force slammed into me with the speed of a truck. I went flying, rolling over the side of the ring and onto the regular floor.

"Jade! I-I didn't mean—" Dylan floundered. He started toward me, but Palo sent him a look telling him to stay back. Dylan obeyed.

"Jade," Palo said, eying me knowingly. He knelt down, keeping his voice low so the boys couldn't hear. "Are you hurt?"

"No," I said, shoving myself up. My hands were carpet burned, and I'd busted the knee out of my sweatpants, but other than that, I seemed okay. I didn't feel that way, though. I'd had so much luck sparring with Henry that I had thought going up against Dylan would be easy. Who was I kidding? I didn't stand a chance against someone with actual like, useful powers. Seeing the future wouldn't help me stay safe...in fact, it made me *more* vulnerable. The headaches, blackouts...I'd be a goner if I was in an actual dangerous situation.

Palo put his hand on my shoulder. It was a surprisingly gentle gesture for someone with those wicked sharp claws I'd seen yesterday. "I think that's enough for tonight."

"Palo, why am I even here?" I asked, stepping out of his grip. "Wouldn't I be better off just working with Yan Mei?"

"Jade, look, that was an accident," Dylan said, running up to me. "I would *never*—"

"I know, Dylan," I snapped, instantly regretting how irritated I sounded. I took a deep breath. "People are going missing, and I can help."

"Jade, learning how to harness your powers takes time," Palo tried again. "I'm sure when Skylar gets back, she'll know how to explain this better."

"It's just...this is a waste of time—it's not like any of this will help me in the end anyway," I said, thoughts churning back to the mega-vision.

Dylan froze. "What?"

Henry jerked to attention, too, not caring that he'd re-spilled all the popcorn he'd just picked up. His face was unreadable. "What do you—"

"Jade, there you are!" Yan Mei called, materializing in the door of the sparring room and saving me from having to awkwardly explain my death. She was out of breath, hair hanging loosely from her bun. "We need you. *Now.*"

I nodded, snatching my bag and hurrying toward my grandmother. Dylan tried to follow, but Yan Mei held up a hand to stop him.

"Not you," she said firmly. "You can't be involved."

"What? That's stupid—Wait!"

Yan Mei guided me out into the main concourse of the mall, walking so fast I halfway had to run to keep up with her. I could tell we were heading back toward the bookstore when we headed down the escalator. "What's going on?"

"Not until we're in the Archive," Yan Mei muttered, eying people warily as we walked. We passed Tyler Martinez coming out of one of the training courses, and I realized why she was being so cautious. If Tyler had super hearing, one overheard word could send the whole mall into a panic.

We rounded the corner into the bookstore, heading past researchers and tables piled high with books. The air in the Archive seemed tense, like everyone had suddenly gone into research overdrive. Once again, Yan Mei led me back under the castle arch to the partitioned-off kid's section.

The four people waiting on us couldn't have looked more out of place. The Core 5.

Dylan's mom noticed me first, shooting a concerned look our way as the same intrusive feeling entered my mind. I imagined mental walls going up. I could not handle someone poking through my brain right now. Skylar was beside her, halting the conversation that we'd just walked in on. Her parents weren't here, but she hadn't lost the same worried expression from earlier.

"I didn't realize she was so young," the man closest to me said, scratching his bald head. He had dark skin and was dressed sort of formally, like a professor or something: green sweater, slacks, polished shoes. He watched me curiously out of his thick-framed glasses, just like he had the other day when I'd fought Henry. "She's just a kid."

"This kid is *my* granddaughter, so show some respect," Yan Mei said protectively, moving to the center of the group. "Vivian wasn't any older when she started helping William and me. Jade can handle this."

The four other adults straightened up, suddenly looking at me very differently. Obviously, none of them wanted to be on Yan Mei's bad side.

"Jade, meet the Core 5, the leaders of the powered community," she said, gesturing to the assembled adults. "You already know me, Skylar, and Jessica, Dylan's mother. This is Nora and Marcus."

"It's lovely to meet you," a woman with tanned skin and long, sleek hair said. Nora. A kind smile crossed her face as she reached for both my hands. She was in her late forties, maybe, wearing a black pantsuit like she'd just got off work. "Lance and Vivian were very dear to us. I was proud to call them my friends."

I smiled, not entirely sure what to say, as Nora let go of my hands. I might have been mistaken, but I could've sworn a sour expression crossed Yan Mei's face at my father's name. Come to think of it, she had said barely anything about my father at all...

"Jade, we brought you here because we need your help," Yan Mei said, the strange expression suddenly gone from her face as she got us back on topic. She pulled something small from the pocket of her sweater and handed it to me: a black lighter, broken and scuffed up like it'd been dropped on something hard. *Odd.*

"Is this about the missing people?" I asked.

She nodded. "Two more were taken...the first time more than one person was snatched at once. This invisible person is getting bolder,

147

increasing the number of people they're willing to take. Whatever it is they're planning, it's speeding up."

Two people? I hadn't noticed anyone else missing from school recently. I thought we were doing well since Tyler had come back. Dylan's mom interrupted my thoughts.

"They aren't from the school this time. They were adults—Susan and Antoine," she said, settling uneasily against one of the empty bookshelves. "They both helped out here like the rest of us. Susan could temporarily reduce her gravity or the gravity of other objects. Antoine could manipulate fire."

"They were aiming to go to a movie together before coming here tonight," Nora chimed in. "But neither one showed up or is answering their phones. Marcus and I found Antoine's lighter in the parking lot when we went to investigate. Their car had been smashed up, and there were traces of burn marks nearby. We think they were taken by force."

"My cousin and Susan were gifted fighters," Skylar added, crossing her arms over her chest. If Antoine was her cousin, that must have been why her parents had come rushing in. They must have known he was missing. "They wouldn't go down without a fight."

"We need your powers to try to find out what happened to them. Some clue as to where they are," Marcus said, pushing his glasses up on his face. "They knew nearly as much about the powered community as the five of us do. That information, in the wrong hands..."

"Got it. Real bad," I said, trying to ignore the sick knot twisting in my stomach. This was all starting to be too much. This was huge—what if I screwed up like I did in the fight with Dylan? I didn't even want to know what he was thinking right now after I'd stormed off like that. "I-I'll try my best."

Dylan's mother took my hand. "We don't expect a miracle. We just want you to try."

"You are powerful, Jade," Yan Mei said encouragingly. I gulped and tightened my grip on the lighter. I took a deep breath and called my mind to focus. *Show me Antoine and Susan. Show me what happened to them.*

My brain was foggy like a dust storm clouded my vision. Faintly, I could make out a door with a marquee sign above, its bright light peeking through the dust. I pushed open the door and found myself outside. It was evening, the sky just fading into a deep purple-ish black. The parking lot was slightly desolate, being a weekday. Colorful lights flashed on the marquee surrounding the name of the latest *Spider-Man* movie, but there were no people around.

Alright, where are they?

I walked toward the steps near the glass doors and peeked inside the theater. There were what seemed to be a few staff members behind the concession stand, but their faces were blurred. I couldn't make out any of their features, just vague blobs of people. The popcorn maker was nearly depleted. Then, out came a couple. A man and woman who looked like they were holding hands. They were so distorted that even as they got closer to me, it was extremely difficult to gauge what was going on accurately. I tried my best to focus, but the longer I stared at them, the more my head started to hurt.

The pair were outside the theater now, walking toward the cars. I could vaguely hear their conversation, but it was muffled, and the ache was coming back, forcing me to blink rapidly. The blurs stopped. I closed my eyes for a second, and when I opened them, there was a quick-moving blur high in the air. A wave of heat gathered around me before a flash of brilliant orange. *Fire.*

I held up my hands in defense and turned away, suddenly finding myself back in the Archive with five adults staring at me.

Yan Mei placed a hand on my shoulder with a concerned look. "That wasn't very long."

"I could see them—but I couldn't really," I said, trying to explain. I could still feel heat on my face from the sudden burst of fire. "It was like they were purposefully blurred out in my mind. Like when I was looking into Mary's past, and I didn't know the woman behind her...I knew she was there, but I couldn't tell what she looked like. I'm sorry, I don't know if I will be much help if I can't see them."

"What about a picture? Maybe that would help?" Marcus asked. The adults nodded in agreement.

"I got it!" Skylar shouted excitedly, yanking out her phone. She tapped the screen insistently, then shoved her phone into my hands. A woman's social media profile was pulled up. "Try this."

I studied the latest picture. The woman, Susan, had fiery red hair in pin-up curls that accentuated her ivory skin and circular glasses. Her eyes were a warm brown. She was curvy and wore a simple white shirt tucked into a flow-y maroon skirt that went down to her ankles. The man, Antoine, was also dressed up. He had dark skin with tight braids that were neatly tied in the back. He did favor Skylar some- something in the curve of his face or the shape of his mouth, maybe. He had a matching maroon sweater, dark-washed jeans, and nice black shoes. The pair had their heads leaned toward the other with candid smiles like the picture was taken in the middle of them laughing. I could tell they were very happy.

"Alright, I'll give it another go," I said. Dylan's mom gave me a concerned frown. I wondered if she had seen my vision and how distorted it had looked.

She nodded, answering my unintentional question. "Yes, and I know it hurt you. Don't push yourself too hard, dear."

"I think I'll be okay this time," I said, gripping the lighter again. The Core 5 watched me expectantly, and the confidence they had voiced in my powers re-energized me. I had been wary about moving to Pinewood, but now I was glad I had. There were people here like me. People who understood what it was like to have powers and be different.

The door to the vision seemed less dusty this time. I rushed through and ran toward the theater. The staff's faces were still blurred, but they weren't my target.

Coming toward me was Susan with her fiery curls and Antoine with his neat braids, holding hands and laughing as they made their way to the exit. As they approached, Antoine kissed her hand before holding open the door. "After you, my love."

Susan laughed before giving an exaggerated curtsy and walking through. The couple immediately joined hands, and Susan leaned into his shoulder.

"That was such a great movie!"

"It was," Antoine agreed, "but I liked getting to spend time with you more."

Susan nodded. "I know. With all these disappearances, it feels like we've just been glued to work."

A rustle in the bushes nearby caused them both to freeze. Antoine reached into his pocket for something small that I couldn't see and gripped Susan's hand tighter. A deep laugh cut through the silence.

"Alright, that's enough playing around," Antoine said, eyes sharp as they scanned the bushes.

"Show yourself, coward," Susan called.

The pair were met with silence before there was another sound: gravel crunching loudly under someone's feet. The invisible force was running toward them.

Susan jumped high into the air, lessening the gravity around her to stay aloft. Antoine popped the lid open on the small black lighter he'd pulled from his pocket, flames erupting instantly. He used one hand to force the flames toward the gravel. There was no sound to indicate that he'd hit anything, and he called the flames back to his hand, letting them spiral impatiently, ready to uncurl at a moment's notice. Susan bounced down and launched toward the cars. The weightlessness slowed her down, but she was able to make long strides.

Suddenly, her arms were constricted by her sides, making her gasp. Susan smirked. "Gotcha."

Her arms grabbed the invisible force and started bringing both of them skyward with a large leap.

"Not very fun being taken by force, is it?" Susan asked. She started to spin, the force still tight in her grasp. "Tell me, do invisible people get motion sickness?"

"Be careful, love. Don't push yourself too hard," Antoine said but continued to stand by. Susan was spinning so fast that she was starting to blur.

Suddenly, Susan vanished from sight. For a second, I thought she was just spinning too fast for my eyes to register, but Antoine's reaction told me that her vanishing was not a usual side-effect of her powers.

"Susan! Susan!" he yelled desperately, eyes searching the dark sky around where she'd vanished.

"I'm here! I'm—" Susan's voice cut off sharply. Something was happening up in the air—some kind of scuffle between her and the invisible force. Wait, had it made her invisible, too?

I jumped as the windshield of the car closest to me smashed in, seemingly on its own. The dent was certainly big enough for two humans, and a small trickle of blood dripped down the silver hood.

"Susan!" Antoine yelled, running forward, though he didn't make it far before something grabbed him as well. He fought and kicked, though the flame in his hand had been extinguished. He hit the ground and rolled. His lighter went flying, leaving him without a source for his powers.

His shirt stretched like something had grabbed him by it, and Antoine was hauled to his feet. His face was scraped up from the black-top. "Show yourself! What did you do to Susan?"

Antoine brought his knee up, hitting something firmly in the stomach and breaking its grip. There was a sound like someone falling, though, within a second, something had lunged right back at Antoine. He toppled, suddenly fizzling out of sight, too.

Antoine and Susan were gone. Taken by the invisible force. I stared, horrified, at the busted car. If the invisible force had attacked Antoine after that fall...was that blood Susan's?

I was about to will the vision to end when something caught my eye on the ground. It was a folded-up piece of paper—bright yellow card-stock with a little cartoon of the comedy/tragedy masks. My stomach dropped. I could have walked forward to see it better, but I already knew what it said.

"*Macbeth*," I gasped as the Archive reformed around me. My knees almost buckled, but Dylan's mom steadied me before I could fall.

"What?" Marcus asked, staring at me like I'd grown a third eye. Wow, was watching me have a vision that traumatic?

"After Antoine and Susan were taken...I saw a paper on the ground. It—it was a notice for the Pinewood Players' performance of *Macbeth* this Saturday."

"How do you know that?" Nora asked.

I fished around in my bag, pulling out an identical, slightly crum-pled yellow paper. "Because I have the exact same one for our English class. We just got them today."

Skylar suddenly looked extra worried. "You mean this invisible dude's coming after someone in our show?"

It took me a minute to realize what she meant. There was a Pinewood Players button pinned to the backpack by her feet.

"You're in the show, aren't you?" I asked, pushing away from Dylan's mom as my strength returned. "Are there others, you know, like us?"

She shook her head. "Not that I know of."

"We're the targets," Yan Mei said ominously, breaking the silence that had fallen. "The invisible force knew that they'd have a much better chance of getting Antoine if they went after Susan first. Now Skylar. We're the most prominent members of the powered community—they're going after us."

"We have to go then," I said, turning back to my grandmother. "Me, Dylan, and Henry...we have the perfect way in. If the invisible force is really planning to go to the show, then we might be able to catch them."

"No, no, absolutely not," Dylan's mom protested. "This is serious. You all are too inexperienced to be getting involved with something like this!"

"Don't you get it? The invisible force had a slip specifically for *our* class!" I protested. "Only junior-level English is studying *Macbeth*. This person might even be one of our classmates!"

Marcus raised an eyebrow. "She may be onto something. That might explain why the last few people taken were high schoolers."

"It's too dangerous," Mrs. Mason insisted. "You, of all people, should know why, Jade!"

An image of the mega-vision bombarded my mind. Dylan cradling my dead body in the apocalypse version of Pinewood. Residual waves of grief washed over me, but I did my best to force them out of my mind.

I stared at Mrs. Mason, wondering how she'd figured it out when I'd tried so hard to keep the mega-vision out of my thoughts at dinner. Suddenly, I realized that she hadn't found out from me. Yan Mei had seen the sketches of the vision in my journal—Mrs. Mason hadn't pulled it out of my head at all.

"We have to go," I said, trying to keep my voice level. I sensed Mrs. Mason was a lost cause, so I turned to plead my case to the others. "Other than the swim meet, this is the only time we've known where this thing was planning to be before they got there. You guys can be there for backup, but if the invisible force really is one of our classmates, then the three of us have the best chance of finding them. Please, let us help."

Yan Mei put her hand on Mrs. Mason's shoulder. "She's right, Jessica."

Dylan's mom didn't look thrilled, but she finally nodded, unwilling to speak against the older woman. "Fine," she said, eying me cautiously. "But you three, let us handle it if things get dicey. You stay within sight of one of the five of us at all times. If we tell you to run, you run. No questions asked."

"Yes, Mrs. Mason," I agreed, feeling a grim sense of determination building in the pit of my stomach. Now this, *this* felt like I was actually helping. Finding out the truth, planning to stop people with powers from getting taken once and for all—feeling like I was actually part of something bigger than myself.

"We'll meet back here tomorrow night," Yan Mei said, motioning for me to follow her back out of the Archive. "The five of us will help make sure you, Dylan, and Henry are ready for the mission. Bring your friend Mary along as well."

"Mary?" I asked. "As in Missing-for-Days-Then-Rematerialized-Out-of-Nowhere Mary?"

"She's in your English class too, isn't she?" my grandmother asked. "I think she might be able to help us out with this one."

I stopped short just as we were almost to the doors leading back into the mall. Shoot. There was Dylan, pacing anxiously as he waited for me to come back out of the Archive. Yan Mei glanced between us and raised an eyebrow, clearly picking up on the tension.

"I don't suppose you'd be willing to give me a ride home tonight instead of Dylan and Henry?" I asked hopefully.

"Please tell me you're not fighting with Dylan three days before we're about to put the two of you on a very important mission together?"

"No, no, we're not fighting!" I said quickly, watching him fidget nervously through the glass. "I accidentally let slip about what happens to me in the mega-vision. I just...need a second to figure out how to explain that to him. Especially all that other stuff."

"If by 'all that other stuff,' you mean his feelings for you, then I understand," Yan Mei said, chuckling slightly. "I'd forgotten how much of a minefield it was having all these teenagers around."

"I assume you're talking about my mom?"

Yan Mei rolled her eyes. "Her, Henry's father, Jessica...your father."

"Is there something you're not telling me?" I asked, unable to stand it anymore. "About my dad, I mean. Every time you mention him, you don't seem very happy."

It was a long time before my grandmother answered. "Your father—Lance...He trained with us for many years. He and your mother loved each other very much, and he loved you and your brother very much."

Okay. One hundred percent Not An Answer, I thought. Why was she being so weird about my dad? Did she not like him or something? If that was the case, then why? What could possibly have gotten him on such rocky terms with Yan Mei?

"Yeah, but—"

"Some other time, perhaps?" Yan Mei said, cutting me off in a way that made me suspect there definitely *wouldn't* be another time to answer that particular question. She glanced back at Dylan, who clearly wasn't leaving anytime soon, and shook her head. My grandmother was smiling, but I could tell there was an uneasiness to her that she was trying to hide. "Come on, I'll help you escape tonight, but you two have to promise to work this out before the play Saturday."

"You got it," I agreed reluctantly, following as she led me toward the back exit of the Archive.

155

CHAPTER
SEVENTEEN

I t was late, later than my usual outings to the mall or restaurant. To the Bensons' knowledge, I was staying with Mary Milford for the night, which wasn't exactly a lie, but it also wasn't exactly the truth either.

Mary, Dylan, Henry, and I were gathered at the mall together, awaiting whatever fun and exciting "training" the Core 5 had planned for the theater. Since we were going to all be involved, the Core 5 said they wanted to see what they were working with, see if they could trust us.

"Are they even going to show up?" Henry whined, pacing up and down the old candy shop. We'd come here to wait since it was the only brightly lit space in the mall. The rest was shut off or heavily dimmed, making it hard to see anywhere outside the shop.

There was something about the mall at night—I'd been several times now but never like this. It seemed...mysterious, but in a good way. I definitely wouldn't mind coming here after dark another time. The mall did host sleepovers from time to time, I'd heard, though that was mostly for children.

"They'll be here. Just be patient," Dylan suggested.

"He kind of does have a point, though. I thought they were coming right after lights out for training. Everyone left a half hour ago," I said, glancing at the time on my phone.

"Hey, Mary," Henry said. "What's the probability that they'll show up sometime in the next five minutes?"

"One hundred percent," Mary said before pointing to the window. "They're actually right over there."

Three adults made their way quietly across the dimly lit mall. The three I was still learning about. Marcus, Skylar, and Nora.

"Oh," Henry said. "Hey, guys!"

"Good evening," Marcus said, his deep voice filling the room. No longer in his usual button-down and slacks, he wore a black tracksuit with shiny white sneakers. "Tonight, your training will consist of a race. You'll be split into teams and will be competing for who can get to Skylar first."

"You can go anywhere in the mall, but you are not allowed to step outside the doors," Skylar added. Her hair wasn't braided tonight but teased out in an afro. She'd donned a similar athletic look with a red hoodie and leggings. What stood out the most were the red lighting bolt earrings that dangled from her ears. The flashy accessories seemed true to Skylar's style.

"But, for a challenge, Marcus and I will also be in the mall to deceive you. If we capture you, you're out of the running, and you *will* have a loser's penalty," Nora said. Her long dark hair was slicked back into a tight ponytail, and she wore a similar black tracksuit to Marcus.

Were they gone so long because they were looking for matching outfits to torture us in?

"What's the penalty?" I asked.

"You don't want to find out," Marcus said. "This will be a girls versus boys challenge, so Jade, you are with Mary; Dylan with Henry."

"Besties will prevail!" Henry shouted, making Dylan just stare at him. I looked over to Mary, who had a small smile. I still didn't really know too much about Mary or her powers, but maybe doing the challenge with her would be fun.

"Save the energy for the race, Henry," Nora said gently. "Alright, Skylar is going to take her place, and we'll get you set up at your starting points."

Personally, I didn't think the blindfolds were necessary. We couldn't even talk strategy during our trip into who-knows-where in the entire mall while someone continued to usher us along. *How big was this place anyway?*

We stopped.

I felt someone pulling at the back of my head, and my blindfold came off. The sudden shift in light made my eyes burn. Nora and Mary were beside me in a tight, enclosed space. An elevator.

"I can't tell you anything except good luck! I'm excited to see how you all perform," Nora said. Nora stepped back through before the doors could shut, leaving Mary and me alone as it closed behind her. Suddenly, the elevator started to rise. It didn't go very far...to my knowledge, the mall only had two floors, an elevator at each of the ends. Why not start us as far away from anything else in the mall as possible?

A voice sounded from the intercom, making Mary and I jump.

"Competitors," Yan Mei's voice said. Of course my grandmother would be here too, "your time starts...NOW!"

The doors opened, and we were surrounded by darkness. The entire mall had peaks of light here and there but was mostly bare. The main hallways had black lights swinging back and forth like they were searching for someone. It was like walking into an entirely different world.

"Where to first?" I asked. Mary's eyes were still wide with shock. I poked her shoulder. "Um, Mary, we need to go now."

She shook her head and stepped out of the elevator.

"I doubt Skylar would be at one of the ends of the mall, she's probably somewhere in the center," I said.

"Seventy-six percent likely," Mary said.

I paused. "Uh, that's a good percentage. I guess."

My stomach felt queasy with indecision. Mary's wide eyes said she was clearly waiting for me to take the lead. I'd never done any sort of challenge like this before. There were several course entrances around us. I tried to recall where I was based on the numbers, but I hadn't been here long enough to have the layout of the mall memorized. I walked further down, checking to make sure Marcus and Nora weren't around, Mary following behind me.

"We should be toward the back of the second floor," I said. "Let's check this room first."

"Fourteen percent," Mary said.

Did she always answer in probabilities? I knew she did when she was taken, but I had chalked that up to her being in that weird trance. Maybe she wasn't comfortable around me? In truth, I wasn't sure I'd ever even spoken to Mary before she'd been taken. She was always quiet, kind of kept to herself. Ironically, like me.

I went over to the door and jiggled the doorknob. Locked. Of course.

"You were right about that one," I said. "Where do you think we should go next?"

Mary looked around. "I need a map."

Ugh, I never even got a map. Do they even make ones for the mall? That would be very helpful.

"I don't know how to find one, but maybe we should start moving through the courses and try to make our way to the middle," I suggested.

Mary nodded. Well, that may be as good as it got for now.

A high-pitched sound startled me. It almost sounded like a *chirp?* A bird?

"Let's go!"

We ran inside the closest course, which I immediately regretted. Mirrors. Ceiling-to-floor-length mirrors towered around us. Our reflections surrounded us from all sides. I could see the panic on my face.

I reached out my hands and tried to feel for where the mirrors stopped and started, trying to orient myself to the maze. My stomach started to churn. I wasn't normally claustrophobic, but the lack of knowledge of where I was or what wasn't a reflection was really starting to boggle my mind.

"Ugh," I groaned. "I can't tell where we are at all."

"Mirror mazes have an average failure rate of sixty-eight percent when under a time limit."

That's really helpful there, Mary.

"I need positive probabilities only," I groaned, slowly easing myself around the maze, hands glued to the wall.

She laughed at my outburst, and I started laughing too. "Sorry, sometimes the probability stuff is an automatic thing. I can't always control it."

I nodded. "I know exactly what you mean."

And suddenly, it made a lot of sense why Mary never seemed to talk much.

I pressed on but kept my voice soft so we wouldn't alert Marcus or Nora. "You know, I get why you don't talk a lot at school, trying to hide your abilities and all, but...you don't have to hide around us. You can be yourself here," I said.

Mary smiled. "Thanks, Jade. I was right about you. You're really nice."

My next sentence caught in my throat. It seemed I was wrong about this place. The people here were nice too. "Did you have a probability on me being nice?" I wondered, nearly bumping my head into a mirror before stepping to the side.

"About seventy percent," Mary joked, causing us to laugh again. "Do you play games?"

My hand smacked into another mirror, forcing me to switch directions again. "Not really. They're cool, but I tend to read more. I assume you do?" I asked. Surely, we had to be almost through the mirrors at this point.

"I love them. Everything is based on an algorithm and player skill. I also love when I'm right," Mary said, eyes gleaming.

"That's cool that you turn your powers into a good thing. I see freaky death visions, and it's very depressing."

"Freaky death visions?"

"Let's just ignore that I said that."

SQUEAK.

We froze. Slowly turning around, we saw a small, white rat with ruby-red eyes. It was looking right at us and continuing an urgent *squeak, squeak.* My eyes widened.

"Nora talks to animals! I think the rat is ratting us out!" I shouted, grabbing Mary's arm as we took off.

"The rat is ratting us out?" Mary said as we briskly tried to finish out the maze. "I think you've been spending too much time around Henry."

"You're probably right," I said, seeing the exit. "There!"

We made our way out into the hallway, flashes of purple swirling around us.

"We should cut across and try to throw them off!" I suggested.

"Sixty-nine percent chance of getting caught running in the open," Mary said.

"Let's take those odds," I said as we sprinted across to the next doorway. Bits of the floor had small puddles that we had to dodge. Where had those come from? The sounds of the squeaking rat got further away until it was gone. The room we were in was dimly lit with recessed lights in the ceiling. Counters full of knick-knacks surrounded us. There was nothing remotely related to training or a course at all here. I saw a rack of T-shirts that just said *The Mall* in cosmic lettering.

Is this some kind of inside joke? Aren't they supposed to be secretive about that? Twenty-five dollars!

"I think we're in a gift shop," I said.

"One hundred percent."

"Whoever priced these T-shirts is ripping people off."

"One hundred percent."

Of course the mall would have a gift shop. What *wasn't* in this mall?

We used this unusual room to catch our breath and look around the shop for any sign of the rat or any other mysterious animal friend of Nora. Talking to animals must have been a weird power. What did they actually say? I couldn't even talk to people my own age.

"Jade?" Mary asked, picking something up off the shop's counter, bringing me out of my thoughts.

"What is it?" I asked.

"Isn't this one of Skylar's earrings?"

In her hands lay a red dangly lighting bolt earring, the same one Skylar had been wearing to match her hoodie. There was no way she just randomly took an earring off over here. It had to be some kind of clue. Oh. *Oh.*

It's for me.

"I can try to get a vision off of it!" I said happily, almost snatching it from Mary's hands.

"That would increase our percentage of winning to seventy-five percent!" Mary exclaimed.

I'd never actually forced a vision like that before, but I really didn't want to tell Mary that. Somehow, I just had to make it work.

C'mon, vision, work your magic for me.

Nothing happened.

I huffed. I knew it wouldn't be easy, but that didn't make it any less annoying. "Okay, come on, earring. Tell me where Skylar is."

Still nothing.

"You can do it, Jade," Mary said. "You're strong and powerful. Make your powers bend to you, not the other way around."

I supposed I had been bending to my powers my entire life. Until I'd moved to Pinewood, I hadn't even known it was an option to try and *control* my visions. So much had changed since we'd driven into town. I'd changed.

"Yeah, I am strong," I said, glancing down at the earring once more. *Make your powers bend to you.* I took a deep breath.

Show me where I'm going to return the earring to Skylar.

A flash of darkness appeared before me. I was in a familiar place. Mattress signs adorned the walls. The Arena? I looked around, catching sight of Skylar sitting in the middle of the fighting ring with a small hand fan. Only one red lightning bolt earring. *Got it.*

I blinked hard, returning to the present.

"I know where she is. Follow me."

We sneaked through various courses with no sign of Marcus or Nora. We dodged objects in the telekinetic course, hopped around in the gravity room, and tried to get closer to the Arena. We ended up in the kid's area, foam pits and trampolines surrounding us.

"There!" I whispered. There, just across from us, was the Arena, a black curtain covering the entrance. How did they find a room-darkening curtain that big? IKEA?

"Our odds of winning are now ninety-seven percent," Mary said with a grin.

"I wouldn't say you've won yet," a deep voice said from behind us.

Marcus. Mary and I both whirled, finding him directly behind us on the trampoline pad.

Panic. I was panicking. We were just *so* close. But Mary's words from earlier came back to me. She believed in me, and I wasn't going to let her down. My powers weren't really that practical for evasion or a fight like Dylan's were, but that didn't mean I was going to go down easily.

"You still have to capture us," I said with as much fake confidence as I could muster in front of the scary, powerful man. "And I've already seen you coming. You don't stop us."

Mary seemed to catch the idea as well. "Yeah, it's, like, one hundred percent probable."

Marcus paused, an excited smirk crossing his face. "You don't say? Well, I've never bet against a psychic before, but if I lose, you're going to have to work for it."

Well, there goes that.

I tried to dash away—to think of something—but my body stayed still.

"You won't be getting away from me that easily."

I looked over at Mary, who was shuffling away. Marcus turned to her, and Mary suddenly froze, like something was keeping her locked in place. That was it!

"Don't let him look you in the eyes, Mary!" I shouted.

I used my chance of freedom to run toward the trampolines. This was a very risky—very much *Henry-esque* plan, but now was definitely the time for that. I jumped behind Marcus as he turned toward me. My body froze and fell down like a rock into the trampoline pad, causing him to falter and land on his backside.

"Let's go, Jade!" Mary shouted. Her arms were filled with foam blocks that she used to throw at Marcus. I shot up as the effect of his powers faded and darted toward Mary, still rapid-firing foam blocks at the poor man's face. We darted out the exit, but Marcus was already up and getting ready to turn toward us.

The gate!

"Mary, let's pull the entrance gate down!" I said. The lever was hidden to the side of the entrance, and we used all our combined strength to pull it down, effectively securing Marcus in the kid's trampoline area.

"The odds weren't in your favor today, sir," Mary said.

I burst out into laughter as we headed across the corridor toward the Arena.

"We could have a really interesting business using our powers together," I said.

"That's true, but it kind of seems illegal," Mary said.

Well, that joke didn't land. Still, she was probably right.

We reached the Arena with the large, black curtain.

Before we pulled it, Mary spoke, "And speaking about earlier, you don't have to hide around me either."

I smiled at her, and together, we yanked the curtain back, revealing a brightly lit Skylar sitting in her chair with a fan.

"Congratulations, girls. You've won the race!" Skylar said, jumping up from her chair.

I smiled at Mary, who wore a proud smile of her own. Is this what it felt like to win at school events? Still, I didn't think any school event could compare to something like *this*.

Before I could say something, Skylar had run out of the Arena into the hallway, leaving me and Mary behind.

"Stay there!" she shouted with a grin. "You'll see!"

Then we saw it.

Her whole body illuminated. She glowed a pale blue that got brighter and brighter until I had to look away. It was so bright the room around me looked like the outdoors on a sunny day. Mary was squinting. Then it was gone. I turned my head back to Skylar, whose light dimmed to a soft glow before disappearing completely.

"I think you need a warning label," I shouted at Skylar.

"Long-term exposure could lead to a thirty-four percent higher risk of eye damage," Mary said.

Skylar laughed at us and jogged back in. "It's easier to signal everyone this way. Plus, I love seeing everyone's faces the first time. Henry calls me *Flashlight*. He wore sunglasses for a week straight the first time he saw my powers."

Somehow, I can imagine exactly how that happened.

Murmurs caught our attention. We looked up to see Dylan and Nora trying to free a trapped Marcus from the trampoline area. A pang of guilt formed in my chest. *Oops, I probably should have freed him right after we finished.*

"What did you do to Marcus?" Skylar asked us.

"We kinda trapped him," I said.

"It was the only thing we could think of," Mary said.

Skylar's face lit up. Literally. *Does she always glow when she's excited?*

"Seriously? I need the full story on this when we all debrief."

The three made their way back to us, and Marcus did not look like he was having a good time. If I were a betting person like Mary, I would say it was because of the way Nora was cackling at him. Dylan seemed to be trying to remain neutral, but even he had a small grin on his face. He was drenched from head to toe...Was that where all those puddles had come from? Did he fall into a pool somewhere during the race?

Wait. Where was Henry?

I almost voiced my question to the three when we heard loud voices near the escalator, the words becoming clearer as two forms rode it up.

"You know that's not what I meant, Henry. I'm just concerned!" Yan Mei said.

"Just give me a chance, Grandma. That's all I'm asking," Henry said, a deep sadness in his voice. Like a boy who had given up. Even when he completely screwed up, Henry still had enough enthusiasm to light up a room—something I was coming to appreciate about my quirky cousin. What could Yan Mei have said to dampen his spirit like that? Had she yelled at him? Said something bad about his performance in the challenge? I mean, yeah, Henry could goof off, but his heart was there.

Everyone stilled, too nervous to speak, as the two reached the mall's second floor. The air was heavy. Henry wore an uncharacteristic frown as he walked off the escalator and dashed past us, disappearing down the hallway.

Yan Mei looked like she was about to call for him when Dylan gave her a soft smile.

"Let me go talk to him," he said.

"Thank you, sweet boy," Yan Mei said.

Dylan ran off after him, leaving me and Mary with the four adults.

165

The tension between them all tempted me to run off in a different direction, but my feet didn't move.

"Yan Mei..." Nora said in a gentle voice. She laid a hand on the older woman's shoulder. "I know you mean well, but...he'll be safe."

Yan Mei nodded, a deep frown on her face. "I know I'm supposed to believe that, but I can't. He's too important. They were all too important."

I froze. The other adults didn't have any words either.

Yan Mei cleared her throat. "Let's have the briefing in half an hour," she said softly. "I'll go on ahead."

She left without saying another word.

CHAPTER
EIGHTEEN

"That was impressive work, ladies," Yan Mei said.

We were back at the Archive, where the entire Core 5 was now present, along with Mary, Dylan, and Henry. Henry still looked ticked, though I wasn't sure if that was because of whatever argument he'd had with Yan Mei or because they'd lost the challenge. They wouldn't tell me about whatever loser's penalty they were facing, and I wasn't sure I wanted to know.

"You both used your powers and intellect to not only find Skylar but also evade capture...even if it was not the most *standard* operation," Yan Mei continued, shooting the still grumpy-looking Marcus an amused glance. Jessica snickered even though she hadn't arrived until after the challenge was over due to Sophie's bedtime, but Nora and Skylar had clearly given her the full play-by-play. "I know you're all tired, but we are going to quickly go over Saturday's plans one more time before we turn you loose. But just remember, I am *always* watching. You have good hearts, but you're also teenagers. Don't get any ideas."

The mission had been drilled into our heads so well I could recite the plan from memory, but I was too hyped up from winning to pay much attention now. The Core 5 slowly filtered out. Henry said something about going to test out his new course and darted out of the room. Dylan came over to me, and, unfortunately, I had a feeling I knew where this was going.

"Can I talk with you?"

I looked toward Mary, reluctant to run off on my newfound friend. In truth, I would have much rather stayed there with her than run head-first toward a depressing death conversation with Dylan. Benson would be so proud. She gave an encouraging *shoo,* and I turned to the boy beside me. He had changed out of his soaked clothes into baggy gray sweats and a Pinewood hoodie, but his hair was still slick.

Dylan and I walked down the hallway, passing various training courses, though neither of us seemed to know where exactly we were going. After a few minutes of wandering and no indication from Dylan of a place to stop, I finally led us toward a rectangular kiosk, yanking the small curtain open to reveal a very compact seat. Not much room for two people, but it'd work.

"The photo booth?" Dylan gulped, his eyes wide in fear.

Huh?

I raised my eyebrow. "Is that a problem?"

"I guess not," he said, slumping his shoulders.

We squished onto the tiny seat that really would have only been comfortable for one person. Our legs were flush against one another. The large screen in front of us buzzed brightly to life with the words *Insert Coins* flashing on the screen.

Dylan was rigid in his seat, not daring to move a muscle. Was I doing something weird? Was this photo booth some stupid teenage make-out spot? Well, I had to make him say *something.*

"Um, not to be rude, but...you and Henry were soaked after the challenge. Why were you *wet?*" I asked.

Dylan cringed. "It's a long story."

"Well, I'm not going anywhere."

"You're stalling."

I frowned. "Okay, fine. Just...give me a second. I'm not good with words."

Normally, being so close to someone, particularly the somewhat-attractive swim-team-telekinetic, would have made me flustered. Dylan was very confusing. Well, he was actually very kind and a really great guy, but everything gets strange when you see somebody confessing their love for you over your dead body at some random point in the near future. *I'm rambling. I hope he can't tell my face is burning because that is so—*

"Um, Jade," Dylan said, breaking me out of my thoughts. "I won't rush you or anything, but you seemed like you spaced out for a minute, and it didn't look like you were having a vision."

"Wait. How do you know when I'm having a vision?" I asked, my eyes wide as saucers.

He paused, grinning uncomfortably. "Well, you just sort of look different. I don't know. Anyway, that's not what we're talking about."

Oh, we *would* be talking about that when I wasn't in the hot seat. Nobody had *ever* been able to tell the difference between me zoning out and me having a vision. Granted, not many people knew I had visions, but still. *Focus.*

"Alright, you remember when we first met?" I asked.

"That sounds kind of cheesy, but yes. At Yan Mei's," he said.

"Sorry, I was having a really bad day and didn't mean to be rude to you or anything," I blurted. Dylan raised his eyebrows, but I continued before he could say anything. "Well, I accidentally touched your hand and passed out and...I had a vision. A big one. One unlike any other I had ever had. The town was destroyed, and there was no one around. It wasn't until I heard your voice...you were crying. I followed that sound until I saw you."

Dylan kept his eyes locked onto mine. I could tell by the way he pressed his lips together that he wanted to say something but remained silent. I continued.

"You were in the street with Benson. I was drawn toward you both like my vision was trying to show me what you were kneeling in front of, or rather, *who.*"

I paused. Unwelcome emotions were starting to spring forward. Panic. Terror. Heartbreak. Never had I spoken about the details of the mega-vision aloud. My chest tightened, and it felt like a beacon of light was shining down on me. Like I was on a stage with the entire world staring at me, judging. The words were reluctant to come out.

Dylan reached for my hand, squeezing it gently. He seemed to understand the rest without me explaining. Which, on one hand, was good because...I didn't think I was ready to say it loud in a way that wasn't some stupid joke. But he was silent, which was almost worse. *What was he thinking?* My heart hammered too fast to be healthy. I focused on the feeling of Dylan's hand holding mine. The softness, the warmth. How his fingers were just slightly longer than mine. I realized that, for the first time, I felt comfortable holding another person's hand. And it had to be Dylan.

Somehow, it's always Dylan.

"I can see why you were terrified of me when you woke up," he said.

I managed a shaky laugh. Tears were threatening to spill out of my eyes, and I willed myself to stop being so embarrassing. "You were a stranger to me, but you already knew my name and were connected to... *that.* Not the ideal first impression."

Dylan smiled and used his free hand to wipe a stray tear that had started rolling down my cheek. "It was still probably better than your first impression of Henry."

I almost snorted at the joke. "I don't think anything could have prepared me for that."

We laughed. As embarrassing as I likely looked, laughing and crying, it felt nice getting some of the tension from the air after such a heavy conversation. I already felt lighter. But I purposefully left out the part about Dylan's feelings. I didn't really know how he felt about me at the moment. Well, I had a possible, slight inclination, but it would just be... wrong to tell him about that. Especially if he didn't feel that way about me yet. It felt intrusive and best left unsaid. After a few moments of a much more comfortable silence, Dylan spoke again.

"Jade?" he asked, eyes finding mine. "Do you think maybe your vision could change, like how you changed your vision about me?"

I shook my head. "I can't change what happens. When I saved you, I only traded you for Tyler. If it's not me...I can't let someone die in my place."

"But...what if it could be the bad guy?" Dylan asked, pleading. My breath hitched. He was trying to save me—this sweet boy whom I'd never heard so serious. So grave. I wished I had something better to say.

"I-I don't know...I don't even know if there is a *bad guy*..." I trailed off. Of course, these were thoughts I'd already had every night when I couldn't sleep. Every possibility, every what-if. Time and time again, I'd debated, but my thoughts were always left to one question: could I really let someone die in my place? Wasn't that the same thing as me *choosing* their death...essentially killing them?

If that was the case, then I wouldn't have been able to live with myself even if I did survive.

Dylan sensed my internal panic and backtracked. "Sorry, I don't want to cause you any more stress. I can't imagine how difficult it must be to hold on to information like that. But...do you know when it happens?"

"At least a year or two," I guessed. "Tommy was taller, and my hair was longer. But we weren't that much older than we are now."

He sighed. "That's not great, but...at least we have *some* time to plan."

I raised my eyebrows at him. "We? I was the only person who...you know."

Dylan shook his head and looked down at our still-joined hands. "Jade, you're not alone anymore. You have a crowded, super-secret mall full of people like you. They care about you, Jade. I care about you..."

I looked up at Dylan, who didn't meet my eyes. A warm feeling spread throughout my chest. A feeling I didn't know if I wanted to grab onto for dear life or run away from and never look back.

He continued, "You saw something terrifying. You don't have to handle that all by yourself. If there's a way to stop it, we'll find it."

I squeezed his hand. "You know, you're pretty good at pep talks. You should stick with that instead of constantly apologizing for kicking my butt."

Dylan winced. "I'm..." He trailed off, seeing my glare. "I won't do that. You are strong, Jade. You'll probably be stronger than all of us once you figure out how to beat me. I've been using my powers longer than you—it's kind of an unfair advantage...unless you get in a good right hook like you did the other day."

I laughed. "Henry can thank Mrs. B for teaching me that one."

"Mrs. B is kinda scary."

"Have you seen your mother?" I asked, raising an eyebrow. "She's a literal lie detector!"

Dylan chuckled, but his heart didn't really seem in it. Like he wasn't fully with me at the moment. He seemed...defeated.

We sat in the dim silence of the photo booth for a long time after that, neither of us in the mood to say anything. I was acutely aware of Dylan in the tight space—the places where our shoulders and knees touched, our still-entwined hands. Were my hands sweaty? That would be embarrassing.

Dylan looked up, his blue eyes locking onto my brown ones. My mind was in shambles. Maybe it was a trick of the light, but I could've sworn there were tears forming in his eyes. Dylan was confusing me in every way possible, but I knew that tears did not suit him. There was nothing more that I wanted than to take his hurt away. *But how?* I gently rubbed my thumb over his. It wasn't much, but I also didn't have any words to comfort him.

I found myself staring at his lips. For a moment, there was no vision. There was no upcoming doom or psycho kidnapper. It was just us. The sweet boy who always cared about other people. He was kind, even when he was mad or confused. And, if I was being honest, it may have made me a bit weak in the knees the way he was staring into my eyes. I hadn't realized how close our faces were before. Did I move closer, or did he? I felt his breath on my cheek. I would only have to lean forward slightly to...

The photo booth's curtain ripped open, blinding both of us.

"SCANDAL!" Henry's voice shouted, his hand clamped tight over his eyes. "What were you two doing in the photo booth?"

"Um, taking pictures?" I lied, blinking hard as Henry peeked out from beneath his fingers. Apparently, he deemed it safe enough to uncover his eyes and yanked us out into the corridor.

"A likely story," he said, shaking his head at us disappointedly. "You know what the photo booth is used for! The place where people sneak off to K-I-S-S!"

I rolled my eyes. "Henry, I can spell."

"Oops. Force of habit. I'm used to Sophie being around," he said.

Dylan rolled his eyes. "Dude, Sophie knows how to spell."

Henry ignored him, jabbing a finger at Dylan's chest. "You said you wanted to talk to her! Not go to the photo booth! Never in my life did I think that my best friend would end up in the photo booth before I did. Especially not with my long-lost cousin!"

"Wow, that's kind of rude," Dylan said with a frown. "Why can't I be in the photo booth first?"

"I'm just saying you haven't exactly made much progress with the ladies."

"I've made more progress than you! At least I've kissed a girl before!"

"That doesn't count!" Henry yelled, rounding on me. "*She* kissed you! Besides, you know my heart belongs only to Victoria. I can't get in the photo booth with anyone else."

"I think you both probably shouldn't be talking about the photo booth in front of a lady," Jessica said, walking toward us.

We all froze. Oh, this was *so* embarrassing.

"Mom!" Dylan groaned.

"Mrs. Mason!" Henry shouted, throwing out his arms. "Dylan and Jade weren't doing anything scandalous in the photo booth! They were just talking!"

We glared at Henry.

"I know, Henry," Jessica said, holding back a laugh. "I can read their minds."

We all shared a sigh of relief.

"But I don't know how I feel about my son inviting a girl who *doesn't* know about the photo booth into the photo booth, even if it is just to *talk*."

Oh, I accidentally took Dylan to an infamous make-out spot. Oops.

"I wouldn't—" Dylan started.

"Actually, it was me who—" I said.

"Wait, wait, wait," Henry interrupted, cutting us off. "*You* know about the photo booth? Aren't you a little...*old* to keep up with that stuff?"

Jessica glared at him.

"Well, if she's old, I'm ancient," Yan Mei's voice sounded as she approached us as well. "And I think it's time for that loser's penalty."

Dylan and Henry's shouts of protest filled the room as I laughed my head off. For the first time in a long time, I didn't feel out of place. I felt like I was somewhere I belonged.

CHAPTER
NINETEEN

"This is so exciting!" Mrs. B said, pulling into a parking space near the Pinewood Performance Center.

"For the last time," I said, unbuckling my seatbelt, "this doesn't need to be a chaperoned event. I'm sure nobody else's parents are staying! It's just a dumb extra-credit thing."

"I'm sorry, isn't that Dylan over there walking in with *his* mom?" she protested, pointing out the windshield. "And that's Henry's grandma standing by the entrance."

Shoot. Why couldn't the Core 5 show up early so Mrs. B wouldn't see them and get any ideas about staying? This was the last place I wanted her to be near when we thought a super-powered invisible dude was coming to snatch someone. I knew that look on her face, though—nothing was going to stop her from coming.

"Fine," I sighed. "But please don't sit anywhere near the rest of my class. Especially not Dylan."

Mrs. B pouted. "At least let me say hi."

"No, no hi's," I said, getting out of the car without waiting for her. I made a break for the marquee where Dylan and Henry were waiting and waved Yan Mei and Mrs. Mason over from where they were talking. "We have a problem. I can't get rid of Mrs. B."

Dylan winced. "What? Why not?" He probably heard the word *doll* in his nightmares.

"She thinks your parents are going, so she wants to stay too!" I whispered frantically. "She doesn't need to be here—especially while we're doing what we're planning on doing because she doesn't know about the you-know-whats!"

The Core 5 had spent two whole days of strategizing to come up with the perfect plan to try to catch the invisible force. I was not about to let that get messed up because Mrs. B wanted to keep an eye on me and my not-really boyfriend. People could get hurt. Maybe taken. Our powers might get exposed. *Mrs. B could get hurt.*

"Oh, hi, Charlotte!" Mrs. Mason greeted cheerfully as Mrs. B finally caught up to me. "So good to see you again."

"Wow, someone's eager to see some Shakespeare," Mrs. B said, giving Dylan's mom a polite hug. "Ran right out of the car as soon as she saw you guys."

"What can we say? We love us some Shakespeare." Henry laughed nervously. His eyes widened as Victoria passed us by without a word, not looking thrilled to be spending her Saturday on school stuff.

Please don't turn into a lamp. Please don't turn into a lamp. Benson would think she'd had a nervous breakdown if I brought Mrs. B home raving about boys turning into household objects.

Stay calm, Mrs. Mason's voice crept into my mind. *She doesn't suspect anything. Let's keep it that way. I have a plan to keep her distracted, but you'll need to play along.*

Suddenly, I felt Dylan's fingers lace with mine, and I instinctively pulled away. Mrs. B looked heartbroken.

I looked at Mrs. Mason. *No, no way. You know what will happen if we walk in there in front of everyone—*

You want her distracted or not? You know why she's really here. Play it up.

I took a deep breath and retook Dylan's hand. His cheeks were a little red, but he smiled at me like this was something we'd done a hundred times. I wasn't sure who looked like they would faint first—Mrs. B or Henry.

"Jylan," he whispered, elbowing her.

"Mrs. Benson," Dylan said, holding the door open for Mrs. B but refusing to drop his hold on my hand.

"Why, thank you, doll." She giggled, striding past him as she chatted with Mrs. Mason. "He is such a polite boy. I wasn't quite sure what to make of the lamp he got Jade, though."

Dylan glared knowingly at Henry as he hurried past us.

"My bad on that one, dude."

The Pinewood Performance Center was a fancy, old-style theater. One of those with elegant gilded moldings and intricate frescos along the ceilings. The floor was patterned in a rich red carpet. The entry hall was loud and echo-y, packed with people streaming in to see *Macbeth*. I spotted Marcus milling around, eyes scanning the crowd for any sign of trouble. Nora was probably already backstage somewhere, giving some extra security to Skylar since she was our designated bait.

"Jade, Dylan, Henry! Over here!" Mr. Goodman called from where a small group of kids from our English class had gathered. I felt eyes on me instantly, hyper-aware of the fact that Dylan and I were holding hands. Why was it so hot in here all of a sudden? Did they have to look at us like that? Half the school had been going on about Dylan and me for a week. Why did they look so surprised? Had they forgotten about it or something? I tightened my grip on Dylan's hand and pressed in closer to him. Mrs. Mason told me to play it up, so I was going to play it up. Who said they got an opinion on who I was or wasn't with?

"Um, Victoria's passing out the tickets," Mr. Goodman said, hands stuffed awkwardly in his pockets. Even he didn't seem to know what to make of mine and Dylan's sudden public display of affection. I didn't know if it was the dim light of the entrance hall chandeliers or what, but something about Mr. Goodman's face looked dull, sort of sickly like he had at the beginning of the school year.

"I guess you two want to sit together?" Victoria asked, materializing beside us. She didn't look like she felt too good either—dark circles under her eyes, hair yanked up in a messy bun, and her Pinewood Cheer Squad hoodie was so wrinkled that I wondered if she'd slept in it. She was bouncing anxiously, face pale like she might be sick. Maybe there was something going around? Her hands were so shaky she seemed to barely be able to hand me and Dylan our tickets. It wasn't just me who

177

noticed it either—Henry was staring at her, which wasn't *unusual*, but his face was suddenly very worried.

"Um, you don't have any more seats by you, do—Oops!" Henry asked, knocking all the tickets out of her hand in what I was sure was a very purposeful move.

"Henry!" Victoria groaned, bending down to pick them up. Henry knelt to help.

I shot Dylan a confused look, but he shrugged. Mrs. Mason was waving to him from where she and Mrs. B were talking.

He let out an audible sigh. "I'd better go see what that's about. Probably Escape Plan 387 if things go wrong."

I watched as Dylan wove his way across the room. Henry and Victoria were still on the ground, though neither seemed very dedicated to picking up the tickets. They were whispering fiercely, like they were arguing. Henry seemed to be insisting on something, his hand barely brushing her arm. Finally, Victoria gave a reluctant nod.

"Hey, we're seat buddies," a voice behind me said. I turned so fast I practically smacked into Julian—who the heck taught him it was okay to stand so close to people? "Sorry. Didn't mean to scare you."

"Oh, have you suddenly decided you want to talk to me again?" I snapped without thinking. Julian looked a little hurt. I remembered all the sadness and loneliness I'd felt emanating from him when I'd had that vision in the cafeteria. "Sorry, that was mean. You just startled me."

"I startle a lot of people." Julian chuckled. He raised an eyebrow curiously. "So...you and Mason, huh?"

I looked around desperately, hoping for someone to rescue me from having to talk to Julian Graves about my love life. Mrs. B seemed to have captured Dylan in an embarrassing conversation by the ticket office, and Henry was still on the floor, hurriedly gathering the fallen tickets. Wait, where had Victoria gone? I didn't see her anywhere in the room.

"Um...yeah, I guess—me and Mason," I repeated, thankful that the ushers had started opening up the doors to the main entrance of the theater. "I-I'd better get back to Dylan."

Julian nodded, clearly disappointed. "Well, I guess I'll see you in there."

"Alright," I said, waiting for him to leave. Julian made no such move, staying firmly planted beside me. Inexplicably, him standing there silently was even more awkward than him trying to talk to me.

"Is everybody ready to go in?" Mr. Goodman called over the noise, clearly trying to get a headcount. "Wait, where'd Victoria go?"

"Um, she's in the—" Henry started, but Victoria cut him off, suddenly beside him again. I blinked. I would've sworn she wasn't there a minute before.

"I'm here, Mr. Goodman!" she said, looking a lot better for some reason. She seemed much less jittery, and was she actually *smiling* at Henry?

Mr. Goodman started leading the class up into the next section of the theater. Fingers laced back through mine as Dylan returned. "Julian," he greeted curtly.

Julian smiled, though he was fussing anxiously with the bottom of his cardigan's sleeves. I don't know why the motion even caught my attention, but the sight of Julian's hands stopped me so fast that Henry walked into my back. Julian kept walking, unaware that I'd stopped.

"Jade?" Dylan asked, keeping his voice low as the rest of the class pushed past us. I caught sight of Mary and pulled her aside as well.

I tried to find words, but I was hyper-aware of Victoria beside us. Henry waved for her to go ahead without him, and for once, I thought she might have looked a little disappointed. What on earth had he said to her while they were crawling around?

I waited until she was long out of earshot before I spoke. "We need to find Yan Mei. Now."

"What? Why?" Mary asked, looking around in concern.

I didn't see any of the Core 5 nearby beyond Mrs. Mason, who was chatting with Mrs. B as they went into the auditorium. This was bad. This was very, very bad.

"Julian's hands," I said, trying to catch my breath. "They're bright red, scraped to pieces. Antoine knocked the invisible force down when it attacked him in the parking lot—probably sent him skidding across the concrete."

Dylan's eyes widened. "You mean, you think Julian—"

"I thought he might've had powers, but—"

"Wait, wait, wait, *what*?" Henry interrupted, head obviously spinning.

"It makes sense," I said, running a hand over my face. "The way he's always popping up without people noticing. I saw him in my swim meet vision before Tyler disappeared."

"He could have been at school when I was taken too," Mary agreed. "Lots of clubs and teams stay late. I calculate a sixty-two percent chance of—"

"Bad guy vibes?" Henry suggested.

"Sure, let's go with that," Mary said.

"I knew that guy bugged me for a reason," Henry said. "We have to let the others know. From here on out, we use code names, right, Fortune Cookie? Calculator? Guppy?"

Dylan looked mortified, eyes wide. "Guppy? Why do I have to be Guppy?"

"Because you swim, and I don't have adequate time to come up with a good codename!" Henry said, eyes searching for our grandmother in the crowd. "Julian will be Earl Grey. I'll be the Illuminator. Stay calm and wait for my signal."

Without another word, Henry disappeared into the crowd to alert one of the adults.

"Stay calm," I said, swallowing hard. "I just have to sit beside Julian for the next two hours. Piece of cake."

"Earl Grey," Mary muttered helpfully.

"Don't encourage him," Dylan and I said in unison.

~

The performance could have had dancing penguins, and I still wouldn't have noticed anything but the potential arch-nemesis sitting beside me. I did my best to act calm, but I could tell I was failing miserably. My mouth was sandpaper, my hands sweaty, and I was probably shaking the entire aisle with how much my leg was bouncing from anxiety. We had to be close to intermission, didn't we?

I glanced over at Julian for what had to be the millionth time, only to find he was already looking at me. Both of us looked away awkwardly.

How was I supposed to keep an eye on him if he kept looking back at me? Every few minutes, the exact same thing: I'd glance over and find him staring at me with that same weird expression, we'd both look away, he'd look back when he thought I wasn't paying attention like he was trying to memorize everything about me. His eyes made me feel like a bug under a magnifying glass as they studied me: the curve of my face, the way I was sitting, my hand still gripping Dylan's like I was holding on for dear life. I basically was.

I don't know how much more of this I can take, I thought, glancing back and feeling the familiar presence of Mrs. Mason's powers in my mind. She had settled into a seat directly behind Dylan and me, close enough to provide backup if needed, though the fact that Mrs. B had magically gotten a seat beside her did nothing to reassure me.

Just a few more minutes, Jessica's voice came, slow and reassuring. *Yan Mei got word to the others.*

Still nothing?

Mrs. Mason shook her head almost imperceptibly. *I haven't been able to get a good look at him. I can't read his mind if I can't see into his eyes.*

Great. As if I hadn't been scared enough before our fool-proof mind-reader said she couldn't read Julian's mind. Maybe I could get him to turn around somehow? But how could I do that without drawing a bunch of attention, specifically from Mrs. B?

You know the plan, Mrs. Mason's voice came inside my mind again. *Once intermission hits, Skylar will come down and wave Yan Mei backstage. You, Dylan, and Henry will go with her—invite Julian along. Nora, Yan Mei, and Skylar will be back there to protect you; Marcus and I will come in the theater's back exit when we can follow without getting too much suspicion.*

I swallowed hard, feeling Dylan's eyes on me in the darkness. He'd turned enough that I suspected he'd heard the plan as well.

Just keep Mrs. B safe.

Mrs. Mason didn't answer, but I got the feeling she understood. The music surged as the curtain dropped onstage, signaling the end of the first half of the play. The lights of the theater came up in a bright burst, making everyone blink wearily.

"Alright, everyone, you know the drill," Mr. Goodman said, standing up so our class could see him. "If you have to use the restroom, go now so you're not getting up and down in the middle of the show."

Our English class muttered grudgingly. Some of the other kids streamed back toward the lobby in the lazy crowd drifting out of the auditorium.

"Pretty good show so far, huh, kids?" Mrs. B asked, leaning forward onto my seat. Her eyes locked excitedly on mine and Dylan's still interlocked fingers.

"Yes, indeed, Mrs. Benson," Henry said, materializing with Yan Mei at the end of our row. He was grinning like crazy, probably thrilled that he got to sit by Victoria instead of a potentially superpowered evil teenager for the whole of a Shakespearean tragedy. Henry was probably only giving me any attention because she'd vanished off to the bathroom or somewhere. "One of Grandma's friends said we could bring Jade and Dylan backstage if we wanted to look around. If that's okay with you guys, of course?"

"Why, of course, you can, honey!" Mrs. B said, waving her hand dismissively. Oh, no. Honey. There was no stopping her once she went full Southern twang. "I'll tell your teacher where you went if you're not back before he is."

Yan Mei and Henry started heading for a curtained-off entrance at the base of stage left. I could see Skylar poking her head out, looking for us. Dylan gave me a nervous glance. Someone would have to ask Julian to move so we could get out of the aisle. He was sitting dejectedly in his seat, clearly pretending like he hadn't just heard our conversation or that Dylan and I were running off somewhere together. I suddenly felt very self-conscious of our hands, but I didn't know why. There was something else too, something odd in his expression...almost worried.

Mrs. Mason's blue eyes stared at me as sharp as knives. *Invite him, Jade.*

I coughed awkwardly. "Um, do you want to come too?"

Julian looked up at me in surprise, beaming from ear to ear. "Really?"

"Sure," Dylan said, not sounding too thrilled. His grip on my hand tightened ever so slightly as the three of us made our way toward backstage.

THE VISIONARY

dittered over so she didn't, the three of us made our way toward backstage.

CHAPTER
TWENTY

This was it. The moment we had spent days planning and training for. The invisible force wasn't getting away from us this time.

At least, that's what I thought for the first five seconds the plan actually worked.

"Jade, are you sure this is such a good idea?" Julian asked, his torn-up hands still fiddling worriedly with his sleeves as he, Dylan, and I slipped behind the curtain leading backstage. "I mean, I really don't think we should be going backstage right now—"

"IT'S TIME TO SWIM, GUPPY!" Henry screamed, lunging at Julian before our grandmother even had time to yell at him not to. What was he doing? We had practiced the plan over and over, and *this* definitely was not it. I don't know what Henry was trying to execute with this change of plans, but apparently, "Guppy" didn't either since Dylan just stood there looking as confused as I felt.

Julian dodged out of the way, inadvertently toppling into me and knocking us both backward. Henry, suddenly surprised Julian hadn't stayed put and let him ram into him (even though I *told* him that screaming-tackle-runs never work), kept going with too much momentum, slamming into a platform cut-out of a tree and the actor brushing up on his lines behind it instead.

"My ankle!" the actor playing Macbeth screamed, hands clamped tight over his foot as Henry tried to disentangle himself from the wounded actor. "I have to go on in five minutes!"

"Sorry, sorry, I-I can fix this!" Henry promised worriedly, clearly not sure what to do. He pointed at the nearest stagehand. "You! I'm going to need an ice pack and a script!"

"Henry! What are you doing?" Yan Mei snapped. "That was not part of the plan! Stay on mission!"

"But the show has to go on, Grandma!"

"Come on!" Julian yelled at me, fumbling to his feet while the others were distracted.

"What?" I asked in surprise, body aching from the fall.

"We need to run! Now!"

When I made no move to stand, Julian yanked me to my feet, tugging me through the chaos of backstage. There were black-clothed stagehands everywhere—lugging heavy props into position behind the curtains, scrambling around and talking hurriedly into their headsets, giving us confused looks as we tore past them. We slammed into a painted backdrop of a manor, tearing straight through the center with a sickening *RIPPP!* Yan Mei was yelling for us, trying to follow. Skylar and Dylan had gotten blocked by two teens carrying a table. The stage manager was cursing. Nora plowed out of one of the dressing rooms just in time to see us stagger past.

"Let go of me!" I yelled, trying to shake out of his grip. There was no way I was about to let him take me like Mary and Tyler and all the others. Still, something nagged at my brain. If Julian really wanted to take me, why not just have gone invisible instead of dragging me out of here in plain sight?

Julian started to respond but was silenced as a platform of a cauldron dropped in front of us out of nowhere, busting into a spray of splintery shrapnel.

Dylan had finally gotten past the crew, his hand extended toward the ceiling. I hadn't realized it, but there were at least half a dozen heavy-looking scenic pieces suspended from the ceiling up above mine and Julian's heads for extra storage space. Dylan had dropped one—a warning shot, not close enough to hit us but near enough to scare Julian into stopping.

"You need to let Jade go. *Now*," Skylar commanded, raising her hands threateningly. I tried to shake out of Julian's grip again, 100% sure I did not want the sunburn to end all sunburns. Nora was running toward us now, too, Yan Mei not far behind. Henry had gotten lost in the fray, but I could've sworn I heard him arguing somewhere.

"Release her," Yan Mei said, coming to the front of my allies. Her voice was low and dangerous.

Julian didn't drop his grip on my hand. There were four mega-strong people with powers threatening him. Why wouldn't he let go of me? Momentarily, his eyes met mine...He looked terrified.

Suddenly, everything went dark.

"No, no, no!" someone—probably the stage manager—hissed from my left. "We still have two minutes to lights down, people! Who hit the switch?"

"Skylar, we need light!" Yan Mei said from somewhere.

I felt Julian's grip on my arm break, his hands shoving me further into the darkness before a faint glow started up from around where Skylar had been. A strange feeling washed over my mind just before he let go of me. It wasn't the same as Mrs. Mason's powers, but something inside my brain suddenly felt an incredible, panicky desire to run. I knew Yan Mei and the others were there to keep me safe, but something told me I *needed* to get away from them. They were dangerous. They wanted to hurt me.

My eyes were slow to adjust, but I staggered down the hallway, away from the others. Yan Mei and Dylan called for me. I'd lost sight of Julian. Actors ran frantically to their places, clearly unprepared for the sped-up start.

"Behold!" Henry's voice boomed from all around me as if it was coming through the stage monitors. Was he *onstage*? "It is I, Macbeth! You may not recognize me, for I was cursed by the witches to change appearance and wear these modern adornments, but I promise it is still I. And I have not forgotten my quest to save my one true love, Victoria... Juliet...I mean, whoever this play's about!"

"Who let that kid onstage?" a horrified stagehand whispered somewhere in the darkness beside me.

This was a total disaster. Not only had we taken out the principal actor, destroyed probably hundreds of dollars worth of props and set, but now Henry—*Henry*—was onstage in front of a packed house and Mrs. B, jabbering blindly in a terrible Scottish accent with no signs of stopping. And why did he keep saying Victoria's name? I was pretty sure he would definitely have her full attention by now. Why had he gone AWOL two seconds into the plan?

That inexplicable feeling of terror was starting to fade from my chest, but I'd lost all signs of the Core 5 or Dylan or Julian in the darkness. I dodged around a couple of quick-moving stagehands and into what I thought was an empty dressing room. I put my hands on my knees, trying to catch my breath.

Someone cleared their throat.

I whirled, finding myself face-to-face with an older woman. Gray was just slightly mixed in the long, dark hair that hung over her silver dress suit. Her skin was dark and wrinkled with age, and she was grinning at me like she'd just won the lottery. I wondered why she wasn't in costume.

"Why, hello, dear. You seem to be a little lost," the woman said, approaching me slowly. Okay, I was *not* getting good vibes from her at all. I started backing up. Something about her seemed oddly familiar, yet I couldn't recall where I had seen her.

She grinned at me, stepping closer. "I just want to help, dear."

Her hand grabbed mine before I had the chance to run. Suddenly, my mind calmed. What had I been thinking a moment before? I was supposed to be doing something, wasn't I? I could still hear Henry yelling onstage, but it seemed...muffled, far away somehow. Everything was quiet. I liked it.

"Tell me who you are," the woman instructed.

The words flew out before I could even think about it.

"I'm Jade Kastel. I'm sixteen—almost seventeen years old," I felt myself jabbering. Why couldn't I stop talking? I didn't *talk* to people. "I live with the Bensons, but I'm not really related to them—I'm adopted. That would be weird if I had a different last name than my real family.

Nobody knows where they are, though. Supposedly, I have a brother... Do you think he'd have powers like me, or could you have a twin that didn't have powers?"

The woman's eyes narrowed sharply. Why'd she look so serious all of a sudden? Had I said something wrong? I wasn't sure why exactly, but I *wanted* my answers to please her. The longer I talked, the more a warmth seemed to fill my chest.

"Your brother...the second Kastel twin," she said cautiously. "You've never met him? You don't know his location?"

"Nope. Long-lost. I did find my long-lost cousin. Ooh! And my grandma! No brothers, though."

The woman seemed relieved. I was glad I could help.

"Your powers. Tell me about your powers, dear."

"Well, I can see the future and the past—"

"The future *and* the past?" the woman interrupted in surprise. Why was everyone always so shocked that I could do that?

"Uh-huh. I actually had this super scary mega-vision where—"

"Let her go!"

My words cut off at the sound of the woman in front of me struggling. Suddenly, I was aware of the world again. I was in the theater, supposed to be looking for the invisible force. As I regained my bearings, I saw the woman with Julian behind her, his eyes shut tight as his fingertips gingerly touched her temples.

"Julian?" I asked, still feeling a little foggy. Had that woman messed with my mind?

Noticing the older woman's face, I could imagine that was *exactly* what was happening to her. Her eyes rolled back in her head, and suddenly, she went running, frantically scrambling into the darkness of the hall like she'd seen a ghost. Whoever that was...she definitely wasn't the invisible force. An accomplice, perhaps? Someone like Yan Mei had suggested covering their tracks? Just how many people were working with this guy?

"You saved me," I said, dumbfounded. Why would Julian save me if he was the one after everyone with powers? And why would he attack his own ally? If they were working together, they could have snatched me easily. I would have been powerless against them with their mind powers. Julian was clearly not the person we were looking for.

"It was nothing," Julian said shyly, hands still twisting nervously around his sleeves. He looked like he was going to be sick. "Did you tell her anything important?"

I shook my head. I didn't think I had...had I? I could hardly remember now. My head was pounding—having someone poking around in your mind was suddenly very high on my Do-Not-Recommend list. Still, something didn't make sense. If I had been wrong about Julian, then...

"What happened to your hands?" I asked, eyes serious.

Julian smiled sheepishly. I raised my eyebrows at him in confusion.

"Well, you see, I was making some tea and trying out my new glass kettle. I accidentally boiled it too long, and it may have...exploded," he said, looking at the ground. "Scraped my hands up good when I was trying to clean it up."

I looked at him like he'd grown a third eye. "How did you make a tea kettle explode?"

"It's a long story. It took hours to clean up, but luckily, my dad wasn't even mad that I exploded it. He said it was bound to happen eventually...I can be a bit clumsy sometimes," Julian said, embarrassed.

Understatement of the century, I thought.

While I still didn't know Julian all that well and I had heavily suspected him to be our bad guy, some strange feeling told me I could trust him. He had been distant, maybe a little cold in the past, but he had saved me from that crazy mind lady. If he hadn't stepped in...I was already dreading having to tell Yan Mei and the others I might have blabbed about my powers to a total stranger. My list of mistakes just kept piling up.

The sound of a crash startled us, quickly followed by a loud battle cry that could have only come from Henry. The way he was yelling, it sounded like one of the stage managers had purposefully yanked him from the stage.

"But someone has to be Macbeth!" my cousin's voice complained loudly.

I opened the door behind me and saw Dylan and Yan Mei rushing toward us. Henry wasn't far behind.

"Hey—" I turned around to tell Julian he didn't have to hide from them anymore, but he wasn't there. The window was open, the old fire escape creaking with retreating footsteps. Why would he leave so suddenly? Why was he so afraid of the others?

"Jade!" Dylan shouted as I caught up with them. "Are you alright?"

I frowned. "I'm fine, but I was wrong. It wasn't Julian."

The group looked at me in confusion. Henry spoke first.

"But you said—his hands..."

"I know what I said," I interrupted, "but I was wrong. His hands were hurt from—"

"You let him get away?" a calm but irritated Yan Mei cut me off. I flinched under her piercing stare, the guilt of today's mistakes starting to weigh heavy on my shoulders.

"I didn't let him get away. He saved me and left," I said.

"Saved you?" Dylan asked, reaching out worriedly toward me. "Did someone try to attack you guys?"

"It doesn't matter right now. We need to find Skylar and..." I trailed off. Running toward us was none other than Skylar herself, out of breath and panting. There was a small cut on her forehead.

"Skylar! You're alright!" Yan Mei said, relieved. They must have gotten separated when the lights went out.

Skylar looked up at us grimly. Something was wrong. Terribly wrong.

"It gave up on me," Skylar said, eyes on the verge of tears. "The invisible force got Nora. I-I think I got a lucky shot with my powers, but it threw me into one of the platforms before I could save her. I lost track of him after that."

My jaw dropped, stomach sinking. Everything about this was *wrong*. The play was in shambles. Macbeth had broken his ankle, I had falsely accused Julian—now Nora was gone, and our bad guy was still on the loose. If I hadn't put all the attention on Julian, the real invisible force might never have had a chance to take any of the Core 5. This was so much worse than anything that had happened with Ashley or being expelled from school last year. I would take those any day over this. I wanted to sink to the floor and cry my eyes out. They relied on *me* to be their guide, their visionary, and I had failed them all.

Yan Mei's eyes softened, anger fading slightly at my obvious hurt. "They may still be nearby...I know Nora wouldn't go lightly."

"Yeah, we can still save her!" Skylar agreed, not sounding super convinced but clearly trying for my sake.

Dylan looked at me like I was about to shatter into a million pieces. Maybe I was. I had just turned away from him when I saw a sudden flash behind me.

On a normal day, I would've just said it was a trick of the light, but not today. There was something about it—almost like someone moving just in the corner of your eye, hard to see but definitely there. It *had* to be our guy. Maybe the invisible force really hadn't made it out of the theater yet.

I dashed toward the flash.

"Hey! Stop!" I yelled, taking the stairs toward the back exit two at a time and trying not to fall on my face. The person in front of me was fast, but I could tell they were tiring, shimmering in and out of sight as they slowed. They stumbled slightly as they whipped around the final curve in the stairwell, smacking into the release on the back exit to the theater.

By the time we were both outside, the person was fully visible, their powers tapped out for the moment.

I froze. The runner had hit the door with such force that their hood had fallen down just enough to give me a quick glance at their face. Fair skin. A flash of blonde in the sunlight. A gray hoodie with unmistakable green and purple lettering.

For one brief second, Victoria Harper and I locked eyes. Then she was gone, disappearing out into the alleyway behind the Pinewood Performance Center, running fast toward the corner of Main and West Broadway.

"Jade! Jade! Who was that?" Mrs. Mason yelled as she, Marcus, and Mary finally rounded the corner of the theater. Had it taken them all that time just to get away from Mrs. B? The others were coming out of the stairwell now, all out of breath and frantic after how I'd run off.

Mrs. Mason met my eyes, silently processing everything I'd just seen. Victoria. Nora being taken. The woman in the silver dress suit—

Abruptly, Mrs. Mason's powers withdrew from my mind, her face ashen as she locked eyes with Yan Mei. If it was possible for my grandmother to look even more worried than before, then she did.

"Skylar, take Jade back to Mrs. Benson. Don't let her out of your sight until then," she said, voice completely unreadable. "Henry, go wait for me in the car."

"Grandma, we can help—"

"I think you've helped enough for one day," Yan Mei said, cutting him off with a stern look. "You three wanted a chance to prove yourselves, and we gave it to you. Jade jumped to conclusions. You sabotaged the mission for your own validation. The invisible force captured Nora, something I now unfortunately have to go explain to her family, and we came within a breath of losing Jade again as well."

"Wait, what?" I interrupted. "You mean that mind-control lady? Do you know who she is?"

"Nevermind that now—"

"You *do* know who she is! She was asking about my brother," I said, wheels turning inside my mind. What about this woman had put Yan Mei on the defensive? Did it have something to do with why Dylan's mom pulled out of my thoughts so fast? I thought back, trying to connect all the clues floating around in my brain. Was it possible I'd seen this woman before? "Wait, was that the lady I saw talking to Mary in my vision? Was she—"

"Jade, enough!" Yan Mei snapped, raising her voice just enough to make me sure she was *real* worried. "From now on, there will be no more missions. You will resume your self-defense training and continue trying to master your powers."

"You're shutting us out?" I asked. "But you'll still need my help to track down the invisible force."

"The Core 5 will contact you if we need you."

"Contact her?" Henry asked incredulously. "I only did what I did today because Jade was so sure it was Julian! Why does she get to help when she screwed up, but I don't?"

Yan Mei ignored him, motioning for Skylar to take me back to Mrs.

B. People were streaming down the sidewalk now. The show must have been over.

"Come on, Jade," Skylar said, tugging me back toward the parking lot. She still seemed upset, but forced a calm look across her face. She waited until we were out of earshot of the others to speak. "This isn't your fault, Jade."

"But it was my call-"

"This is *not* your fault," Skylar insisted, dark eyes pouring into me. "Blaming yourself is only going to make yourself feel worse. The Core 5 was in charge of this mission- it wasn't like we were communicating great either."

"There you are!" Mrs. B said in relief when we finally found her waiting by her car. "You were gone so long, I wasn't sure where you'd gotten to. You missed like half the show."

"The kids just got so interested watching everything from behind the scenes," Skylar lied, squeezing my shoulder slightly before heading back the way we'd come. I imagined the Core 5 was going to have a whopper of a meeting tonight, probably laying out in detail all the ways we'd screwed up. *This is not your fault*, Skylar's voice rang in my ears.

"Hey, are you okay, Jade?" Mrs. B asked, cutting into my thoughts. "You look upset."

I shook my head. "It's nothing. Just tired, I guess."

Mrs. B didn't look like she believed me, but she smiled anyway. "Nothing a little ice cream can't fix, huh? We don't have to tell the boys when we get home."

"Sounds good, Mrs. B," I said, finding a small smile despite myself. I was suddenly very relieved I got to ride home with Mrs. B and wasn't facing an awkward, angry car ride with our grandmother. I doubted Henry was getting ice cream on the way home.

CHAPTER
TWENTY-ONE

"I t's Friday, everyone, so you know what that means!" Mr. Nicholson announced happily, picking up a stack of papers from his desk. "Crossword Day!"

Fifth-period psychology let out a collective cheer as he started to pass around the printed-out puzzles. Thank God at least one teacher was cutting us some slack on midterm week. If I had to memorize one more calculus formula or important date for some dead dude in ancient Egypt, I was genuinely worried my head might explode.

"Um...Do you want to work together on the crossword?" a quiet voice asked, nearly making me jump out of my skin.

"How do you keep doing that?" I asked Julian in exasperation, halfway shocked that he'd even approached me at all.

It had been over two weeks since the fiasco at the Pinewood Performance Center, and Julian and I had said little to each other after he'd saved me from the mind-control lady. He seemed to have shrunk back into his quiet way of avoiding me again almost immediately, but every once in a while, I'd see him hurrying down the hall away from me as if he'd tried to say something then chickened out.

We were starting to draw attention, him standing over me like that. Mr. Nicholson always let people work together on Crossword Days, but while the rest of the class piled together and did it all at once, I always stayed put and finished it myself. Julian usually did, too.

I motioned for him to sit.

"So..." we both said at the same time. We laughed, though I felt like that only made things more awkward. Julian fidgeted nervously with the sleeves of his sweater, his hands no longer scraped up.

"Nice weather we're having?" he commented after a long silence, nodding over his shoulder at the downpour lashing the classroom windows.

"I can't tell if you're joking or not," I said.

Julian chuckled. "I'm not really good at talking to people."

"Eleven Across is *Amygdala*," I offered, turning my attention back to the crossword. Julian quickly scribbled down the answer. "Five Down is—"

"I'm sorry about taking off like that at the theater," he interrupted, keeping his voice low. "I just...I had to go."

"They could help you, you know," I said, keeping an eye on the girls working a few rows behind us to make sure they couldn't overhear. "They know how to teach people. Help them get better control. There's more of us than—"

Julian shook his head worriedly. "I can't get involved with them. I'd like to go with you, Jade, but...well, my dad's really strict."

"So strict he won't let you use your powers?" I asked, horrified. "That's terrible!"

"It's not that exactly," he said, shrugging. "My dad's always taught me how to keep my powers under control. It's just...all the others—it wouldn't work out."

That wasn't much of an explanation, but I didn't know how to convince him that Yan Mei could help. It had only been a few weeks since Palo and Skylar first started helping me try to get better control over my powers, and I'd drastically improved. I had smacked straight into Benson this morning and not had to endure some dorky flashback of him and Mrs. B when they were in college. That was a win in my book.

Though even if I could convince Julian, I doubted it would do much good now. Whoever that lady in the silver suit was, she had sent the Core 5 into full-blown crisis mode. Self-defense classes had been doubled for every student at the mall. The remainder of the Core 5 stayed holed up inside the Archive, trying to figure something out. I'd been called in twice in the last two weeks to see if I could get a vision off of something, but Yan Mei had insisted that Henry and I not go anywhere beyond home, school, the restaurant, and the mall. Dylan's parents had implemented a similar rule, though I wasn't sure if the sudden curfew was out of precaution or a punishment for how bad things had gone at the theater. Skylar was the only one of the Core 5 who hadn't gone all icy on us- in fact, I'd hung out with her so much for training in the last few weeks that it seemed like we were starting to become good friends. She still maintained that what had went down wasn't on us, but it was hard not to feel that way after my bad call with Julian.

None of us knew what was going on other than the adults were really worried. Susan, Antoine, and Nora had yet to be returned like all the others, even though they'd all been gone well over a week. Their families were going crazy. More people seemed to be vanishing, too— Dylan said he'd overheard his mom tell his dad that at least eleven people from the powered community were MIA. It was so stupid. One little mistake and I'd been shut out of nearly all of the Core 5's efforts to find the missing people. Who was that going to help? Not Antoine or Susan or Nora, that's for sure.

Two of the groups across the room brought me back to reality when they started arguing over the answer to Fourteen Across. Mr. Nicholson sighed and pushed himself away from his desk to resolve the situation.

"Can you at least tell me what you did to that lady?" I asked, grateful for the distraction to talk freely. The question had been bugging me ever since the theater. "I mean, I've never seen anybody who could—"

Julian looked reluctant, then suddenly smiled like he had an idea. "Tell you what, if you guess my powers, I'll guess yours. Fair enough?"

"I guess so."

Julian raised an eyebrow, looking at me expectantly. What were Julian's powers? He had saved me in the theater by touching that lady's head, and...then what? Making her run off? That didn't make much sense, but that's what I'd seen.

"You can do something with people's minds...Make them see things?" I whispered, thinking how Dylan's mom had let me see memories of her and my mom. An icy feeling suddenly crept through my chest. "Wait, you've not been able to read my mind this whole time, have you?"

Julian let out a loud laugh, something that almost seemed out of place with the rest of him for some reason. "No, no, I can't read minds."

"But you can do the other stuff?"

"In the theater," Julian said, ignoring my question, "when I saved you, you didn't seem shocked that I had powers. You know things before they happen, don't you?"

"That's only part of it," I said, glancing around to see if anyone was paying any attention to us. They weren't. "I can see the future and the past."

Julian's pencil clattered to the floor as he dropped it. "You—You can do what?"

"I could watch you brushing your teeth this morning if I wanted to."

Julian suddenly looked worried. "How does that work? Like can you just see it, or do you have to touch someone...?"

"Touch usually," I said, not really sure how to explain it. "I imagine that the memories are doors, and I just walk through the one I want."

He raised an eyebrow. "Why doors?"

"Haven't you seen *Monsters, Inc.*?" I asked incredulously. "Besides, it doesn't always work like that—I think that's just how my brain makes sense of it. I don't really know how it works. Sometimes I can see people really clearly, then sometimes I can't, like they're all blurry or something."

Julian pursed his lips. "Maybe you can't see people if you haven't actually *seen* them," he suggested curiously. "Like your brain can't make sense of them because it's never seen them before."

"Huh," I said. "I never thought about it that way before. Thanks, Julian."

"No prob—" The bell signaling the end of class cut him off. He looked a little sad that we'd run out of time.

"You'll need to bring those back next time if you want your class credit, kiddos," Mr. Nicholson said, eyeing our half-finished crosswords as he headed back toward his desk. He didn't really look mad that we'd spent the whole class talking, though—probably thought it was good that the two class introverts were actually socializing.

"Well, I guess I'll talk to you later," I said, hurriedly gathering my stuff. Where fifth period Friday meant calm crossword puzzle day, sixth period Friday meant Death-Match Dodgeball in PE. It was never a good idea to be late on a dodgeball day. I was dreading it, though at least Henry would be there for moral support. And cover. People always aimed for Henry before me.

"Yeah, later," Julian agreed, trying to stuff his crossword into his backpack without crumpling it up too badly. "Hey, Jade...would—um, would it be okay if I sat here again next time?"

"Sure," I said, smiling slightly. "And Julian, watch your back. There's someone going after people...you know, like us."

Julian nodded his head sadly. "Yeah, I know. You be careful too, Jade."

❧

"I'm telling you, I know what I saw, Henry!" I said, trying to keep my voice low and avoid a barrage of red rubber dodgeballs at the same time. "It had to be Victoria—blonde hair, a Pinewood Cheer hoodie! Exactly how many people at the theater were dressed like that?"

Henry scowled, dropping onto the basketball court to avoid getting nailed by a shot headed straight for his chest.

"No lying down during the game, Henry! On your feet!" Mrs. Ward barked, sending an ear-splitting whistle blast across the gym. The pack of jocks on the opposite team laughed, sending another volley toward the corner where we and a few other kids had taken refuge.

"It's not that I don't believe you, Jade," Henry said, yanking me back as the kid beside me got smacked in the shoulder by a ball. "I'm just saying, why would Victoria be backstage at the theater? She's never even been on Grandma's radar for people with powers."

I ducked. A kid yelped a few feet away as another ball hit his legs and sent him toppling. Henry and I ran for the opposite corner while the coast was clear.

"So what? Nearly everyone I've met since we moved to Pinewood has had powers! Is it really so impossible that Victoria could, too?"

Henry looked like he was going to be sick, and I had a feeling it wasn't from the dodgeball that had hit him in the stomach in round one. He was hiding something to do with Victoria. That much was obvious, but would he really cover for her if she was the one taking people with powers? I mean, sure, they had been friends once, but I couldn't believe Henry would do that.

I was so distracted I barely had time to catch a ball before it smacked into my face.

"Oh, come on! Knocked out by the swim nerd's girlfriend!" a basketball guy complained, sulking over to the bleachers to wait with the other kids who'd been eliminated.

"He is *not* my boyfriend!" I protested, hurling a dodgeball back at one of the smirking football guys. It missed horribly, and I had to dodge as Victoria scooped it up, sending it back at me with blinding speed. Henry half-tackled me to keep me out of the way.

"Ooh, trouble in paradise!" a dark-haired girl said in a sing-songy voice.

"I heard the two of them snuck off during that stupid show for English class," another boy snickered.

"That's not what happened, and you know it, Brian!" Victoria snapped. I was so stunned she was standing up for me that I nearly got taken out by one of her teammate's throws.

"Yeah!" Henry called, suddenly empowered. "What Jade and Dylan do behind closed doors is their own business!"

The whole gym burst into laughter.

I glared at Henry. "In what universe did you think that was a helpful thing to say?"

Brian wiped his eyes like he was crying. "Oh, this is too funny!"

Victoria lobbed a ball straight into the guy's gut, glaring daggers at our teacher for not getting involved. "Hey! Leave them alone!"

He raised his dodgeball to hit her right back, but another sharp whistle blast sounded from Mrs. Ward.

"Team One, no friendly fire! Resume play!"

As expected, the first dodgeball thrown went hurling straight at me. Henry pushed me down, and we dropped hard onto the floor.

"Jade and Henry, what did I say about laying down during the game!"

Henry rolled his eyes and ignored our teacher. "See? I told you Victoria wasn't bad. Would she stand up for you like that if she was the invisible force?"

Brian and his team seemed to have newfound energy. I barely had time to get out of the way before three shots took out the two girls crouching by the wall behind us.

"Not unless she was covering her tracks. Something *is* going on with her, Henry!" I said, ducking as another ball flew over my head. "I know you know what!"

Another two dodgeballs flew straight at us. There were ten people still left on Team One and only four—*SMACK!*—make that three people left on ours. There couldn't have been much more time left in class, could there?

"I don't know anything about Victoria!" Henry said, his voice cracking as he waved his hands dismissively.

"You know *everything* about Victoria!" I argued. "Tell me!"

"No!" Henry looked like he was about to say something else but was cut short by a dodgeball smacking right into his face. I winced. Oops. Maybe I had distracted him a little *too* much. "OW! My face! My beautiful face! It just healed, too!"

Another whistle blast. Everyone froze as Mrs. Ward marched onto the court and looked Henry's face over. "Eh, you'll be fine," she said, eyes turning to the other team. "Alright, what wise guy threw a headshot?"

The other team shrank back under the full evil eye of Molly "The Warden" Ward. Victoria cringed and reluctantly raised her hand.

"That wasn't on purpose, Mrs. Ward," she said quietly.

Henry suddenly straightened up and finger-combed his hair. "No, no, it's cool. I'm fine—no big deal."

Mrs. Ward rolled her eyes. "I ought to give the three of you detention for all the disruptions today—"

"But it's literally the last day of school before fall break," Henry protested. "And I got hit in the face!"

"I thought you said it was no big deal?" I asked innocently.

Henry shot a wary glance at Victoria's still mortified face. "Of course, it isn't. I'm made of steel, practically indestructible—"

The final bell rang, signaling that the weekend and the first break of the school year had arrived. Mrs. Ward waved us off, a clear sign we should go before she changed her mind about detention.

"Sorry about that," Victoria said, falling into step beside Henry and me as we headed out of the gym. "I really didn't mean to hit you in the face."

Henry opened his mouth, but nothing came out—as if he'd hit his daily limit of things he could say to Victoria, and his brain had shut down. I didn't get a chance to see if he'd snap out of it before Mr. Goodman stepped out in front of us.

I knew Mr. Goodman had been sick off and on since the beginning of the year, but he looked even worse now than he had before his treatments. His skin was pale and gaunt like he hadn't rested in weeks, he'd lost weight he couldn't afford to lose, and his hair was greasy and disheveled. He looked like Benson had when he'd tried to write his dissertation the week Tommy was born. It was not a good look.

"Victoria, could I speak with you for a moment?" His eyes flicked to me and Henry. "Shouldn't you two be heading for the bus?"

"Um, I drive," Henry said, clearly aware of the irritated look in Mr. Goodman's eyes. Something in my brain sounded alarm bells. I had never seen Mr. Goodman be unkind to anybody, yet here he was, glaring at me and Henry like we were demon spawn. Victoria sent me a wary glance, and I could tell she was picking up on the bad vibe, too.

"I'm actually late for cheer practice right now, Mr. Goodman," she said, choosing her words carefully. "Can we maybe talk another time?"

His face was so harsh I was suddenly worried he was going to start yelling at us. Mr. Goodman looked at Henry and me again with that strange, angry look before shooing us on. "Fine, fine. Later then," he said, clutching his side like he was in pain. "But we will talk later."

"Uh-huh," Victoria responded, sounding very much like they would definitely *not* be talking later. She grabbed Henry's arm and started tugging him forward. "Well, come on, guys."

"Are we all going to cheer practice?" Henry said dreamily, a goofy smile plastered across his face.

I glanced back, keeping an eye on Mr. Goodman until we rounded the next corner. His dark eyes watched us sharply until we were well down the hall. Why did he look so sick again all of a sudden? Why be so snippy? I'd never even heard him raise his voice since I started at Pinewood. Maybe he was having a bad day?

I was so focused on him that I didn't realize my phone was buzzing until Henry pointed it out.

Victoria suddenly dropped her hold on his arm, as if just realizing she was still holding it. "Well, I've gotta go. Sorry about your face, Henry."

"It's okay! It was a pleasure!" he said, though suddenly his face fell. "Wait, no! That's not what I meant—and...she's already gone. You know, if you two don't stop hitting me, you're not going to have this gorgeous face to look at anymore."

"We might have bigger problems than that," I said, eyes frozen to the words on my cell phone's screen. My stomach felt like acid.

"Why does Grandma text you and not me?" Henry asked incredulously, reading over my shoulder. Suddenly, his goofy grin faded.

Marcus taken. Have Henry drive you straight home. Stay there. Will contact when we know more.

"They got Marcus?" Henry squeaked, suddenly herding me toward the closest doors to the parking lot. "That dude was super powerful. If they got him...there's only three leaders of the powered community left: Grandma, Skylar, and Mrs. Mason."

"It's getting worse," I whispered as we passed a crowd of kids in the computer lab. "More people are vanishing, and no one's come back since Susan and Antoine. Things are out of control."

Henry nodded gravely. "I'll take you home, then find Dylan. Maybe he'll be able to get something out of his dad. Mr. Mason couldn't keep a secret if his life depended on it."

We hit the doors and strode out into the parking lot. The storm had stopped for the moment, but the sky was dark and churning with anger. I felt the same way. I hadn't seen a sky so sad since the one my mother had summoned in the vision I'd seen of her and Yan Mei.

We were supposed to all be doing this together—me and Lance, Michael and Trisha, and now Jessica and Chris, my mother had said.

I suddenly wondered if all the disappearances would have been stopped weeks ago if mine and Henry's parents were still around to help lead. Maybe the reason the powered community couldn't get a handle on the invisible force wasn't because they weren't strong enough, but because they weren't working together enough—like the way Palo and Skylar had been teaching Henry, Dylan, and I to do in training. Sure, the theater had been a disaster, but we hadn't really been working together then either. Maybe if we could, though...

"Call me the second you know something," I said, clambering into the Yan Mei's Cafe van beside Henry. He looked at me worriedly.

"But what if we don't find out anything? The grown-ups have had us boxed out for two weeks—"

"We're gonna stop this thing, Henry," I said, startled by how confident my own voice sounded. "And we're going to do this together."

CHAPTER
TWENTY-TWO

Regret may have been one of the things crossing my mind as I lingered outside the basement window to Henry's bedroom—something that was fairly obvious with said window's curtains being open and the nerdy figurines in spacesuits and superhero costumes all over the room.

Sneaking out of the house had been easier than I'd thought. Benson was working late at Graves *again*—something about DNA, comparative mapping, and a bunch of other things I didn't understand. Tommy had a cold, so Mrs. B was fully occupied. I didn't *have* to sneak out, per se. But talking to my adoptive parent while she was in "My poor baby!" mode was definitely not something I had the energy for. The distressed mother was bustling around the house, armed with an ice pack, Tylenol, and a steaming bowl of chicken soup. Last time, I'd gotten roped into a movie marathon while she checked my temperature every fifteen minutes. No thanks.

With my bedroom door locked, I did what Henry couldn't: climbed out of my window. It wasn't nearly as bad as I had initially thought, and I was able to climb down the old ivy-covered lattice with ease. Something I fully intended to rub in Henry's face.

That was, after I made him spill what he knew about Victoria.

She was suspicious, and I was certain Henry was protecting her. He'd tried to brush me off during gym, but there was no way he was avoiding me this time. I kept trying to tell myself that Victoria wasn't another Ashley situation like at my last school, but I'd learned my lesson after that one. Never trust anyone blindly, no matter how much you wanted to believe they were good.

I reached down to check if the window was unlocked. To my surprise, though it really shouldn't have been surprising, it was. I made a mental note to chastise him for leaving himself and his home vulnerable when there was a supervillain on the loose as I slid the window open and hopped through, stepping down onto Henry's desk.

The stench of body odor and cologne lingered in the air. I could see why my cousin chose to leave the window open. It was worth the safety risk. If I was ever brave enough to come here again, I would not be returning without Febreeze and some room fans.

Once I had gotten accustomed to the rank teen-boy stench, I could fully appreciate the rest of the room. The glimpse of nerd memorabilia from the window was nothing compared to the entire room. The comic book-themed covers were at least made on his twin bed. That was probably the only thing tidy about the room. Ramen containers, chips, and soda cans littered the small wooden desk. There were candy wrappers on the floor, and the laundry was neatly tossed just outside of the hamper. What a slob.

On the bedside table, next to an empty two-liter of soda, was a small picture frame. Henry and Victoria cheesing together at the carnival. I recognized the younger pair from my vision. I smiled, recalling the events like I was actually there.

The doorknob to the room jostled. I braced myself for the chaos and unexpected that was Henry in his natural habitat.

When the door opened, Henry screamed. Like a girl.

And with a *poof*, he turned into a lamp.

I slapped my hand to my face. Of course he would do that.

What I wasn't expecting, however, was the concerned voice of Dylan rushing over to Lamp-Henry.

Crap. What was he doing here? Well, I guess it wasn't too out of the ordinary, but today of all days when—

"Henry? Why are you a—" Dylan's words were cut off when he looked into Henry's room and saw me grinning sheepishly. He gave me a half-wave. "Jade?"

"Hi," I said.

Dylan nudged Lamp-Henry. "Snap out of it."

With another *poof*, Henry emerged, sitting on the floor with wide eyes. "I never expected *you* to sneak into *my* room."

"Why not? You did it to me!"

Dylan frowned. "And nobody invited me?"

"Aw, sad Dylan," Henry said. "But clearly, you are the only person in this room who has yet to sneak into someone's window. Sometimes, you're going to miss out if you're not brave enough, my friend."

"But you came in to talk about...you know what? Never mind, forget I said anything," I said nervously.

Henry shot me a wink as he sat down at his desk. "Exactly."

Dylan rolled his eyes before turning toward me. "First off, if I left my room or someone came in, my mother would know, and it would defeat the purpose of not using the front door. Second, not that we don't love to see you, Jade, but why are you here?"

I felt both pairs of eyes on me and cleared my throat. *Here goes nothing.* "I came for the truth about Victoria." I took a seat on the edge of Henry's bed. "Henry, I know you know something about her. I know you like her, but she could be dangerous."

His happy smile instantly dissipated into a sharp frown. "I'm telling you, Jade. She doesn't have anything to do with this. Drop it, please."

"Then why was she backstage at the theater? Why was she running away from us after the adults showed up—if she didn't have anything to hide, she would've stayed put!"

Henry opened his mouth, ready to defend his precious crush, when Dylan put a hand on his shoulder.

"Jade," Dylan said calmly, eyes pleading with me to drop the subject, "maybe we shouldn't bring Victoria into this."

I rolled my eyes, feeling a bubble of anger rising up in my chest. I didn't want to fight with Henry, but I wasn't about to drop the matter just to spare his feelings when all the evidence pointed toward Victoria. There were over a dozen people missing! Lives could be at stake! "But

206

what if she's the one taking people? She was with Mary before she vanished. She was at the swim meet—"

"Wait, what?" Dylan asked. I'd never actually planned to explain my visions in detail to the boys unless I was certain about Victoria—which, after the theater, I *was*—I didn't want to bring it up to them. "What do you mean she was with Mary?"

"Victoria was the last person Mary talked to before she vanished. I saw it in a vision when I looked through Mary's tampered memories," I said.

"It doesn't matter if she was," Henry said. "Victoria didn't kidnap Mary Milford!"

"You don't know that, Henry!" I snapped, clenching my fists so tight they hurt.

He glared at me. "Neither do you! You were so confident it was Julian until...what? He stopped ignoring your existence for two seconds? Wasn't he at the swim meet, too? Didn't he have marks on his hands? Oh, but of course, it can't be him!"

"He saved me from the woman with freaky mind powers!" I shouted.

"Or he made you *think* he saved you. You could be his next target for all we know."

"Trust me, as vulnerable as I was, no kidnapper would've missed that opportunity. You're just trying to throw the blame off Victoria," I said.

Dylan looked at both of us with a worried expression, but we paid it no mind. Henry shot up from his seat.

"Because I *know* she's innocent!" Henry huffed, throwing his hands up in frustration.

I shot up as well, staring him down. "How do you *know*, then?" I asked. "Tell me why she's innocent, and I'll believe it."

He paused, his temper faulting for a moment. Henry looked down at the ground with a somber look. "I can't tell you."

Seriously? Did he not see how shady that looked?!

"Why not? If you want to prove her innocence so bad, what is it? Henry, if she's hurting people, you can't just—"

"She's not hurting *anyone!* Just back off, Jade!" Henry snapped.

Dylan stood between the two of us, ready to stand as mediator as always, but this was not something I was willing to let go. She had evidence against her, and he knew *something*.

"Jade," Dylan said softly. "Maybe we could talk about this another time."

"No! Are you kidding me? If that invisible person is taking people, going after people like *us*, then we don't have time to talk about it later. We need to catch them *now*!" I said.

His frown deepened. "I know, and I agree with you, but maybe we should calm down a bit."

"So we're just going to ignore all the evidence against Victoria and wait until another person gets kidnapped? Dylan, they went after *you*. They went after our classmates. They're not even scared of the Core 5! What if they try to take you again or someone you care about?" I asked.

Dylan stood silently, looking at the ground. It was clear I had made him uncomfortable. Perhaps he had been thinking similar thoughts to what I said. But maybe Dylan *was* right. Maybe we did need to calm down. I didn't want to yell at Henry. I just needed to solve this before someone else got hurt...and if Victoria was the bad guy, then Henry *would* get hurt.

"So, now you're taking Jade's side? Is that how it is now? Stupid Henry being ridiculous again?" Henry said.

"You know that's not—" Dylan said.

"Yes, it is! Nobody takes me seriously. Nobody listens to me. It doesn't matter what I do. I will just be the funny guy who tries too hard," Henry said. "But not Jade. She's the shining *star* around here."

My jaw dropped for a moment before I put my hand on my hip. "Excuse me? Weren't we *both* being chewed out by our grandmother?"

Henry scoffed. "Oh, please, you got off with a wag of a finger. I'm the one who really took the fall. Like always. Grandma never let me into the Archive. She didn't even want me to *go* to the theater. You've only been here a few months, and you're already the golden grandchild."

"Now you're being ridiculous," I said. "I'm not competing with you. I'm trying to help you!"

He threw his hands up in frustration. "I don't need help from *you*! Before you got here, I was doing alright. The Core 5 didn't let me into meetings, but it seemed like I was getting *somewhere*. I didn't have to hear about how amazing you are every five seconds..." Henry trailed off.

Dylan tried to put a hand on Henry's shoulder, but he shrugged it off. "Henry, you're out of line."

Henry narrowed his eyes. "No, Dylan. Someone needs to say it to her, and clearly, it's not going to be *you.*"

Why was he so angry with me? I knew he was irritated recently, but I never thought it was because of me. Did I really bother him that much?

"If this is about Victoria..." I trailed off, suddenly unsure.

"This isn't just about Victoria! This is about how you are ruining everything! I've had nothing but embarrassment since you showed up, Jade. You know how many times I've been hit in the face or covered in food or heckled for trying to look out for you? I'm sick of it! We would be better off if you'd never showed up!" Henry said.

I staggered back like he'd slapped me in the face. Honestly, a slap would've hurt less. My chest felt like ice. Hot tears brimmed behind my eyes. All the air had been knocked out of my lungs.

My long-lost family didn't even want me.

Dylan was shouting at Henry, but I couldn't make out what he was saying. I stayed silent, feeling the warm droplets slide down my cheeks.

"If that's how you feel, I won't bother you again," I said, interrupting whatever Dylan was saying. He snapped his eyes toward me as I made my way back toward the window.

"Wait! Jade!" Dylan shouted after me.

I ignored him and climbed back out of the window, dusting my pants off and wiping my eyes. It was embarrassing enough that not one but two people saw my sob fest. Dylan followed shortly behind me, clearly not getting the memo.

"Dylan," I said as more tears decided to leak from my face, "I think Henry needs a friend right now."

He was silent for a moment, his mouth slightly ajar, before composing himself. "But what about you?"

I tried to laugh, but it came out as a half-choked sob, and I wanted to slap all emotions out of me. "I think I need some space."

He paused for a second, face torn. "Okay, but please promise me you'll keep in touch. Henry is important to me, but so are you. I'm here for you, too," Dylan said.

I rushed over before my mind changed and quickly hugged the very confused Dylan before running off. He stood in the same spot, frozen, when I turned away from him and started up the driveway.

I was halfway across the yard before the tears really started falling. I tried to keep them in, but it felt like there was a dagger in my chest. The tears blurred my vision, and I fought the urge to break out into a run. I didn't even see someone coming out of the house next door.

CRASH.

I fell to the ground with a less-than-graceful fall. Ugh. Groaning and disoriented, I looked to see what I had clashed with.

"We really have to stop doing that," I said.

Julian was rubbing his head, also plopped onto the ground from our sudden impact.

"I would make a joke, but my head hurts," Julian said. He brushed himself off as he stood before offering his hand to me and helping me off the ground. Suddenly, his eyes went wide with panic. "Oh, Jade! I'm so sorry. I didn't mean to hurt you!"

I stared at him for a moment, wondering where his sudden panic came from before I realized that he had likely seen the remnants of tears from my prior conversation. I hated emotions.

"Oh, you didn't. It's just been...a really bad day, that's all."

His face was an open book. First, he was relieved that he hadn't, in fact, injured me with our random collision. Next, he panicked. If he was anything like me, he probably had no idea what to do when another person was upset. Something told me that we had that in common.

"Well, I'm not really good at fixing things—really I cause a lot of harm, especially to ceramic mugs, but we could go get some tea..." He trailed off, seeing my frown. "Or coffee. I know a place that has really good selections of both. I think you'll like it...If you want, that is."

I pondered his offer for a moment. Honestly, I was emotionally drained and had planned to wallow my night away with ice cream and my favorite movie. But I could tell that Julian was really trying to be helpful. And, given what Henry said, it felt nice to have someone *want* me around.

"Alright, show me the caffeinated place."

Julian laughed at my antics and started to lead us further down the street. It was then I noticed the house where Julian had been coming from. Henry's next-door neighbor: Victoria Harper herself, the girl I was trying to prove was our invisible kidnapper and the reason Henry was very angry with me.

Thinking of my cousin only made my chest ache. The fight mere minutes ago was still raw in my mind. Henry, the boy who had invited me so eagerly into his group, who seemed so happy that we were a family...I didn't think I could screw things up this badly after such a short amount of time.

Realizing I had been lost in my thoughts, I looked to Julian, who gave me a soft smile before looking on. Whether he didn't know what to say or if he was giving me space to sort out my thoughts, I was grateful.

We made our way toward the center of town, not too far from my house. An area I was *very* familiar with and not particularly happy to be walking toward. A pit formed in my chest as we got closer to the neon sign for Yan Mei's restaurant. I turned toward Julian, ready to demand we go somewhere else, when he led us to a small building nearby.

The London Fog. The place Julian had come out of when we first met. A time we had also crashed into each other.

"Isn't this where you bought a bunch of boxes of tea?" I asked.

Julian flushed. "You remember that?"

"I can't say I've ever seen a person carrying that much tea. I hope you weren't planning on dumping any into the harbor?"

Julian gave an exaggerated gasp. "As if I could waste such fine tea. Have some respect!"

We laughed. I was happy to see Julian more comfortable, and after that fight...I really needed a laugh. My darkening thoughts caused the almost forgotten tears to make a reappearance, but I did my best to shake it off and at least try to have a good time.

"I hope this place has espresso. I need a double," I said, opening the door.

We walked inside, and I was immediately calmed by the charming atmosphere. It was a small cafe with dimmed lights and large windows on the side. Fairy lights were scattered across the ceiling, with at least a dozen hanging plants. A chalkboard menu on an easel displayed the various drinks of the day. Soft piano music played in the background. The smell of coffee beans and freshly baked muffins almost made me sigh.

"Alright, I love this place," I decided.

Julian chuckled. "Just wait until you place your order. Have you ever had a scone?"

I shook my head, very intrigued. Though, to be honest, it wasn't really that hard to capture my interest with food.

"Try the chocolate one. I've heard that goes well with coffee. I'll be getting my usual."

The normalcy of the conversation put my mind at ease. I didn't have to think about powers, missing people, or anything connected with the Chinese food restaurant a few steps away. For now, I could just be Jade. And Julian was very easy to talk to. I felt comfortable around him. Not in the same way as Dylan...more familial, like he could be a long-lost family member as well.

"Jade?" a familiar voice called.

Julian and I looked over to see none other than Benson, with another man sitting beside him.

"Benson?" I asked.

"Father?" Julian asked.

"Wait, what?" I said, really confused, until I realized he was talking about the other man.

We walked over to the table they were sitting at.

So this was the infamous Dominic Graves Benson worked for? He had dark hair with light blue eyes that contrasted Julian's brown. He must have shared the same eyes, curls, and skin tone with his mother, whom Julian had never mentioned. I made a mental note to bring up the subject at a later time.

Dominic was dressed nicely in slacks with a navy blue sweater vest and tie, complementing a white button-down underneath. It was clear who Julian's style was inspired by. The coat slung over his chair matched the one Benson had on, the Graves Research logo embroidered over the heart.

"Jade, it's so lovely to meet you," Dominic said, his voice low and soothing. For some reason, I almost thought it sounded familiar. "I've heard so much about you...from both of these two, actually."

I briefly wondered what Julian had said about me to his father. Did Dominic have powers like his son? At this point, I wouldn't have been surprised if the Bensons were the only people in Pinewood who didn't have powers.

I nodded politely. "Thank you, it's nice to meet you too."

"How about you guys join us?" Dominic asked.

Julian looked at me, and I shrugged, pulling up a chair to the table.

"I'll go take our order," Julian said before walking to the counter, leaving me with Benson and Dominic.

"Small world, isn't it?" Benson asked, dumping a massive scoop of sugar into his coffee. "It's so weird that we would be running into each other like this."

Dominic nodded. "Yes, indeed."

"Do you guys stop at the cafe often?" I asked, curious. I knew Benson had been staying late at Graves almost every night recently and how tired he was. He hadn't been to one of Tommy's soccer games in over a month. He'd never missed those before.

"Unfortunately, we've been very busy recently," Dominic said apologetically. "We've had a small breakthrough in our research, and while that's wonderful...work can be a bit hectic. I'm just showing Benjamin a token of my gratitude. After all, he was the one who made the discovery. We're very lucky to have him."

Benson smiled and scratched the back of his neck. "I'm just doing my job. I do appreciate the coffee, though."

I smiled at Benson. He was shrugging it off, but I figured you had to do something pretty important to get the CEO of your company to take you out for coffee. Benson had been offered the Graves position so out of the blue that I knew he'd been nervous about switching—I was glad he was excelling.

Julian returned with two full hands of coffee, tea, and baked goods. Dominic gave him a strange look of approval, like he was happy he was being such a gentleman.

"One chocolate scone and vanilla latte—double espresso," he said, setting my items down in front of me. The scone smelled delicious, but

I was extremely eager for the coffee and took a quick sip. I sighed, the warmth flooding down my chest. Nothing like caffeine to drown out sadness. In an odd way, I felt like I was going through a breakup. A family...breakup.

Clearly, I needed to focus on the conversation at hand because I had three pairs of eyes staring at me.

"Maybe next time I should order one of those." Benson chuckled. Julian and his father smiled.

"It is delicious," I said, turning to Julian, who was setting his items down. "What did you get?"

"Earl Grey, no sugar, and a blueberry scone," he said. His tea had a very distinct smell, like black tea, but with something else, I couldn't put the name on.

"He's rather fond of that," Dominic said. "He gets it every time we're here."

Julian gave his dad a look but didn't protest. He sighed pleasantly as he took a drink.

Benson sipped his coffee. "Will you guys be going to the festival coming up? We haven't been here that long, but I've heard how big it is."

"Oh, yeah." Julian laughed eagerly. "I wouldn't miss the chance to pie Dad in the face."

Dominic rolled his eyes. "Graves Research always sponsors the pie-throwing booth. Julian here always makes it his goal to land one on me. I think he just enjoys tormenting his old dad."

"It's fun." Julian shrugged, taking a bite of his scone.

"I'd love to see that—no offense," I said, turning to Dominic.

He gave a gentle smile. "None taken. In fact, you should join us. We'd love to see you there with the rest of your family."

Benson looked at me nervously. I was never exactly thrilled with going on family outings with them. I had honestly thought I would be going with Dylan and Henry. Thinking of the two now just made me sad. Even if Dylan had no part in hurting my feelings, he was so closely tied to Henry that being around the two again...just hurt. So much for that. But I needed to give the Bensons a fair shot. They at least deserved that for putting up with me.

"That sounds great," I said.

Benson looked like he visibly exhaled. I wanted to laugh at him but chose not to and took a bite of my scone. I was unprepared for the sweet, chocolatey goodness. It had a warm, flakey breading. It took actual restraint to not shovel the entire thing down.

"Julian, this is delicious!" I said.

"If you think this is good, you should try the kind he makes at home," Dominic said.

Huh, maybe there was a lot more to Julian than I realized. "You bake too? Can you do everything?" I asked.

"He's exaggerating, but I appreciate that you don't think I'm some weirdo," Julian said.

"No, that's really cool. If they're anything like these, I will happily try them anytime," I said, probably a little too enthusiastic.

"Well, that settles it," Dominic said. "Jade seems like someone you shouldn't deny."

Benson paled. "She gets it from my wife."

Everyone at the table laughed. Dominic's phone buzzed. He frowned at the message before tucking his phone away.

"I'm so sorry to be rude, but unfortunately, I'm needed back at the lab," Dominic said.

"Do I need to head back with you?" Benson asked, starting to get up as well.

"No, no. You should enjoy your time with your family. But I will see you tomorrow," he said, waving him off. "Oh, and Jade, it was so nice to meet you. I do hope to see you at the festival. I'm sure this year will be the most exciting one yet."

"I look forward to it," I said.

Julian stood up as well. "I guess this is my cue to go home. I've got homework I need to finish anyway—Victoria and I barely got anywhere on that stupid English project tonight. I'll see you at school, Jade."

Even though I'd never really hung out with Julian before, I was surprised to find I was sad to see him leave. I was actually starting to feel a little better.

"See you! Thanks for the coffee and...everything," I said, waving to him as he walked away. I didn't want to say in front of Benson why he had offered to take me here in the first place.

"So, uh, do you really want to go with us?" Benson asked, eyeing me cautiously. "We figured you were planning on going with Dylan and Henry."

I cringed at their names. "I won't be going with them. We...sort of had a disagreement. With Henry, not Dylan. I'm just...getting some space."

Benson looked concerned. "Is everything alright, Jade? I mean, this isn't like before...with Ashley, is it?"

Meaning they pretended to be my friends then gossiped about me to the entire school. Completely cut me out when I got in trouble. Dropped off the face of the earth after school was over. Normally, I would have been angry with him for prying, but I could tell from his expression that Benson was genuinely worried- I did have a pretty tough time after last year. I guess maybe the Bensons had always cared more than I'd given them credit for. It's not like they knew I had powers.

"Yeah, yeah. Just, you know—high school stuff. It's complicated," I said.

Benson nodded in understanding. "Yes, definitely. I remember those days for me—they weren't very fun. But we're here for you if you need anything...You know that, right?"

I smiled. Suddenly, Benson paled. I raised my eyebrows.

"Charlotte is going to be crushed," he said, sipping his coffee morosely. "She liked Henry."

"Ugh," I groaned. "She's going to start stress baking again."

"You know what, let me talk to her about it. I'll handle it," he said. "And don't feel pressured to go with us to the festival if you don't want to. We respect your space."

"I would be happy to go with you guys," I said.

Benson smiled. We chatted a little longer while I finished my scone and coffee—for the first time in a long time, it was surprisingly easy to speak with Benson.

"This stuff is delicious!" I said, putting down my now-empty mug.

Benson chuckled. "What kind is that?"

"I think Julian said something about a vanilla latte."

"I'll have to try it out sometime," he said. "Well, would you like to go home?"

I could tell he was nervous again, probably wondering if I wanted to walk home myself. I really had been kind of harsh with him.

"Sounds good," I said, yawning. "I'm beat."

"You just had coffee." Benson chuckled.

I shrugged. "It's been a long day."

"That, I understand."

CHAPTER
TWENTY-THREE

2 *new messages from Dylan.*
1 new message from Julian.
46 new messages from Henry.

I tossed my phone to the other side of the bed, flopping back against the pillows. Two days. It had been two days since Henry and I had fought, triggering an almost constant stream of apology texts from my cousin. Dylan kept telling me that he hadn't meant any of it—that Henry was notorious for bottling stuff up until he couldn't deal with it anymore.

We would be better off if you never showed up!

I wished I could believe that.

A small knock drew my attention to the door. Tommy poked his head in, Benson and Mrs. B behind him.

"Can we come in?" he asked, eyes locked worriedly on the small flock of plush owls roosting on top of my bookshelf.

I sat up, not sure what to do. Why was everyone here? Had I done something wrong? No, that didn't seem right. They didn't look angry. Just...tentative. Cautious.

"Is this an intervention?" I asked, deciding humor was the safest option. Well...unless this really was an intervention, in which case that joke might not have gone over great.

"No," Mrs. B said, fighting off a smile as she nudged Tommy forward. "Tommy has something he wants to say to you."

Well, this definitely can't be good, then...

"A few weeks ago," he started, blue eyes fixed firmly on his sneakers, "when I took your journal...I didn't know why it was so important to you. I didn't know all that stuff about your real mom's name and how Mom and Dad got you. I-I just wanted to say I'm sorry."

My jaw was on the floor. I didn't know what to say. "You already apologized for that, Tommy."

He shook his head, eyes darting up to mine for the first time. "I know. But until Mom explained...well, I just wanted you to know that I get it now. I won't bother your journal anymore. Promise."

"Tell Jade the second part, bud," Benson said, smiling at his son encouragingly. "Your idea."

"Idea?" I asked, not sure where this was going. Tommy's ideas concerning me usually involved hiding my stuff or sneaking fake spiders into my bag (a plan that *totally* backfired on him, by the way).

Tommy's gaze flicked up to me shyly. "Well, Mom and Dad explained how they used to live here in Pinewood...how they got you but didn't know anything about your birth family. So, I just kind of said, 'Well, aren't there records?'"

"Something your da—" Mrs. B caught herself. "Something Benji and I hadn't thought about having access to again now that we were back in town."

My heart started to pound against my chest. I wasn't sure I'd heard her right. "What are you saying, Mrs. B?"

"I'm saying that your brother decided to do some digging," she said, fighting off a proud grin as Tommy stepped forward, holding out a file folder.

"It's not much, but we were able to find out a little bit," he said. "If you want to know. You don't have to read it if you don't—"

"No, I want to!" I said, doing my best not to snatch the folder straight out of his hands.

Never in my life did I think that my brother—annoying, obnoxious *Tommy*—would have done so much just to try to make me feel better. Is that what he'd been up to all this time? I noticed he'd been acting differently around me over the last few weeks—no pranks, no jokes—but I never would have imagined he was up to all this. Better question: why hadn't *I* thought to go look up my own records?

"Have any of you seen this yet?"

The Bensons all shook their heads.

"We figured you'd want to see it first," Benson said, putting an arm around his wife.

Trying to keep my hands from shaking too badly, I opened the folder.

"Birth Certificate: Jade Olivia Kastel," I read, ignoring Tommy as he climbed on the bed to read over my shoulder. "Date of birth: October thirtieth. Name of parents: Lance Reeves Kastel; Vivian Walker Kastel. Birth: single, double, or multiple."

"Yours says double," Tommy said, looking up curiously. "What's that mean?"

"It says what now?" Mrs. B asked, breaking away from Benson to look at the paper in my hands as well. Her eyes darted across the page. "My goodness...it does say that. The copy the hospital gave us didn't mention anything like that."

"Meaning?" Tommy insisted, raising an eyebrow.

"Meaning I have a twin brother," I said, voice barely above a whisper.

Benson sat down on the edge of the bed. "We can't be sure if it was a boy, Jade."

Pretty sure we can, I thought, though I knew I couldn't very well explain *how* I knew that.

"Just a gut feeling," I said, tracing my fingers over the names of my birth parents. I mean, I already knew their names from the journal and from what Yan Mei had told me, but there was something different about seeing the words written out on paper. Something more official. Confirmation that, at some point, my parents' were real people. That, for a moment, we were all a real family. Together. A warm feeling started to spread throughout my chest.

"You have a *twin*?" Tommy asked in surprise. "That's so cool! Do you have telepathy? Is that why you're zoned out all the time?"

If only you knew...

"I don't think I have telepathy, Tommy," I said, chuckling despite myself.

"Jade," Mrs. B said, drawing my attention back to her, "your mother's maiden name...Isn't that the same last name as your friend Henry?"

I swallowed hard, trying to ignore the lump in my throat at the mention of Henry or the fact that Mrs. B's voice had cracked slightly on the word *mother*. All eyes were on me, but no one said anything for a long time.

"I have a confession to make," I said, fumbling for the right words. "Back when we first moved to Pinewood...when I started hanging out with Dylan and Henry, well, I might have had more reason to hang out with them than just a school project."

I waited for someone to interrupt me, but no one did. Benson looked like his brain was going a mile a minute. Tommy seemed confused. Mrs. B squeezed my hand, encouraging me to go on.

"Mrs. Yan Mei, Henry's grandma, she recognized my last name when we were introduced," I said, trying to figure out how much of the truth to spill without saying anything about, well, you know...everything. "We swapped stories. I knew my mom's name from the journal; Yan Mei's daughter was named Vivian. Yan Mei had a granddaughter born around when I was. Basically, things started to match up."

"So, you're saying the lady from the Chinese food place..." Benson started, apparently not sure how to finish the thought.

"Is my grandmother, yes. Same as Henry," I said, fidgeting anxiously with the edge of my blanket. "His dad would have been my uncle."

Tommy still looked confused. "But you don't look anything like Henry."

"Yan Mei's husband looked more like me," I said, not sure how else to explain it to a nine-year-old. "Me and my mother."

"So, you've known your birth family this entire time," Benson said, shaking his head in amazement. "I-I just thought you really liked hanging out at work. I never thought—"

"I know. It's a lot to process," I said, feeling a little relieved to admit out loud that I'd found at least some of my family. I hadn't realized how heavy the weight of keeping that secret had been. "I should have told you sooner. I just didn't know how."

Mrs. B's eyes met mine, clearly not sure where to start. "Did Yan Mei—your grandmother—know what happened? To your parents, I mean? Before Benson and I got you."

I shook my head. "She'd lost all contact years ago. Hadn't heard anything about her daughter's family until the day I walked into her restaurant a few weeks ago. She didn't even know what her grandchildren's names were."

"Grandchildren," Benson said, watching me curiously. "Meaning she knew there were twins. Which is how you know your twin was a boy."

"Exactly." I nodded.

"Do you think he's still here?" Tommy asked, clearly not knowing what to do with the information that I had a biological brother as well. That, or he was just ticked that he'd spent time researching a bunch of stuff I already knew.

"I mean, I guess my brother could still be in Pinewood," I said, mulling the thought over. "I've never really thought about it before, but the only reason we left here was because of Benson's job. If my brother got adopted like I did and his family didn't leave—"

The thought ran me over like a truck. If my brother had never left Pinewood like I did, then it was probably highly likely that he was still here. A boy. My age. I racked my brain, thinking of anyone around my age who might have even remotely looked like me. I could have walked past my brother at school or the mall or in the street every day and never even known.

Mrs. B seemed to sense I was spiraling and tightened her hold on my hand. "Yan Mei doesn't know if your brother's still here?"

"If he is, then she doesn't know about it."

"Jade, this argument between you and Henry...It didn't have anything to do with all this, did it?" Mrs. B asked tentatively. "It must have been pretty hard on both of you for all of this stuff to come out of nowhere. To suddenly have a family you didn't know about before..."

222

"I'm not the one who started this argument," I said, pretending not to notice that my phone had at least one new text from Henry.

Mrs. B eyed me knowingly. "Jade, if he's family—"

"I'll work it out with Henry when I'm ready," I said quickly, desperate for a subject change from my cousin. "Is my birth certificate the only thing you found?"

"There wasn't much else to find," Benson sighed, shaking his head slightly. "Tommy and I tried everywhere we could think of: public records, the adoption agency, newspapers. There's almost no mention of a Lance or Vivian Kastel anywhere."

"Isn't that weird?" I asked, feeling sure there should have been some sort of proof of my parents somewhere. Tommy had gotten his picture in the paper nearly any time there was a soccer game at his last school... How could two people live their entire lives in Pinewood and not leave any trace of their existence?

Unless someone didn't want *there to be any trace...*

I shook the thought out of my mind. I had enough trouble on my hands with Victoria and Henry without going all conspiracy brain about my parents.

"Thank you, guys," I said, voice catching slightly in my throat. "Thank you for finding this for me."

"We're your family, Jade," Mrs. B said, giving me a tight hug from behind. "If you want answers, then we do too."

"Yeah, but does this mean we get free Chinese food now or what?" Tommy asked, earning a round of laughter from all of us.

"I'll put in a word with Yan Mei," I said, earning a glare as I messed up his hair. "Better yet, it means now I've got a better middle name than Margaret."

Benson and Mrs. B feigned protest, but both of them were smiling.

And for the first time in a long time, the Bensons and I actually felt like the way we used to be.

~

Fall break plans: visit Nana Benson's, gain twenty-five pounds as a result of visiting Nana's, "help" Tommy work on his soccer (translation: get repeatedly hit by soccer ball), make cookies with Mrs. B, crush Benson at his nightly game of chess...Oh, yeah, and prove that I had been completely right about Victoria Harper being the invisible force.

As expected, this proved unusually hard.

For one thing, I was down a few team members. I still wasn't talking to Henry, though he'd sent me about sixty more texts in the few days we'd been gone to Nana's. There was always Dylan, but I figured he'd be all weird about going behind Henry's back to investigate Victoria. This left me two options.

Option One: Julian Graves, who I knew had powers but had been weirdly MIA for the last few days. He must have been busy. Luckily, Option Two, like me, apparently had no social life and was free.

"She couldn't just disappear," Mary Milford said, looking around the Pinewood Boardwalk in confusion as we tried to find Victoria for, like, the millionth time. We'd been following her for well over an hour since she'd left her house for a run, but Victoria was proving notoriously hard to track. "Teleportation seems to be a really rare power among us. Only eight percent probability."

"You've really been reading up on those books in the Archive, haven't you?" I said, trying to push through the crowd the way I thought Victoria had gone. "Besides, we know she can't teleport because she has invisibility. That's probably why we keep losing her."

Even for a weeknight, the boardwalk was crowded since school was out. Lots of kids from Pinewood High were roaming around with their siblings or friends, flitting in between the restaurants and arcades and rides. Brightly colored lights danced across the wooden sidewalks from the Ferris wheel as Mary and I tried to weave our way through all the people. Distant screams echoed as the slingshot ride whipped its next victims into the quickly darkening sky.

"I still only calculate a thirty-six percent chance that Victoria Harper is the invisible force," Mary said, repeating the same probability she'd been telling me ever since I'd texted her to pick me up. I had to bum a ride to my own stake-out. I really needed to get my driver's license. "Plus, Yan Mei is certain that neither of Victoria's parents have powers. That only leaves a seventeen percent chance that she would have powers at all."

"But literally everyone in Pinewood has powers!" I insisted, dodging a pack of teenagers coming out of the haunted house.

"Not every—" Mary started but stopped short when she saw my glare.

"Victoria was the last person you talked to before you vanished. Doesn't that increase her likelihood at all?" I said, eyes scanning the crowd for any sign of a tall, blonde, potential supervillain. "Where on earth does she keep disappearing too?"

"We've lost her approximately twenty-two times since she left her house," Mary said, totally not helping. "She tends to reappear every ten to twenty seconds, usually several yards from her original location. Meaning we should be catching sight of her again, right about... there!"

I looked where Mary was pointing, and sure enough, there was Victoria, ducking away from the boardwalk's main thoroughfare into a slightly quieter section. Within seconds, Mary and I were running, careful to keep her in sight before we could lose her again.

This stretch of the boardwalk was much less crowded, most people milling around outside an ice cream parlor or the few shops that hadn't already closed up for the night. Victoria finally came to a stop beside the pier's railing, leaning on her elbows and staring down at all the lights reflecting on the water.

"What's she doing?" I asked, tugging Mary down behind an empty refreshment kiosk. Close enough to keep an eye on Victoria but enough cover to stay out of sight. "Catching her breath?"

"Considering she ran all the way across town without stopping once? Probable," Mary said unsurely. "What's she doing now?"

Victoria had pushed herself away from the railing, looking up at the lamppost above her suspiciously. After a long moment, she rolled her eyes and gave the pole a light punch, like she might do to someone's arm.

"If that's your idea of incognito, you might want to try again," Victoria said to no one in particular.

"Is she talking to a pole?" Mary asked, looking at me in confusion. I could practically see her calculating the probability that our class president had gone insane.

Victoria rapped on the lamppost again, apparently expecting something to happen. Nothing did.

Then suddenly, the light on the lamppost behind Victoria blinked out, and something shifted in the darkness, turning my blood to ice.

"I was actually this one, but you were pretty darn close," a voice said, making Victoria whirl.

"No, no, no, no, no," I muttered, starting to get up, but Mary yanked me back down.

"What do you think you're doing? Using your powers like that out here in the open!" Victoria hissed, yanking Henry further away from the crowd in the ice cream place and, ironically, closer to us. "Someone could have seen you!"

"The only thing those people are interested in are their sundaes," my cousin said. "Easiest place to use your powers is in plain sight. Always has been."

Victoria didn't look convinced. "You know how your powers are, Henry. That was risky."

Henry shrugged, digging around in his jacket pocket before pulling something out. Was that a bag of chips? He held the bag out to Victoria, who bit her lip before reluctantly taking it. She had to be hungry after running all this way.

"Thanks."

"You feeling better?" Henry asked. "You really had me worried back at the theater."

Victoria went back to leaning against the railing. "I know. I overslept. I shouldn't have let it go so long."

"You have to take care of yourself, V. I thought you said you had it under control?"

"I do!" she said, not sounding very sure. Victoria took a breath and seemed to collect herself slightly. Her voice sounded a little more confident now. "I do have it under control."

"I brought more snacks if you need them," Henry said, digging in his pockets again, but Victoria waved him off.

"You didn't ask me out here for snacks, Henry," Victoria said, "What's going on?"

Henry leaned back against the railing, watching all the kids and families in the ice cream place like he wished they were inside with them instead of having this conversation. "They're onto you. The Core 5."

Victoria dropped the chip she'd been eating. "What? *How*? You didn't tell, did—"

"Do you really think I'd tell, Victoria?" Henry interrupted, raising his voice just enough to silence her. It wasn't angry, just...sharp. Like he couldn't believe she'd think he'd do such a thing. He took a deep breath. "I promised I wouldn't say anything, and I haven't. Not ever. Jade saw you coming out of the theater."

Victoria hung her head. "I knew it. I knew I shouldn't have gone backstage."

"Hey, you were just trying to help. If anything, I was the one who yelled for you to come back there—"

"It doesn't matter now," she said, cutting him off. "Damage control. What can we do?"

Henry sighed, running a hand through his hair. "Honestly? I don't know. The Core 5 is still a little wary of Jade's predictions after she called the invisible force wrong last time, but I know they're digging. Jade's convinced you're the bad guy...it's only a matter of time before they come looking."

"But I didn't *do* anything!" Victoria protested.

"You know that, and I know that, but nobody else does, V!" Henry said, shaking his head sadly. "I tried to convince Jade it wasn't you, but then everything got all out of hand. I started yelling, then she started yelling, and now she won't even talk to me."

A long silence fell between the two of them, definitely long enough for me to feel terrible about not answering the seventy-plus texts my cousin had sent me over the last few days. As bad as I felt about ignoring Henry, I still wasn't sure what to make of this little scene. All the evidence we'd seen so far pointed at Victoria, yet here he was, warning her that the Core 5 were investigating her. How was it he could be so sure that she was on his side? I knew how Henry felt about Victoria—it was obvious enough...the friendship I'd seen them have in his memories, him chasing after her constantly in hopes of just a word or a smile, the way he was always looking out for her even though she hardly said anything to him in return. Did having feelings for someone really justify helping them out, even if you knew they were on the wrong side of things?

Would I have been doing the same thing if it was Henry in Victoria's shoes? Or Dylan? Or my brother?

I didn't like those thoughts.

Victoria nudged Henry slightly with her shoulder. "At least she didn't give you a black eye again."

Despite himself, my cousin laughed. "Nope. You've still got the last word on hitting me."

"I said I was sorry about that," Victoria said, fighting off a smile.

Henry looked like he wanted to return it, but he held his ground. I'd never seen him look so determined. "You've got to tell somebody, V."

"Henry, we've been over this a hundred—"

"It's the only way to get them off your back, Victoria," he interrupted, eyes pleading. "I can't explain, and it's your secret to tell. You have to tell."

Victoria was fidgeting so badly I could almost believe this was the same anxious little kid I'd seen on that fairground in Henry's memories. For the first time since that vision, I almost wondered if I was truly seeing the *real* Victoria Harper.

Henry dug a couple of packs of gummies out of his jacket and pushed them into her hands. "Just think about it, okay?" he said, voice softer now. "I'll do what I can to convince them it's not you, but that's not going to happen without *you*."

Victoria pursed her lips. "Henry, I can't just walk in there out of nowhere, alone..."

"You've never *had* to be alone, Victoria. You wouldn't have to be for this either. Not if you didn't want to be," Henry said as he pushed away from the railing to head back toward the main part of the boardwalk. He made it about five steps—nearly on top of me and Mary—before Victoria stopped him.

"Henry?"

"Yeah?"

"I'm sorry. I-I can't."

My cousin's face fell, though he managed to find a small smile. "That's okay. It was nice talking to you again, V."

"You too, Henry."

It seemed like an eternity before Henry's footsteps faded into the crowd along the boardwalk. Victoria stayed a few minutes longer, frowning at the lights on the water. I don't know how long she was there, but I swear, one second, she was there. The next, I'd lost sight of her again. Probably vanished into the crowd. Or turned invisible.

"Did that make any more sense to you than it did to me?" I asked Mary hopefully.

The red-haired girl shrugged. "The snacks were obviously to compensate for metabolism, judging from Victoria's approximate height, weight, and previous observations. Her powers must use up quite a bit of her strength...Victoria does snack a lot, doesn't she?"

"I thought you said it wasn't likely she had powers?"

"Judging from Henry's insistence on her 'telling the truth' to the Core 5, I think it's safe to say she does."

"But why tip her off?" I asked. "He could have just blown any chance of the Core 5 catching the invisible force!"

"As I said, it's only thirty-six percent likely that Victoria even *is* the invisible force," Mary said. "Also, in short, hormones."

"Hormones?"

"I calculate a 99.87 percent chance that Henry will propose to Victoria at some point in their lives. 99.95 that he does it before they're twenty-five," Mary rattled off as if that was a perfectly normal thing to say. "There is a ten percent chance she'd say no, though."

"Just ten percent?" I asked in surprise. Honestly, the way she avoided him, I was expecting it to be higher.

"There is a .05 percent margin of error, but yes. Ten percent," Mary confirmed. "Comparing possible combinations of their features, there's over ninety percent chance that their children would be well within the parameters for social definitions of beauty based on potential symmetry and genetic variations."

"O-kay then. Beautiful children...I guess that's good to know," I said, 100% sure I would never be telling *that* nugget of information to my cousin. "Are you saying you can calculate people's relationships? Why didn't I know you could do that?"

Mary chuckled. "Because then people would be asking me to calculate their relationships. Obviously. Not a pastime I'd want to have."

"But just theoretically though, you couldn't calculate a relationship concerning someone like, say...Dylan, could you?"

"What about Dylan?" Dylan asked, suddenly crouching right behind me.

"OH MY GOD! WHERE DID YOU COME FROM?" I screamed, scattering away from him and Mary and toppling out from behind the cart. If Henry had been right about the people in the ice cream place only being interested in their sundaes, then he was definitely wrong now.

"I was out with my dad and Sophie," Dylan said, staring at me like I'd grown a third eye. Mary looked like she was trying hard not to laugh. "I saw two of my friends hiding behind a lemonade cart and decided to see what they were doing. Now, what about Dylan?"

"Jade was just asking—"

"Nothing. Jade was asking absolutely nothing," I said, clamping my hand over Mary's mouth. "We've got some bad news...about Victoria."

Dylan's amused smile suddenly fell. He seemed to be torn between several responses, though one must have finally won out. "Like what?"

"Like we just watched Henry tip her off that the Core 5 was on her trail," I said as Mary pushed my hand away.

Dylan closed his eyes and sucked in a breath. "Henry, what did you just *do*?"

"The question is, what do we do now?" Mary asked, shifting unsurely as she got to her feet. "We have to tell the Core 5."

"Agreed," Dylan said, running a hand over his face. "I'll tell my mom as soon as we get home. If Yan Mei was mad before, then she's definitely going to be ticked now."

"That's Henry's call, not ours, Dylan," Mary said, standing up and brushing the dirt off her jeans. "We've all got to do what we think is best."

Dylan nodded, standing as well and offering down a hand to help me up, too.

"Hey, Mary! Over here!" a voice called, drawing our attention back toward the ice cream place. There was a girl our age coming out of the restaurant with her family, waving at Mary. She was about my height, with dark curly hair. It took me a second, but I realized I recognized her as one of the empathic kids from the mall. Elyse, that was her name. Mary's friend who'd convinced her to talk to Yan Mei.

Now it was Mary's turn to look flustered. "Um, you don't mind if I go over there for a few minutes, do you, Jade?"

"I'll meet you at the car," I said, nudging Mary forward.

"I guess I'd better be getting back then," Dylan said, nodding back toward the boardwalk's main thoroughfare. "Dad's probably let Sophie buy half the clothes in the new Make-A-Meerkat by now. Want to walk with me?"

"Only if I get a meerkat out of it." I smirked.

"I knew getting you a stuffed owl was a bad idea," he muttered, trying hard not to smile. "I'm going to go broke before this is over, aren't I?"

"This?" I asked without thinking.

Dylan tensed, not sure what to say. Apparently, I didn't either.

Good job, Jade. Now you made it weird.

"Don't worry about Henry," Dylan said after a long moment, scrambling for a subject change. "I'll talk to him...Maybe you should, too."

I blew a curl out of my face. "He tell you how many texts I've ignored?"

"I believe the last count was a hundred and twenty."

"A hundred and seventeen if you account for the bad cell service at Nana Benson's."

"Sounds like Henry's not the only one who's counting," Dylan said, raising an eyebrow. "I know what he did tonight was stupid, but he's only trying to look out for Victoria. Henry's always looking out for someone...unfortunately, that someone never seems to be himself."

The crowd was thinning out now that it was getting late. People were still screaming their heads off on the slingshot and lining up for the haunted house. The Make-A-Meerkat where Mr. Mason and Sophie were probably waiting was just in sight at the end of the boardwalk, meaning my walk with Dylan would quickly be coming to an end.

I stopped short, glancing up at the lights of the Ferris wheel as it completed its slow cycle. I bet you could see all of Pinewood from up there.

"You think your dad would mind if I borrowed you for a few more minutes?"

Dylan followed my gaze, a small grin already taking shape. "I think he'd be okay with it. Sophie definitely would."

"Well, then, what are we waiting for?" I asked, tugging him forward.

CHAPTER
TWENTY-FOUR

The Bensons were getting concerned. Even as I made my way downstairs, I could already hear the loud music blaring from outside the house.

I rolled my eyes. "'We Are Family?' Really? That's the song he went with?"

Mrs. B gave me a worried look from where she was peeking out the kitchen curtains. "He's out there again, Jade."

I sat down at the table and poured myself a bowl of cereal. "I told you I'm not talking to Henry at the moment."

"Honey, he's been out there for two days straight," she said, looking at him sadly. "I don't know what you're mad at each other about, but he's at least *trying* to make up for it. Can't you cut him some slack?"

"Not before his boombox runs out of batteries," I said firmly as Tommy staggered sleepily into the room.

He groaned. "Oh, not again. Mom, can't we call the police or something?"

"No, honey," Mrs. B chided, taking her seat as well. "Henry's just trying to apologize. I imagine that's what he would have done last night, too, if your sister would have actually come down to the door and talked to him."

Tommy gave me a look like, *You'd better fix this before my eardrums explode.*

I kept my eyes on my cereal.

In truth, I had known Henry had come. After going to the door hadn't worked, he'd climbed the lattice and knocked on my window, even after I'd closed the curtains on him.

Benson squeezed my shoulder as he set a mug of fresh coffee down in front of me. Besides Morning Guilt Jamz with Henry, another new tradition had been put into place in the week since I'd been to the cafe with Julian. Benson had almost burned the house down the first time he'd tried to use the espresso machine, but with the great Henry/Jade war raging, he seemed determined to replicate something at least close to the comforting drink I'd had at the London Fog. It was a very nice gesture, and I *always* appreciated caffeine. Still, it did little to help me with all the problems raging outside the kitchen.

I hadn't heard much from anyone inside the powered community beyond Dylan and Mary, but I had to assume things were getting worse. Susan, Antoine, Nora, Marcus...they were all still MIA, along with over a dozen people from the mall. Palo and Skylar were working double-time on self-defense classes, and the remaining three members of the Core 5, I suspected, were keeping us all purposely in the dark. I didn't know what our grandma knew about mine and Henry's fight, but I'd noticed our training sessions had been mercifully reassigned to avoid each other. Maybe she thought it best to give us our space after I'd ignored the first hundred messages he'd sent me.

"Oh, not *High School Musical*!" Tommy groaned as the song outside changed into "We're All in This Together".

I got up and went to the window. Henry was in front of the Yan Mei's Cafe van with a boombox that had to be older than he was propped on the hood, full-blast. I'm sure our neighbors loved that. His face lit up momentarily as he saw me, then fell as I closed the window.

Benson's phone beeped loudly as I went back to the table.

"Shoot," he said, eyes furiously scanning the text. He'd only got in about one bite of his gluten-free bagel (Benson's stomach hates all normal foods) before he was scrambling for his coat.

"Where's the fire?" Mrs. B asked in concern.

"Something's gone wrong with some of the samples at the lab," he groaned, wincing as he finished off the rest of his coffee. "We thought we finally had the cell combinations stable, but they've all suddenly started to deteriorate. The adapted strain is literally eating the host tissue from the inside."

"Ew, that's gross," I said.

"Cool!" Tommy disagreed.

Benson shook his head. "It doesn't make any sense...There were elements in the adapted strain that should have kept this from happening. The concentration must not have been high enough. Who knows how long it'll take for us to figure this out."

"But you were supposed to take me to Fernando's!" Tommy protested. "The *Chronos-Blue* tournament is tonight! MegaKoolKid is gonna try to challenge CobaltChaos for his spot back in the top twelve!"

Benson stared at Tommy like he'd just started speaking a different language. I remembered Katie and Kazi teasing Spencer about losing his top spot in the video game at the lunch table a few weeks ago. I had no doubt that Spencer would have the handle MegaKoolKid.

"I'm sorry, bud, but this is really important," he said, not sounding *too* devastated. "Charlotte?"

"I have to be at the PTO booth all day," Mrs. B said. "Sorry, dear."

Tommy pouted. Henry's music was getting louder outside. The song "Wannabe" was blaring, and I could hear him screeching along with it at the top of his lungs. Maybe it was time to go somewhere he would never look for me.

"I can take Tommy...if you want," I offered.

"*Who are you?*" Tommy whispered, eyes wide in horror.

"Great!" Benson said, completely ignoring Tommy's hesitant face. "Jade takes Tommy to his game thing, Charlotte does her booth, and we'll all meet up tonight for the fireworks, huh? Good? Great!"

He was out the door before any of us had time to answer.

"Well, I guess that's that." Mrs. B chuckled, snatching the rest of his bagel.

∿

Ever since I'd gotten to Pinewood, I'd heard rumors that the harvest festival was the biggest party in town, but the crowds on the street were nothing compared to that of Fernando's Comic Shop.

Every inch of the room was packed with people in the weirdest assortment of clothes I'd ever seen: full medieval ball gowns done in sleek futuristic material, spacesuits painted gray like suits of armor. Some even wore quivers on their backs beside their oxygen packs. It all put a whole new meaning to Kazi's description of *It's like King Arthur but in space.*

"Hey, Jade," a quiet voice said beside me. I recognized Mary's frizzy red hair immediately.

"Mary. What are you doing here?" I asked, ducking as a couple in matching clothes pushed past me.

"Fernando wanted me to run some numbers on whether his live streams were running at optimal speeds." Mary shrugged. "You know how good I am with numbers."

I nodded knowingly as Tommy tugged at my sleeve. "Can I go closer to the screens? I don't need you to babysit me, you know."

"Fine, but stay in sight!"

"I'll be like three feet away, Jade," he sighed, running off to get closer to what I guessed were the gaming stations. A loose ring of people had formed around the wall monitors at the back of the store. I recognized Tyler Martinez, talking hurriedly with ten other people I guessed were the game's top players. Kazi and Katie were up at the front, trying to reassure a worried-looking Spencer. He was decked out in an intricately embroidered tunic and breeches, both of which were steely gray. His gaming headset had been built into a shiny chrome crown.

I had just started to wonder where the gamer he had challenged was when the entire store fell deathly silent. A wide path suddenly cut through the crowd beside Mary and me—though how there was that much room to be found in a place that was so packed, I had no idea.

A tall figure strode inside silently, their thick-treaded boots impossibly loud on the carpeted floors. Okay, CobaltChaos 100% won the cosplay contest—they had the fanciest outfit by far. The gamer wore a sleek bodysuit, though the circuitry-like pattern of the fabric echoed chainmail. Same with the helmet—it seemed like a standard spacesuit helmet, but there was something about the design that gave it a Renaissance style. A wide cape billowed around their shoulders, hiding most of their body. Even though the suit was decently form-fitting, it was impossible to tell if it was a guy or girl. The entire costume was deep blue and silver.

Spencer gulped as he stood to face his opponent, staring down his reflection in the sunshade of their helmet. He was a whole head shorter, and his hand trembled terribly as he shook the one CobaltChaos had extended.

"This might be the most dramatic thing I've ever seen," I whispered, making Mary laugh.

"MegaKoolKid, former knight of Kingdom Pinewood," a balding, middle-aged guy with tanned skin boomed, extending his arms wide to the audience. I assumed this was Fernando. "Do you wish to proceed with your challenge against CobaltChaos, highest ranking knight of Kingdom Pinewood?"

"I-I do," Spencer said, his voice cracking terribly. "I wish to reclaim my honor by a duel to the death."

The room gasped as if this was very shocking. I heard Tommy's voice yell, "WHOA!"

"If his avatar is killed in the duel," Mary said, noticing I was looking for an explanation, "then he has to start all the way at Level One with a new character."

Fernando turned to Spencer's opponent. "Do you, CobaltChaos, wish to accept the challenge?"

The blue knight gave an unconcerned nod.

"Then assume your stances, players!" Fernando yelled, causing the room to cheer. A group of dudes beat their fists against their shields.

"Am I supposed to clap?" I asked Mary.

Spencer and the blue knight took up their controllers, their respective characters popping up on screen in similar costumes. I noted that Spencer had given his character a much fuller mustache than the wispy little thing he kept on his face.

"Begin!" Fernando yelled.

The two characters on screen went after each other with blinding speed, slamming and parrying attacks with their futuristic-looking swords. Spencer seemed to be holding his own, but it was clear Cobalt-Chaos was better. Faster. It was only a matter of time before he was defeated.

FVOOM!

Every monitor along the wall went out all at once, sending up a roar of protest from the crowd. Spencer and the blue knight were still rapidly clicking at their controllers for a solid five seconds before they seemed to notice their characters had vanished.

"Hey! I was winning!" Spencer yelled angrily. I couldn't see their expression, but the way the blue knight had their helmet turned made me seriously doubt he'd been anywhere near winning.

Suddenly, an icy chill ran up my spine. A couple people yelled at the back of the store as something shoved past them. The crowd shifted anxiously. No one seemed to know where the commotion was coming from.

Not again, not now. I desperately wished I'd talked to Henry this morning now.

"Run!" I barked, shoving Mary toward the emergency exit. "Tommy! Where are you?"

The whole store was in chaos now. People were trying to get out of the way as something big tore through the crowd. Something they couldn't see.

"Tommy!" I yelled again, getting delayed as a guy in a jester hat ran into me.

"Jade!" Definitely Tommy. He sounded scared. "Jade! What's going on?"

"Stay where you are!" I said, trying to weave my way to the front of the monitors where Spencer and CobaltChaos had been playing. Tommy had been near the front, close to the right side of the store.

Fernando was trying to wave people out the emergency exit. Kazi, Spencer, and Katie were nowhere to be seen, and I'd lost Mary in the crowd. Hopefully, she'd gotten out all right.

"Jade!" Tommy prompted urgently.

"I'm coming!" I said, getting smacked in the face by a girl holding a bow.

A guy near me let out a blood-curdling scream as his feet suddenly lifted off the floor. He drifted and hit the ceiling like someone had unhooked a tether, which was sort of ironic since he was wearing one. There was no way the invisible force could have held someone up that high...wait, was he using Susan's powers? Could he *absorb* powers?

"Run!" I yelled at the blue knight just a second before something slammed into both of us. CobaltChaos and I toppled, pinned down and fighting against something I couldn't see. I couldn't move, couldn't breathe. Marcus's powers? Suddenly, I *really* regretted being so awful to Henry this morning. He hadn't walked out on me. I'd walked out on him. Now I was going to get taken like everybody else, and no one would even know.

Suddenly, the weight on my chest was ripped away, and a shriek tore through the air. Something slammed hard into the wall of monitors, cracking the screens.

"You alright?" Dylan asked, hands extended and voice straining with the effort of trying to hold the invisible force in place.

"Yeah, yeah, I'm good," I said breathlessly, turning to check on the crumpled form beside me. CobaltChaos had taken the worst of the blow, groaning as they tried to push themselves up off the floor. "You okay...um, CobaltChaos person?"

They tried to wave me off, but I could tell it was a struggle to get back up. Something green caught my eye as I noticed it poking out from under the sleeve of their costume. It was a necklace—little, like a kid's, with a tiny plastic frog charm on the end. Much too small for someone my age to wear, which was probably why they'd fastened it around their wrist. The kind of thing that was probably a dime a dozen in a toy vending machine.

I had seen this before. I knew who CobaltChaos was and why they never showed their face at gaming tournaments.

"*Victoria?*"

The blue knight hung their head, grunting painfully as they yanked off their helmet and shook out a tangle of blonde. I couldn't believe my eyes. There, sitting in full cosplay, was Victoria Harper—head cheerleader, class president, frequent wearer of the color pink and...supreme gamer?

Victoria opened her mouth to say something but got cut off as

Henry came charging into the comic book store, his hands fumbling with some sort of white container.

"ATTACK PLAN BP!" he screamed. "GET DUSTED, INVISIBLE DUDE!"

Henry threw the container at the wall of monitors where Dylan was still holding the invisible force. A massive burst of white tore through the room, coating everything—me, Victoria, Henry, most of the store, and the invisible force with...powder?

I coughed, a familiar smell choking my lungs. "Is this *baby powder*?"

"Pretty smart, huh?" Henry beamed, looking like a ghost under the explosion of white. "If you'd talked to me in the last few days, you'd know I had a plan!"

"You've had a week, and all you came up with was baby powder?" I asked, dumbfounded.

"It's simple, and it works," Dylan said, looking embarrassed and proud at the same time. "Look."

The invisible force had stopped fighting, probably more from surprise than anything. There, now coated in a sheen of white powder, was the form of a man. Mostly his back and shoulders were visible, but it was very clearly a man: scruffy hair, broad shoulders, button-up shirt. The man sputtered and must have tried to wipe his eyes because a white streak of powder smudged across his face.

"HA!" Henry said triumphantly. "I told you it was Julian!"

"Okay. One: Julian looks nothing like this guy!" I said in exasperation. "Two: he's literally right there!"

Henry followed my gaze outside the window to where the Graves Research booth was plainly in sight. A boy who was very clearly Julian Graves was grinning in front of it, having just drilled a cream pie straight into his dad's face.

"Oh, my bad," Henry squeaked. "But if it's not Julian—"

"And it's not Victoria..." I agreed, staring at the girl still sprawled out on the floor.

"Then who is it?" Dylan finished, starting toward the invisible force.

"WHAT IS GOING ON?" Tommy yelled, ducking out from behind a shelf full of comic books.

"Tommy!" I said, crushing him in a hug.

"Get off of me!" he protested, eyes flitting between all of us. His gaze locked in on Dylan's outstretched hands, clearly still holding an invisible man in place. "Why is that dude invisible? How is your boyfriend holding him back without touching him? AND WHY DID HENRY JUST TURN INTO A LAMP?"

I turned, groaning at the sight of a stained-glass Tiffany lamp sitting on the floor behind us. Great, as if Tommy wasn't going to need enough therapy after this.

Victoria flicked the lampshade. "Snap out of it!"

"Sorry!" Henry apologized as he reappeared. Tommy's face was pale like he might faint.

Another fit of coughs came from the man, then suddenly, an ear-splitting screech ripped through the air. It seemed to be coming from the man. Tommy screamed. I clapped my hands over my ears, the force of it nearly making my knees buckle. It was unnerving only being able to see the invisible dude's eyes, but they were locked straight on Dylan. He was doing his best to hold his ground, but I could tell it was only a matter of seconds before he wouldn't be able to hold him.

"Dylan, no!" I yelled, but it was already too late.

With Dylan's concentration broken, the semi-visible man ripped away from the wall. He made a break for the emergency exit, but suddenly, Victoria was in his path. She cried out as her leg crumpled, her foot twisted at an odd angle. She'd probably hurt it when we'd fallen the first time. How had she gotten across the room in less than a second?

I kicked myself—the nervous energy, the random appearances, the take-out from places other than Pinewood. She had *super-speed*. That's why Henry had wanted her backstage at the theater and why Mary and I had kept losing her trail the other night. It seemed so obvious now.

The man grabbed Victoria's arms, dragging her toward the exit.

"Hey! Don't you kidnap my future wife!" Henry yelled, running past me. He jumped at the man, his form shifting in midair. I half expected a lamp to crash to the floor in his place, but the thing that emerged was nothing of the sort. A massive black wolf slammed into the man, teeth bared and jaws snapping. The man cried out as Wolf-Henry's fangs clamped down on his shoulder.

Dylan was on the ground, hands clamped over his ears. Victoria was trying to get back on her feet, but her ankle wouldn't hold her weight. The man was trying to shake Wolf-Henry off—I could see a lighter in his hand. Antoine's powers! I figured I only had seconds before Wolf-Henry got charbroiled.

"Tommy! The console!" I yelled.

Thankfully, he seemed to understand. Tommy ripped one of the consoles out of the fried monitors and tossed it to me. I charged at the invisible force, whacking the console into his back. Wolf-Henry released him, falling back and losing his grip on his powers as he hit the floor.

The man whirled on me, his eyes angry and bloodshot from the powder.

"Jade, your signature move!" Henry yelled.

I balled my fist and decked the invisible force the second he was close enough. Painful images ripped through my mind, but they were all disjointed—nothing made sense, as if the man wasn't capable of keeping a coherent thought. I saw a lab with bright lights, IV tubes, the pool, the movie theater, the Pinewood Performance Center. There was a long corridor in his mind, with lockers and a trophy case glinting in the dim light.

I saw Mary's empty desk in the English classroom, and a surge of fear washed over me. *They were going to find out. They were going to find out.* A shrill scream battered my senses even worse than the howl he'd let out a minute before. I saw a stuffed owl flying at his face from a tiny fist. A flash of blonde.

"You took Sophie!" I yelled, stumbling back from the man.

His eyes widened suddenly as if realizing something very important. His voice was a rough growl, eerily familiar. "You're the one they're looking for."

A blast tore through the air and sent the man flying away from me. Dylan was back on his feet, though he looked like he could barely stand. The man was getting up again, his eyes darting around like a caged animal.

"Tommy, move!" I yelled, but the man was too fast. He barreled into Tommy like a linebacker and the two vanished out of sight. Victoria tried to run at him again but ended up face-first on the floor. The door to the emergency exit flew open and I tried to chase after them, but there was no sign of them anywhere in the crowd outside.

Silence suddenly filled the store when I came back in as if everything had returned to normal. Broken glass and baby powder littered the floor. Henry slipped his arm under Victoria's shoulder and tried to ease her to her feet. Dylan looked shell-shocked. I felt the same.

My brother was gone.

CHAPTER
TWENTY-FIVE

It had only been twenty minutes, but each second was another reminder that Tommy was slipping further away. Still, that didn't stop me from trying to chase after my brother.

"What do you mean we can't go back?" I snapped, halfway running to keep up with Palo's long strides. "That thing just took my brother!"

"And my sister!" Dylan added, popping up on the tall man's other side.

"It's too dangerous," he grunted, pushing his way through the double doors into the mall's food court.

The invisible force had only been gone a few minutes before Palo had found us in the comic store. With the large crowds expected at the Pinewood Harvest Festival, Yan Mei had put the powered community on high alert, thinking that would help keep people safe. Once it became clear, though, that people were being taken from within the crowd, she had ordered everyone to leave and regroup at the mall for safety.

"You've all done well, but it's time to let the adults handle this," Palo said. "It's a miracle he didn't take any of you."

"But he did!" I insisted, trying to block his path. Palo wove around me easily. "He probably took Tommy because he knew I had powers. What's he going to do to him once he realizes he's normal?"

I thought about that dark room where Mary had been interrogated, Tommy being confronted with questions he didn't have answers to. He didn't know anything about the mall or the powered community or me and my twin brother. What would they do to him if he didn't know anything useful? If he didn't have powers? Worse yet, what on earth was I going to tell the Bensons if we weren't able to get him back?

Palo stayed silent. His dark expression remained unreadable and only made the pit in my stomach feel worse as we entered the main atrium of the mall.

Every person with powers in Pinewood must have been present. Hundreds of people of various ages were milling around—a small amount compared to Pinewood as a whole, but a huge amount, considering I was the only powered person I knew of up until a few months ago. Most of the younger kids had been herded into one of the empty stores to watch a movie, probably to keep them calm. A large group of adults stood in the middle by the fountain, talking urgently and swinging on coats like they were getting ready to go somewhere.

"Oh, thank goodness!" Mrs. Mason cried, breaking away from the group as she caught sight of us. She caught Dylan in a bone-crushing hug and kissed the side of his face. "Why is your face all cut up?"

"Broken TV," he gasped, trying hard to catch his breath. Mrs. Mason reluctantly released him.

"These four had a run-in with the invisible force at Fernando's," Palo explained. "Seems he was going after the blonde one."

"Victoria, right?" Yan Mei asked, slinging her arm under Victoria's other shoulder and helping Henry ease her down on the edge of the fountain.

"You remember me? It's been years since I've been over." Victoria winced, stretching her injured ankle out in front of her.

"Of course. Henry wouldn't let us forget." Yan Mei chuckled. She cupped Henry's face, brushing a streak in the baby powder that was still all over him. "Ah, you sweet boy." She sighed in exasperation. "Do I even want to know why you're covered in...all of this?"

"Attack Plan: Baby Powder." Henry beamed. "We got enough on him to see what this guy looked like! And guess what? I actually turned into something that wasn't a lamp!"

"Yeah, he went full werewolf on the guy." Dylan smiled.

"Yeah, a real wolf!" Henry agreed. "Not like Palo here—"

"Watch it," the older man grunted.

"Wait, wait, wait," Dylan's dad interrupted, cutting through the crowd. "You actually saw the invisible force?"

"It was a man," I said. "Broad-shoulders, maybe six feet tall. Short hair, we couldn't tell what color with the powder all over him. He took my brother."

The momentarily hopeful faces of the adults around us faded. Mr. Mason looked like he might start crying at any second.

"He's not the only one," Yan Mei said, placing a gentle hand on my shoulder. "The disappearances have been ramping up over the last week —one or two a day, maybe a whole family taken."

"We think he's using the festival as a cover," Mrs. Mason added grimly. "Lots of people to hide behind, everyone in one central location. Sophie was only out of our sight for a second before—" She stifled a sob. Mr. Mason laced his fingers through hers.

"We've counted twenty-four people missing since this morning," Yan Mei finished. "All with powers, all taken somewhere around the festival grounds."

"Twenty-five, counting Tommy," I said. "But why? Why take so many all of a sudden?"

"Something's changed." Palo shrugged. "Desperation, fear...we never even knew why he started taking people with powers in the first place. Our best chance is to go back to the festival and try to find him again."

"We might not have time for that!" I snapped, fear gripping my chest. "Tommy doesn't have powers! What if he hurts him or worse?"

"We're going to find them, Jade," Yan Mei said confidently, though her eyes still seemed unsure.

"It should have been me," I said. "Tommy had nothing to do with this."

She frowned before pulling me in and wrapping her arms tightly around me. "Jade, dear. You can't beat yourself up over this. It's not your fault. Even with the power to see the future, you can't predict everything."

My resolve was slowly breaking. I grabbed onto the older woman and laid my head on her shoulder. "But he's my family too."

She laid a gentle hand on the back of my head, stroking gently. "I know, dear. We'll find him."

Tommy was just a little kid—sure, he could be mean and gross and annoying, but he was my brother. He couldn't defend himself against a guy with powers. Not to mention this man's powers. I was scared. I was angry. But mostly, I was ready to storm the entire festival ground if it meant finding him.

Suddenly, I remembered the things I'd seen when my fist had connected with the man's face. Sophie getting taken, the places the others had disappeared. The school. That long hallway and Mary's empty desk—the fearful feeling washing over me. Why would I be seeing that? Mary hadn't been taken anywhere near the English classroom. Neither had Tyler, the only other person who'd vanished from Pinewood High. Why had I felt like the man hadn't wanted me to see it?

"The school," I said, pushing away from Yan Mei's grasp, not even realizing I was talking before the words were already out. "I-I think he's at the school."

Yan Mei raised an eyebrow. "What? Why?"

"I saw things when I touched him—visions. The places where people disappeared...I saw the school more than anywhere else," I tried to explain. My mouth was as dry as sandpaper. "I think that might be where Sophie is."

"But the school isn't anywhere near the festival." Mrs. Mason asked in concern, "Are you sure? Yan Mei said your emotions can hinder your powers when you're upset...Could losing Tommy—"

"It doesn't work like that!" I protested, feeling my anger rising. I could see the doubt in their eyes, wondering if I was leading them astray like the mishap at the theater. "My emotions mess up my control over the vision, not what I see. The school was all over this guy's mind! I think that's where he's taking them—"

"Jade, we trust you," Mr. Mason said, trying to keep his voice calm. He got that same worried look Dylan always did when he was nervous. "But we can't be wrong about this."

"I'm not wrong! He's at the school!"

247

"Are you willing to bet Tommy's life on that?" Mrs. Mason asked, cutting me off sharply.

I could tell from her expression that she hated going against me like this.

Mrs. Mason sighed. "I will not gamble with my daughter's life, Jade. We're going to the festival."

"But you're going to the wrong place!" I insisted. "At least let us check out the school! This guy was using multiple powers at Fernando's! The same powers as the people he'd taken!"

"Out of the question," Mrs. Mason said. "It's a wonder you all got away from him the first time with as little training as you've had if he's got powers like you say. No, you're staying here where it's safe."

"Mom," Dylan said, choosing his words carefully. "If Jade's right about this—if you really are going to the wrong place..."

"Yeah, do you really want to bet against someone who can see the future?" Henry agreed.

"She's been wrong before," Mrs. Mason said sadly, slinging on her coat. "Palo, can you keep an eye on the kids while we're gone? Make sure they don't do anything rash."

Palo nodded. Dylan's dad waved over some of the other adults to signal that it was time to leave. Skylar shot me a sad look out of the passing faces.

"Mom—" Dylan tried again, but she held up a hand.

"I said no, Dylan James," Mrs. Mason said, sounding like she'd aged twenty years in the last ten minutes. "You all have done enough for tonight. Your job now is to stay safe—I *need* you to stay safe, understood?"

Dylan nodded reluctantly. Mr. and Mrs. Mason joined the crowd, heading out into the parking lot. This was wrong, all wrong.

Yan Mei was watching me curiously. I had the feeling she was at least considering what I was saying. If she was, though, she didn't let on, giving both Henry and me a quick hug and then heading off with the others.

Palo cleared his throat awkwardly. "Well, come on, kiddos. Let's go get some ice on that ankle, young lady. You all want to watch *Finding Nemo* with the others?"

"You mean the five-year-olds?" Henry sighed, helping get Victoria back to her feet.

I locked eyes with Dylan as Palo turned to lead us deeper into the mall. His face was confident, deadly serious. We came to a silent understanding. Both our siblings had been taken, and we'd been sidelined, basically put on house arrest. It was time for a jailbreak.

Think.

I pondered our options as we dug around for pieces of a puzzle. Almost half an hour had gone by and I still had no ideas about how to get away from our babysitter. Palo had backed off our case when he saw the four of us pull out a 1,000-piece puzzle but sat at a distance reading a copy of *Gone with the Wind*. We had settled into the Archive after cleaning up the remains of Attack Plan: Baby Powder. Unfortunately, now, we were near the back of the mall and Palo had locked the Archive's back exit—leaving unnoticed would be quite the challenge.

"Why are there so many edge pieces?" Victoria groaned, bouncing the knee of her uninjured leg. Dylan and I looked at her, confused. Neither one of us had ever heard her complain.

"I know!" Henry agreed, not a surprise. "And why are there so many blue pieces? This is a city puzzle, not the ocean!"

"I bet I can find more than you." Victoria smirked.

Henry cracked his knuckles. "Bring it on!"

I poked Dylan and pointed to a pair of bean bags nearby. He nodded at my unvoiced question, and we moved to the more private area. Palo briefly looked up from his book at our movement when Henry let out an excited yell. Palo rolled his eyes before going back to his book, satisfied that we were just getting away from the pair. I turned toward Dylan.

Honestly, I hadn't had time to process everything. Well, maybe during the break, I'd had too much time to process. The frequent visits and stereo music had only made me more irritated, but I couldn't deny that they had both defended me and taken my side against their own families. That took guts against the likes of Mrs. Mason and Yan Mei.

"I'm sorry about Sophie," I said. It wasn't a great start, but it needed to be said.

"I'm sorry about Tommy...and the boombox. I told Henry to tone it down, but I don't think he listened," Dylan said.

I chuckled. "My cousin has an interesting method of asking for forgiveness. Tommy wasn't pleased to hear "We Are Family" on blast so early on a Saturday. Remind me to never argue with Henry again so he can't apologize."

Dylan smiled before it dropped. All seriousness on his face. "Okay, but for real, are you alright? You know that Henry didn't mean what he said. We are all happy you are part of our lives...you know that, right?"

"It's kind of crazy. Before I got here, I didn't really have any friends and wasn't on great terms with my family. I'd been so happy when I found out I could have part of my original family, and when Henry said those things...I felt like I had screwed it up. My own family didn't want me," I said.

Dylan took my hand, and I felt paralyzed by his intense stare. "I'm so sorry that stupid fight happened. Henry will talk to you—he's been going over *exactly* what to say. I know he shouldn't have lashed out at you, but he really is sorry. He cares about you. We both do."

I smiled, trying to catch my breath. My chest felt heavy, the words harder to speak. "You say that a lot."

He leaned in closer. All I could see were those deep blue eyes. I felt heat on my cheeks and reminded myself to breathe. "Well, I just want you to know that I do. I care about you." Dylan's thumb drew feather-light circles on my hand, sending tingles all the way up my arm.

"You know, for a shy person, you're kind of bold sometimes," I said.

Then he dropped my hand and leaned away from me, looking ahead with a conflicted expression. Did I say something wrong?

"Jade?" his voice whispered.

"Yes?" I asked. My heart was racing so much I was thankful to be sitting down.

"I have a plan," he said, turning to look at me.

Okay, now I'm really lost.

"Uh...yeah? What is it?" I asked, raising my eyebrows at him.

"Be bold."

Before I could ask what he meant, he pulled me forward. My eyes widened, his hands grazed up my arms and glided to my cheeks. The heat of his breath ghosted over my lips before I was enveloped in warmth. Feather softness pressed into my lips, and my entire body started to simmer. He gently pulled back and smiled.

"Let's go!"

What? What!?

"But you just—" I whisper-shouted.

"Yes, I did." Dylan beamed with pride. Clearly, he was taking this bold thing to heart because I had never seen Dylan this way before. "And now, I'm getting us out of here!"

Now I was really confused. "You are? But how? We didn't even talk about a plan!"

He smirked. "Leave it to me. Go get Henry and Victoria and...stand back."

I stared at him dumbfounded for a moment before heading toward Henry and Victoria, trying to keep my pace even. My heart pounded in my chest. I told myself it was because of the plan, but if I said that was the only reason, I'd be lying. But I definitely wasn't complaining.

Henry and Victoria were still wrapped up in their game of finding the pieces. Henry was trying to shove two pieces together that clearly did not match, while Victoria studied the picture on the box intently as if that would miraculously solve the rest of the puzzle. I sat down with the pair.

"Guys, we need to move," I said, trying to keep my voice quiet. "Now."

Henry raised an eyebrow in confusion. "How are we getting past wolf-boy?"

"Dylan said to leave it to him," I said. Victoria and Henry looked at me as if I had grown a third eye.

"Dylan said that?" Henry asked.

"That doesn't really sound like something he would say," Victoria said.

"Look, I don't understand it either, but we have to trust him," I said, trying to hurry them up. They looked at each other and nodded. We all stood up, and I nodded at Dylan, who started walking toward Palo.

Palo immediately noticed and looked up from his book. "Something wrong, Dylan?"

The air was tense. Palo looked like he knew something was about to happen. He sat up, putting down his book.

"We're leaving now," Dylan said.

We gaped at the boy not too far ahead of us. He really was taking this *bold* thing to another level. I felt a nudge from Henry. "Is that really Dylan?" he whispered.

Victoria shushed him, but her eyes flashed to mine with a smirk. I panicked. For someone who wasn't a mind reader, I felt like she could read me like a book.

Palo scoffed. "Yeah? What are you going to do?"

Suddenly, all the books in the surrounding ten feet started hovering over the shelves. Palo didn't have time to react before a barrage of books from all directions surrounded him. At least a hundred barreled at him, forcing him down with a groan.

"Run!" Dylan shouted.

We made our way out of the door, Dylan following close behind. An explosion of books scattered throughout the Archive, Palo with his wolf-like powers glowered menacingly as he tried to shrug out from under their weight.

"Shut the door! Shut the door!" I shouted.

Henry and I slammed the door shut, trying to hold it closed while Dylan used his powers to crush the locks from the inside. He threw up his hand, and a wire metal security door snapped into place in front of the Archive, firmly blocking the entrance. I held my breath as we saw Palo's shadowy figure emerge from the stacks on the other side of the door. Palo's clawed hands tried frantically to open the door, but it wouldn't budge. He kicked several times before deciding it was no use. He glared at us through the glass and metal security frame.

"Dylan." Palo's voice was slightly muffled through the door. "Now *that* was an attack!" he said proudly.

Dylan scratched the back of his head. I looked at him, confused. Wasn't he supposed to be happy about the compliment?

"So, uh, I guess you won't mind us borrowing your truck then for a bit?" Dylan asked nervously.

We all gasped at Dylan, who pulled out a set of keys from his pocket, jingling a keychain with a giant plastic tooth in front of the door. When had he gotten those? Had he swiped them off Palo with his powers?

"You guys are in *so* much trouble," Palo said.

CHAPTER
TWENTY-SIX

"**W**ho are you, and what have you done with my best friend?" Henry asked as we sped toward the school in Palo's truck.

Victoria elbowed him. "Leave him alone, Henry," she chided, wincing as she stretched out her ankle. It seemed to be doing better since Henry had helped her get some ice on it, but I was still worried about how well it would hold up if she tried to use her powers. "I, for one, like Confident Dylan."

"Me too," I agreed with a grin. Dylan shot me a warm smile from the driver's seat.

"Wait, wait, wait," Henry said, throwing out his hands. "Why are you two all smiley at each other? Did I *miss* something?"

"This is the greatest day of my life," Dylan said, glancing at Henry in the rearview mirror.

"WHAT?" Henry yelled. "JYLAN HAPPENED?"

"Why is that so shocking?" Dylan asked incredulously.

"Again with the ship name?" I asked. "When did you even come up with one?"

Henry shrugged. "August? Whenever Dylan first started going all heart-eyes for you. Don't worry though, it wasn't nearly as long ago as Operation: HENTORIA."

"Wait, when did I get dragged into this?" Victoria asked worriedly.

"YOU CRACKED THE CODE THAT QUICKLY?" Henry pouted jokingly. "I should have expected no less from our class president and gamer queen."

Victoria ignored him, leaning between me and Dylan as Pinewood High came into sight. "So, do we actually have a plan, or are we just running in, powers blazing?"

"Honestly, I don't know," Dylan admitted sheepishly. "I didn't think we'd get this far."

"Find Tommy and Sophie and anyone else in there. Fight bad guys? Try not to die?" Henry suggested.

"That's all great, but how do we do that?" I asked as Dylan brought the truck to a stop in the parking lot. There were three or four other cars parked nearby—a sleek black car and a couple of white corporate vans, though the sides weren't labeled with any company in particular. The others seemed to get a similar bad vibe. No one had been at school for at least a week during fall break, and no one definitely should have been here now with the festival going on.

"We can go through the gym...I have a key for practices," Victoria offered, digging around in the folds of her blue gamer costume and pulling out a drawstring bag. She glared at Dylan when he snickered. "Don't laugh. This thing doesn't have pockets."

"I think you look stunning." Henry beamed. "I thought you gave up gaming after...you know, we didn't hang out anymore?"

Victoria shrugged. "It's a good way to burn off energy. Let's go find some missing people."

She slipped out of the truck without another word, leaving the rest of us no choice but to follow. Even with a hurt ankle, Victoria was still faster than the rest of us—she had the side door of the gym unlocked and open by the time Dylan, Henry, and I scrambled over.

"Looks clear," she said, squinting into the gloom.

Together, the four of us crept into the darkness, wincing at how loud our sneakers were against the basketball court. It was eerie being at the school at night with nobody around. All the lights were off when we got into the hallway, too, but loud voices sounded off to our right.

"The cafeteria," I said, taking the lead as we crept closer.

"I guess it's too much to hope that the lunch ladies are getting a jumpstart on cookies for Monday?" Henry said.

Dylan shushed him as we ducked into a hallway across from the cafeteria. The doors were open, and the lights were on, illuminating what looked like a triage hospital. Portable monitors and beeping machines were spread out all over the room, hooked up to dozens of people lying on top of the lunch tables. Yan Mei had said that twenty-four people had been taken today *before* the invisible force had grabbed Tommy. There were easily that many here, if not more.

Most seemed to be unconscious, though there was a group at the far end of the room who were still awake. Two men in lab coats were hauling a struggling boy over to one of the tables where a woman with dark skin was waiting. Her graying hair was pulled back into tight braids, and she wore a silvery pantsuit under her lab coat. The two men restrained the boy on the table, and the woman knelt down to whisper something to him. Instantly, the boy's body slacked, calming enough for the men to begin hooking him up to one of the monitors. The woman staggered slightly, catching herself on the table.

My breath caught. I knew her. It was the woman Julian had saved me from at the theater. The one that Yan Mei and Jessica had all but gone into panic mode over. Those powers...she had to be the same lady I'd seen in Mary's hidden memories, too—the one who'd put her into that weird hypnotic state for her Q&A with the voice in the speakers.

Familiar faces started to emerge in the sleeping crowd: Nora, Marcus, Susan, Antoine. They were all here, hooked up to machines like lab rats. A person with powers experimenting on other people with powers? Suddenly, a blond form sprawled on a table near the back caught my attention.

"Tommy!" I gasped. He was out cold like the others, a monitor beeping steadily by his head. No one seemed to be paying him much attention yet, but I figured it was only a matter of time before someone realized they'd grabbed a kid without powers. I started to move forward, but Dylan held me back. "Let go! I can't leave him like that!"

"You're more help to him out here than in there," Victoria said, putting a hand on my shoulder. "We've found them. Maybe we should call the adults now...let them handle it?"

Despite how much I wanted to run into the cafeteria and rescue Tommy, I knew she was right. There had to be at least twenty doctors in that room, plus the scary hypnotist lady. I nodded reluctantly, forcing myself to look away from my brother. We needed to get out, call the grownups for backup. They'd know what to do.

"Grandma's not answering," Henry said, face pale in the blue light of his phone. "I've sent an S.O.S. text to her and Dylan's parents, but I don't know if anyone's seen it yet."

"I don't think they're going to," I muttered, feeling my heart sink as a group of men in white coats marched Mrs. Mason and Skylar down the hall toward the cafeteria. Both looked like they'd been put through the ringer: scuffed faces, disheveled hair. Skylar's jacket was charred like it'd been smoldering at one point. Their hands were bound behind their backs, but that didn't stop Dylan's mom from shouting more curses at the men than I'd ever heard. *Whoa, Mrs. Mason.* A guard barked at her to be quiet.

A familiar feeling crept into the back of my mind. Mrs. Mason was looking up, blue eyes scanning the dark hallway knowingly. I couldn't tell if she was more relieved or annoyed to see us crouching down beside the lockers. Skylar followed her gaze, making a point to distract the guards for a second so they wouldn't notice where she was looking.

Get out of here, Mrs. Mason's voice whispered in my mind. Judging by the way Henry jumped, I guessed the others were getting the same message. *Help is coming. Go back to the mall and stay safe.*

"Hurry up, Mindreader!" one of the men ordered, pushing Mrs. Mason a little harder than necessary. There would only be a few seconds before they were in the cafeteria, and I could tell she was trying hard not to draw attention to where we were hiding.

Dylan, keep Jade safe. I can hear it in their minds: she's the one they want. You can't let them—

The message cut off as Mrs. Mason's eye contact was broken. The men herded her and Skylar inside the cafeteria, slamming the doors shut behind them and blocking our view.

"They've got all of the Core 5 except Grandma," Henry whispered worriedly. "All the leaders of the powered community."

"And they can make them talk," I said. "That lady in the silver suit..."

I've seen her powers before. She can put you into some kind of trance, make you answer things."

"But my mom said that help was coming," Dylan said hopefully. "Why don't we go back to the truck? Regroup and wait for backup?"

We all nodded, hurrying back toward the gymnasium once we were sure that the coast was clear. Jumbled thoughts bounced around my head. Why would these scientists be trying to find *me*? The woman from the theater, who'd also been present during Mary's interrogation, was here with the missing people. It all had to be connected. Nearly all the questions the voice had asked Mary had been about the Kastels...my parents, then all those questions about twins...

"Do you hear that?" Victoria asked, stopping us short a few dozen feet from the gym.

She was right. There was a noise now: the faint rustle of footsteps on a hard floor, the click of a door handle being turned. Someone was coming out of one of the classrooms in front of us.

"There's nowhere to hide!" Henry said, looking around frantically. The walls around us were dominated by lockers.

Victoria tried the closest classroom door. "Locked!"

"This one, too!" I agreed. "Dylan, can you unlock it like you did in the locker room?"

"I'd need time," he said, wringing his hands worriedly.

We could have tried to make a break for the gym, but there was no way we could have run that far without being heard. Plus, we didn't have time. Before I could even blink, one of the classroom doors opened, and a familiar form stepped out.

"Mr. Goodman?" I asked, dumbfounded.

For a moment, our teacher looked just as surprised as we were. He slung his bag over his shoulder and drew a key out of the door to the English room. Maybe it was just the dark, but Mr. Goodman looked more weary and gaunt than ever.

"What are you kids doing here?" he asked in surprise, lumbering toward us with a pained stride. "You shouldn't be here on a Saturday."

"We could say the same thing about you," Victoria said warily, taking a step backward and nearly tripping over Henry.

"I had to get some papers for Monday," Mr. Goodman said, raising an eyebrow in confusion. "What's going on? You all look scared to death."

"Oh, thank goodness—somebody normal," Henry said, letting out a sigh of relief. "You're never going to believe this, but bad guys have infiltrated the school! Look, there's a bunch of people missing, and they're here—laid out in the cafeteria! We've got to call the police or my grandma or somebody!"

"Have you all been drinking?"

"It's the truth, sir," Dylan attempted. "We need to get out of here. We're all in danger."

Victoria gave me a worried look. I nodded, a knot cinching tight in the pit of my stomach. Something didn't seem right about this—Mr. Goodman was running around the school at the same time as a bunch of evil scientists and hadn't even noticed? Plus, he'd given that response about getting papers just a little *too* quick. He listened intently as Henry explained the situation as best as he could without mentioning our powers, but still, Mr. Goodman seemed barely able to keep himself upright. He swayed on his feet, and his eyes were sunken, his hair wet like he'd just gotten out of the shower. A small dot of red had soaked through his dress shirt on his right shoulder, and what was that all over his shoes? They were spattered in white dust like...

Baby powder.

My heart pounded as puzzle pieces clicked into place. Mr. Goodman had been at school when Mary and Tyler were both taken. He would have had permission slips for *Macbeth* and been at the show to snatch Nora. That's why I'd seen the English classroom in my vision, felt that terrible guilt. Mr. Goodman had known *he* was the one who'd taken Mary. The blood on his shirt—it was from where Wolf-Henry had bit him at Fernando's. He'd gotten sicker and sicker looking as the disappearances increased...could taking other people's powers be hurting him?

"Guys, we need to leave. *Right now.*"

"What—" Henry started but got cut off as a pair of arms wrapped around his waist from behind. "Hey!"

Dylan tried to grab me, but another man had a hold of him as well.

259

Victoria might have tried to run for help, but her ankle crumpled underneath her. A woman yanked her roughly to her feet, securing her hands.

"You want these with the others, sir?" one man asked, tightening his grip as Dylan tried to send him back into the lockers. I could tell it was a losing battle, though. Dylan's powers weren't back to full strength yet from his fight with Palo. The man barely budged.

Mr. Goodman nodded. "Knock them out so their powers can be copied. The Kastel girl stays with me."

A worried look crossed the guard's face. "But, sir—"

"She stays with me," my *former* favorite teacher insisted, catching my arm tightly. "Bring me the other one."

I felt my heart stop. *The* other *one?* No, there was no way...

"Sir, you know the boss explicitly said—" the woman holding Victoria attempted, but Mr. Goodman whipped out his hand. The woman and Victoria slammed roughly into the ceiling as their gravity momentarily decreased. Both dropped to the floor hard but slightly gentler than if he'd just let them fall.

The three guards wasted no time hurrying back toward the cafeteria, unfettered by my friends trying to fight them off. Dylan yelled my name until they were well out of sight.

Mr. Goodman reopened the door and dragged me into the English classroom. All the tables and chairs had been pushed haphazardly against the walls. The only furniture now was two chairs and one of the portable monitors in the center of the room. He shoved me into the chair on the left, quickly securing my hands and feet.

"Sounds like someone's going off script," I said, trying to keep my voice steady. "Going against your boss, huh? He's the guy who ordered you to take all these people? Is that what you can do—swipe people's powers?"

"If you're asking about my abilities, Jade, then no," he said, sounding ridiculously normal for a guy who'd just duct-taped one of his students to a chair. "I can only use the abilities I have been given."

"Given? You mean someone *made* you like this?" I asked in horror. "How? Why?"

A dark look fell across his face. "A little experiment. Some small hope for a dying man," Mr. Goodman said, pushing himself up painfully from the floor to fiddle with the monitor. My heartbeat rang out loud and much too fast.

"A dying man...That week, you were gone at the beginning of the school year, you were sick. You went to get some kind of treatment."

"Treatment, yes—I felt better, stronger than I had in years. Though, unfortunately, my newfound health began to deteriorate after a few days," Mr. Goodman said sadly. "I seemed to feel better each time a new ability was introduced to my physiology, but we quickly found out that giving powers to people without them is a tricky business. Abilities don't always take. Mine helped sustain me but also caused greater harm whenever I used them. My system is trying to reject my powers...my genetic code was never set up to be able to handle them like you or your friends in the cafeteria."

"That's why you've been taking more people?" I asked. "To keep yourself going?"

"It's not like I had a choice," Mr. Goodman snapped. "You think I wanted to hurt anybody? I didn't even know I was the one taking people until recently!"

"The lady with the mind powers...She forced you to take people?" I asked.

"At first...until I got worse. They offered me a chance to be healthy again," he muttered, keeping his eyes low. "Nobody's supposed to be dying at thirty-eight. What about my wife? My daughter? I-I had to take the chance, no matter what."

"Who offered you a chance, Mr. Goodman? It's more than just that mind-control lady...who does she work for?"

Mr. Goodman shook his head. His laugh sounded more like a gasp than anything remotely humorous. "There's one who's been searching for you even longer than I have, Jade. Someone who wants to close the gap between those with and without powers once and for all."

Suddenly, a crowd of loud voices sounded at what seemed like the far end of the hallway, sending Mr. Goodman running outside. One of them sounded suspiciously like Henry's banshee-karate battle cry. Had something happened? Had my friends been able to escape?

"Psst! Jade!" a voice whispered from somewhere behind me. "Jade, over here!"

I turned my head as much as I could to look at the windows behind me. There, barely visible in his dark clothes, was someone I was very, very happy to see: Julian Graves.

"What are you doing here?" I asked worriedly. "Mr. Goodman's going to be back any second! He's the one who's been taking the missing people, the one who came after us in the theater—"

"Yeah, I know," Julian muttered, trying to pry the cracked window open more than a few inches.

"You know? How do you know?"

Julian raised an eyebrow at me. "Haven't you ever seen a TV show? No one named *Goodman* is ever a good man."

"Oh, forget it," I said, rolling my eyes. "Hurry up! He's going to be back soon!"

"I'm trying! Just—just hang tight. I'll get you out in a second."

"I'm duct-taped to a chair, Julian. Where am I supposed to go?" I groaned.

Heavy footsteps were approaching from the hall. Mr. Goodman was coming back.

"Hide!" I hissed.

Unfortunately, I forgot that this was Julian Graves, the clumsiest teenager on the face of planet Earth.

So, of course, the second Mr. Goodman reopened the door, Julian fell straight through the window onto the floor of the English classroom, in plain sight. If I could have facepalmed, I would have. So much for my daring rescue.

"Perfect!" Mr. Goodman said, face stretching into a sinister grin. "I suppose I should thank you, falling right into my hands, Julian. You've been much more helpful than usual lately, though I assume that's because of this one here?" I didn't like the way he was looking at me. "I probably would've wasted hours hunting you down, but here you are."

Julian stepped in front of me protectively. "You know this is a bad move, Goodman. You need to let us go."

"I'm dying, boy!" our teacher yelled, voice cracking with emotion. "I've heard the stories. The Amalgamation might be the only thing powerful enough to sustain me."

"I'm sorry, is anyone ever going to bother telling me what the Amalgamation is?" I complained. It had been a *long* day: getting attacked by angry invisible teachers, busting out of malls, kissing Dylan, and *then* getting kidnapped. I was done with everything.

Julian and Mr. Goodman ignored me. "The Amalgamation is a myth. No one really knows if it's even possible.

"He believes that the Kastel children could manage it," Mr. Goodman said, shaking his head emphatically. "The first set of twins born with compatible powers in decades. The only ones who might have the power to save me. Please, *save me.*"

Tears streamed down Mr. Goodman's cheeks, and he stumbled as he tried to step closer. Julian didn't budge, extending a hand threateningly.

"You stay away from my sister," he ordered.

CHAPTER
TWENTY-SEVEN

S ister? *Sister?!*

I gaped at Julian. "What did you just say?" I asked.

Julian stared at me with wide, panicked eyes. He hadn't meant to say that. "I—um, well, you see..."

"Is it true? Yes or no?" I commanded.

"This is all so touching and sweet, but—"

"Shut up, Goodman," I hissed. He raised his eyebrows in mock defeat, and I ignored him. "Julian, answer the question."

Julian gulped. He looked like he was debating on his answer. He turned to face me. "Yes, I am your brother, Jade."

I stared into the eyes of my long-lost brother. A missing piece of my family that I didn't know I'd found. Curly hair, light brown skin tone—why didn't I see it before? We had gotten along like we'd been friends for years when we'd only spoken a handful of times.

"You..." I trailed off, seeing Mr. Goodman approach at a rapid pace. "Julian! Look out!" I shouted, but it was too late. Mr. Goodman had his hands on Julian's shoulders, erasing his gravity. Julian's shoes drifted off the floor until he was hovering well over three feet in the air. Mr. Goodman cursed, his body rigidly still like he was in pain.

"Argh!" he shouted, painfully stretching out his arm to lift Julian higher. "Quit messing with my head!"

Julian's hands were forced away as he was pushed further toward the ceiling. Suddenly, Mr. Goodman dropped his arm, smacking Julian onto the floor with a thunderous *plop*.

"Julian!" I shouted as I fought my restraints. He wasn't moving. My eyes scanned him over with bated breath. I nearly gasped for relief when he groaned, a clear rise and fall in his chest.

"Ugh," Julian groaned.

"Thank goodness you're okay," I said.

He looked worse for wear, sluggishly trying to sit up. Honestly, he looked like he had been hit by a bus. I'm sure that wasn't far off from how he felt. He gave me a weak smile and a small thumbs-up.

"Aww, you two are so cute," Mr. Goodman sneered, hooking Julian up to the monitor as well. Our heartbeats chimed together in a nervous rhythm. Mr. Goodman coughed, hoarse like he was trying to hack up a lung. "We don't have much time. I might not be able to do an Amalgamation, but you two should be able to."

"I don't even know what the Amalgamation is!" I protested, yanking against my restraints. "I can't do something I don't understand!"

"Good thing Julian is here," Mr. Goodman insisted, waving me off. "He seems to know plenty. You both could never channel enough power alone. But together...the possibilities are endless."

"Mary," I said, trying to reason with him. "Her probability powers. She said there was barely a fifty/fifty chance that something like this would work. Those aren't great odds."

"Better than the ones I had before my abilities were given to me," Mr. Goodman said, slicing the tape around my wrists. I tried to lunge at him, but it was pretty pointless, with my feet still secured to the bottom of the chair. "Now, now, none of that, Jade. Join hands with your brother—your powers only work through contact, correct?"

"Like I'd tell you."

Mr. Goodman shoved me forward, nearly knocking me out of the chair. "Join. Hands."

"It's alright, Jade," Julian said, trying to keep his voice calm, though

265

his brown eyes looked terrified. "Just do as he says. Let's not give him any extra reason to hurt us."

I swallowed hard, staring at Julian's outstretched hands. I didn't want to take them—to give Mr. Goodman what he wanted, to try to attempt some crazy mega-power that no one seemed to know whether or not was real. I still had no idea what Julian's powers were other than they had something to do with the mind.

Could I even trust Julian? He'd known we were twins the entire time—but then again, how would you go about explaining you were long-lost, powerful twins? How had he even figured out that information?

But he had tried. Julian wasn't supposed to look for me when he'd first bumped into me outside the London Fog. He had checked on me when I was dizzy from that first vision of Victoria...he had tried to be my friend. I supposed, even if I didn't have all the answers right now, one thing was clear—Julian was looking out for me. I could trust him.

I slipped my hands into my brother's, feeling a tingle of electricity spark up my arms. Julian closed his eyes as if he was concentrating hard on something. I didn't want to take my eyes off Mr. Goodman, but something inside me told me I needed to do the same. I relaxed my mind, focusing on connecting with Julian.

What had Mary said about the Amalgamation? That it was something only twins with compatible powers could do? I could feel Julian's powers reaching out, searching for my mind. I would have to let him in, totally surrender my powers the same way he was doing with his. Our powers would link together, combining into...something completely new.

Breathe.

Then it happened. We were no longer in the classroom, there was no Mr. Goodman.

We had done it.

And we saw the future.

I screamed as the classroom re-formed around us.

Our breath was labored. The air was ash. Julian was clutching his chest with his right arm, though his left still had my hand in a vice grip. I shoved his hand away and latched onto both his arms. Tears streamed down my face, and for once, I didn't care.

"NO!" I screamed.

Julian was just as frazzled. Tears pricked at the edge of his eyes, and he seemed to have trouble catching his breath.

"Jade! *Jade!*" he called out.

"Julian—this can't happen. It *can't*. It can't," I chanted. Julian pulled me in and clutched onto me. He pulled back and grabbed both my hands.

"Jade...we have to forget what we saw," he said.

I was tempted to smack him. "How can we forget *that*?"

Julian steeled himself, taking a deep breath. "I'll make us forget for now until we can discuss it with the others."

"You can do that? Make us forget?" I asked, hoping desperately for anything that could get those awful images out of my mind.

"Temporarily. Long enough to make sure we get out of here with our sanity," he said. "Breathe, Jade."

I tried to do as he asked, but it was shaky and labored. Julian's grip tightened. In my head, images flashed rapidly: when we first met, Dominic Graves taking a ten-year-old Julian to a baseball game where he complained the entire time about the heat, and a blooming flower garden. His memory started focusing on another person, someone with pale blonde hair and blue eyes—

"That should be enough," Julian quickly said. He was right. My mind was completely blank. I was filled with peace and happiness, even though I could still feel the remnants of tears rolling down my cheeks and an ache in my throat from screaming.

I was about to comment about that last memory when a slow clap behind us signaled our attention. Mr. Goodman had a sick grin on his face.

"Amazing," he gasped. "You actually did it! And that was quite the performance there, too. I'm moved."

We glared at the older man in front of us.

"You sick, piece of—" I started.

"Now, now, that's no way to talk in school. Wouldn't want to get expelled again."

I froze.

"Leave her alone!" Julian snapped.

"Aren't you the protective brother? It's actually refreshing to see you get all worked up," Mr. Goodman said. "But no-can-do. See, now I know that the Amalgamation is not only real—but you two have the ability to do it. The girl who can see through time and the boy who can make you see anything he wants with his touch...combined to see something so terrible you forced yourself to forget? That's no fun. But I need a copy of your powers anyway."

He started toward us with a small electronic device.

"Try it, and I'll deck you," I spat.

"That might be a bit more of a threat if your feet weren't tied to a chair," Mr. Goodman said.

He had just raised the device when something massive swooped through the window at lightning speed and slammed straight into his face. Mr. Goodman screamed, sending the device skittering across the room as he desperately tried to swat his attacker away. Something he was not having much luck at, considering it was a fully-grown bald eagle. Man and bird grappled, screaming and scratching as they slammed into the pile of desks across the room.

"You kids alright?" Mr. Mason's voice asked worriedly as he toppled through the open window in a very Julian-esque move.

Mary and Palo followed shortly behind him. Palo's claws were out, his teeth barred. He rushed over to us and sliced through our restraints.

"We're okay. They took Dylan and the others to the cafeteria—they're knocking them out, taking samples to study their powers," I said breathlessly, happy to finally be free.

"I was sixty-eight percent worried about that," Mary said. "It's just like when I was taken, but they're leaving them here for some reason."

Across the room, the screeching had stopped. The eagle had vanished, and Yan Mei towered over Mr. Goodman's slumped form, face full of anger as she stared icily down at the bloody cuts across his face. As small and old as she was, I had never been so terrified of someone in my life.

"Where is he?" she snarled, yanking Mr. Goodman up into a sitting position in an amazing show of strength. "The man you work for—tell me where he is!"

"Yan Mei..." Mr. Mason started, but a scream from the direction of the cafeteria cut him off. It was impossibly shrill. I had a terrible feeling it was Henry.

For a moment, the older woman's hard expression gave way to worry, but then it iced over into a placid anger. Her eyes suddenly focused on Julian as if she was just realizing he was there. She looked at him, then me, then back at him.

"Is that...?"

I nodded. "Yeah, it is."

Yan Mei gasped. "You're both here." She smiled before glaring at Mr. Goodman. "Go. Help the others. Keep the twins safe," she called to Palo and Mr. Mason.

"And leave you here with *him*?" I asked, baffled.

"Given her power, she has a ninety-five percent chance of winning in a confrontation," Mary said.

"You heard her, let's go!" Palo said, rushing us out the door.

"You know all these people?" Julian asked me.

I pointed back toward the English classroom. "It's a very long story, but that was our grandma. This is Mary from class, Dylan's dad, and Palo, a pediatric dentist who is secretly a werewolf."

"Jade! Not funny!" Palo snapped as we made our way down the hallway.

"Oh, and Henry's our cousin," I said.

Julian blinked a few times and shook his head. "That's...How are we all related?!"

"I'll explain everything later," I said.

"We need to figure out how to get everyone out safely," Mr. Mason said as we approached the cafeteria doors, slowing our steps.

Palo spoke first. "We should split up. We can't all sneak into the cafeteria."

"You can cut through any restraints like you did with us, Palo," I said.

He nodded. "Er, your brother—"

"Julian," Julian said.

269

"Yes, so Julian, what power do you have?" he asked.

"I can make people see what I want by touching them," Julian said.

"We'll need your powers then to divert the scientists long enough to rescue the others," Palo said before reluctantly turning to Dylan's father. Mr. Mason's face lit up in a grin.

"We need to wake them up, yes? Leave it to me," he said.

"Wait a second..." I said, thinking back to my dinner at the Masons', where Dylan's father had a passionate conversation about exotic fruits. "Are you talking about—"

"The papayanapple! Yes, I am." Mr. Mason beamed with pride. The group looked at us, highly confused. "The fumes will help wake them up. I'll start on that. Julian will help distract the workers, and the rest of you can focus on getting everyone freed."

"Provided we don't get caught off guard...our plan has a forty-three percent chance of success," Mary said.

"We'll have to take those chances," Palo said grimly. "Get the Core 5 out first. We'll need their powers."

Julian stared at Mary, confused.

I sighed. "Mary has probability powers."

Julian looked surprised but nodded. Palo gave the order to start. I didn't have time to think about it. We had to keep going. We had to win. For everyone's sake.

CHAPTER
TWENTY-EIGHT

A s it turned out, the hostages didn't need as much saving as we
thought they did.

As Julian cracked open one of the doors to slip into the cafeteria for
our plan, we got our first glimpse at how Team Taken was doing.

Palo let out an uncharacteristic laugh. The noise inside was like that
of a full-scale food fight, and in truth, it didn't look that far off from
one. The enemy in lab coats shuffled frantically about, trying to find
cover. Dylan, Henry, and Victoria were on the right side of the room,
thrashing in their restraints and basically causing a full-scale prisoner
riot. Four lunch tables were flipped and scattered about, something I
imagined was Dylan's doing, especially the way he was smirking. Henry
was squirming away from a scientist with a syringe, shouting nonsense
about a painful death by needles. Victoria was the calmest of the trio,
death-glaring the scientists as she tried to get her to her feet. *Bad move,
making the class president angry.*

"Has he been able to attack this whole time and just been holding
out on me?" Palo asked in confusion, looking at Dylan's dad for some
kind of answer. Mr. Mason shrugged.

"Julian's got one," Mary said. I followed her gaze to see my brother behind one of the closer scientists, his fingertips pressed gently to the man's temples. The scientist seemed to calm instantly, turning and heading toward the far exit at the other side of the room without a word. Julian flashed us a small thumbs-up.

"A few more, and it's game time," I said, trying to sound confident.

"Is it just me, or is it weird none of them seem to care that he's just walking around?" Mary asked, watching curiously as Julian easily overtook two more scientists and sent them away as well. In a way, she was right—none of the scientists ran from him. The few that weren't trying to avoid getting beaned by Dylan throwing things across the room didn't even seem to question his presence until Julian was close enough to use his powers. It was odd...they had to notice him. Julian Graves might have been a lot of things, but stealthy was *not* one of them.

"The others are keeping them pretty busy," Palo said, dark eyes scanning the scene. "The Core 5 are clustered toward the back. You four start there and work your way out. I'll try to keep the scientists away from you as much as I can. Do you have the papayanapple? Chris? Chris!"

"What?" Mr. Mason said, jumping slightly. He had been staring worriedly as the scientists swarmed on Dylan, trying desperately to keep him under control. Another table went flying, sending half of them skittering for cover again. "Oh, oh, yeah. I've got it right here."

Mr. Mason pulled a small plastic container out of his backpack, the inside packed with neatly cubed yellow fruit.

"Do you just keep that stuff on you?" Mary asked, raising an eyebrow.

"It's a healthy and nutritious snack," Mr. Mason said defensively, nearly dropping the container as a loud crash sounded from the inside of the cafeteria. Palo swore as the second pop machine ripped away from the wall and went flying across the room. Scientists scattered as sparks and shards littered the floor, barely missing some of them.

Holy cow, Dylan could do that?

"GET HIM UNDER CONTROL!" a voice yelled as a familiar face emerged in the crowd that hadn't scattered: the older woman in the silver suit. She looked furious but was still leaning heavily against the table of the latest person she'd put to sleep with her powers.

"He's using up too much of his powers," Palo said, shaking his head slightly. "We can't wait on Julian. We have to move soon."

"That woman over there is the person putting everyone to sleep!" I said, ice spreading through my chest at the memory. That feeling at the theater when she'd got the better of me was indescribably terrifying. The moment when I had no control over my body, spilling my secrets against my will...it was one of the first times I'd felt *powerless*. I never wanted to feel that way again. "She's calling the shots. We have to stop her if we want any chance of freeing the missing people."

Palo's eyes widened as the other two followed my gaze. He'd gone absolutely rigid. "It can't be..."

"Do you know her, Palo?" I asked in confusion.

Mr. Mason nodded grimly. "An old friend, actually. I haven't seen her since—well, in a very long time."

"Julian's waving at us!" Mary interrupted. "We have to go now!"

"Free the Core 5, then the kids," Palo said, kicking open the cafeteria doors and charging at the closest scientists. Henry let out a shrill scream, followed by a *poof* and a lamp on the ground.

"We're on your side, you dork!" I yelled, running toward the tables where the Core 5 lay.

Lamp-Henry lit up brightly before another *poof* as Henry returned back to normal. His eyes widened, and he was looking at his hands in surprise, like he was seeing them for the first time.

"I did it! I'm free!" he shouted, waving his now unrestrained hands at Dylan and Victoria, both of whom were gaping at him. "Did you guys see that? The lamp worked! It's not useless after all!"

"Then get us out too!" Victoria prompted, holding her duct-taped wrists out to him.

Henry grinned at her helplessly, patting his pockets for something that might help. "Can you turn into a lamp?"

"I've got it!" Palo yelled, slicing through Victoria's bonds with a claw. "Help them wake the others."

Mr. Mason helped his son to his feet as Palo cut him free as well. "Dylan, find Sophie and get out of here—"

"Wait, we can't just start unplugging people," I protested, stopping Victoria before she could unhook Marcus. "We have no idea what these guys are pumping into them. We might be doing more harm than good. Mr. Mason says to use the papayanapple."

Victoria stared at the container of fruit in my hands. "You're not serious?"

"There's a seventy-three percent chance the consistency of the fruit will be enough to wake them up," Mary said, waving a cube of papayanapple under Nora's nose as if to make her point. Nora winced in her sleep as if being woken abruptly from a pleasant dream.

Victoria looked at the fruit in horror, though she took a piece anyway. "What is *in* this stuff?"

"Hey!" a scientist yelled, charging toward us as he realized we were trying to release his prisoners. I flinched as Dylan sent the nearest empty table hurling at him, pinning the man back against the far wall. Dylan slumped painfully like he had a headache. His powers were running out...which was a problem since others were starting to notice us, too.

Another scientist made a break for us. Victoria snatched a larger chunk of the papayanapple and hurled it straight at the woman like a star quarterback. Unfortunately, the shot went wide, missing just slightly and exploding into a citrus-scented burst of juice beside a young guy I had seen at the mall. The juice splashed his face, causing a reaction like a vampire to sunlight. He jerked bolt upright, swatting the juice off his face like it was toxic. It might have been.

"It's working!" Mary prompted, helping Nora sit up sluggishly. Marcus was starting to groan as well.

"I've got more!" Mr. Mason said, producing a few small containers of cut-up fruit squares from his backpack and passing them out to Dylan and Henry.

"How much of this stuff do you have?" Dylan asked incredulously.

"Just be thankful I didn't leave it back at my booth at the festival," his dad said proudly, running off to wake up the nearest row of people.

"Jade!" Julian yelled urgently.

I had lost track of him in the chaos, but now I saw my brother was in deep trouble. The woman in the silvery suit had him in a tight grip. She still seemed worn out from using her powers but had regained enough of her strength to get back on her feet.

"Alright! Enough!" the woman shouted, her voice echoing through the cafeteria with a stern determination. She kept a tight hold on Julian, her lips close to his ear—ready to give a command at a moment's notice. I doubted his powers had recovered enough from the Amalgamation and the scientists to fend her off like he had at the theater. One word from her and Julian could turn us all on each other. "Stop waking people up and stay where you are."

I felt her words wash over me, persuasive whispers twisting into the corners of my mind. I didn't need to try to rescue Julian or wake up the others. I should just stay put, let the scientists get everything back under control. Everything would be fine.

Don't let her in, Jade, Mrs. Mason's voice came, sharp and determined. She looked dazed but was sitting up on the table to my left, her husband having just woken her up. *Fight it.*

My mind started to clear some, though I doubted many of the others could say the same. Victoria had a dazed look on her face, hovering over a still-asleep Sophie like she couldn't quite remember what she was doing there. Henry had dropped his container of papayanapple. Dylan looked reasonably coherent, but I didn't feel confident enough to bet on him being ready to help.

"Let go of my brother," I said, taking a cautious step toward the woman. Her sharp eyes leveled at me, and she tightened her grip on Julian, but only slightly—like she didn't really want to hurt him. I couldn't read his expression. Fear? Anger? Confusion?

Dylan seemed to shake himself out of his daze a little. "Wait, did you just say Julian—"

"I'll explain later," I said, taking another step forward. The woman and Julian moved back, closer to the emergency exit. I put my hands up cautiously. I couldn't force her back too far, or she'd just run. "What's going on here? Why has someone been trying to study people like us?"

"You can see the future, you tell me," she said, smirking knowingly.

"Who's doing this?" Dylan tried, stepping into place beside me and raising his hands. Ready for a fight. Henry wasn't far behind.

"Yeah, lady, start talking," he agreed, trying to sound threatening. He might have even managed it if his voice hadn't cracked.

275

The woman let out a humorless laugh. "A Kastel, a Walker, and a Mason standing against me...been a long time since that's happened."

The woman leaned down and whispered something in Julian's ear. His eyes instantly got a clouded look to them.

"Julian," I said carefully, feeling a knot twist in the pit of my stomach. Between the two of them, they could make me see anything, *do* anything. Suddenly, I wasn't reassured by the boys' presence. One word, one false memory, and we could be turned completely against each other. The lady could let us duke it out and walk away without even a punch thrown at her. "Julian, you need to wake up. I *need* you to wake up right now."

"He's not listening to you anymore, dear," the woman said, shaking her head sadly. "I can be very persuasive when I want to be: your adoptive father's boss recommending him for a new job in Pinewood out of the blue, your former principal insisting you be expelled after that little mishap...What happened again? You broke some kid's nose?"

"He would have done a lot worse if I'd let him get to the girl he was headed for," I protested, teeth clenched tight. My sudden removal from my last school was still a sore subject—even though I knew I'd done a lot more good by stopping that bully I'd seen in my vision. It had all happened so fast: a thrown fist, a quick suspension, a letter saying I wouldn't be allowed back for the next school year. No charges or questions as long as I'd agreed to leave peacefully—almost perfectly timed with Benson's new job halfway across the country anyway. Almost *too* perfect, now that I thought about it.

I swallowed hard, a sick feeling building in my gut. "Someone wanted me here? In Pinewood?"

The lady smiled. "We first found you from the searches you made about your birth parents online. It was almost too easy to get you here. One well-placed operative to befriend you, a false vision from yours truly, and a little orchestrated mishap. Over sixteen years of searching, then it was like you weren't even trying to hide. Thanks for the help, Miss *Kastel*."

My heart skipped a beat. Of course. I hadn't known it at the time, but I had single-handedly let everyone on earth looking for the missing Kastel children know right where I was. I'd been so mad about getting suspended from my last school that I'd run off. Benson had finally found me at 2:30 the next morning, staring at a destination chart at a bus station, trying to figure out someplace where a kid with a couple hundred bucks and no known family could go. It'd been the final straw—Benson had caved in an argument we'd had for years, desperate to get me home and not sure what else he could offer to make me agree.

Okay, you win, he'd said, rubbing his face wearily in the pale light of the bus terminal. *We can go by the clerk's office tomorrow. You can change your name—Jade Kastel. New start. Just...please, don't ever take off like that again.*

I'd promised. The next morning, Jade Benson had vanished with the stroke of a pen, and Jade Kastel had put a big red target on her back.

Still, the woman's words sent a chill up my spine. *One well-placed operative to befriend you...a false vision...a little orchestrated mishap.* I had never been particularly close to anyone at my last school, no one except...*Ashley.* My head started spinning, puzzle pieces clicking together: the way she'd never invited me over to her own house, the way she'd all but vanished after the incident that got me expelled. But how could she have been connected to this woman unless...I felt like I was going to puke. *Unless she had powers.*

"Jade?" Dylan's voice asked worriedly, stirring me back to reality.

"Who's doing this to me?" I asked, ignoring him and keeping my eyes locked dangerously on the woman. "Why was someone so desperate to get me to Pinewood? Was it because Julian was here? The Amalgamation?"

The woman smiled at me, pleased that I was starting to catch on. "My employer and I have searched many years for the Kastel children, the first twins born in decades believed to be able to complete an Amalgamation."

"Something you'd dare not ask them to try if you had any conscience, Winifred," Yan Mei's voice said as she came into the cafeteria. Mr. Goodman was nowhere in sight. The other leaders of the powered community had gathered behind her, still groggy but all on their feet. Mrs. Mason, Marcus, Nora, Skylar, Palo, Susan, and Antoine. "Didn't you learn anything from what happened to William?"

"Don't you dare speak to me about William!" Winifred snarled, dark eyes flashing dangerously. "I have spent seventeen years trying to figure out what went wrong that day! Don't you understand, Yan Mei? The power your grandchildren hold? They could fix everything! *Save* everyone! I tried to convince Vivian, but she refused my offer—"

"My grandchildren will have nothing to do with you if I have any say in it," Yan Mei growled. She looked about two seconds from reprising her bald eagle routine on Winifred.

I stepped between them, drawing the silver-haired woman's attention back to me. "What do you mean? What offer did Vivian Kastel refuse?"

"Jade..." Mrs. Mason's voice warned. There was a small shuffling noise, but I didn't look back—probably her pulling Dylan and Henry back to a safer distance.

"The chance to be on the right side of history," Winifred said, clearly a practiced speech. "The chance to improve our knowledge of who we are. The chance to actually help our people instead of teaching them to hide in the shadows. Unnoticed, unrewarded when we use our powers to help people—just like you were rewarded at your last school."

"We shouldn't need a pat on the back for helping people," Skylar said, balling up her fists. Her face was covered in stray chunks of papayanapple, but she was clearly itching for a fight.

"And anyone who deludes themselves enough to think that you and your cronies are actually helping people is a fool," Yan Mei agreed, face hard. "Look around, Winifred. You're taking people against their will, experimenting on them. Vivian knew there were lines that should not be crossed. She never would have sided with your bunch."

Winifred let out a loud laugh. "Now who's the deluded one! I bet it drives you crazy, Yan Mei, that your children never had the same hatred toward me that you did. I *helped* Trisha. And is that Chris back there? He and Michael and Lance worked for me. Vivian always considered my advice...All of them were able to see the importance of what I was doing."

"Your actions drove my family to ruin! My husband is dead! My daughter's family scattered! Michael might still be alive if it weren't for you and your meddling!" Yan Mei yelled, breaking her stoic composure more than I'd ever seen her. Henry let out a strangled noise for the first time, clearly at a loss for words. "We knew you were the one who set the fire! Vivian never would have let you near the twins! She couldn't—*wouldn't*. Michael was her brother!"

"And *I* offered her the chance to save him," Winifred sighed, eyes turning on Mrs. Mason. "You can tell I'm not lying, Jessica. I offered Vivian everything: prosperity, a place to raise her children where they'd never be hunted or in danger, a chance to save her father, brother...and still, she refused."

Dylan's mother swallowed hard, nervous under all the eyes watching her. "Vivian knew some deals weren't worth taking."

Winifred shrugged. I could sense a boredom taking root in her eyes like she had things to do and was getting tired of keeping us entertained. She kept glancing at Julian, his face still pleasantly vacant. She looked like she didn't want to leave without him.

"I'm just saying, Yan Mei...I tried to convince Vivian there was a way to make everything right again," she said. "With just a little practice, her twins could do it. You could have William back, Michael..."

"You can't bring back the dead, Winifred," Yan Mei said, though her voice was shaking.

"All we want is understanding, Jade. Equality," Winifred said, looking me straight in the eyes. Her tone was so convincing that I almost wondered if she was using her powers. I didn't think she was. "People should use their powers to improve the lives of others, not lurk in the shadows. You and your brother could do wonders for this world, Jade. Vivian couldn't see it, but you can. Let me help you."

"Well, I'm not Vivian," I said, startled by the calm in my own voice. "I'm Jade Kastel, and I want you to let go of my brother *right now*."

Winifred started to laugh again, though she wasn't laughing when I ran forward and put my hands on either side of Julian's face. I was vaguely aware of someone yelling my name—maybe Dylan—but the cafeteria was already fizzling out of sight.

Julian's mind was sluggish, weighed down by Winifred's powers. I could feel her presence everywhere, keeping him calm and slow to respond. A wave of animosity pushed back against my mind. She didn't want me here. I could feel fear growing in her control over him—there was something here she didn't want me to see.

I had to search deep for Julian's memories. They were buried under her powers, blocked off so he couldn't concentrate on anything. I willed them to come to the surface—everything, anything. Good, bad, ugly. Even that disaster of an Amalgamation we'd just seen. Julian needed to wake up, needed to remember. Think for himself.

"Wake up!" I yelled, feeling my brother shudder under my grip.

It was like a dam had broken. Visions ripped through my mind like they had when I'd touched Mr. Goodman at Fernando's: places, people, voices. All of them flashed by at a hundred miles an hour. I saw Julian at five, twelve, sixteen. A winning science fair project, his first day of high school, *several* trips to the doctor's office for bruises and breaks due to his terminal accident-proneness. I saw Dominic Graves scooping up a tiny Julian and hugging him tight after he'd fallen off his bike. I saw a much older Julian having a bad argument with his dad. I saw myself—plowing into him outside the London Fog, sitting in class, holding hands with Dylan at the theater. Emotions battered my mind: anger, sorrow, loneliness, hope. It was all so personal, so *intrusive*. I was invading my brother's mind, forcing him to show me memories I had no business seeing without his permission.

A wave of clarity filled my senses. Julian was waking up, starting to fight back against Winifred. He was forcing her out, taking control again. This was good, considering I felt like I was about to pass out.

I love you so much, a man's voice crept lazily through my mind. *Everything's going to be alright.*

An old, old memory—blurry and half-constructed, maybe one Julian himself wasn't even aware of. His face looked sort of familiar—young and handsome despite the worry woven into it, black hair slicked with rain, eyes lit up blue behind his glasses from the lightning in the sky. I knew I should have known him, but my vision was starting to dim. I felt myself falling into a sea-sick sort of sway like when the Bensons had forced me to go on that cruise.

Finally, I felt Winifred lose her hold on Julian's mind. My eyes opened back on the cafeteria. The lights were all too bright, the monitors too loud. The world was tilting...or was I falling? Julian looked worried. Dylan was still yelling for me. Winifred was running for the exit, though Yan Mei and most of the others were right behind her. The remaining scientists didn't need to be told twice—all of them made a mad scramble for the cafeteria doors, hoping to get away as well.

Somebody caught me before I hit the floor...I'm not sure who, other than they seemed to have about three heads.

CHAPTER
TWENTY-NINE

S omeone was poking me. My eyes were shut tight, but I could tell that there were bright lights on above me. The air was cooler, less echo-y, like a much smaller room than the cafeteria. There was a strong, greasy smell close to my face—dough, sugar—almost like...

"Donuts?" I asked, sitting up much faster than my head appreciated.

Henry laughed, his face slowly coming into focus. "And to think Victoria wanted me to use the papayanapple."

"Chinese food works faster," I agreed, snatching one of the sugary pastries off the plate. I hadn't realized how hungry I was until I'd inhaled about half of them. The donuts weren't very pretty—misshapen, a bit too big, too much sugar—but they tasted almost as good as Yan Mei's. "You make these?"

Henry shrugged sheepishly, munching one of the donuts himself. "I owe you a huge apology. I was angry but not at you, and I took it out on the wrong person. We're so much better off with you, and I'm happy you're my long-lost cousin."

Emotions bubbled in my chest, the taste of the donut suddenly like lead. I did my best to swallow it. "I understand. I'm sorry I kept pushing about Victoria."

"Friends?" he asked, offering me the last donut.

I split it in half and handed him back the larger piece. "No. Family," I agreed, finally feeling like I could move my head enough to take in the familiar room. "When did we get to the cafe?"

"Maybe an hour ago?" Henry guessed, chewing up the last of his donut. "You've been out cold since you did that crazy mind thing on Julian."

I looked around, my heart suddenly pounding. Yan Mei's Cafe was nearly deserted except for us. The *Closed* sign was over the door, and one of the cooks was mopping up the kitchen, silently bopping to whatever music was in his headphones. Tommy and Victoria were stuffing their faces in bowls of lo mein up at the counter, still oblivious that I'd woken up. Dylan and Sophie were propped up against the wall at one of the tables near the front. Dylan had his arms around her, his sister's face tucked into the crook of his shoulder. At first, I thought she might have been asleep, but every once and a while, she'd give a tiny shudder like she was crying. Julian was nowhere in sight.

"Is Julian—"

"Second long-lost cousin was going to stay until you woke up, but his dad called. Said he needed to go back home."

I nodded, still a little dazed. I'd been out an hour? It seemed like there might have been a vague memory of someone putting me back into Palo's truck, but that seemed more like a dream than something that had really happened.

"What happened at the cafeteria? Did they catch Winifred? Any of the scientists?"

Henry frowned. It was a strange expression for him. "They're still looking, but Grandma didn't sound too confident about finding her when she called to check-in. Victoria tried to follow the scientist's cars, but she didn't get too far on her bad ankle. Got a few license plate numbers, though...Grandma's going to give them to a friend at Pinewood PD and see if it goes anywhere."

"And Mr. Goodman?" I asked.

"Already in custody. Once we got all the missing people cleared out, we placed an anonymous call that someone was trespassing at the school," Henry explained, scratching absently at a gouge on the tabletop. "We couldn't get him for taking people since most of them had had their memories manipulated, but Principal Porter apparently showed up in a rage. Looks like we're getting a new English teacher."

Judging from the state our last one had been in, I doubted Mr. Goodman would have been able to hold out much longer anyway. As much as I didn't want to feel bad for the guy, I wondered just how long he'd be able to last without trying to sustain himself on other people's powers.

Luckily, I didn't have to think about it long.

"Jade! You're awake!" Tommy yelled, jumping down from the counter and running over. I should have been flattered—I'd never seen him forget about food for anything before, let alone me. "That was so cool the way you grabbed onto that dude and un-zombied him! Then you passed out, and I thought you were dead, and I was like, 'Oh, no, Mom's gonna be super mad if she's dead!' but then that weird fruit guy said you weren't dead, and I was like, 'Okay, cool' and—"

"Tommy!" I interrupted, head pounding as it tried to make sense of his mile-a-minute words. "Breathe."

"Oh, right," Tommy said, grinning awkwardly. His little nine-year-old face suddenly got that same pensive look all the Bensons got when they got serious. "All those times you zoned out...was that because of—" He waved his hand over me in a broad gesture.

"My powers?"

Tommy nodded.

"Yeah," I said, feeling weird about admitting to a secret I'd kept longer than he'd been alive. "Yeah, it was. Look, Tommy—"

"I'm not going to tell," my brother promised, holding up his hand like Scout's Honor. "I can't jeopardize your secret identity. That's like Rule Number One of knowing a superhero."

I didn't choke up. It was just...really bad allergies. "You think I'm a superhero?"

Tommy gave me a mischievous grin. "I think you're much more interesting than you were this morning."

I punched his arm, though maybe a little lighter than I normally would have. A loud series of pops sounded from somewhere outside, making us all jump. A wave of color flashed through the restaurant's windows as embers fizzled in the night sky.

"Hey, look, the fireworks are starting," Henry said, grinning as another burst of blue and red and green sizzled up over Pinewood.

For a moment, they were pretty. Then my stomach dropped with realization.

"Oh, no!" I yelled, shoving myself up out of the booth and grabbing Tommy's hand. "Oh, no, no, no, no, no. This is bad. Where's my bag? Henry, where'd you put my bag?"

"It's over by the door." Dylan pointed, blue eyes suddenly alarmed. He looked like he wanted to get up but couldn't really manage it with Sophie on him. "Where's the fire?"

"Tommy and I were supposed to meet the Bensons at the fireworks! They're going to freak out!"

"Then let's go make sure you guys get to the fireworks!" Victoria said.

I smiled at her. For someone who could see the future and the past, I was so wrong about Victoria. She was actually completely different than I originally thought. It wasn't fair for me to complain about people judging me without knowing me when I had done the exact same thing to her.

Dylan gave Sophie a questioning look, and she nodded. He swung her around, placing her gracefully on his back.

"For The Owl Kingdom!" she shouted, a little sleepy sounding.

Henry thrust his arm up in the air. "For The Owl Kingdom!"

We all gave Henry a look, and we ran out the door. Thankfully, Yan Mei's restaurant wasn't that far from the festivities. We briskly ran through the crowd, apologizing constantly for being in the way or stepping on toes as we tried to find our way to the Bensons in the crowd. Where had they said they'd be?

"There!" Tommy yelled, yanking me toward the far edge of the park where most of the crowd had gathered. Mrs. B and Benson turned at the sound of his voice, smiling confusedly at the sight of him dragging me forward.

As we got closer, the Bensons noticed Dylan, Sophie, Henry, and

Victoria trailing behind us. Mrs. B beamed like no fireworks could have lit a candle to me showing up with friends. I found myself smiling and waving at the Bensons as we caught up with them.

"Sorry we're late!" I said, panting as we stopped.

"I see you brought some people," Benson said.

"Just a few friends," I agreed.

"And they're awesome!" Tommy shouted, making our parents laugh. Both looked shocked that Tommy could have thought any friends of mine were "Awesome!"

Mrs. B looked at Henry. "So I take it the boom-box days are over then?"

Henry gave her a big thumbs up. Victoria eyed him curiously.

"No longer needed."

Benson gave an apprehensive glance to Dylan, who was still carrying Sophie on his back. Mrs. B nudged him before smiling at Dylan. "Oh, Dylan, I take it this is Sophie?"

Sophie perked up at the sound of her name. "That's me! I like owls."

Mrs. B chuckled. "You are such a doll!"

Henry leaned close to Dylan out of Mrs. B's earshot and whispered quietly. "Oh, no. You're being replaced."

Dylan bopped him lightly on the shoulder.

"Well, you didn't miss much. Let's all sit down and enjoy the show!" Mrs. B said.

The pair sat in lawn chairs they'd brought while the rest of us found a spot on the soft grass. Sophie sat in between Henry and Victoria, oohing and ahhing at all the larger fireworks. Tommy sat near the Bensons, happily accepting a bag of gummy worms from his mom's snack stash and leaving me and Dylan sitting next to each other. If I had to take a guess, I would say it was planned.

Dylan leaned in close, unable to speak over the loud booming of the fireworks. I found myself feeling warmer as our arms touched. He smiled at me.

Before long, the fireworks gave one last thunderous roar before dissipating into the night sky, leaving just the stars in their wake. People started to clear out. Julian wasn't anywhere in the crowd—he and his dad probably couldn't make it back in time if they'd had to go home. I looked to my friends, realizing the day was now over, and we would all be going our separate ways. It felt like an entire week had passed since this morning, and I certainly was starting to feel like it.

Henry offered to drive Victoria home since they were neighbors. Mr. and Mrs. Mason had showed up to collect a very sleepy Sophie. Judging from their somber expressions, the Core 5 hadn't had much luck finding Winifred. They glanced at Dylan, and Mrs. Mason gave him a knowing look. I couldn't help but think they were having a silent conversation in their minds. She nodded, consenting to whatever Dylan had silently asked.

Benson and Mrs. B were packing up their chairs. Tommy was already headed for the car. I was about to follow when Dylan grabbed my hand. He nervously glanced between the Bensons and me before speaking.

"Jade, can I talk to you for a second?" he asked before turning to the Bensons. "If that's alright with you, of course?"

Benson didn't look happy, though his wife could barely contain her excitement. Mrs. Mason blinked rapidly, and I wondered if Mrs. B was shouting in her mind. That would not be surprising.

"Of course, you can!" she said.

Benson cleared his throat. "Make it quick...We'll meet you at the car, Jade."

He reluctantly turned to follow his son back to the parking lot. Mrs. B stayed close behind, trying not to grin at me over her shoulder. I rolled my eyes.

He's lucky to have you, Jade, Mrs. Mason said in my head, smoothing a piece of hair out of Sophie's face before she and her husband left as well.

With everyone gone, Dylan turned to me. Most of the crowd had trickled away now, too, leaving us in the semi-darkness of the park. My heart started to race. Even after what happened at the mall, I still found myself nervous. Had that only been a few hours ago?

"You did it, Jade. You saved everyone."

I smiled at him. "You believed in me."

My words seemed to make him nervous. He stepped away from me ever so slightly, his smile dropping into a serious look. "Listen, about earlier...I know people like us—together, that is," he started.

"My adoptive mother especially," I added.

"Right. But I don't want you to think you should be with me because other people want you to or just because I want you to," he said, fiddling nervously with the zipper on his jacket. "Does that make sense?"

I turned my head to the side, confused. A silent cue for him to continue.

"I just...I understand that at the swim meet, you were trying to protect me, and at the theater, we were just trying to play a part. I don't want you to feel like you should like me if you don't feel the way that I do. I mean, you just found your long-lost twin brother! And you're like —this super special and amazing person who's the reason all the missing people, like my sister, are saved. You are like so out of my league it's crazy, and I'm a dork who has trouble being confident and always says the wrong thing, so I understand if—now that we don't have to pretend if you don't want—"

I put my hand over his mouth. His blue eyes were wide, not sure what I was doing. I was tempted to laugh. Nervous Dylan was so cute, but I didn't want him to get the wrong impression.

"Well, why don't you ask?"

He stammered. "Ask you...what?"

"Ask me what I want."

"Okay..." He trailed off. "What do you want?"

"A lot of things, actually," I started, making him laugh. "First, I want you to stop beating yourself up. You weren't forcing me into anything— I'm Jade Kastel, I do what I want. Second, I want you to never talk about kissing me with Henry ever again. And lastly..." I said, trailing off. The words seemed to be stuck in my throat. In just a few months, he had changed my entire world. How do you tell somebody that?

I gazed into his eyes.

Dylan, the boy who caused me to see a vision of my own death. The boy who never saw me as an outsider but instead believed in me against all odds. The boy who I now knew I cared for just as much as I'd seen him feel for me in my vision. I was still terrified of the future—but, at least now, I wasn't alone.

I reached up, gently cradling Dylan's face in my hands. His eyes locked onto mine. "Last, I want to be with you, Dylan Mason."

He smiled as I pulled his face down to mine, kissing him softly before pulling away. Just slightly, though.

His hands rested gently on my waist. "Yes, ma'am."

CHAPTER
THIRTY

"But it's not the same!" Henry complained, biting sadly into his hamburger. "I'd already started making our costumes!"

"Oh my gosh, Henry! We were *never* going to do the play!" I said for the hundredth time. Henry had not taken well to Mr. Goodman's replacement changing the instructions on our *Macbeth* group projects. "Just be grateful for the paper and be done with it."

"But we'd already been working on it for like two months—"

"You didn't even read your script," Dylan commented, squeezing my hand underneath the table. I could tell he was trying hard not to laugh. "Until a few days ago, you were confusing Macduff with Montague. They're from two completely different plays."

"By the *same* writer," Henry insisted, taking another massive bite of his burger. "You're just agreeing with Jade so you can make a good impression on the in-laws."

Julian looked up from his lunch tray, suddenly startled by all the attention on him. He'd been sort of quiet and distracted since he'd sat down beside me, but I wasn't sure if something was bothering him or if that was just naturally how he was. It was clear he had no idea what we were talking about.

"What?" he asked blankly.

"Wouldn't you be his in-laws too, Henry?" Mary asked, trying hard not to smirk as she took a drink. Elyse nudged her to leave him alone, but she was grinning too.

"That...is beside the point," Henry fumbled, rolling his eyes as he turned to the rest of the table. "Back me up here, guys!"

"After you spilled Dr. Pepper all over the model *Enterprise,* I'd just spent six hours painting?" Kazi said, narrowing his eyes at Henry with disdain. "I don't think so."

"I told you it was an accident!" Henry defended. "Spencer? Katie? Tyler?"

Spencer and Tyler ignored him, not even pausing in their conversation. Katie looked like she wanted to say something but pursed her lips when Kazi glared at her.

"I'd just take the paper," she said, busying herself with breaking crackers into her soup thermos.

A fast-food bag suddenly plopped onto the table as Victoria sat down in the empty spot between Henry and Mary. WUZZIES. Again. I'm sorry, why couldn't I have a *useful* power like super-speed to get takeout anytime I wanted?

"You know, you really don't have to show off," I said, watching her pull out a Ginormous-Size Wuzzyburger and a large order of fries. My school chicken tenders looked remarkably sad in comparison.

"I know." Victoria grinned, smacking Henry's hand away as he tried to swipe some of her fries.

"I'm sorry...What are you doing here?" Tyler asked, gaping at her like he couldn't quite understand why one of Pinewood's most popular people had just sat down with us. I mean, the nerd table had grown significantly in membership over the last few weeks: first me, then Julian, then Mary, then Elyse...but Victoria Harper? If I hadn't seen what I had at Fernando's that night, I wouldn't have even believed it myself. Apparently, several other people were thinking the same thing— the pack of cheerleaders and swim and football jocks at her usual table looked thoroughly confused without the presence of their supreme leader. "You lost?"

"Better yet, do you have my list?" Spencer interrupted, nervously smoothing out his only slightly thicker mustache. "You were supposed to give me the names of all the gamers at Pinewood so I could find out who CobaltChaos is."

"I'll save you some time," Victoria said, plopping a big glob of ketchup out onto a napkin. "It's me."

Spencer choked on his Mountain Dew. "*What?*"

Victoria looked up, unconcerned. "CobaltChaos. It's me," she said nonchalantly. "Oh, by the way, I beat the quest for the Black Sword last night. You're gonna need a whole four thousand more points to reclaim your spot now."

"Dang, girl!" Katie cheered, high-fiving Victoria across the table.

Spencer didn't know what to say. Kazi started laughing, low at first but then so much he was almost crying. More people were looking at us now. Victoria didn't seem to care. Suddenly, I realized she looked different too—posture less stiff, jaw not so tightly set. Confident, but more comfortable. Still Victoria, but more real. Henry beamed, noticing it too.

"T-The Black Sword," Spencer echoed, unable to manage anything else.

Victoria nodded calmly. "Better practice up. I'm going to have a lot more time on my hands now that I've resigned as class president."

"Nineteen percent more time," Mary muttered under her breath, though luckily, no one seemed to notice.

"You're quitting?" Julian asked, leaning around me in confusion.

"I decided I needed some time to focus on other things," Victoria said, eyeing those of us from the mall knowingly.

I hadn't heard all of the story except for what Henry knew, but apparently, after he'd dropped her off from the festival, Victoria and her parents had a long talk about letting Yan Mei try to help her with her powers. Judging from the way she was grinning, Victoria must have felt better about her powers than she had in a long time.

"Ooh, there's Mrs. Sawyer!" Henry said, dropping his hamburger and scrambling out of his seat. "I'm gonna see if she'll change her mind on the play—"

"NO!" Dylan and I said in unison.

Henry ignored us, shoving his stuff back in his lunchbox and checking both ways for incoming students ready to throw away their trays. "Remember, six o'clock sharp, everybody. You know where. I'd better see you there too, Victoria."

"You will," she promised, making Henry grin from ear to ear before he hurried off to chase down our new English teacher.

"What's at six o'clock?" Julian whispered, leaning over to ask me once Henry was gone.

I smiled at him. "You free tonight? I think there's something you need to see."

~

"It's a mall," Julian said, looking confused as he stepped out of his car. His driver—who was still inexplicably wearing sunglasses at night—gave me a curt nod before pulling away. "Why are we at a mall? I've never been to this mall before."

I grinned at him. "I think you'll find all the answers inside."

"I feel like that has to be a line in some movie."

"Improving your taste in movies is second on my agenda," I said, bumping him slightly as we made our way into the food court entrance. Julian stuck his tongue out at me. One of my favorite things about Julian was that he had the demeanor of a serious person if you didn't know him, but when you did, you quickly learned he was basically a total goof.

"Wow," he gasped, face awestruck as he took in the overhead courses and training rooms. He looked like a kid at Disneyland. "Also, you lied. I have *so* many more questions now."

I tugged his arm forward to hurry him along—people were waiting on us. On our way to the Archive, I suspected I answered approximately a million questions before I finally snapped at him to hush.

"Yes, ma'am," he said with an audible gulp.

People waved at us as we passed, and I was suddenly surprised by how many I knew: Palo and Skylar, Mr. and Mrs. Mason, Marcus, Nora, Susan and Antoine, Mary and Elyse, Tyler. We passed Sophie and some of the other super-strength kids hefting hundred-pound barbells over their heads. Henry had planned to give Course Seven another go since he'd yet to manage another non-lamp transformation since the wolf at Fernando's. Tommy, despite not having powers, had talked Dylan into letting him tag along in the newly opened blackout course (AKA, the *Dodge-All-the-Things Room*). I could hear him inside the course, laughing maniacally about how he would not be defeated. Henry was definitely going to be proud his hard work to convert the mini-golf course was successful.

"He certainly seems to be enjoying himself," Julian noted as we caught a brief glimpse of Dylan running past the course's doorway, yelling for Tommy to be careful.

"Too much." I nodded darkly. "He's having so much fun he might never go back to soccer practice again."

The door to the Archive finally came into sight just as a quick flash of blonde whirled around us.

"Hey, guys!" it said cheerfully before rushing away in a burst of wind.

"Victoria?" we asked in unison, but the blonde blur was already gone.

The door to the Archive opened, Yan Mei's head peeking through.

"Come in," she said, holding the door open for us. We walked inside, and I once again got to marvel at Julian's reaction to the place, even if this was one of the less tampered-with areas of the mall. The Archive seemed the same as it had on my first visit—strong coffee smell, soft music for the few researchers milling around. Our grandmother led us under the arches of the storytime castle, where several new bean bag chairs had been added to the Core 5's secret meeting place. I gave Yan Mei a questioning look.

"Henry figured they would be comfortable," Yan Mei said, sinking into one of the plush chairs. "Have a seat."

Julian sat on a pizza-print one while I chose a plain black seat, obnoxiously sinking further toward the ground than comfortable. Julian chuckled at my annoyance.

Yan Mei smiled fondly at us. "I never thought I would see you both in the same place at the same time again. For a long time, I had almost given up hope that either of you was alive..." She trailed off before clearing her throat. "I asked you both here because there is something very dangerous coming, and I want you to be prepared. It's time you knew everything."

We stared at her in silence for a moment. The air was already thick with tension. Only Yan Mei would be able to set a tone like that with just a single sentence.

"The fact of the matter is," our grandmother began, voice trembling slightly, "that you two are not the first set of twins able to complete an Amalgamation."

"Um, what?" Julian asked, hugging his knees awkwardly to offset the shifting beanbag.

"Yeah, I thought Mary said—"

Yan Mei raised a hand to cut us off. "I never said that Mary's analysis was incorrect. It is very difficult to align all the factors needed to produce a complete Amalgamation—even if you had a set of twins with compatible powers, it might never be possible for the two to harness their abilities in such a shared way. My researchers have barely found a dozen instances where such a combination has been recorded. As Winifred obviously hoped and I feared, you two have proven you are able to wield such a power as well."

"But isn't that a good thing?" I asked, a bubble of curiosity building in my chest. "If an Amalgamation isn't such a new thing—"

"The Amalgamation is a *dangerous* thing," Yan Mei said, cutting me off sharply. "Only made more dangerous by the combination of you two and your specific powers."

"You mean us seeing the future when we did the Amalgamation... that doesn't normally happen?" Julian asked, fighting to sit up straighter against the pizza beanbag.

Our grandmother shook her head. "An Amalgamation is specific to those who use it, Julian. In some instances, harnessing an Amalgamation might be perfectly harmless, but you two have inherited gifts of awesome potential. I'm afraid the consequences of Jade's power fusing with your own could have disastrous consequences. When you told me what you saw, how *real* you said it felt...did it ever occur to you that maybe it felt real because you were *really* there?"

I nearly fell off my beanbag. "Are you saying that instead of just

295

seeing through time, we actually *traveled* through it? That—that *mess* we saw, was our actual future?"

"Unfortunately, I suspect it was," Yan Mei said grimly. "The combination of one who can see through time and one who can shape the appearance of reality. That is what Winifred meant when she said you two could fix everything. With you two at her side, she could become a master of time itself."

"Meaning she could speed up whatever project her boss is working on," I said, feeling puzzle pieces start to click together in my mind. "Mary said it would be delayed sixteen years."

"Project?" Julian asked.

"Jade was able to find out some information when she saw Mary Milford's memories from when she was taken," Yan Mei explained gravely. "Winifred and someone—presumably her boss—were probing for information on you two and some kind of device they were building. A device to mass distribute powers."

"I thought the missing people had their memories tampered with?" Julian asked, suddenly looking very confused. He looked pale, and I was worried we were hitting him with too much new information too fast.

"I was able to get through the tampered memories," I said, reaching over and squeezing his hand reassuringly. I didn't think it helped.

"I believe Jade's right. Winifred would have much cause to change the past, but she obviously has an agenda for the future as well," Yan Mei said. "Much of her previous research dealt with discovering how powers work, though she's obviously made some progress since I last saw her. I imagine the experiment with Mr. Goodman was a trial run, some lead up to this device she's so concerned about."

"Do you think it has something to do with what we saw?" I asked, trying to keep my voice low as one of the Archive workers passed by the doorway to the kid's section. "I mean, Julian saw the date. Sixteen years in the future, just like Mary said with the device—"

"I think it's best we agree not to mention what you saw to anyone beyond me or the Core 5," Yan Mei said firmly, steely eyes leveling at us. "I know it was frightening, but we can't let fear take over us. Actually, I would think you'd find some comfort in it, Jade, seeing yourself alive that far in the future."

In truth, I *did* feel relieved. I had never had a vision that hadn't come true before, but if what Julian and I had seen in the Amalgamation really was the future, then maybe the impending doom I'd seen in the mega-vision wasn't so impending after all. I mean, we had both seen it: me alive, clear as day, sixteen years from now. But still, with the rest of it...

An ashy taste filled my mouth. Julian didn't look much better.

"If we can change time, though," he said quietly after a long silence had settled over the three of us. "What's to stop us from going back to the future and stopping everything from happening?"

Yan Mei looked like he'd slapped her across the face. "Didn't you hear anything I just said? Combining your powers is extremely dangerous! You don't know how much power you'll exert. You don't know what point in time you'll go to—"

"But the Amalgamation snapped us to a specific moment in the future," I protested, standing up. "There had to be a reason we went there! Nearly every vision I've had has shown me something important. Surely, this would work the same way!"

"Shown you, yes. Allowed you to change, no," Yan Mei protested, standing to meet my gaze. I'd never noticed it before, but we weren't too far off from the same height. "Jade, you told me yourself that's how it works."

"But the Amalgamation directly contradicted the mega-vision!"

"Meaning your abilities allow you to see *potential* realities," Yan Mei said, running a hand over her face wearily. "Still, we have no idea which course of action your life will take. Will you die a year or two from now or be alive in sixteen years? It's impossible to say."

"But we could make sure she's alive!" Julian said, clambering to his feet as well. He grabbed my hand, and I smiled softly at him. "I'm not going to just stand by and let people die without a fight. Especially not my sister. I'll do whatever it takes to stop it."

"Time is not meant to be messed with!" Yan Mei said worriedly. "Don't you understand that's the opinion Winifred wants you to take? If you two control time, you can control anything—any event, any person, any consequence. People with powers are not meant to be gods."

"Even if it could save our mom?" I asked, knowing it was a low blow. "Even if it could save *us*?"

Yan Mei looked like that one question had aged her ten years. For the first time, she watched me with a strange expression, as if she'd looked up and been surprised to find me standing there instead of someone else.

"The Core 5 and I have decided. No mention of the Amalgamation is to be shared with anyone else," Yan Mei said, steeling herself with a shaky breath. "Not Dylan, not Henry, not anyone. Though you have this power, you two will never attempt to use it again. Is that clear?"

"What?" Julian and I asked in unison.

"What do you mean, never use it?" I asked, beating my brother to the question. "The future—"

"The future will come in its own time with its own problems without any help from you two," Yan Mei said, looking at us pleadingly. "I just got the two of you back. I will not risk you again. Not for the past. Not for the future. Not for anybody."

She tried to reach out for us, but I pulled back just out of reach.

"What is it about the Amalgamation that scares you so much?" I asked in confusion. "You've been terrified ever since Mary mentioned it. There has to be a reason."

Yan Mei took a deep breath, obviously trying hard to hold it together. "There are some things that just shouldn't be messed with."

"There's more to it than that, though, isn't there?" Julian agreed, keeping his voice gentle. Yan Mei's eyes darted between us like she was cornered by a room full of ghosts.

I reached out and grabbed her hand. "If there's something about the Amalgamation we need to know, it'd be better if it came from you... Grandma."

Yan Mei put her hand on my face like she'd done with Henry before and gave a reluctant nod.

"As I said, you two inherited powers with awesome potential," she said quietly, pulling Julian close as well. "When we first learned there were two of you, I never even thought about what that could mean power-wise, but once you all disappeared, I knew those who wished to exploit the Amalgamation must have been what caused your parents to flee."

"Because twins are so rare among powered people?" I asked, remembering what Mary had said.

Yan Mei pursed her lips, clearly unsure. "Rare among powered people, but not among our family. Powers are a complicated thing... sometimes people develop ones that are unique, other times they are passed straight down genetically."

"Like Henry being a shapeshifter like you, but our mom having storm powers," Julian said.

"Exactly," she confirmed. "Much like Henry, you two inherited your powers directly."

"Your husband," I said, feeling silly for not realizing it before. "That's how you knew so much about the way my powers worked and why you were surprised that I could see into the future and past. He couldn't see both, could he?"

Yan Mei frowned slightly. "No, he couldn't."

"But if Jade got her powers from our grandfather, then whose did I get? Our dad's?" Julian asked.

Yan Mei shook her head, fighting off that same little wince she got any time our father was mentioned. "Lance had an extraordinary gift, but it was not like yours. No, your gift, much like Jade's, comes from Vivian's side of the family."

Realization hit me like a truck. I would've stumbled back if Yan Mei didn't still have my hand. Her eyes watched me sadly, grimly confirming something I'd never imagined in a million years. It all made sense...why all the grown-ups had known each other in the cafeteria, why Yan Mei had been so worried when she'd heard I'd been mind-controlled at the theater...

"Your husband's name was William," I said, unable to figure out a better place to start. Julian looked at me worriedly, waiting for an explanation. "Willam, who had the same powers as me. I have a twin, and you said twins weren't uncommon in our family..."

Yan Mei said nothing, waiting for me to piece it all together for myself.

"When you said we weren't the first twins able to do an Amalgamation, you weren't talking about history, were you? You've seen it done before, haven't you?"

Julian suddenly braced himself against the closest bookshelf. "William and Winifred...like Jade and Julian. I-I inherited *her* powers?"

Yan Mei rubbed slow circles on his back like he was a little kid who suddenly felt sick. Julian didn't look that far off from it. "Where one's powers come from doesn't matter. It's how you decide to use them that counts."

"The reaction makes all the difference," I mumbled, echoing her words from when we'd first spoken about my powers at the cafe. "They have roughly the same powers as us...You knew what our Amalgamation would be this entire time, didn't you?"

"I suspected, assuming you'd be able to use your powers in such a way," she said quietly. "William and Winifred...As far as I can tell, they were only able to manage a complete Amalgamation once. Not long after the two of you were born. I don't know how or why they suddenly decided to try it again after years of failed attempts or why their Amalgamation finally worked."

"But they would have traveled to the future, too?" I asked, feeling the wheels turning in my mind. "Did they see the same thing we did? Did they go to some other time?"

"I don't know," Yan Mei said, taking a shaky breath. "I never found out where they went—only what happened afterward. That's why I can't let you experiment with the Amalgamation anymore. The risks are just too high."

Julian looked dumbfounded. "But, Yan Mei, the future we saw—"

"Is nothing compared to what will happen if you combine your powers the wrong way," Yan Mei said sharply, cutting him off. "You two were lucky to have gotten through the Amalgamation safely at the school. I won't have you attempt it anymore, not for anything."

"Something happened, didn't it?" I asked, a knot already twisting tight in my stomach. "When William and Winifred combined their powers—something went wrong? That's why you don't want us messing with it?"

Yan Mei leveled her eyes at me. She looked more serious than I had ever seen her, eyes filled with seventeen years of loss, fear, and anger.

Sometimes, it was easy to forget that this was a woman who had lost nearly everything, everyone. Yet for the first time, she had been given a small chance at getting back some of what had been stolen from her. It was clear she was not about to let it be lost again.

"You two cannot combine your powers," our grandmother said firmly, "because the Amalgamation is what killed my husband."

EPILOGUE

JULIAN

I was nervous. Well, that wasn't too surprising, but *everything* about this mattered. They had to trust me. *Jade* had to trust me. For a brief amount of time, I got to be selfish—something I planned on fully taking advantage of. How well I did now would determine how long I got to be selfish, and for the first time in my life, I was going to do *exactly* as I was told.

"Everything okay?" Jade said, a small frown on her face. It's funny; I always knew I had a twin, but I was fully unprepared for how it would *feel* to have a twin. She could read me like a book... which was both wonderful and frightening, for more reasons than one. I gave her a soft grin. I imagined my father's business smile. *Be charming.*

"Yeah, thanks. Just a little nervous," I told her. She nodded, and I let out a shaky breath. It was bad enough she had seen my memories when I was under Winifred's control. *Ugh.*

Jade placed her small hand over mine. "I am, too. But we're in this together. You helped me keep it together at the school. I'll be here for you today."

302

I vowed for the fifty-seventh time that, above all else, I would protect my sister.

We were walking inside the giant mall—the abandoned one that served as Yan Mei's hideout and training facility. I had thought about asking Jade if I needed to show up in a tracksuit, but our dear cousin Henry would probably love that idea. The last thing we all needed was matching exercise clothes that said *Cuz Crew.*

Still, the place was endless: dozens of half-set-up training courses or unused rooms like the one we'd just stepped into. An old movie theater? Everyone had said it would be an easy place to hide, and I could see why —this side of the mall was practically deserted. Yan Mei had basically made all talk of the Amalgamation a big no-no. Her reasoning was solid, so I was surprised at Jade and the others' willingness to go against her words. It *did* kill our grandfather...*If only it had taken the other one instead.*

Inside the small movie theater was a giant screen that took up the entire back wall, rows of black carpeted seats filing downward, and large red curtains on either side of the screen. The others were already waiting for us: Victoria, munching contentedly from a giant bucket of popcorn; Henry, chatting aimlessly as always; and Dylan, the lovesick boyfriend, staring lovingly at my sister. I'd known Dylan for a long time, and it was clear he would be good to her. Only somewhat attractive, though.

"Hey! You're back!" Henry shouted, completely missing the point of *covert meeting.* We made our way down the front row toward the trio. Jade opted to sit next to Dylan, so I took my rightful place on her other side in between her and Victoria.

"So...how do we do this?" Dylan asked.

"Julian can share his memories through touch. He's basically going to *replay* what we saw when we did the Amalgamation," Jade said.

"That's still so freaky that you can time travel," Victoria said, shoveling a handful of popcorn into her mouth.

"It's *awesome!*" Henry exclaimed. "And it can't be that risky. You both did it already, and nobody died."

Jade and I nearly choked. It was her idea not to tell them everything our grandmother had told us, only that it was too risky. Victoria nudged him.

303

"Not funny, Henry," she chided.

"Sorry! So, do we form a kumbaya circle or something?" Henry asked.

I did my best to clear my throat. "A circle is fine. We just need to all be touching, so...grab hands, maybe?"

It was awkward touching people in general, but all circled up, I could definitely see how this would be very weird if someone accidentally wandered in.

"Okay, let's do this," Jade said with a forced look of confidence. I don't think I had to be her twin to see how hard this was on her. Experiencing the Amalgamation the first time was traumatizing enough. Her shaking form haunted me sometimes. To think that the Amalgamation shook her more than seeing a vision of herself dying...she didn't realize how truly selfless she was. I squeezed her hand.

"Wait!" Henry shouted, breaking free from the odd circle. "I have to pee! I'll be five minutes—seven minutes tops!"

We all gave a collective groan.

"Henry!" Victoria whined.

"Seven?" Jade asked worriedly.

He was gone almost as fast as Victoria.

Untrue to his word, it had been fifteen minutes, and there was still no sign of our chaotic cousin.

"Ugh," Jade groaned.

"Well, maybe it would be best to just tell him about it later," Victoria said, earning puzzled looks from the rest of us. "You said the Amalgamation was pretty rough. Maybe Henry's taking his time on purpose?"

Jade and I shared a knowing look. We had warned them all in advance that the vision would be a brutal experience, and if there was anyone who seemed to be able to read Henry, it was Victoria. She did have a point, though—Henry might take the news better by *not* reliving it. Especially with what we saw.

The three moved closer to me, and we joined hands once again. I closed my eyes, focusing on connecting with the three of them. *No going back now.*

I focused on the memory of our Amalgamation. Sixteen years in the future.

~

The town was ash. Smoke permeated the air from what remained of the buildings, making my nose sting. I looked to Jade, who was frozen. Her eyes were wide, arms hugging herself.

"I've seen this before," she said. Never a good sign. She started running. "This way!"

I ran after her, my shoes crunching with every step over glass shards and ashy remains. I had been trained in mental and physical endurance for years, but still I struggled for breath in the smoky air. Jade coughed mercilessly as we ran.

Suddenly, she came to a halt, looking around frantically.

"I don't understand," Jade said. "Everyone was supposed to be here."

"Are you sure you've seen this before?" I asked.

"This looks *exactly* like a vision I had a few weeks ago. I don't have that many visions of destroyed towns, Julian," she said.

I threw my hands up in submission. "Okay, I believe you. What happened in your vision?"

She paused, rubbing her arm again. "Well...the Bensons and Dylan were there, and I...I was dead."

Oh.

What?

Suddenly, there were two figures that were running a short distance away. A man and woman who looked strikingly familiar but were too far and too fast for me to tell who exactly they were.

"Let's follow them," Jade said. She said it like a suggestion, but her tone was meant to be taken as an order.

"Alright," I said, and we took off once more. "Do your visions always require this much exercise?"

She huffed. "No, I've never run this much in my life. Also, if this is an Amalgamation, where do your powers come in?"

I really wanted to stop running, but I kept on as I thought of her question. "No idea."

The pair started to slow down as they approached what looked to be the remains of the Pinewood library. Jade and I settled into a spot behind a fallen sign just close enough to the library entrance to not be seen. The door was smashed, but the majority of the building remained intact, with books littered everywhere.

I got a closer look at the duo: the woman had light brown skin and shimmery brown curls thrown into a disheveled updo. Her clothes were tattered, and there was a nasty cut on the arm she was clutching with her other hand. The man was tall with long, dark hair with gray streaks on the sides and the start of wrinkles around his eyes. He looked to be in better shape than the woman, with neater clothes and a shark tooth necklace around his neck.

"They look so familiar," Jade whispered.

"Jade," the man said. We both looked up at the man who was gently holding the arm of the woman beside him.

I looked to my sister, whose mouth was agape.

"Is this the future?" I whispered.

"I'm alive?" Jade gasped.

"The van should be about to go. You can still leave...if you want. No one would blame you," the man said.

The woman—Jade from the future—shook her head. "No, Palo, I'm staying. I have to."

"Jade!"

A blonde woman came rushing in, forcing us to creep closer to the entrance to hear them. It was a younger woman with blue eyes and a dress suit and tailored pants. Why was a businesswoman in the apocalypse?

Future Jade rushed over to the young woman and embraced her tightly. "Soph!"

Sophie? As in the tiny girl with super strength and a slight obsession with owls?

Future Palo pointed to the back of the building. "I'll go check on the others."

"Sophie, it didn't work. We still couldn't do an Amalgamation."

Future Jade was trying to combine powers again? Had we reached a point where we couldn't do that anymore? Was the Amalgamation a one-time thing?

"It was something we had to try. The important thing is you're safe," she said. "Where's Dylan and Julian?"

We couldn't see Future Jade's face from our hiding spot, but we could see Sophie's. The joy from seeing Future Jade vanished. The younger girl's arms dropped from their embrace, mouth agape and tears pooling in her eyes.

"Jade...Where is Dylan?" she asked.

Future Jade fumbled her words. "He's gone."

My sister's form shook beside me. I found myself in shock, too. Clearly, she and Dylan still cared deeply for each other years into the future. They could have even had a life together, a *family*. I'd known Dylan Mason since...since we started school. In a sense, we'd grown up together. We weren't friends, but...even sixteen years in the future, he was so *young*. Too young.

"He died protecting me and Julian," Future Jade said.

Future Sophie took a deep breath and cleared her throat, nodding. "Then he had no regrets and lived his life the way he wanted," Sophie said. "I'll go tell the others to prepare for Plan B."

Future Jade said nothing as Sophie walked off, meeting a guy about her age in the doorway. She took his offered hand and walked toward where Palo had gone. I'd known Dylan's sister was supposed to be strong physically, but her future self must have been made of extremely tough stuff to hear about her brother's death and then have to immediately stay focused on the mission at hand.

I turned to my own sister, who stared at her future self's form, both of them frozen in silence.

"That can't happen," Jade muttered.

I didn't have any words that could help her, so I gave her my hand. She took it, and I didn't complain when my hand started to ache from the pressure.

"Should we...see who else is left?" Jade choked out, her voice hollow.

Suddenly, Future Jade rushed over to a wall, searching worriedly as if she'd dropped something. She rifled through piles of fallen books and rubble before she seemed to find what she was looking for. A crumpled flier blew out in the wind, brushing momentarily against my shoe. *August 25th*, it declared, but the other date...Did that say *sixteen years* from now? Future Jade finally seemed to find what she was looking for, slinging something back around her neck as she quickly reapproached the front of the building. Wasn't everyone else leaving from the back? Where was she going?

"Rushing off into danger again, Jade?" a familiar voice said.

"What?" Jade whispered.

Future Jade turned around to see Benjamin Benson, who looked exactly the same as he did now except with streaky gray hair, forehead lines, and thick glasses.

"I can't sit back and do nothing, Dad," she said.

"And I can't let you go alone, my dear," Benson said.

As if the woman's walls finally crumbled, Future Jade threw herself into her adoptive father's open arms. She clung to him, sobbing. Her voice was hoarse, but she continued to cry out while Benson gently rubbed her back.

"I loved them, Dad," she cried. "I loved them *so* much. What am I going to do without them?"

Benson's eyes widened, his grip slacked for a moment before continuing on, tears flowing gently down his cheeks.

"They knew, love. They loved you more than anything. They were... both like sons to me. I loved them too."

We knew Dylan, but who was the other like-a-son to Benson? Surely not Tommy—he was his biological son. Henry, perhaps? Just the thought of guessing who was dead made me sick. But there was a feeling in the pit of my stomach. Was it...*me*?

"Is everyone alright? Violet and B—" the sobbing woman asked, getting choked up on her words.

Benson nodded. "They're safe. Victoria and the others are all loaded up, waiting to go. Charlotte and Tommy just got the last of the children in the van."

Future Jade didn't say anything, and Benson continued to hold her.

The eerie unknown sent a chill up my spine. *Who* was the other? The one Benson viewed as another son.

"Dylan always adored you, you know. I knew it the second I met him," Benson said. Her sobbing faded into silence, but she remained in her adoptive father's arms. "He did, too. I'm so glad you both found each other, even if it took years. We were one big, giant family. I even got to marry him off. There really was nobody else like Julian."

And there it was.

The answer.

Me.

Was this how Jade felt when she saw a vision of her own death?

Wait...I got *married*?

What was my life like? Did I have children...Was I happy? I had to have been, right?

There was no mention of my father, or her, or anyone else—which meant they either died or I deserted them. But...I had a life, a person, and then I died.

I betrayed them, and then I died.

Was it worth it?

Was *Jade* worth it?

I turned to the girl in question, eyes bloodshot, tears leaking down her face, looking at me as if I were going to disappear. I looked down at our hands to see that we weren't holding on to each other anymore.

"I just got you...I can't lose you," my sister said.

I froze. I tried to speak, but the words failed me.

"Dad...will you help me?" Future Jade asked, drawing my attention back to her.

Benson didn't even hesitate. "Always."

"Don't forget about us," Sophie's voice said. The blonde emerged with the man she'd left with earlier, Palo, and what looked to be an older version of Victoria.

"We heard what happened, Jade," Future Victoria said. "We'll make them pay."

Future Jade nodded, stepping away from Benson. "I owe my life to them."

"We'll stop the device, for good," Palo said.

"We're all that's left that can fight. We can't afford to make mistakes. We were caught off guard today with the attack, and too many people lost their lives because of it," Sophie said.

Benson, Sophie, Palo, Unknown Guy, Jade, and Victoria were the *only* people still on their feet who could help? Out of the hundreds of people with powers that filled the mall, they were down to *five*?

"Yan Mei was right to put you in charge, Soph. You're a natural," Victoria said. The woman smiled at her.

Future Jade spoke up. "Dylan would have said the exact same thing. He was so proud of you. We'll never forget anyone who...died today, but let's not forget that if it weren't for Henry, none of us would be alive right now."

Future Victoria flinched, clutching her necklace—*Was that a frog?*—but nodded. "He died a hero."

"Let's take them down! For Henry!" Future Jade shouted.

"FOR HENRY!"

∼

We were all crying.

That was to be expected. It almost felt *worse*, reliving it a second time. Jade looked to be in the same condition: eyes red, breathing labored. Victoria looked *frightened*. She stared at us with disbelief, maybe even a little nauseous. Dylan was the oddest of them all. He was calm. He stared at his shoes for a moment, deep in thought. None of us dared speak a word.

I wondered how different it was for Jade, seeing it through my eyes. I had been trained to use my powers effectively since I was three, so I was very good at making people see only what I *wanted* them to see. So, the three of them only got the events. They didn't get my thoughts or secrets while I showed them what had happened when we traveled to the future.

The silence was maddening. I was a quiet person, and even *I* couldn't stand the overwhelming nothingness.

Suddenly, the door flew open.

310

"Okay, so I know I'm a little late," Henry said, barging into the room with a tray full of snow cones. "But I had to pee, and then I had to go find my phone charger, and I figured we needed artificial sugar for our trauma bonding session and... *Wow*, you guys look like you've seen a ghost."

ACKNOWLEDGMENTS

This story has come a long way from the initial random conversation at our grandparent's kitchen table where we decided to write together to the finished book in your hands. It took a long time, and we never would have made it without the help and support of lots of people along the way:

Jonathan Black, our Oreo cousin, who read this story first.

Our fabulous friends who believed in us, cheered us on through our entire journey, and offered helpful feedback: MaKayla "Onesie" Brown, Makayla "Roz" Brown, Perry Logan, and Dusty Salyer.

The knowledgeable people without whom KrisKam Publishing L.P. would have never gotten off the ground: Rachel Bowling from Morehead State University's Small Business Development Center and Aimee Carter, CPA, from James & Holbrook, CPA'S.

Aprampar for bringing Jade to life through his beautiful cover art, despite how confusing our initial ideas probably were. We love it!

Maryssa Gordon at Pocket Editing for her fantastic editorial skills. Your comments gave us confidence in our story and we loved reading your feedback. We shall always remember "facial expressions/body language" in the future.

Euphemia A. and Alexia, two sensitivity readers crucial to making this book better. We understand as writers there will be times when we need to portray characters that might be representative of a different background than us and the utmost care must be taken to do so authentically and respectfully. To Euphemia, thank you for your patience, your honesty, and your time— your feedback and advice made us better writers and *The Visionary* a better story. To Alexia, whose encouragement and confidence in our story was monumental. We'll try and get that second book to you ASAP!

Jacob, thank you for your continued support and confidence, and for believing that we could actually turn an idea into a full-fledged book. Sorry you've had to listen to us talk about this idea for nearly a decade.

Last but not least, we'd like to thank Becky and John Black for their enormous support throughout this entire process. Without them, *The Visionary* would not have come into existence. Thank you for always believing in our dreams. We love you!

ABOUT THE AUTHORS

Cousins Kristin Harris and Kamryn Black have been sharing an imagination and love of writing for their entire lives.

Kristin has a bachelor's degree in Elementary Education, enjoys guessing plot-twists and crochet. She lives with her husband, Jacob, her son, Leo, and dogs, Percy and Poppy.

Kamryn is a theatre lover who has helped in the production of over a dozen shows within her community. She has a bachelor's degree in Marketing, and plays several instruments.